S THE ATAPUR MOONSTONE

Books by the Author

THE PERVEEN MISTRY SERIES
The Widows of Malabar Hill
The Satapur Moonstone

INDIA BOOKS
India Gray: Historical Fiction
The Sleeping Dictionary

JAPAN BOOKS
The Kizuna Coast
Shimura Trouble
Girl in a Box
The Typhoon Lover
The Pearl Diver
The Samurai's Daughter
The Bride's Kimono
The Floating Girl
The Flower Master
Zen Attitude
The Salaryman's Wife

S THE ATAPUR
MOONSTONE

—

SUJATA MASSEY

Published by
Soho Press, Inc.
853 Broadway
New York, NY 10003

Library of Congress Cataloging-in-Publication Data

Massey, Sujata, author.
The Satapur moonstone / Sujata Massey.
ISBN 978-1-61695-909-8
eISBN 978-1-61695-910-4
I. Title.
PS3563.A79965 S28 2019 81'/.54—dc23   2018046843

Map illustration © Philip Schwartzberg

Interior design by Janine Agro, Soho Press, Inc.

Printed in the United States of America

10 9 8 7 6 5 4 3 2 1

For Tony

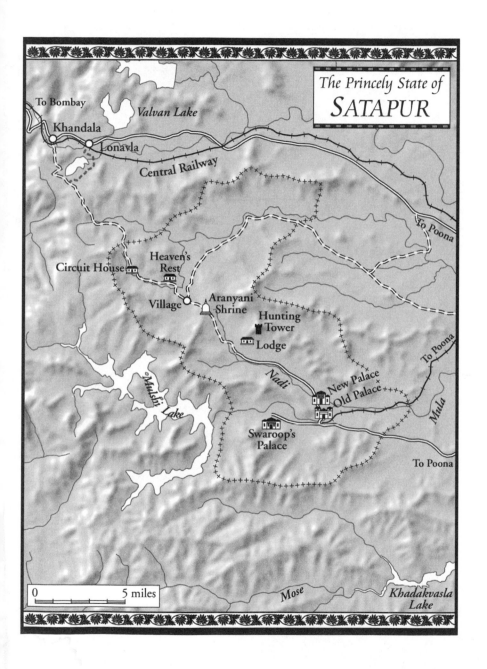

The Princely State of
SATAPUR

THE ROYAL FAMILY OF SATAPUR

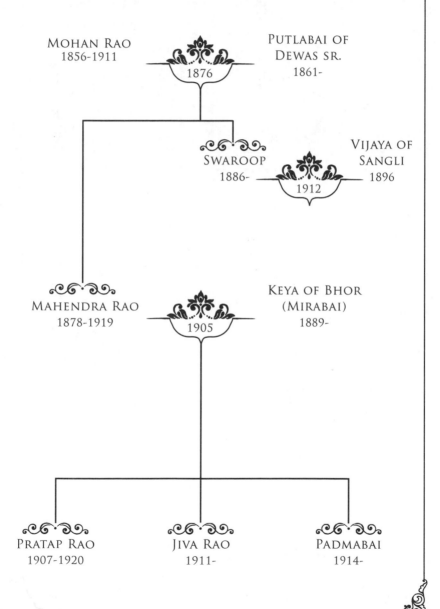

MOHAN RAO
1856-1911

1876

PUTLABAI OF
DEWAS SR.
1861-

SWAROOP
1886-

1912

VIJAYA OF
SANGLI
1896

MAHENDRA RAO
1878-1919

1905

KEYA OF BHOR
(MIRABAI)
1889-

PRATAP RAO
1907-1920

JIVA RAO
1911-

PADMABAI
1914-

1

THE RIDING RING

*P*erveen Mistry sighed, adjusting her hat on her sweating brow. It was six-thirty in the morning and already eighty-two degrees. Cantering around the riding ring at the Royal Western India Turf Club, never quite keeping up with her friend Alice, was vigorous exercise.

Alice Hobson-Jones was cantering on a large bay, Kumar, who had been born from racing stock. He'd wound up as an exercise horse because his stature was a few hands too short for the race-track. Still, Kumar was a prince of a horse, and since Alice was almost six feet tall, their union dominated the ring.

Perveen, five feet three inches, had been delighted to be assigned a female pony, which she had assumed would be gentler. Dolly was so short Perveen had been able to swing herself over the saddle without being propped up by the grooms, an awkward ritual she'd had to repeat most of the times she'd ridden. However, the little horse was hardly amenable to the directions Perveen tapped out with her feet. She was no horsewoman, and it seemed that Dolly sensed it.

Still, this horseback ride was less frightening than the times Perveen had ridden huge animals during house-party weekends Alice had brought her to in England. Now the shoe was on the other foot. Perveen had come home to practice law in Bombay, and Alice was on an extended visit trying to find a teaching position. In a city where the Mistrys had resided for almost 350 years, Perveen's family connections opened doors, and it looked likely that Alice would be hired as a lecturer in mathematics at Wilson College.

Alice had campaigned hard to get Perveen to awaken early enough to ride at six o'clock three times that week. At the outset, it had seemed like a pleasant idea. The rains had stopped, making the city navigable, although as the sun rose, it became a hot and windy place again.

As Perveen came around the ring, she noticed Alice's father, Sir David Hobson-Jones, standing at the edge. He was a Western India Turf Club trustee, despite the fact that he'd been in Bombay for only two years. That was the kind of thing that happened when one was part of the governor's ring of top three councillors.

Sir David smiled, making a sweeping gesture with his hand. Perveen trotted around the ring, concentrating on keeping her back straight. As she passed Sir David, he made the same gesture, only more vigorously.

He was calling her over.

She felt her stomach sink. Perhaps he'd come to say someone in the club had complained about an Indian rider; she was the only one she'd seen.

Perveen hated to kick the filly, but this was the way she'd been taught to make horses move. Dolly ignored her. It was not until Perveen kicked a few more times that the horse reluctantly walked from the ring into the area near the gate where grooms waited to assist. A scrawny boy held the horse while she half-fell off. She was brushing her dusty hands on the sides of her split skirt when Sir David strolled up. He wore a sharp white suit that looked utterly unsuitable for riding.

"Good morning, Sir David. Did you ride earlier?" She tried to sound less shaken than she felt. If Perveen was going to be thrown out of the European-established club because of her race, she could not let the matter pass without protest. But Sir David didn't know she was a member of the Indian National Congress, an all-Indian group advocating for civil rights. He understood only that she was his daughter Alice's former classmate at Oxford, a young woman who was rising in Bombay's legal scene.

He shook his head. "I came for a quick breakfast before going over to the Secretariat. The eggs are very good here. Would you care to join me?"

So she wasn't being thrown out, which was good news. Still, she disliked the idea of going off without telling Alice.

"But I'm . . ." Perveen gestured at her riding clothing, which was not a sporty tweed habit like Alice wore but a light cotton jacket and a voluminous split skirt, the slightly out-moded garment her mother had presented her with as being suitable for an Indian woman doing something as outré as horseback riding.

"Don't give it another thought. People wear riding clothes on the veranda. I'll be the odd one out."

She still felt uneasy. "But Alice—"

"She'll know where to find us." Lowering his voice, the governor's chief councillor said, "I've business to discuss with you anyway, before she arrives."

Business was a welcome prospect for a Bombay lawyer who was well known but not as busy as she'd like. In the ladies' lounge, Perveen scrubbed the track's dust from her face and hands and brushed out her hair before fixing it up again in a coronet. She left off the pith helmet she'd been wearing, although its absence revealed a bright red line running straight across her forehead. Walking out to the veranda, she felt multiple pairs of English eyes on her. Was it because she'd been seen with Sir David, or was it the silly split skirt?

Sir David waved encouragingly at her, and this set off a chorus of whispers.

"I've taken the liberty of ordering you breakfast," he said. "You go straight to work after this, don't you?"

"I try to open up the office before eight," she said, putting on her best business voice. "It's the only time one can attack one's papers without interruption."

"Yes. As I mentioned, I may have a good prospect for Mistry Law."

She leaned forward so eagerly she almost knocked her empty teacup out of its saucer. "Does someone you know need a lawyer?"

A slender waiter in a crisp, high-necked jacket righted her cup and poured a golden stream of Darjeeling into it. Sir David smiled benevolently. "Yes. I do."

She looked at him hard. Was he in trouble at work? "Remember that I'm a solicitor. The Bombay court does not yet allow women advocates to approach the bench, but my father can—"

"That is irrelevant," he said, cutting off the rest of her explanation. "Have you heard of the Kolhapur Agency?"

She was surprised by the simple question. Spooning sugar into her cup, she said, "Certainly. It's the branch of the civil service that oversees Kolhapur State and falls under purview of Bombay Presidency."

"It's a bit more than that," he said. "The Kolhapur Agency has authority over twenty-five princely and feudal states in Western India. The agency's officers are political agents and residents who maintain relationships between British India and these states."

Perveen was embarrassed she hadn't known how many states were overseen by the Kolhapur Agency. But why was he asking about it, anyway?

The young waiter came back with a plate of scrambled eggs, toast, and kippers for each of them. The eggs looked fluffy, the toast appropriately buttered, but Perveen did not like kippers. She resolved to try one, out of courtesy to her host.

It was like that with the British. An Indian could not prosper without contact with them, but one did not have to become a Britisher in habits. As she shook green chilies over her eggs, she considered the picture that Sir David was painting. Although the British government had power over approximately 61 percent of the subcontinent, the rest of India was a patchwork of large and small states and landholdings ruled by Hindus, Muslims, and a few Sikhs. In exchange for being exempted from British rule, many royals paid tributes to the British, most often soldiers in the form of cash and crops. And as Sir David indicated, the states still had to cooperate with the desires of the political agents.

Sir David slid one of the kippers into his mouth, chewed with relish, and continued the conversation. "At the moment, the Agency is challenged. They've sent out a request for help finding a legal investigator to step in and assist with business in one of their northernmost states."

"How interesting," said Perveen, the wheels already turning as she thought about the suitable lawyers she might refer. "Tell me more. How long has the position been open? And how much time will the job take?"

"The matter came up at a meeting last week, and the others agreed with me that you are probably the only person in India who could do it."

Perveen almost lost her grip on her teacup but steadied herself. The hell if she'd be the one to work for Britain, which had kept India under its elephant feet since the 1600s. But she had to be diplomatic. Carefully, she said, "I'm honored that you'd consider me for a government position, but I'd never leave my father's practice. He just promoted me to partner last month."

"Congratulations! But you do serve clients who are willing to pay a fair rate—isn't that the reason to have a firm?"

Perveen nodded warily.

"Rest assured this is a one-off job—it will probably take a week, with a little more billing time afterward when you're back in Bombay writing the report." He paused. "Have you tried a kipper yet? They're made from a local fish, not the usual Scottish herring."

A tiny, bony local fish that she considered bait, not good eating. Reluctantly, she put it in her mouth. As she chewed the unpleasant fish, she thought.

Things weren't especially busy at the office; she had a few

contracts to finish, but the prospect of more than a week's work for a prestigious employer would please her father, Jamshedji Mistry, who saw the British as allies, not adversaries. Still, it was out of town, and he wouldn't like that. Working some eggs over the top of the rest of the kippers, which she was determined to avoid, Perveen said, "Kolhapur is more than three hundred miles from Bombay. Is that where I'd have to go?"

"Not quite that far. Have you heard of Satapur?"

"It's a minuscule state somewhere in the Sahyadri Mountains." Perveen remembered its shape, rather like a rabbit posed on hind legs, from her school geography book. "I don't know that I could point to it on a map or name its ruler."

"It's just forty square miles," he said. "And there isn't a royal sitting on the gaddi at the moment. His Majesty Mahendra Rao died two years ago from the cholera. His son, the maharaja Jiva Rao, is just ten years old."

Perveen tried to imagine the situation at hand. "So although Jiva Rao is already the maharaja in name, it will be at least eight years till he takes power. Does his mother rule until then?"

"Women don't hold power in most princely states. Because Satapur's ruler is underage, the state's decisions are made by its prime minister and our political agent, who happens to reside at the circuit house on the border between Satapur and the hill station of Khandala."

"Running a princely state must be a challenge for a British political agent," Perveen said skeptically, "especially if he's not even living in the palace."

Sir David waved a dismissive hand. "A palace minister does the day-to-day, sending reports to Mr. Sandringham on all that transpires. And the prime minister, Prince Swaroop of Satapur, is the maharaja's uncle, so that's cozy."

Perveen took a bite of toast. Buttered toast was one thing the British did very well. "What can you tell me about the political agent?"

"Colin Wythe Sandringham has been at the post for about ten months. He is responsible for the well-being of the royal children and the late maharaja's widow."

"What children? You only mentioned Prince Jiva Rao."

"He has a little sister, but I don't know her name."

Perveen didn't like the way he had almost forgotten about the princess, nor that he had labeled the young maharaja's mother a widow, when she should have been called a queen. Pointedly, she asked, "What is the maharani's given name?"

"Mirabai." He pronounced the name slowly, in his Oxbridge accent. "At least she's not alone—the late Maharaja Mahendra Rao's mother, the dowager maharani, is still ruling the zenana. I don't recall her name."

Of course, she thought. Sir David was better than most English administrators—and he certainly had been respectful of her own professional accomplishments—but he seemed to share the common belief that the vast majority of Indian women were faceless, nameless, and passive.

He sipped his tea. "I think it's splendid the mother and daughter-in-law have each other for company. But according to Mr. Sandringham, a bitter dispute has arisen between the two maharanis about the prince's education."

This was a common enough problem, regardless of whether one had royal blood. In Perveen's own family, there had been disagreements about whether she should study law, as her father wished, or literature, which was her own choice. It hadn't been until she'd been out of school for years that she had realized practicing law could bring her a lot more excitement in life than analyzing novels.

Unaware of her thoughts, Sir David continued. "Maharaja Jiva Rao's mother wishes him to attend Ludgrove, where several other Indian princes are studying. But the grandmother, who still sees herself as superior to her daughter-in-law, doesn't want him to go."

Perveen had finished everything except the kippers. She wanted something sweet to take the edge off. She signaled the waiter. "Have you any guavas?"

He grimaced. "No good ones today, memsahib."

"Very well. I'll take another piece of toast." She turned back to Sir David. "Where in India is Prince Jiva Rao studying?"

"In the palace. He receives lessons from the Indian tutor who taught the last two generations of maharajas."

"I suppose he could be a good teacher. Certainly an experienced one," Perveen said, imagining this man would be over sixty.

"These are answers you could find out for us when you visit the palace. Mr. Sandringham paid a call in September, but he was not admitted due to the maharanis' custom of seclusion."

"Hindu maharanis often observe purdah," Perveen said. "If the agent is determined, he should return and ask to speak to each lady through a screen. That is common when purdah ladies are needed to testify in a court of law."

"Going back to try again has its problems. You see, Mr. Sandringham is a cripple," Sir David said bluntly.

"A cripple!" Perveen's eyes widened. She was quite surprised the British had put someone with a disability in a position of great responsibility and dispatched him far into the countryside. Probably he had a gigantic staff to assist him. How else could one manage?

"Others in the Kolhapur Agency suggested sending him again; however, I don't wish to compromise his health when the interview with purdah ladies could be accomplished with more ease by a woman lawyer."

Sir David remembered what she'd done in Malabar Hill at the beginning of the year. She felt a rush of gratitude, knowing how easily things could have gone another way. Few lawyers could help women in seclusion, and she'd been involved in just such a case. Women who observed purdah could not meet with men outside of their immediate families. Nodding, she said, "You wish me to get behind the curtain, interview both maharanis, and report my opinion on the maharaja's schooling."

"There's another aspect to the interview," Sir David said. "There are ongoing concerns about land improvement, such as bringing in railway lines, building dams, and so forth. What the maharanis and any other nobles in the palace think about these possibilities is valuable knowledge."

"It truly is an investigator's job." Perveen took a bite of toast and chewed slowly, allowing herself time to think. This sounded like a straightforward consulting assignment. And the twenty-five states included in the Kolhapur group were home to hundreds of royal women. If word slipped through their purdah screens that a lady lawyer stood ready to assist with their concerns, Mistry Law might receive a tremendous number of new clients.

But what was the financial value of the endeavor? Sir David might hope she'd perform the job at a discounted rate due to their connection. But the British government wouldn't get away with underpaying her the way they did Indians in general. They wanted her. She had power.

Pursing her lips, she said, "I'm trying to fathom how this job could be billed."

He answered promptly. "Twenty rupees a day—the salary of a district sub-inspector."

Not terrible, but nothing to boast to her father about. She shrugged.

"However, your traveling expenses would be on par with a commissioner's. All rail travel will be first class, and you'll be able to stay in rest bungalows for ICS officers as needed. There will either be some horseback riding or palanquin travel."

"A palanquin is one of those awful boxes on poles, isn't it?" She had a dislike of closed-in spaces.

"Sandringham suggested it. He says that part of the route is not easily negotiated by horses. Local men handle the palanquin, start to finish. And you'll enjoy the scenery as you travel."

She raised a cynical eyebrow.

"The Sahyadri Mountains are beautiful beyond compare. This month is post-rainy season. It is at least fifteen degrees cooler than Bombay." He finished with a flourish, reminding her of the hawkers near the Royal Bombay Yacht Club who proclaimed the splendor of the tourist boat ride out to Elephanta Island.

Gentle rains in the mountains sounded better than the hot winds of early October in Bombay, but she didn't want to seem too excited. "There's always a load of contract work at our office. Making twenty rupees sitting at my desk isn't hard to do in a day's time."

He was silent for a moment and then grunted. "Understood. I'm fairly sure I can persuade them to commit twenty-five rupees per day."

This was phenomenal. Keeping a poker face, she said, "Duly noted."

Her happy reverie was interrupted when Alice strode onto the veranda, showing no signs of having washed hands or face. "Hallo, Perveen! Here you are!"

"Sorry. Your father invited me to breakfast. I hope you weren't worried that I'd vanished."

"Not at all. Has he convinced you to take the job yet?"

"What? You knew about it?" Perveen's gaze went from her friend to the smug-looking Sir David.

"Why else do you think we've been riding around the ring all week?" Alice yawned. "I've been refreshing your skills."

"How dare you trick me?" Perveen hooted with laughter. She was relieved and excited, but she didn't want Alice to keep secrets from her. "You're a dreadful excuse for a friend."

Alice grinned and said, "Don't look a gift horse in the mouth."

2

A VISITOR TO KHANDALA

Aditya, the official jester attached to Satapur Palace, was feeling sore from a long horseback ride. Satapur Palace was four hills away from the Khandala Railway Station. Because of the thick fog and broken, muddy paths, the journey had taken six hours instead of five. The sun had just risen when he'd set off on a short, sturdy gray mare. People had traveled the narrow path for centuries, so it was easy to see where to go; but the long summer's rains had left it treacherously slippery. He had been in a constant battle to keep the nervous horse moving forward to reach Khandala Station.

Now he sat half-hidden in the shadow of the station's roof. He preferred traveling to trying his jokes on the palace's people, who had given up laughing years before. He'd had a cup of tea and was smoking his third cheroot. There were no travelers waiting to board, but sticking to the schedule, the train would still stop. He anticipated the people on board would step out and exclaim at the beauty of the tall, silent green hills, the streams of water running down them like silver tears. All this nonsense he'd heard before.

The horn sounded well before the black steam engine train chugged up to the platform. A young conductor opened the door and jumped out, and a small flood of local boys appeared from out of the trees, quickly tying red scarves around their heads to signify their status as coolies approved by the stationmaster.

Khandala was most popular in spring, when it was a delightful respite from Bombay's heat. In rainy season, the hill station became unreachable. The rains were so long and hard that the train, which ran a steep route from Neral Junction, temporarily stopped.

Aditya watched an elderly man totter out of the train's general section, followed by two more men and a family.

The conductor was poised at the steps of the first-class carriage, looking impatient. A boy sprang down, easily balancing a small trunk on his head. From the warm brown leather and geometric golden pattern, Aditya recognized it as Louis Vuitton, a brand favored by both Europeans and wealthy Indians.

Aditya moved out of the shadows to get a closer look. A dainty foot in a beige leather boot emerged before its owner: an Indian woman swathed in a butter-yellow sari embroidered in blue and gray paisley designs. She wore a white lace-trimmed blouse underneath her silk sari, which made her look like some of the wealthy Parsi women he'd seen at the races and society parties in Poona. Yet instead of a delicate parasol, she carried a brown bridle-leather briefcase.

He gaped at the briefcase, not quite believing his eyes. It must have belonged to her husband, who was surely coming off the train, too. Her husband would be the P. J. Mistry, Esquire, mentioned in the letters the maharanis had received.

But nobody else stepped off the train.

As if feeling his gaze, the woman turned. Impertinent greenish-brown eyes regarded him from above a hooked nose—a Parsi nose; of that he was certain.

Aditya felt deflated. His body was sore from the long journey, and now the lawyer everyone was worried about hadn't come.

The lady turned from him to speak to the coolie who'd unloaded her suitcase. She gave him a coin; although Aditya could not see what it was, he guessed it was more than the usual paisa, because the boy had pressed it to his forehead and was beaming like a fool.

Idly, he wondered why she was going on holiday by herself. Perhaps she was meeting someone; Khandala was popular with Europeans and wealthy Indians.

A man dressed in shabby brown clothing came out of the

train's third-class compartment, carrying a sack marked with the symbol of the Imperial Mail. He dropped it on the platform.

As if on cue, the region's only postal cart, a small wooden stagecoach driven by two locals, Pratik and his teenaged son, Charan, came up the rough path. Aditya was friendly with them, but he drew back because he didn't want them to call out to him.

"You're late!" The stationmaster rebuked them loud enough for Aditya to hear. "It's not just letters that are waiting. There is a memsahib."

"What is late, and what is early?" was the amiable response of Pratik. Pratik lumbered down from the driver's seat and took a long stretch before accepting the bundle of mail.

Aditya was startled to see Charan approach the woman. Aditya could not make out her reply, but Charan began gesturing as if she should follow him. When she reached the postal cart, the boy pulled down the back gate. From his watching place, Aditya could see the woman's shoulders curling downward as she looked inside. Perhaps she was afraid.

Aditya soon realized the woman traveler had stooped for reasons of practicality. She placed her right foot on Charan's hands, which he had clasped together, making a step for her. In the next instant, she'd tumbled into the back of the postal cart, clutching the briefcase to her chest. As she fell, her sari flared, and he glimpsed cinnamon-colored skin over the top of her kidskin boots. This was a titillating sight, something he could exaggerate into an unseemly joke for the palace.

Charan latched the back of the wagon and went swiftly to the bench seat at the front. Aditya watched as the young man seated himself next to his father and took the sack of mail between his ankles.

Pratik rapped the horses with one stroke of his whip, and they were off.

3

THE AGENT OF SATAPUR

"Miss Perveen Mistry?"

Perveen opened her eyes, and then shut them fast in response to a harsh white light.

"Welcome to Satapur," boomed a cheerful English voice. "I hope you aren't feeling poorly?"

"No, I'm fine. I must have dozed off," Perveen said, struggling into a sitting position. How undignified she must have looked—she hadn't meant to arrive this way, especially in front of the Englishman who was presumably the Satapur agent. "I can't see you with that light in my eyes."

The light swung away from her eyes. "Sorry! I'm Colin Sandringham. I'm here to walk you up to the circuit house. That is—if you're P. J. Mistry, Esquire."

She was confused because Sir David had mentioned the man having a disability. "I am indeed. And it was most kind of you to meet me. It must have been a dismal wait in the dark."

"Oh, I was on the veranda until ten minutes ago. I saw the lantern and knew it had to be the postal cart. Pratik, how are you?" He said the last bit in English-accented Marathi.

The postman answered, "Well enough. I also have letters for you."

"What time is it?" Perveen wondered how long she'd been sleeping.

"It's about six-thirty," Mr. Sandringham said.

Perveen stretched her legs down the four feet of space between the cart and the ground. As she touched the earth, she felt the telltale sinking of mud. She bit back the Gujarati curse that came to mind. She was wearing brand-new beige kidskin boots that buttoned up to the ankle, a special pair that her mother, Camellia, and sister-in-law, Gulnaz, had helped her buy a day earlier in Bombay.

"How practical!" Camellia had enthused. "They cover the whole foot and even the ankle. With all the traveling in the mountains, they will serve you better than sandals."

"But you mustn't wear them in the palace!" Gulnaz warned. "English boots don't suit saris. The palace's maharanis will probably wear jeweled slippers. Perveen, you can borrow the ones from my wedding trousseau. I hardly wore them."

Perveen wistfully remembered her own bridal trousseau: dozens of fine silk saris, embroidered cashmere shawls, and fancy slippers like the ones Gulnaz had. Four years earlier, Perveen had abandoned the loot in Calcutta, along with her marriage. In her new life as a lawyer, she dressed practically—but she sometimes missed what she'd once owned.

"I'm not worried about you being in a palace," Camellia had fretted. "As Pappa said, when stories go around about this job, it could promote the law firm. But I worry about you traveling alone in the wilderness. If something happens, you might never be found!"

"It won't be like that," Perveen had promised. But if her mother had known she'd traveled three hours in the back of a postal cart—treated like luggage, rather than a lady—she'd want Perveen to turn right around and go back to Bombay.

Perveen stood, stretching. The closed-in cart had been musty with the scent of damp paper. Now she breathed in refreshing cool air. Sir David had been correct about the weather. She wondered about the rest.

Mr. Sandringham's voice cut into her thoughts. "Can you see well enough to follow me up to the circuit house?"

"Yes. I'm glad to stand and move about." She rotated her ankles, feeling her feet come back to life.

"Please follow me closely; there are obstacles along the path. We're a quarter mile away, and we'll walk near a bluff with a rather steep drop. What did you bring?"

She knew from experience it was important not to let her Swaine Adeney briefcase out of her hands. "I've got two pieces. I can carry my briefcase myself, but I'm afraid the trunk is too heavy."

"Charan and Pratik will bring it up—and in thanks I'll offer them a chance to stay the night. Rain has been coming in fits and starts, and I wasn't sure if the cart would make it."

"Do you typically bring people up by postal cart?" she asked, following along in the wake of the bobbing lantern he held. He leaned toward his right, where she caught sight of a walking stick. So he was lame; that was hardly what she'd call being crippled.

"I'm afraid tonga carts are only at the station when weather is dry. But the post comes on every train, and it's met by these two postmen. Hence, we've developed a system."

"That seems efficient." She didn't want to say the ride had been comfortable, because it hadn't been. But there was no reason to complain. She was still in shock that the Kolhapur Agency had confirmed her to serve as a "lady legal investigator." They must not have heard she was a supporter of Mohandas Gandhi, the freedom activist who was agitating throughout Bombay against British products. Perveen's father, Jamshedji, had been worried about Perveen's attendance at Gandhiji's most recent public meeting. If the government thought that Mistry Law was aligning itself with political protest, the firm's property taxes could be raised. It had happened to others.

But Perveen was thrilled that Gandhiji had spoken to her directly in their shared language, Gujarati. He'd asked if she could encourage more women to join the cause.

The maharanis she was about to meet were fabulously wealthy. Would she be brave enough to bring up the idea of supporting the freedom movement? Would that be in conflict with her assigned job to recommend a plan for Prince Jiva Rao's education and to understand the family's sentiments about the state's development?

Absolutely it would be.

Perveen sighed inwardly and kept her eyes on the dark shape of Mr. Sandringham.

"When the sun's shining tomorrow, you'll see some spectacular views!" he called back to her. "It's thick jungle, but from Marshall Point, one can see the five surrounding hills."

"Yes," Perveen said, feeling slightly breathless from the uphill climb. She wasn't used to exerting herself.

"It's only a bit farther."

Indeed, they'd come up to a stone path lined by torches illuminating the way to a massive house with a steeply pitched roof. A lantern hanging from the porch's center shone on a dark brown monkey settled inside an eave. The nestled monkey had a fluffy lion's ruff of golden hair.

Perveen sighed with pleasure. "I've never seen that type of monkey."

In the half light, Sandringham smiled. "He's a lion-tailed macaque. I call him Hanuman, after the monkey god in the *Rāmāyana*."

Perveen had noted earlier he spoke some Marathi, and now it sounded as if he'd read the Hindu epic. "He has a most intelligent face," she said, keeping her eyes on the monkey, who looked impassively at her. "And he looks so calm. He's quite different from the gray monkeys one sees in the city."

"Those gray monkeys—the rhesus—always look absolutely disgusted with us." With a snort, he added, "It's as if they're pointing out we've destroyed their habitat. But there are no paved streets or high buildings here. Hanuman's family lives in the trees out back, and they have plenty of sources of food."

As the two of them came into the warm golden light of the veranda, Perveen saw Mr. Sandringham in full. He was a young civil service officer, perhaps still under thirty, although his wire-rimmed glasses gave him an aura of intellectualism. But he did not wear the typical linen suit that ICS officers like Sir David did. Instead, his lanky frame was clothed in a rumpled white shirt with an ink stain on the chest pocket and wrinkled khaki jodhpurs tucked into riding boots. Sandringham looked like a scholar who'd stumbled into the jungle—and his uses of zoological nomenclature and the *Rāmāyana* added to that impression.

She belatedly realized he was also studying her. He blinked behind his glasses and said, "It's the oddest thing, but you look familiar. Where have we met?"

There were Parsi families who socialized regularly with the British for the sake of advancement, but the Mistrys weren't like that. Perveen's only British friend in India was Alice Hobson-Jones, whom Perveen had met during her Oxford days. "I don't recall a meeting. Have you worked in Bombay?"

"No, all my postings have been in the mofussil."

"If you've been in the countryside, we haven't met." She shrugged, wanting to put the matter to rest. She had liked him better in the dark, when he'd been talking about monkeys and the land.

A thin, silver-haired old man wearing a homespun lungi and vest came out of the bungalow and took the trunk on his head. He turned neatly and practically skipped up the stairs and into the house.

"Who is that spry gentleman?" Perveen inquired as she went up the few stairs that led to a long, wide veranda covered in red and green encaustic tiles, more practical than wood in such a damp climate. Behind the veranda, the whitewashed circuit house was a long, utilitarian rectangle with a dozen doors facing outward. The windows were covered by heavy shutters—more defense against the rains.

"Rama. He's the head bearer, who cooks and does . . . other important things."

"He seems very strong for an old man!" Perveen wondered what the other important things he did were. She followed Mr. Sandringham, whose limp was now clearly visible. She wondered if he'd been hurt in the war but decided it was too personal to ask.

"Your room is on the end here. I'm sure you'll want time for rest and washing up. But first, let's go into the office so you can sign the guest book. We maintain records of all who've stayed here going back to the 1870s."

The high-ceilinged room was lit only by a hurricane lamp burning on the table. There was a series of glass-doored cabinets with books and folios stored within, and a big teak desk with a marble top. Mr. Sandringham ushered her toward the desk and the book lying on it, its leather cover smudged with mildew. He opened it up to a page full of names written in many variations of cursive handwriting, followed by dates, addresses, and short personal messages. The last line showed a visitor with a date in the previous week. He was Graham Andrews, MD: a doctor, most likely in the Indian Medical Service. The names above Dr. Andrews's were also English. Perhaps she was the first Indian to stay in the circuit house. It was the kind of thing her father would have been proud of, but that made her uneasy.

Perveen picked up the waiting fountain pen, filled it with ink, and neatly wrote *P. J. Mistry* and the address of the firm on the line.

"When you leave, you may write your comments on the experience!" Sandringham said brightly.

This immediately made her nervous. "Actually, the person on the line above me didn't comment."

"That's because Dr. Andrews is a regular caller. His surgery is a few miles away. He dines here at least once weekly," he said, looking down at the page. "Perhaps we'll see him tonight or tomorrow."

So they were friends.

Turning her attention back to the room, she noticed that behind the table there stood a high-backed chair that looked fit for a judge. Along the side of the room were more high-backed chairs.

"This place is called the circuit house. Do you preside over a court?" she asked, wondering if she should have addressed him differently.

"Oh, no!" He gave a light chuckle. "I've no judicial degree. Judges from nearby courts travel in when needed."

"But this is princely India, not British India. How could you hold trials here?"

"In cases of conflict. Theoretically, a citizen could say the maharaja had treated him unfairly and ask for a second opinion. Just as a judge must preside here if one of the maharanis chooses to argue against our decision on the maharaja's schooling."

Perveen knew the government expected her to broker an agreement between the royal women. If she didn't accomplish it, she would have failed. Pushing down her feeling of anxiety, she tried to change the subject. "It's a lovely building, but rather remote. How does Mrs. Sandringham like living so far from civilization?"

"Sorry?" His narrow eyebrows rose.

"I was asking about your wife."

A slow flush spread over his cheeks. "I'm afraid I have no better half. Typically, bachelors are given remote posts like this one."

Perveen went rigid. Had Sir David known all along Colin Sandringham was a bachelor? Her father would never have accepted the prospect of her staying overnight in a solitary male's dwelling. Now her name was written in the guest book. There was a chance this evidence of her staying under a single man's roof could spread all around Poona and Bombay. It could ruin her good name.

Mr. Sandringham spoke quickly, as if he'd realized she wasn't pleased by the situation. "Besides Rama, there's Hari, who helps him in the house, and Mohit, who works with horses in the stable. Hari sleeps on the veranda, and Rama and Mohit share a hut in the garden. There is additional space for servants traveling with guests, and that is where Charan and Pratik will bunk tonight. We have the protection of a guard dog, Desi, who will be loose from after suppertime into the morning hours. Nothing's ever happened here—but if you feel nervous, ring the bell, and we'll all come running."

Except that he couldn't run. And he seemed to think the danger to her was from the outside, not from him. Striving to sound neutral, she said, "This is a remarkable bungalow with an interesting arrangement of rooms, all stretched out along the veranda. Is it typical of British officer housing?"

"Yes. These mountain bungalows need to be built quickly, between rains, and all materials for building are hauled up by donkey. You may have noticed the house has a very steep pitched roof to allow rain to drain quickly."

"Yes. That is sensible." Perveen's family had a construction company that had built offices and bungalows in Bombay for more than two hundred years, and she had an intuitive feeling for buildings. This looked like what her late grandfather would have called a pukka house—well built and free of defect— although it was relatively modest, with none of the ornate moldings and inlaid marble tile designs that were a feature of her own family's home. Was Sandringham's character also pukka? That was the question.

"You asked about the arrangement of the rooms," Sandringham said, interrupting her thoughts. "The tall double doors at the veranda's center lead to the drawing room and dining room, where we'll eat tonight. Cooking's done in a separate house out back. Now that you've arrived, I'd like to give Rama our order for supper. Firstly, do you eat chicken?"

"Certainly." She had endured English cooking for three years, so she could imagine how dreadful supper would be.

"Good, because it's all we have. Rama has a repertoire of just ten chicken dishes. I'll let you choose which one."

She nodded, thinking this was a surprising way to offer

hospitality. But then again, he was a bachelor. Everything was bound to be topsy-turvy.

"We can offer you chicken kabob. Chicken cutlets. Roast chicken. Curried or stewed chicken!" Mr. Sandringham affected the accent and manner of a Cockney hawker. "Boiled chicken. Smothered chicken. Fried chicken. Chicken mince. Chicken biryani."

Perveen's anxiety was somewhat lessened by his silliness and at hearing Indian dishes were a possibility for dinner. "I'm curious about smothered chicken. It sounds rather mysterious."

"Chicken splayed apart, dusted with spices, and pressed between hot rocks. I like it as well, but it takes an hour."

She nodded, imagining the flavor. Food could take her mind off many tensions. "I don't mind. I'll use the time to freshen up."

Rama had already lit the sconces and candles in her rooms, so Perveen spent the next hour unpacking and looking around. The long, stone-floored bathroom had an old-fashioned commode with a wooden seat and a bucket of water for flushing—this was better than she'd anticipated, although there was no sink with taps, just a washbasin on a teak stand with a round mirror behind it.

A deep zinc tub was filled with warm water. She realized that the water must have been heated on the fire she'd seen blazing in a pit in the garden, and some poor lackey must have quickly carried buckets through a short doorway to fill the tub. The lifestyle of the place, with its lack of electricity, running water, and indoor stoves, was reminiscent of a half century earlier. She would never have imagined a British officer in 1921 would live this way; but if he could manage, so would she.

Perveen picked up a fresh bar of soap that smelled like neem leaves. Scrubbing away the dirt and sweat from her long ride in the post wagon, she decided that Sandringham was strange for an Englishman. She had been expecting someone like Sir David, and from Sandringham's accent, she guessed he came from the upper class. But he lived modestly and had a sense of humor about it. And at least he hadn't requested Rama make a boiled chicken; he'd let her choose what she wanted.

After Perveen had bathed, put on a wrapper, and gone back to her bedroom, she opened up her Vuitton trunk and lifted out the saris, each folded into a perfect square by Gulnaz, who had lent them to Perveen. She looked at the layers of glowing pink, cream, and light green silk: very fancy saris Gulnaz had deemed appropriate for hobnobbing with maharanis. Perveen feared creasing them, so she picked one of her own saris, a blue watered silk shot through with golden threads. It was a subtly formal sari that was heavy enough to offer warmth against the cool evening air. Underneath, she wore a silk blouse with gold embroidery on the cuffs, which came to just above her wrists. She was glad of the long sleeves because she'd heard the whining of a few mosquitoes making practice laps before beginning the night's work.

"You could catch dengue," her mother had warned when they were talking about safety precautions for the trip. "Do not go about after dark. And watch your step in the gardens. Perveen, I'm not at all convinced it's a good idea you take this job for the government."

"Two days' work that pays as much as twenty client hours," Perveen had told her. "All travel expenses covered and a good chance for more work with royalty in the area. Pappa will be so pleased after I'm done."

She'd counted on all of that—but not how strange and far-away this world would seem. Worrying about mosquito bites would be the least of her concerns.

4

OLD HOME WEEK

Perveen gaped as she entered the circuit house's drawing room. Even though she'd seen the pitched roof outdoors, she was amazed by the height of the drawing room's ceiling—at least thirty feet. As if trying to live up to the exaggerated ceiling, the rosewood chairs and settees ranged along the wall had backs that rose ten feet. They looked more suitable for giants than ordinary people.

Well, that was how most British people thought of themselves in India.

Perveen continued her covert inspection, noting that instead of open bookcases, there were ten-foot-high, glass-paneled almirahs. She would have gone closer to look at the titles, but she realized that Colin Sandringham was entrenched in one of the room's few soft, lower-backed chairs with a mass of letters spread out before him on a teak coffee table. In the same moment, she realized she shouldn't have worried about dressing formally for dinner. He was wearing the same jodhpurs and boots. The only effort he had made was changing his shirt. She didn't know whether to take offense that he didn't consider dinner with her worth dressing for, or to feel reassured he wasn't trying to seduce her.

There was a funny Parsi Gujarati phrase to describe such dishevelment: jeethra peethra. Hearing it in her mind, she laughed silently. Remembering her roots was one way to feel more certain in this strange environment.

Mr. Sandringham looked up at her. "Good!" he said in a

relaxed voice, not seeming to notice her change in appearance. "Supper's ready. Are you feeling well enough for it?"

"Yes. That hot bath was just what I needed for my tired bones."

Sandringham rose and walked with his lopsided gait toward the table in the dining room. "You'll see Rama set everything out for us: the smothered chicken, roasted potatoes, and a curry made with the local spinach. He's at work on rotis and dal. I'll open a bottle of claret, if you'd care for any."

Perveen hesitated. Not only was she staying alone overnight with a man, if she accepted his offer, she could also be criticized for drinking alcohol with him. Looking at the bottle made her feel uneasy. Still—she drank a bit of wine on celebratory evenings with her family. And she wasn't sure about the purity of the drinking water. "How's the water at the circuit house?"

"Boiled but not particularly tasty. It's very good at the palace, I hear."

"I'll take a large glass of water and a tiny taste of the wine. I can't risk a headache when I travel tomorrow."

"Yes—I'm going to tell you all about that," he said, pouring her a few ounces of wine and filling his own glass halfway. "Shall we say cheers?"

"Yes. To a successful venture in Satapur," Perveen said, raising her glass before taking a sip. The claret was a good one—it seemed to change in her mouth, leaving a soft floral taste at the end.

"Is it all right?" Mr. Sandringham was smiling, as if he already knew how good the wine was.

"It tastes like violets," Perveen said after a second sip. She'd decided to put aside her anxiety and make small talk. This was the way the British behaved before business. "It's quite a nice taste. I haven't drunk Château Margaux since my time at Oxford."

He looked startled. "Which college?"

"St. Hilda's."

"When did you come down?"

"Last year. I had a brief clerkship in London before returning to Bombay and joining my father's practice." Perveen was grateful he hadn't asked what had brought her to study in England. He didn't need to know about her bungled first attempt at studying law in Bombay and her failed marriage in Calcutta.

"We're practically batch mates! I read geography at Brasenose and came down in 1919." He grinned. "You're looking at me doubtfully. Why is that?"

She didn't want to offend him, so she spoke carefully. "I believe you're a Brasenosian, but you seem older than me."

"I'm twenty-eight. I was at Oxford before the war. Then I spent a few years in France."

"With the army?"

He nodded. "Like a lot of my friends, I believed the war would be over by Christmas."

"And of course, that did not happen." She thought again about his slight limp. He had got off lightly, compared to so many veterans. "Why did you choose geography?"

"Before the war, I was interested in zoology. But while in France, I became keen on maps. An accurate map can mean the difference between life and death. So when I returned to my studies, I shifted my focus to geography. I realized the best way to get into mapping uncharted territory was to serve the government outside of Britain."

"Does the ICS employ geographers to draw maps?" Perveen asked before tasting the evening's main course. The chicken had been smothered with sliced onions, which had melted into soft sweetness that offset the savory, salty flavor of the bird.

"Yes. I'd be delighted to have that assignment, but junior officers generally must serve first as collectors."

"Collectors are the people who count every rupee or grain of rice that Indians owe," she said sarcastically.

"Not just that. The collector reports on the conditions and morale of the people and settles non-criminal disputes. The job requires a great deal of traveling."

Rama came in carrying a bowl of dal and a brass platter laden with rotis. Instead of going around the table and formally serving both of them, he placed the bowls between them and left.

"He's a very good cook," Perveen said after she'd tasted everything on her plate.

"Yes. I was very lucky to get him, because he's a Brahmin. Typically he would only serve vegetarian cuisine and work in a Hindu household."

Perveen guessed that Rama had made a hard decision based on economics to become a chef dealing with chickens. But it was fortunate for Mr. Sandringham. "Brahmin cooks are known for very good hygiene. I had a case once where a family believed they'd hired a Brahmin cook, but they found out the cook was of a lower caste. The family wanted to take him to trial."

Sandringham leaned forward, looking interested. "Who prevailed?"

"I brokered an out-of-court settlement. The cook was not sued and agreed to work elsewhere." She raised her hands. "The cook wasn't overjoyed, but at least he still had a job and didn't owe them money he didn't have."

"You must see a lot of unfairness in your work." Sandringham's sharp jaw set in a disapproving line. "What do you think of the caste system? How does it affect your own family?"

"In my Zoroastrian faith, we don't have such a built-in hierarchy, although only priestly families can do the necessary rites in our fire temples, and certain community members handle the dead." As Perveen took a bite of the savory chicken, she remembered how her mother-in-law had once said she wasn't pure enough to spin sacred thread at a ladies' gathering. She'd felt insulted, but this was nothing to tell Colin Sandringham. "As a lawyer who serves clients of all faiths, I must accept what is present in Hindu law. Yet I did pity the cook for losing salary."

Mr. Sandringham raised an eyebrow. "Was he a good cook?"

"Yes, but he certainly wouldn't prepare meat. What excellent chicken!" Perveen said, taking another forkful. "But I digress. Tell me, how long were you a collector?"

"About a year. I became political agent for Satapur the first of January."

This was a significant promotion after one short year as collector. And Sir David had made it seem as if Mr. Sandringham wasn't doing well in this position. She wanted to understand what the truth was. "So you are now the very important liaison to the Satapur palace. Does your geography background come into it?"

Mr. Sandringham smiled ruefully. "Not at all. But I can draw my maps during the monsoon months, when there isn't much else to do."

"Is the rainy season really six months?" Perveen asked, still wondering how he'd nabbed the job.

He rolled his eyes. "This year it was one hundred eighty days. The season is officially over, but I wouldn't be surprised if we have a few more showers."

"I'd go mad being confined in one place for so long."

"One adjusts. The real problem is that mail ceases, sometimes for months. The two maharanis' letters to me were dated from May, but I didn't get either one until September. Can you imagine such a delay for a distance of twelve miles?"

"So Charan and Pratik couldn't come through with their cart?"

He shook his head. "No. I'm certain that the prince's mother, the maharani Mirabai, is very frustrated that I didn't pursue admission for her son at Ludgrove. The Kolhapur Agency read me the riot act. It's too late now, which means he'll miss entering this year."

"I'm not sure I understand," Perveen said. "The prince's mother wished you to make an application for her son to school in England—yet she wouldn't allow you to come see her at the palace to talk about it?"

"That's the case," he said shortly. "Whether keeping me out was her idea or her mother-in-law's, I don't know."

Her interest rising, Perveen leaned forward. "It could also be orders from a male relative or a palace administrator. Have you ever been allowed into the palace?"

He pressed his lips together. "No, but the estranged relationship predates me. Just before I moved here, Maharani Mirabai's older son, Pratap Rao, suffered an untimely death. According to the last political agent, Owen McLaughlin, the ladies cut off all contact with him after that tragedy, although he'd regularly been allowed inside when the Maharaja Mahendra Rao was alive. I traveled there by palanquin to make a social call—first upon my arrival, and secondly after these letters—but was not admitted."

"Oh dear!" Perveen hadn't realized that more than one maharaja had died. The situation was proving complex. "How old was the young Maharaja Pratap Rao, and how did he perish?"

"Prince Pratap Rao was thirteen years old at the time of his death in 1920. He was on a hunting trip with his uncle and others from the palace. He went missing and was found dead the next day."

"What was the cause of death?"

"Our local Indian Medical Service doctor, Graham Andrews, performed the autopsy. He said the prince was mauled by an animal—most likely a leopard or tiger." Wincing, he added, "The culprit was not found."

Perveen looked at the smothered chicken and knew she wouldn't be able to eat any more.

"Sorry," Sandringham said, putting down his own silver.

"It's all right. I'm not too delicate to hear things like that." Perveen forced normalcy into her voice. "I've know very little about the late Maharaja Mahendra Rao. Was he ill from cholera for a long time?"

"It happened in 1919 and was quite sudden." Sandringham detailed how the forty-one-year-old Maharaja Mahendra Rao had taken a personal interest in the well-being of his subjects. When cholera broke out in one of the villages, he traveled to speak to the people about the importance of quarantine and taking medicine, since Dr. Andrews had been turned away. The maharaja came into contact with a villager who was ill, and then caught the disease himself. "Despite Dr. Andrews's best efforts and twenty priests' prayers, he died five days later."

"What a loss." Mahendra Rao sounded like a noble who'd died trying to help others—not the usual picture of an imperious, decadent maharaja.

"Yes. McLaughlin wrote that the late maharaja was very interested in progress—in using the land's resources for community gain, in modern health practices, education."

Sir David had said that the political agent was almost entirely in charge, but she felt curious about how this inexperienced, casual young man approached things. She began with an easy question Sir David had already answered for her. "So if the maharaja's gone and his only surviving son is underage, who is making decisions?"

"The late maharaja's brother, Swaroop, serves as prime minister."

She was startled that Sandringham hadn't talked about his own role. "He makes the decisions, not you?"

He shrugged. "Nothing has come across my desk that raised concerns something needed to be done differently."

In her mind, a hands-off British government was a good idea. But she wanted to know more about the prime minister. "I've heard just a little about Prince Swaroop. He owns some very fine horses at the Royal Western India Turf Club."

"He's also reputed to have a lavish bungalow on Malabar Hill where his mistress of five years stays."

"Is he more often in Bombay than at the palace?" Perveen had noted the sarcasm in Sandringham's tone.

"I don't know. The prince and his wife have their own palace about four miles from Satapur Palace. I get occasional letters from a palace officer, but they don't offer much other than saying the family's health is good." Sandringham shifted, looking uncomfortable at Perveen's challenging his lack of involvement. "Frankly, since the allotted crops are being delivered on schedule to the government, nobody's felt a need to be involved. It really is the maharanis' letters that have gotten my attention."

"I'm surprised the uncle can't decide the schooling for his nephew, the young maharaja," Perveen said.

Mr. Sandringham smiled wryly. "Remember, the dowager maharani Putlabai is the prime minister's mother. What man would cross his mother?"

As a solicitor, Perveen had witnessed plenty of situations where adult children dominated their parents and sometimes treated them very badly. But there was no point in arguing when she needed to know more. "Do the maharanis know you're sending me to talk to them?"

"I sent them a letter advising that P. J. Mistry, Esquire, would come calling." Sandringham gave her a long look. "My letter did not mention your gender. My goal was to catch them off guard."

"Ah. So that if they refuse on the basis of gender, I can take off my hat and let them see who I am!" Perveen imagined it as a piece of theater: a suspense drama without a script. "I think if the women want a resolution to the education conflict, they'll be eager to admit me. I'll get the situation sorted out."

"Sorted!" Sandringham repeated slowly. Then he snapped his fingers and laughed.

"What is it?" Perveen was disconcerted.

"During your Oxford days, did you ever play cards?"

She was taken aback. "Certainly. But I played in the evenings at St. Hilda's with other women."

He looked disappointed. "Nobody else?"

She thought hard. "I played bridge once with a mixed group at Brasenose."

"Yes!" He thumped his hand on the table. "Yes! There was a most exciting bridge club meeting where two female students came unchaperoned—one Indian and one English."

Perveen laughed aloud. "Mr. Sandringham, you're speaking about my good friend Alice, who is now living in Bombay. Her father is Sir David Hobson-Jones, the government councillor who suggested me to the Kolhapur Agency."

"This really is turning into old home week." A wide smile spread across his face. "Will you please call me Colin? After all, we studied and played cards together."

This was not literally true. It also was a violation of etiquette to be on first names with an Englishman. But the claret was working its subtle magic, shifting time backward, so the man across the table had become a peer. "Very well. Colin."

He beamed at her. "What does P. J. stand for?"

"Perveen is my first name. My middle name is Jamshedji."

"Isn't that a man's name?"

"Yes, my father's. Parsi women always have their father's first name as their middle name." Until they married, and the husband's first name was swapped in. According to the records kept in the Parsi matrimonial court, Perveen's name was still Perveen Cyrus Sodawalla. She was a woman who was separated but not divorced. This was a twilight status that she downplayed by using her maiden name.

"I'd suggest cards tonight if there wasn't so much correspondence for you to see. I've got letters from the royal household and more."

She was glad to be back on professional footing. "Yes, I'd like to see the letters."

"I brought everything in and put it on the small table where I was going through letters earlier. We could have our tea while we read."

They carried their teacups back to the spot with low chairs, and Perveen took the leather folio he handed her. A stack of letters lay inside.

"Most recent are on top," Colin said, settling into his chair.

In the glow of a hurricane lamp, Perveen studied the dowager maharani Putlabai's letter dated May 10, 1921, and written on fine cotton paper with a palace crest. It was in English; Perveen wondered if the lady had written it herself or spoken to a palace scribe, who'd translated.

Dear Mr. Sandringham,

Greetings from the Royal House of Satapur. As the seasons change, the weather grows hotter. Rain will be welcome. I trust that you are comfortable in your residence, which must be better suited to the English life than our palace.

However, the palace is the only home my grandchildren have known. My daughter-in-law has proposed sending the maharaja away to England. This is against my permission. To send him off to live with commoners in a cold place could be ruinous to his health. Danger befell his brother in the forest. I could not bear to lose the maharaja after experiencing the loss of his brother and of his father. My own son was not educated in England. We should not break tradition because she has a silly idea.

You may also question why the junior maharani would wish to send her son away. I know the answer. Since the death of her husband, she has not had a clear thought. Her mood is bad; she has no interest in children. Mostly I am spending time caring for the maharaja and his sister in my quarters while she follows her own pursuits.

For the love of my grandson and the future of the state, I beg you to stop any plots to tear him from Satapur.

With best wishes for your health,
Putlabai
Maharani of Satapur

Perveen knew people were sometimes more likely to exaggerate in writing than in spoken language. It was easier to be dramatic. She wondered if the letter truly expressed the dowager maharani's position or that of the palace officer or prime minister. She picked up the second letter. Dated on May 20, 1921, it was not on official stationery but the type of lined notepaper that students used. The script was neat Marathi.

My dear Sir:

I greet you with respect and prayers for the continued strength of Satapur. As mother of the monarch of a princely state, I am seeking assistance.

My son is now ten years old. In eight years, he will take responsibility for every aspect of Satapur. I seek to send him to Ludgrove School in England. My late husband believed an English education is necessary for a prince to rule wisely. I also believe that to ensure my son's physical safety, he must attend school in England.

I am calling on you to assist with inquiries to the school on behalf of His Highness. Certainly there is money in the royal coffers to pay for the education, travel expenses, and any suggested gifts to the school. Please inform me by return letter of your progress. I should like to shift with both my children to a residence in Poona before rainy season becomes intense. This will make it possible for Jiva Rao to sail from Bombay in July to England.

I trust you will honor this lawful request.
Mirabai
Maharani of Satapur

"Both letters are signed with the title of just 'maharani.' Clearly Putlabai doesn't want to call herself 'dowager,' and Mirabai doesn't want to call herself 'junior,'" Perveen commented as she considered the letter. "That shows us competition—and they both have presented valid arguments for the boy's welfare. How difficult this is, because you've never met any of the people involved."

Colin took a long, appreciative sip of tea. "I have read reports from McLaughlin about Prince Jiva Rao. Apparently he's got quite an imperious nature, even at his young age. He doesn't enjoy maths or literature, but he likes drawing pictures of animals."

"I heard from Sir David there is also a young princess?"

"That is Princess Padmabai, who I believe was born in 1914, which should make her seven." Colin sipped more tea. "I don't know anything else about her."

Because the princess wouldn't inherit the throne, she must have been of no interest to the Kolhapur Agency. Perveen sighed and pushed back her shoulders, trying to ease their stiffness.

"Does your body hurt?"

She was startled, both by his observation and his frank language. "Just a little."

"I recall how uncomfortable the gari ride can be."

"It was fine. I'm just a bit sleepy." Perveen was embarrassed that he'd noticed her discomfort. She didn't want him thinking she wasn't fit enough for the journey to the palace. "May I take the letters into my room? I want to read just a bit longer."

He nodded. "Take the whole dossier. It includes the original agreement made between the government and Maharaja Mohan Rao, who was the ruler two generations ago, and continues through to correspondence from his son, Maharaja Mahendra Rao."

Gathering it up, she said, "I find it strange that Maharani Mirabai would think her son could get out of these mountains to sail for England in July. That's the height of rainy season. Also, I wonder if there's evidence here of what Maharaja Mahendra Rao wanted for his sons."

"I know that he read history at Fergusson College in Poona, but he never explicitly stated he wanted the same for his son." Colin put down his empty teacup. "In any case, the decision about schooling is yours to make."

"It's not my aim to be the decider." At his startled expression, she added, "It would be best to bring the two maharanis to an agreement about the prince's education. Then there'd be no feeling of one person being a winner and the other a loser."

He raised his eyebrows. "What about where the boy would like to go?"

Perveen paused to consider. She could not imagine a situation where a child was allowed to decide on a school. Slowly, she said, "I understand that you were able to choose your field of study. Maybe it's like that for young people in the West. But not in India—and this boy is just ten years old."

"Cultural sensitivity has its place," he said. "But this boy will be ruling in eight years. I'd like to improve the relationship between the state and the Kolhapur Agency. Why not let him feel we are on his side? According to the contract made between our government and princely states, the British will serve as a prince's guardian if his father is not living. You are the personification of that guardianship."

Perveen mulled over what this meant. "Is the maharani Mirabai guardian to the children who are not heirs to the throne?"

He shook his head. "Because there is no ruling male, all the palace women and children come under our protection."

This shocking piece of information gave her an opening. "If we are responsible for all, we cannot ignore the fact that in these letters, both maharanis have voiced concerns for Prince Jiva Rao's safety."

"The grandmother spoke of worries about his health. The mother said something a little different—"

"Physical safety," Perveen said, looking over the letter again. "There have been two deaths of male rulers in the last two years."

His eyes narrowed as he looked at her. "Are you hinting at something?"

"More than hinting. We are getting a message loud and clear that the prince is at risk of losing his life."

5

THE MISSING LEG

Once the words were out, she wished she could take them back. Colin's jaw had stiffened, and she could imagine what he was thinking. She was overdramatic, because she was Indian and because she was a woman. She knew the stereotypes.

He cleared his throat and said, "That is a strong statement."

"I could be wrong," she said quickly. "I hope so. But both of the women are anxious, and Maharaja Jiva Rao is the last male in the family line. If he were to die, who would take over as ruler?"

"I've been told those decisions aren't made until the event happens. The government sometimes chooses a very distant relative, or a fine young man of the same caste who is outside the family tree, depending on the age or suitability."

"It confounds me that British India has control over who the rulers are in non-British India. Tell me, who's the most likely candidate in Satapur?" she persisted.

He shook his head. "I agree it seems like overreach, but right now, the royal succession is not our business. The only matter before us now is the maharaja Jiva Rao's education."

"The maharaja's well-being," Perveen corrected in a crisp tone, because she had a sense he was holding something back, "certainly includes safety as well as education. That is the reasonable legal interpretation of the role of the British government in relation to the ward."

Instead of answering, Colin rose stiffly and walked from the parlor. Perveen had the sinking feeling she'd overstepped her role. But he returned a moment later carrying another folio.

"Because you mentioned safety—these papers will give you a better understanding of the palace's structure. We have a map based on McLaughlin's observations."

Perveen looked with interest at the large, brittle map he unfolded. It was dominated by two structures. Colin explained the one in front was an old palace built in 1704 where the dowager maharani still lived, and across the courtyard garden behind it was a palace built in 1905 where Maharani Mirabai and the children stayed. There were also many outbuildings for servants, kitchen gardens and leisure gardens, storehouses, stables, and even a riding ring.

"There are entrances to the compound on the north and south sides," Colin said, pointing. "North is the one you'll see when you arrive."

After studying the layout, Perveen thought the walled complex seemed impenetrable. "I hope I'll be admitted. Otherwise all our debating about the prince's education and safety is for naught."

"I hope so, too." Colin refolded the map gently and put it atop the documents she was taking to her room. "Rama serves breakfast at seven. The palanquin should come by nine. You should be at the palace before noon."

"Thank you for arranging that, and for letting me have a look at these papers."

"No need to thank me." He went to the side of the easy chair and picked up his cane. "I hadn't thought about there being any peril for the young prince. I realize now that I should have."

So she hadn't come off as badly as she'd thought. In a subdued voice, she bade him good night and walked the length of the veranda to her room.

After she'd locked the bedroom door that opened to the veranda, she washed her face and brushed her teeth using the porcelain bowl on the teak washstand. She studied the map a while longer, trying to commit it to memory. In her experience, it was not good to go into a place without knowing how to leave it. Then she blew out her candle and went to the bed.

Sleep did not come easily. Despite the mosquito netting, at least one bug whined close by her ear. Was it inside the netting or out? She couldn't tell. The mosquito buzzed off, returning every so often just to awaken her when she was almost asleep. There was plenty of other noise to contend with: tree frogs outside and, later on, the hooting of owls. Eventually she drifted off, but she jerked awake at the sound of a scream.

She sat bolt upright before the scream came again, and she realized it was a cockerel crowing early in the dark.

It seemed too dark to be morning. She used the matches left on the night table to light the candle. According to her French wristwatch, it was only five o'clock. Over the next ten minutes, as if prodded by the lord of chickens, the bulbuls and cuckoos and koel birds in the garden began to chatter. The birdcalls reminded her of Lillian, her pet parrot at home in Bombay. She wondered how Lillian would react to such a wild environment.

Perveen read documents by candlelight until six-fifteen, when the sky lightened enough that through her window, she finally had something to look at: an impressive range of green hills. Perhaps she could get a picture of the sunrise. Dressing quickly in a comfortable cotton-silk sari, she picked up her Kodak Brownie and went out the door to the veranda, where a large white dog lay sprawled.

In the pale daylight, the dog lifted his head and appraised her. She realized this must be the guard dog that Colin had mentioned.

"Desi," she cooed to him, trying to act as if they were already friends.

Desi thumped his tail before lowering his head again. Perveen was glad he hadn't perceived her as a threat. Had it been her confident greeting, or did the dog know that people coming out of the guest rooms were not dangerous?

Stepping off the veranda's last wide step, Perveen gazed around at everything she'd missed on arrival. The garden was planted with erratically spaced champa trees, rui shrubs, Burmese cassias, and tamarind. She surveyed overgrown stands of flame-colored hibiscus and purple orchids and tall grasses. It was hard to tell flowers from weeds; maybe there was little difference.

After snapping a picture of the sunrise over the mountains, she walked around the bungalow and stopped short at the sight of animal movement on the grass. A whole family of lion-tailed macaques was gathered under a cassia. The large one that Colin had called Hanuman stood at the outward edge, giving her a look that felt challenging. *Do not come too close.*

Slowly, she raised her camera to her eyes.

"Go, go!" cried a young boy, running toward the monkeys. At his arrival, the monkeys scattered.

Perveen stifled her desire to tell the boy off for spoiling her chance at an endearing photograph. "Are you Mohit or Hari?"

"I am Mohit. I tell you, Hanuman and his family come just to steal our food." The stable boy offered up a sweet grin. "Rama is making breakfast for seven, but do you wish it earlier?"

Smiling back at him, Perveen shook her head. "No need! I'll eat with Sandringham-sahib at seven. I'm just taking a walk."

"To where?" Mohit asked cheerfully. Clearly he hadn't been trained to be seen and not heard like the waiters in the Royal Western India Turf Club. She liked that.

"I hear Marshall Point has a grand view of the mountain range. How far is it?"

"Mmm, a few minutes. Through the ironwood forest—there is a path. But be careful, memsahib. There are many snakes hiding in the leaves."

She lifted the edge of her sari, showing him the buttoned kid-skin boots. "I will be careful. Thank you."

As Perveen headed from the garden into the forest, she thought about how the servant had seemed unruffled by the sight of her walking about so early. She wondered if other women travelers had come alone. If so, they had likely been British, stopping by on their way to join their husbands at their posts.

Maybe British women wouldn't be troubled by the thought of staying at this place with a bachelor. They didn't have family in Bombay worrying about their safety and reputations. And the fact was, they might fancy Colin Sandringham's company. He was neither too young, nor too old; and he had a straightforward way about him that she'd appreciated. She had disputed several points the previous evening, but he had not badgered her into agreeing that his opinion was right. He'd seemed to be a good listener.

She thought all this while keeping a careful eye on the path. The sky was lightening, and ahead through the ironwood trees, she saw a grassy bluff. This must have been Marshall Point. But as she drew closer, she hesitated.

On the bluff, she saw two human figures. Instead of standing upright, they were crouched just as the family of monkeys had been. Drawing closer, she realized they were two men, each positioned on a mat and apparently stretching. With surprise, she recognized the smaller man, who was wearing a dhoti and vest, by his thick head of silver hair: Rama. The Englishman with him was Colin. He wore loose cotton pajama trousers and the same kind of vest as Rama. Colin's arms were finely muscled and his skin more golden than pink.

"Push backward. Higher." Rama spoke Marathi and laid his hands on either side of Colin's waist as he contorted into a position that looked like a triangle.

Perveen made her way quietly forward, wanting to get a better look. Colin had moved back down onto the mat and now was curved like a bow, his stomach on the ground. After some time, he moved from the bow position onto his side, and then he was standing. He and Rama faced each other; then they were laying their hands on the mat and stepping forward, shifting so that their haunches rose up, as a dog did after awakening. As she watched the men's bodies flow, her own body suddenly felt tired, hunched, and inflexible. She considered how it might feel to stretch in such a way—which should have looked disgraceful but, in reality, seemed rather beautiful.

Colin's body stretched as flat as a board on the ground. He stayed there for a long minute. Then he pulled his body back into the strange curve that reminded her of an animal until one leg shot high and straight in the air. The pajama leg fell loosely away.

Perveen blinked, not believing what she'd just seen.

Colin Sandringham had a stump where the bottom half of his right calf and right foot should have been. Not a lame foot—no foot.

She recalled him in the jodhpurs and boots the night before, using a cane from time to time. Because he had worn boots, she'd assumed he had a bad foot. Now she realized he must have worn a wooden leg in order to give the appearance of normalcy.

It was strange; with all the camouflage he'd used the night before, his handicap had stood out to her. But now, as he flowed through exercises without his prosthesis, he seemed almost as strong and graceful as Rama.

Colin was upside down now, with his head on the ground braced by bent arms on either side. She marveled at the strength of his abdomen and arms. How could one balance like that? As her gaze stayed on him, she suddenly realized that through his arms, he had seen her.

She was too far away to read the expression in his eyes, but she saw his upper body toppling to the right; with a short step, Rama was there, righting Colin so he didn't fall.

Perveen turned and ran clumsily, wondering if he'd been able to identify her or just suspected some person had been looking. Would it be better to pretend she hadn't been there, so he could feel reassured his privacy about his handicap hadn't been violated?

She wanted to say that she was sorry, to explain that she'd stumbled upon the sight of the two of them and been fascinated by the beauty of their exercise. But that was half the truth. She'd stayed because she'd wanted to fill her eyes with the sight of Colin.

The question of what to do was answered when she stepped out onto the veranda for breakfast. Two places were set, each with a boiled egg, two chapatis, and a small bowl of purple berries. Rama came forward and stood silently next to the table.

"Is Sandringham-sahib missing breakfast?" she asked uneasily in Marathi.

After a pause, he answered her in the same language. "I don't know if he will come. He was surprised that you watched us this morning."

Sensing the reproof in his tone, she began explaining herself. "I intended to take pictures of the mountains. I didn't know you'd be there. Is that a morning custom?"

"Yes. We practice there daily, when it is not raining."

She was embarrassed that her discovery might be keeping Colin from feeling comfortable facing her. But curiosity overcame her shame. "How long have you been teaching Sandringham-sahib those exercises?"

"Almost a year." Sounding defensive, he added, "It's good for his health."

"I saw how strong you've made him."

The deep creases in Rama's brow relaxed slightly. He nodded, as if accepting her praise.

Perveen ventured a bit further. "Yesterday he said he served in the war, but he didn't say he'd lost his leg."

"The injury did not happen there."

"Oh?" She watched Rama, hoping for him to continue.

"He does not talk much about it."

"I can see he functions very well," Perveen said.

Looking past her into the garden, he spoke in a low voice.
"When he was working as a district collector, he once traveled
to a hamlet. Many people had come to report their troubles, and
there were unwatched children wandering the area. A girl got too
close to a snake. A saw-scaled viper."

Perveen shuddered. "But that is one of the most poisonous
snakes in the world!"

"Yes," he said shortly. "The snake hissed, and the people implored
the girl to stay still. But the viper was still pointing toward her.
Sandringham-sahib suddenly ran forward, wanting the snake to
turn away from the child so she could escape. But it lashed out
at him instead."

"It got him?"

He nodded grimly. "The nearest doctor was two days' ride. By
the time we reached Dr. Andrews, it was very late. The doctor
had to take his foot to save his life."

Perveen winced. "And after that, he was forced to keep working
in the civil service?"

"Nobody forced me to do anything," said Colin in a cold
voice. Perveen whipped her head around and saw he'd stepped
out onto the veranda. "Sorry to interrupt, but I don't fancy listening to stories being told behind my back."

Rama bowed his head as if ashamed of betraying Colin's confidence.

Flushing red with embarrassment, Perveen said, "I was the
one who pressured him to explain. You see, I thought your exercises were splendid."

"Not today," Colin said with a snort. "I almost fell on my face.
Rama saved me, just as he did before."

"Do not say that," Rama demurred.

"It's true. You saved my life by having me drink that god-
awful tree sap on the journey out of the hamlet." Colin settled
himself at the table.

"It is quite impressive that you are willing to stay in the

mofussil," Perveen said as the boy she'd seen in the garden appeared with a teapot.

"Why shouldn't I?" Spreading a cloth napkin in his lap, Colin said, "It was damned hard to get into the ICS. I could still work—just not run about. While I recuperated, my department head searched for a position where I wouldn't need to continuously travel. This post was considered suitable because political agents here don't have to travel for the six months of rainy season. And they were good enough to allow Rama to become my permanent bearer. I could have had a cook from the village, but I've liked what he's made for me."

"It is an Ayurvedic diet. The proper food aids in healing," Rama said as he poured tea into Colin's cup.

Perveen smiled her thanks as Rama poured for her. "And do you always practice those exercises in the dry months?"

"If anything, I practice all the more in the bad weather. We can use the veranda." Colin looked intently at her. "Ayurvedic food and exercise not only helps my body. It does something to my head. Makes me feel calmer."

Perveen watched Rama travel the length of the veranda and down the steps, disappearing into the garden. His soft-footed, fluid walking style reminded her of the unusual movement she'd witnessed. "Is there a name for those exercises?"

"The proper name is yoga. Have you tried it?"

"All I know of yoga is it's a Hindu worship tradition done by holy men. I'm surprised that Rama knows it so well that he can teach you."

"Rama didn't start as a servant." Colin spread a little ghee on his chapati. "He was a priest in the area where I had my accident. The villagers called him for assistance, and he went all the way with me to the hospital. I found him comforting. And I could pay him—which was something the villagers could not. He and his family subsisted on very little; now he can send them money."

Perveen tasted the berries, expecting them to be sour but finding them pleasantly sweet. Rama's story was the classic tale of why rural people abandoned their native places. Her own household employed six people, five of whom had left home in order to earn enough to support their loved ones.

Her thoughts were interrupted by the sound of Rama's distant voice. She turned to see he was still in the garden but addressing a lean, muscular man wearing a threadbare vest and dhoti. She hadn't known they had a visitor.

Colin followed her gaze. "That's Lakshman."

"Does he work here as well?"

"No, he has his own business in the village. He is a highly experienced and dependable fellow who leads the team of men carrying the palanquin."

Rama's voice dropped, and he and the man looked at each other for a long, silent moment. Then Rama walked back to the breakfast table. Gravely, he said, "Lakshman reports the palanquin and the bearers are not in station."

Colin frowned. "But he knows we scheduled the palanquin ride for today."

"Two days ago they traveled to Lonavala for a short job. They intended to return yesterday, but there was a problem with the palanquin. A carpenter is making a repair."

Perveen had always been loath to ride in a palanquin. It was not only embarrassing to be carried on top of men's shoulders; it was bound to be uncomfortable. "Must I really travel by palanquin, when the palace is just twelve miles? I can ride a horse." She pushed back the thought of all the challenges she'd had riding Dolly a few days earlier.

Slowly, Colin shook his head. "It's hard to make a horse go willingly through some parts of the jungle. Especially if it hears a tiger's or leopard's roar."

Perveen didn't like the idea of hearing such sounds but wasn't going to let on. "Could the postmen take me in their wagon?"

Rama shook his head. "They've just left."

"Might another palanquin be hired?" she asked reluctantly.

"The circuit house has some old carriages in the stable, but no palanquins," Colin said. "I've always used Lakshman's palanquin. But don't worry. Eventually they will come, and you will be able to leave."

She hated the idea of arriving late to the palace. "Could word be relayed about the transportation problem to the Satapur palace? Surely they could send a palanquin for me."

"As Rama mentioned, the postal wagon's gone, so I'm afraid we can't send a letter," Colin said. "In any case, I don't think it's wise to ask such a favor. It would make us beholden to them."

She hadn't thought of that.

"Another day here shouldn't be a waste." Colin's voice brightened. "We can talk more about the palace situation. And tonight I could gather a few local people for dinner. They'd be thrilled to meet a woman lawyer, especially in these parts."

She didn't want to be a burden on him—after all, he had expected her to be gone by nine. "Dinner with your friends is fine, but what else could I do today? Is there a village that I could visit?"

"Yes, there's a village nearby—but it's not very scenic, and there's little to buy. What are you looking for?"

"I thought I'd check if someone knew about another palanquin. In case I could actually leave soon."

"I'm sorry—but I don't think there is one," he said.

"One never knows. Might I ride there using one of the circuit house horses? I've brought my own riding clothes."

He looked at her warily. "You may, but I won't be able to go with you. I've got a visitor coming today."

She realized he didn't understand she was trying to make the situation easier for both of them. "That's quite all right. I don't need an escort."

He shook his head. "It's easy to get lost or fall off a cliff if the mist rises. Lakshman must lead you there."

"Thank you." Perveen finished her breakfast thinking that the weather looked quite fine. It seemed suspicious that the transportation had suddenly fallen through. Colin wanted her to visit the palace, but what if someone else did not feel the same?

6

SUBJECTS OF THE MAHARAJA

Despite two weeks' practice at the Royal Western India Turf Club, Perveen was still uncomfortable on horses. It seemed clear that Rani, the horse assigned to her by the stable boy, Mohit, knew this from the start. As did her guide, Lakshman.

As they traveled through the forest on narrow paths that came close to the mountain's edge, the scrawny spotted mare refused to heed the kicking of her heels or any pulling on the reins. After ten frustrating minutes, Lakshman, who'd been walking along-side, chewing paan that Rama had given him, took the reins in hand and led the two of them into the village. Perveen could understand Lakshman's irritation. She had already asked if he knew anyone with another palanquin, and he'd said no.

They proceeded through an area of broken, burned buildings. It looked as if people were living in the ruins; they'd cobbled together bits of wood and tin and cloth to make roofs. The monsoon had done its months of damage, raining straight through the holes.

"What happened here?" Perveen asked Lakshman. "It looks like there was a fire."

"After the maharaja died of cholera, the royal soldiers burned everything."

Perveen was dismayed. "Is it necessary to burn buildings to control epidemics?"

"Sometimes. But the palace was angry at us. We were the ones who polluted the maharaja and made him die." Lakshman's words were matter-of-fact.

Perveen shook her head. She recalled Colin saying Maharaja Mahendra Rao had had an enlightened attitude toward public health and wondered if he would have disapproved of these actions taken after his death. "Is there a post office?" She thought a postmaster would be a reliable source of information on the existence of another palanquin bearer.

Lakshman shook his head.

It really was a small place. "What about a school?"

He shook his head again and spit red betel juice on the ground.

Feeling uneasy, she asked, "Which village does have a school?"

"No need for schools in Satapur. Everyone is farming."

So the previous maharajas hadn't thought it worthwhile to better the minds of their subjects. Feeling cynical, she asked, "Are there other jobs for people besides in the fields?"

His thin shoulders rose in a weary shrug. "Men like me who care for horses and donkeys and take travelers places. And there are a few shops. You will see in our bazaar."

Perveen wondered what comfort natural splendor could provide to people who had so little. She felt some irritation that Colin had not mentioned the condition of these villagers.

As a teenager studying both history and current affairs, she had fantasized what India would be like if it were entirely a tapestry of small kingdoms, each ruled by an Indian. Young Perveen had thought of a diverse, independent subcontinent as a glorious prospect. But now she was disturbed to see how little care this ruling family had taken with its subjects.

"Here is the bazaar," announced Lakshman.

Perveen peered ahead at the muddy lane punctuated by a few weathered wooden stalls. Sitting on the edges of them were men wearing rough homespun and wary expressions. There were no cries about how delicious their wares were, or how well made. It was not at all tempting, as Bombay's markets were. But she was determined not to turn away.

Lakshman's mouth had settled into a smug line. It seemed as if he was reminding her that he'd told her she shouldn't have come and pointing out that here was her reward.

She forced a cheerful note into her voice. "Lakshman, will you please take the horse? I'd like to get down and walk through the market."

Lakshman nodded and steered Rani to one of the shops, where there was a step for Perveen to disembark. She thanked him and began her walk, feeling the eyes of everyone on her. It was only a split second before the charge began.

"Memsahib, memsahib, come and buy!"

The vendors looked so thin and anxious that she wished to buy something. But all she saw were the nuts and grains that were grown locally, as well as sugar and salt priced the same as in Bombay. She continued and found a sweet stand. It sold just one item: the cashew brittle known as chikki. She bought three one-pound boxes. They went into a jute bag she bought at another shop for more than she would have paid at Bombay's Crawford Market. She could have bargained harder, but she felt sorry for the men.

"I am not a cook, so I'm sorry; I have no use for grain," she said with a smile to the elderly man who'd sold her the bag.

"You are going to the palace?" he asked with a wheeze.

She was startled, having assumed the matter was confidential government business. "Where did you hear that?"

"Everybody knows that a lady traveler is leaving from the circuit house."

"Yes, but the palanquin is in Lonavala."

"It is broken."

It seemed strange that the news had traveled from Lonavala without benefit of telephone or telegram. "How did you know about the delay?"

He pointed back to where Lakshman was waiting with the horse. "He is the one who walked back from Lonavala alone."

"Does anyone else have a palanquin?"

The man shook his head. She asked a few other people, and then, convinced that she'd exhausted her possibilities, she returned to find Lakshman sitting in the shade of a tree. His eyes were closed, as if he was napping. She thought about the roughness of the long journey he'd made on foot and felt guilty for having suspected dishonesty about the palanquin situation.

As he jerked awake to look at her, she said, "Thank you for bringing me here. I've seen everything. I shall ride back to the circuit house by myself. I know the way."

"The horse does not like you."

He had a point. She might be unable to get the damn horse to go the way she wanted. But she also knew that she needed to learn how to move horses by herself if she was going to be independent during her time in Satapur. "If she stops and won't go my way, I'll get down and lead her with the reins. My boots are good for riding and walking."

Lakshman gave her a grudging nod. "Yes, but . . ."

He was probably thinking that if he didn't take her back, he would get only half the money.

"What is your fee?" she asked.

He told her an anna, and she doubled it.

Before clambering back on, Perveen looked Rani square in the eyes and informed her that they were going back to the circuit house. It was unrealistic to think the horse understood Marathi, but she did belong to the circuit house, and seemed more amiable about the idea of returning home. Being up on the horse by herself was frightening at first, but then it was exhilarating. She was riding without a guide—and perhaps because Perveen was the only human around, Rani responded. After five minutes, Perveen felt relaxed enough to glance away from the horse and examine the surroundings. As they traveled back into the woods, she took a longer look at a bungalow she'd noticed on their ride into the village. A brass plate on its wrought iron gate said HEAVEN'S REST.

Through its iron gate, she surveyed the large, new-looking stucco bungalow, built in the fashionable neo-Georgian style.

Beyond the house's stone wall was a large garden with elegantly clipped trees and bushes, a dramatic contrast to the lush overgrowth at the circuit house. She wondered who lived in the bungalow. It appeared double the size of Colin's government residence and surely was too grand for the local doctor.

Perveen nudged Rani to move on. They continued at the same pace until a sound from behind alerted Perveen that someone was coming up fast on the narrow path. She kicked lightly but frantically at the horse's side to get her to sidle to the edge of the road. They made it just as a tall black horse cantered by. She would have expected the rider to tip a hat to acknowledge her courtesy, but he did not.

All she could do was glower. The rider was an Indian man wearing jodhpurs and a pith helmet. He was too fancy to be a villager; perhaps he was the landowner, although he had not emerged from Heaven's Rest.

Arriving at the circuit house ten minutes later, she saw Rama leading the same black horse into the stable. When he finished, he came to her side and held Rani while she slid down.

"Who has arrived?" She decided not to tell Rama how annoyed she'd been.

"The government engineer. He's staying the night."

"I see." Perhaps this was the man with whom Colin had an important appointment that had kept him from going into the village with her.

"Sandringham-sahib has eaten. I will bring your lunch."

After washing off the dust from the ride, she went to the veranda table for a very modest repast: a bowl of dal and small plates holding some greens, a paratha, and a cup of tea. Still, it was tasty. She thanked Rama and retired to her room to read through more of the palace correspondence, which was mostly between the last political agent and the late Maharaja Mahendra

Rao. The letters made it seem that Mahendra Rao had made inquiries into the cost of a prospective school in the village she'd just toured, and he had suggested building a processing plant for grain, rather than having it sent away. She was glad to gather these bits and pieces so she could bring up the ideas when she spoke to the maharanis.

At four-thirty, she heard voices. She remembered Colin's mention of local people possibly coming to dinner. It was far too early, she thought with irritation. She wouldn't have a chance to question him privately about why the late maharaja's plans weren't being carried out.

Perveen had been relaxing in her chemise and petticoat while reading, but now she donned a fresh white Chantilly lace blouse and a violet-colored Pathani sari with a pattern of green parrots woven into the border. Swiftly, she styled her hair into a pompadour. She took care not to touch her pearl necklace when she rubbed herself with the pungent neem oil to keep the mosquitoes away.

Walking out to the veranda, she saw that the teak table where she'd breakfasted and lunched was set for tea. Colin had a hand on the table's edge, as he faced the Indian man she'd seen riding past her earlier in the day. She recognized his solid frame even though he'd changed from his riding clothes into a beige linen lounge suit similar to the one Colin was wearing.

The click of heels announced more guests. Perveen turned toward the sound and saw an Indian couple, both of whom were smiling excitedly. The male was a dapper fellow in his sixties, with thin hair that had been slicked with black pomade in the manner of a much younger man; he wore a suit of a lissome wool that could have come only from Europe. The lady with him appeared to be in her late thirties and was dressed in a chiffon sari of the palest blush color. There was no border at all, making it likely the fabric was from France. She'd left her hair uncovered, revealing that it was cut into a shingle style that ended just below her jaw. As she drew close, Perveen saw robust diamonds hanging from her ears, and that her eyes were lined and lips rouged to a cherry red.

Colin went forward to shake the gentleman's hand. Then he turned to Perveen. "You must meet Yazad and Vandana Mehta. They own a large farm nearby. Perveen is a solicitor from Bombay who is traveling onward tomorrow."

"I rode by your place today. It's beautiful," Perveen said, studying them. While the man had the fair skin and prominent nose that were common to Iranis, the Zoroastrians whose families had emigrated from Persia in the last seventy years, the woman looked different. She had wheat-colored skin, exquisite Dravidian cheekbones, and almond-shaped eyes.

"How exciting to meet an accomplished woman!" Mrs. Mehta said in an accent with hints of England, India, and somewhere else. Was it France?

"I am only at the beginning of my career, Mrs. Mehta," Perveen said, feeling awkward about the woman's gushing.

"You must call me Vandana. There are so few of us in the area, Colin and Yazad are like a family, using first names."

Yazad was a Parsi name as surely as Vandana was a Hindu one. For Perveen, the fact that they were a mixed-faith couple was as stunning as that they used first names, just like Colin.

"We usually see few ladies here," Yazad Mehta said, putting out a hand to her. "And then just English ladies with narrow noses. A lady with a good Parsi nose is a pleasant surprise."

Uneasily, she chuckled and tried to refocus her thoughts. She decided to speak in Gujarati and throw in a Parsi expression for good measure. "My parents would be mortified if I addressed my elders without titles. May I call you Yazad-uncle and Vandana-aunty?"

"Naturally," Yazad Mehta said, but he spoke in English, and then repeated what she'd said, as if his wife didn't know Gujarati. "Consider us as your family in the hills."

"Although 'aunty' feels a little old for me," Vandana said, flashing her beautiful eyes mischievously. "I like to tell people I have just celebrated my twenty-ninth birthday."

"We all have celebrated Vandana's twenty-ninth twice already!" Colin said with a grin. "Perveen, I'd also like to introduce Roderick Ames of the ICS engineering division. Roddy's based in Poona but comes through a few times a year on assignment."

"Good afternoon, ma'am," Mr. Ames said in a rolling Welsh accent. Perveen thought this was like a masquerade party. She had met a woman with a short Western hairstyle and an Indian background; a Parsi man who was married to a Hindu; and now a man with an English name who had Indian bone structure and coloring. And bringing them together was a casual young Englishman who called everyone by their first names.

"I'm very pleased to meet you, Mr. Ames," Perveen said, deciding against employing his first name since he'd given her the cue of *ma'am*. "What kind of engineering do you practice?"

"Electrical is my specialty, though I have training in civil engineering as well," he said with obvious pride. "I'm en route to Lonavala. The dam there has some issues."

Perveen remembered that there was only one palanquin in the area. Would Roderick Ames also wish to use it? She imagined his government business in a British Indian town might trump her excursion to visit Indian royals. "How will you travel there?"

"I came by horse, and that's how I'll continue." He shot her a sideways glance. "You weren't also riding a little while ago, were you?"

"I certainly was," Perveen answered coolly, deciding not to publicly announce that he had almost knocked her off the path. It wouldn't help her image to appear to be a helpless female.

"Roddy knows the way quite well having gone many times. He is fearless," Colin said. "Sit down, everyone. Rama is preparing drinks."

As people settled around the table, Roderick Ames took a

planter's chair, just on the edge of things. From her beaded purse, Vandana pulled an ebony cigarette holder and a golden box decorated with a pattern of diamonds surrounding an amethyst flower. "Who else would like a Sobranie?" she asked.

"I will join you," Yazad said, taking a sleek silver lighter out of his breast pocket. Roderick Ames looked for a long moment at the open cigarette case Vandana proffered, but he shook his head.

"Perveen?" Vandana's thinly plucked eyebrows rose. "You are a sophisticated lady, yes?"

"The taste doesn't suit me." Perveen tried to sound nonjudgmental.

"The Parsis believe fire is a sacred element that should not be polluted. That's why they don't smoke." Yazad gave Perveen a patronizing look as he reached into the box for his own cigarette. She resented it; she felt he was declaring to one and all she was old-fashioned and bound by her community's rules.

"No thank you," Colin said.

Perveen looked at him with surprise. Meeting her gaze, he said, "I smoked Player's when I was a collector. But Rama pointed out that it weakened my ability to do the deep breathing that is part of yoga. So I very rarely smoke anymore."

"Dr. Andrews smokes a pipe. Any doctor would tell you smoking is healthy," Vandana said, puffing a smoke ring heavenward. "I spent my childhood watching males enjoying the pleasure of cheroots, pipes, and cigarettes. Chewing mitha paan was supposed to be enough for ladies, but it turned my teeth the most awful red. So I took up cigarettes in Paris and never regretted it."

Perveen wanted to move the conversation elsewhere. Glancing toward Roderick Ames, she said, "Fire seems to be the main source of light in Satapur. Is there a chance of bringing electricity to the state?"

She had expected the engineer to answer, but Vandana broke in.

"Don't I wish it!" the lady said, raising her hands upward as if beseeching a deity. "You must think us awfully backward with no electricity or running water."

"Of course not—this is how much of British India is, too," Perveen said, giving a sidelong look at Colin. "Just as decisions in British India are made by the government, I imagine it's up to the maharaja's family to decide for Satapur, isn't it?"

"Yes." Colin, who had not yet seated himself, rocked slightly to one side, as if his prosthetic foot was uncomfortable. "They own the land and all bodies of water—so even if the Mehtas wished to put in a plant with their own money, they couldn't."

"I've got a question about that," Vandana said with a pretty pout. Patting the empty seat on the other side of her, she said, "Do join me. I have a geography question for Colin, because that is his training. A waterfall is the result of many streams flowing from other areas, isn't it?"

"You don't need a geographer to tell you! Every child knows that," Roderick answered condescendingly.

So now he was talking. Perveen shot him a chilly look for the disrespect he'd shown Vandana, and he looked back, nonchalant.

"The streams come from bodies of water that are north of Satapur," Vandana mused. "Wouldn't this mean that water isn't the property of the royal family? And that we could use it as we like?"

Roderick drew his lips together in a thin line. "I don't know. That hasn't been broached before."

"What is your legal opinion, Perveen?" Colin looked intently at Perveen. It was flattering—but also unsettling because lawyers were cautioned not to make statements that could be considered pronouncements in the eyes of the public. Yet here was a chance to show Ames that she and Vandana weren't just window dressing.

"It's not straightforward," Perveen said. "One could certainly go to court to make a point about the water's origin, but an easy counterargument from the royals is that nothing can be built on royal land without permission. So even if one could use the water, it would be hard to manage a plant without building on land."

"That is a question for a male lawyer," Roderick Ames said pointedly. "I don't believe women can be barristers, can they?"

"I currently work as a solicitor in Bombay Presidency," Perveen acknowledged. "But royal courts have no bar against woman lawyers arguing cases in their courts. The empire's first woman solicitor, Cornelia Sorabji, Esquire, has argued cases in several princely states."

"Marvelous!" Vandana said, tapping ash from the glowing end of her cigarette into a glass ashtray. "Since we are in a royal state, we could hire you to be our advocate."

Perveen hesitated. The prospect of such work was tempting, but it would be a conflict of interest. "For now, I'm just working on behalf of the Kolhapur Agency. But I can refer you to someone later."

"Vandana, why don't you just ask the prime minister for permission?" Colin said. "You've got the blood connections."

Perveen's curiosity shot up. "Are you part of Satapur's royal family?"

"Is she ever!" Yazad said merrily. "My wife almost married the late maharaja. But I stole her heart."

"He's exaggerating." Vandana's rouged cheeks went even more pink. "I'm not a princess at all. But my family has always had ties to the palace, and I grew up spending lots of time there."

Roderick stretched out his legs in the long planter's chair. In a serious voice, he said, "There's a superstition about the Satapur royals being fated for early death. If Mrs. Mehta had stuck with tradition, she might have turned into a very young widow."

Perveen already had heard about the maharaja's death from cholera and his first son's death in a hunting accident. Was Roderick Ames implying there had been other tragedies?

"That superstition is bunk," Colin said, cutting in sharply. "The late maharaja's younger brother, Prince Swaroop, is still alive and kicking at his own palace."

"And at the Bombay racetrack," added Vandana, grinding out her cigarette's end inside the ashtray set on the tea table. "If that playboy dies early, it will probably be a suicide due to gambling debt."

Perveen studied Vandana, who was sitting bolt upright with her shoulders back and her chest slightly forward. She looked ready to spring, not to relax with a drink. Perveen decided Vandana's forthrightness could be helpful; she might provide insights into the palace.

"Where are your children this evening?" Roderick asked Vandana, and although he smiled, Perveen wondered if he was insinuating that women should not be concerned with matters outside the household.

"We have none," Vandana said tartly. "The Parsis made it clear to Yazad they would not recognize his children as members of the faith, and my people, if they were still alive, would have done the same."

"It's hard to be adrift in the world without acceptance of family," Perveen said softly, because she sensed pain behind Vandana's crisp reply. She noticed that Roderick Ames had blushed and settled more deeply into his chair, as if he hadn't expected such a response.

"Frankly, our lives are quite busy without children." Yazad put his hand on the small of Vandana's back, touching her skin. "My wife and I met in Paris, which we thoroughly enjoyed. We've lived in London and spent many holidays in Switzerland. We go here and there like vagabonds. We are not suited to be parents."

"I've visited Paris, too." Perveen smiled, feeling solidarity. She, too was hindered by the Parsi marriage law. The law said she and Cyrus did not have grounds for divorce, which meant she could never marry again. The closest she would ever come to being a mother was in roles like this—serving as a guardian to the maharaja and his sister.

Rama appeared with a small silver tray holding a variety of

drinks. The men and Vandana all picked glasses of golden liquid that was likely whiskey. Rather than take the last glass, Perveen shook her head at him. She didn't want to be overly relaxed. "Do you have sweet lime?"

"In a moment." He gave her a nod and disappeared.

"Aren't you a good girl?" Vandana said with a giggle before taking a copious drink. After she'd swallowed, she continued, "My favorite places in India are our dear Heaven's Rest in Satapur and our lovely bungalow in Bombay. Our Bombay residence is near the Willingdon Club. I play tennis there, and I ride at the Royal Western India Turf Club. Do you belong to either place?"

"We're in three Parsi social clubs, but not because we are sporting. None of the Mistrys have the speed for tennis, although we do tuck away mutton dhansek very quickly."

Everyone laughed except Roderick, who stared into the depths of his glass.

"Is something wrong, my boy?" Yazad inquired in an avuncular tone.

The engineer shrugged. "I've no money for club memberships on my ICS salary. I'm from Kharagpur, where a visit to the Railway Officers' Club is a privilege."

Perveen felt chagrined. She hadn't meant to show off but realized how her words to Vandana could be interpreted.

"Hear, hear!" Colin gave him a sympathetic glance. "I share your pain. The only institutions I belong to in India are libraries: the Sassoon and Asiatic."

"You're a director of a club within the Asiatic Library, I hear," Yazad said with a wink. "Quite impressive!"

"I'm just a cofounder," Colin corrected, as if the praise embarrassed him. "Thinkers for the Future is a group of Indians and Europeans who meet fortnightly to hear lectures from scholars— many of them Indian, some British, others from various nations. Of course, I miss most of these lectures due to my remote posting. But I hear the club has evolved into a friendly gathering that makes people comfortable enough to speak freely. Have you heard of Thinkers for the Future, Perveen?"

She shook her head, thinking it sounded rather fun—like the clubs she'd been part of at Oxford. But that seemed like a long-ago world.

"This is truly a special evening with Perveen here," Yazad said. "I wish a photographer could commemorate it. Where are those people when you need them?"

"Thank you very much." Perveen felt flattered. "Actually, I've got a camera. Not fancy—just a Kodak Brownie."

"We could take the picture on the western veranda, where the light is good. Let's hurry!" Colin got up from the table and waved for everyone to follow him.

Perveen fetched her camera and met the assembled group. There was a nice view of the hills on one side and a bit of the circuit house on the other. From underneath a bush, the handsome Hanuman watched as if they were actors assembled to amuse him.

"All right, everyone, get together!" Perveen directed.

"But what about you, Perveen? The point of the picture is to celebrate your arrival!" Vandana cried.

"And Roddy's," said Colin quickly. "Why are you not gathering with the rest of us?"

"No need for it." Roderick Ames was standing several feet away from the Mehtas and Colin. "But an engineer knows his way around a camera. I'd be glad to take the picture."

"But you are also a guest, Mr. Ames. You must be included." Perveen was aware of how the Mehtas had hardly spoken to him, even before he'd made the comment about the water streams. "Could Rama take our picture?"

The bearer had been standing in the shadow of the veranda almost unnoticed. He came forward at Colin's urging, and Perveen demonstrated how to focus the camera and click the shutter. As they posed, Ames stood rigidly at Colin's right side, looking as unhappy as during all the time since Perveen had met him.

As Perveen looked away from him to pose for the camera, she thought about the engineer's strange social behavior. Roderick was from the Bengali town of Kharagpur, where British India's trains were both made and repaired by a workforce that was mostly Anglo-Indian. This railway employment scheme was resented by full-blooded Indians, who were mostly hired for menial railway positions. But the railway positions that had been set aside for Anglo-Indians also meant they stayed in one field. For Roderick to have landed a sophisticated ICS engineering job meant he'd won scholarships and worked very hard. And wherever he had studied, Roderick had likely been excluded by whites and mocked by Indians.

After two pictures had been taken, the group stepped apart. Perveen put her camera away in her room and came back to find everyone sitting on the veranda around a card table.

"Tell me, how are you traveling to the palace?" asked Vandana.

"By palanquin, if it ever is fixed." Perveen explained the palanquin's breakdown in Lonavala. "I wish I could ride a horse there."

Yazad shook his head. "This area around the circuit house is fine, but as you travel south, the forest is not entirely safe."

"Pish, pish, why say such things?" Vandana interrupted sharply. "Honestly, you're overworried."

"Please tell me more about the forest." Perveen sat forward in the planter's chair she'd taken, which felt too large for her.

"There have been quite a few sightings of men who aren't local." Yazad's voice dropped to a low, dramatic tone. "They may be men who are sought by the government of British India. They live in the forest because they're beyond the reach of law there."

"Is their existence actually documented?" Perveen asked, feeling dubious.

"Oh, it's very real," Yazad said, slapping a mosquito that had settled on his jacket. "I've encountered them once myself. I was on horseback and surprised them foraging for food. Immediately, one chased after and grabbed my horse by the reins. The other pulled out a dagger straight from the *Arabian Nights*. They cleaned my pockets not only of the twenty rupees I was carrying but also my checkbook. Though they certainly haven't presented a check to the Bombay bank."

Perveen wondered why Vandana wasn't concerned about the forest when her husband had experienced such a close call. Did she not love and worry about him? Perveen glanced at the lady, who seemed busy righting the position of the heavy diamond solitaire on her left ring finger.

"You should have told me so I could put it in a report!" Colin interjected. "I've got precious little to say that's considered important by the Kolhapur Agency."

"I must say I'm feeling a bit nervous," Perveen said, casting her eyes over the green hills that rose up behind the garden. Was someone watching them?

Colin looked seriously at Perveen. "It's likely that what happened to Yazad was an isolated incident. After all, I've made the trip out to the palace twice without seeing anyone. And I've made precautions for your safety. Four men will carry the palanquin, and there will be four alternate carriers alongside who will be armed. And then there's Lakshman!"

Perveen wondered why the dour man who'd escorted her was being lauded. Sarcastically, she asked, "Does Lakshman have special powers?"

"In a sense," Colin said. "He has no need of weapons. He is the respected leader; he knows every tree and trail."

"Yes, we have hired him to help with transportation of our visitors," Vandana said. "Lakshman is shy with outsiders, though. He will be very pleased if you ask him to bring you to the right place to make your offering."

"An offering? To whom?" Perveen felt a prickling in her spine. She hoped this would not be some sort of sacrifice.

"Aranyani." Vandana said the name slowly, as if she understood this was the first time Perveen was hearing it. "She's the mother-protector to all the animals of the forest. The local people celebrate her with a puja just before rainy season comes. She is respected all over India, but the ones here know that she controls the rains—if it's a very bad rainy season with floods, it's because someone has hurt an animal."

"Isn't it enough to worship the major gods and goddesses—some of whom have a good many more than two arms?" Roderick said with a laugh.

Perveen imagined he was a Christian, but this was not a good joke to make in mixed company. How could Ames not know that people were protective of their own beliefs? She would never say such a thing aloud to a Hindu.

But Vandana gave him a demure smile. "The more gods, the better. This is a lonely place. I feel sorry for you Christians with your one God to pray to. How can He hear everyone?"

"It's the same trouble for us, isn't it, Perveen?" Yazad chuckled. "That's why I'm doing as Vandana says and leaving a few rupees for Aranyani when I pass the shrine. She must be the wealthiest single woman in Satapur."

Perveen noted the easygoing approach Yazad had toward Hinduism and his own Zoroastrian faith. But if he'd married out of his community, he might have been disowned by his family and the priests of their agiary.

"I've never seen any coins at that so-called shrine," Roderick said with a shrug. "Aranyani or someone else must have taken them for shopping money."

"Just because you didn't see coins, it's not a reason to avoid leaving the offering," Vandana chided. "Aranyani's protection might keep those bandits from killing travelers passing through. Perveen, bring a few sweets for Aranyani tomorrow, and some paise, too."

Perveen took another look at the hills, which were changing color as the sun began to set. It was really quite beautiful. Although she was nervous, she sensed she would be glad for the experience of traveling through a place she'd never been—the mountainous jungle.

Yazad finished his second drink and beckoned to Rama for another one. "When can we start playing cards? That's what you called us for, Colin!"

"I did, but you may regret it. Perveen was an experienced player in Oxford circles," Colin said with a wink.

She rolled her eyes, wondering why he remembered so well an evening she had forgotten. "That's an exaggeration," she said quickly. "However, we're only five people, so we can't play bridge."

"I could sit the game out," Roderick Ames offered. "I'm a wretched cardplayer."

"No. You are here, so you must play—and Dr. Andrews is coming to make the sixth." Vandana turned her gaze from Ames back toward the circuit house. "Must we play bridge? We could play paplu. It doesn't require an even number."

Colin snapped his fingers. "Otherwise known as Indian rummy! Rama taught me during the long afternoons of rainy season."

"Last time I played it was with my grandmother. But why not?" Yazad said with a chuckle that Perveen was beginning to find grating.

Nevertheless, Yazad was better company than Roderick Ames.

Why didn't the engineer fit in? Perveen wondered. He was an Indian Civil Service officer who had an absolute right to stay at the circuit house, and Colin seemed to welcome him like an old friend. Yet Roderick Ames appeared to be doing his level best to remain outside the party. Perhaps it was because the Anglo-Indian was neither Hindu, Parsi, nor English, nor was he wealthy.

Prejudice in India was not as simple as whites lording it over Indians. The sickness was also spread by Indians ranking one another in terms of skin shade, religion, and mother tongue. She imagined that having been born in India with dark skin and an English name must have been a source of endless comments.

7

PLAYING ONE'S CARDS

$\mathcal{P}$erveen had always thought card games were a window to the soul. And sure enough, fifteen minutes after Colin had dealt the cards all around, Yazad's avuncularity disappeared and was replaced by a tight, barking temperament. Vandana was distracted, throwing in cards without strategy while hammering Perveen with questions about various society people in Bombay. Despite his professed lack of interest in cards, Roderick Ames knew the game and played skillfully, every one of his moves frowned at by Yazad.

Colin, on the other hand, seemed indifferent about winning or losing, sipping his drink more slowly than his guests, and occasionally casting a wry look at Perveen. She wondered what the look meant.

An outbreak of animal howling outside made her shoulders go up. Rama appeared with a stooped European gentleman. He was almost bald, with a fringe of red hair ringing his head, and his fair skin was mottled with red marks and sunspots. His eyes were small and a watery blue. It was impossible to tell if India's sun had aged him, or if he was more than seventy years old. In any case, he did not look well.

"Good evening, Dr. Andrews!" Yazad rose and gave a mock-courtly bow to the physician, who was dressed in a heavily wrinkled drill suit. "Our champion player has finally arrived. We started playing without you, I'm afraid, and the game has gone to hell."

"No matter. You may as well carry on." The doctor sank into a side chair away from the table.

Colin put down his hand of cards, poured a cup of tea, and brought it to the man. "You must be fatigued after a long day's work."

"Two more children dead from cholera," he said, accepting the tea with a grateful nod.

"But Perveen here went into the village today!" Vandana said, looking with worry at Perveen. "Did you bathe afterward?"

"I—" Perveen hesitated, not used to talking about such personal issues with people she didn't know well. "I had a sponge bath before meeting you. Nobody there said anything about people being ill."

"There is no sign yet of epidemic, but care must be taken." Dr. Andrews frowned at her. "Who are you? What business have you in these parts?"

Colin interjected, "Miss Perveen Mistry is a government lawyer on her way to the palace. The Kolhapur Agency sent her out, and I'm very glad she's here."

"Government lawyer" wasn't an entirely accurate description, but Perveen didn't think it worth arguing. Now she knew what she should say to explain her position.

"If you are going to the palace, it's quite important that you are well." Dr. Andrews looked searchingly at her. "They have suffered enough. You must not transmit infection."

"We'll all wash our hands and faces as a precaution," Colin said. "There's a washroom just off the dining room. Rama can serve dinner early, if you have the appetite."

"But the game!" Yazad protested.

Colin said, "I don't mind if we end now. What is there to win, anyway?"

Vandana patted her husband's arm. "Too many nights, we play cards because they are the only excitement. Tonight we have the largest gathering of people since last spring. Let's enjoy that."

Perveen wasn't surprised that the main dinner course was roasted chicken. Rama served a chilled tomato soup first, as well as rice, two vegetable pickles, potato curry, and dal. Two bottles of wine were opened: a claret from the same year as the one they'd had the previous night, and a bottle of champagne. Nobody took water except for the doctor.

"I employ a chef trained at the Taj Mahal Hotel in Bombay," Vandana confided to Perveen. "Won't you come to see me tomorrow? I'll give you breakfast or lunch, if you prefer."

Perveen hesitated. "That sounds wonderful, but I'm probably heading out early in the morning."

"It's a three-hour journey. You don't need to leave so early." Vandana sipped champagne and looked pensive.

Perveen wondered about that comment. "So you don't worry about the bandits who robbed Yazad?"

"No, and I'm not the only lady who rides through the woods!" Vandana flashed a defiant look at her husband. "Bandits know better than to cross me. And there were never bandits in my day. Everyone wanted to visit the palace. It was quite a festive and lively household."

Feeling reassured, Perveen asked, "Can you tell me about the maharanis?"

"Oh yes!" Vandana put down her knife and fork, as if glad for the chance to gossip. "The dowager maharani—everyone calls her the rajmata—was such a force. She instructed all of us on how to carry ourselves—even if we were to live out our lives secluded in the palace. Because of her, I learned the importance of what she called signature jewelry. She suggested I always wear diamonds as my signature. A grand idea!"

"For both you and Monsieur Cartier," Yazad commented, and laughed at his own joke. "Even the cigarette case must have diamonds."

Perveen had sold off most of the jewelry she'd received at her wedding five years earlier to fund her Oxford education. Smiling, she said, "I'm afraid I don't have any signature jewelry outside of my wristwatch. I packed very lightly."

Vandana reached out to tap the face of Perveen's watch. "Longines. Very nice."

Feeling slightly mortified, Perveen asked, "Can you tell me more about the dowager maharani's personality?"

"She's terribly stern! She always complained when we children squealed and ran too fast through the zenana. But she is generous with gifts to everyone." Leaning forward eagerly, Vandana asked, "What are you bringing for gifts?"

Gifts? Nobody had told her. "I don't have anything. I didn't—"

"You must bring gifts," Vandana said, worry creasing her brow. "Tell her about what happened to you, Colin!"

Colin expertly mixed dal into his rice before answering. "Last time I went, I carried a tin of Fortnum and Mason biscuits. But they went home along with me, rejected."

Dramatically, Vandana threw her napkin down on the table. "You weren't admitted most likely because of that dreadful offering!"

"Could that be true?" Colin looked thunderstruck.

"Yes, indeed. That is why she asked you to repeat the story!" Yazad joked.

But it wasn't funny to Perveen, who had even less than a tin of British biscuits. "I suppose I could give them the cashew brittle I bought from the village?"

"Not chikki. It sticks to the teeth!" Vandana said, shuddering.

"What about Rama's herbs?" Yazad said with a wink.

Perveen was confused. "Do you mean a gift of herbs to cook with? I don't expect that the maharanis cook."

"No, these herbs are medicine," Yazad said. "There are plants that grow very well here during monsoon that Indian healers use. Rama is known to have that gift, and he is quite a collector of plants, isn't he?"

"He's taught me how to recognize brahmi and ashwagandha," Colin said. "There's a very pretty shrub that grows wild everywhere, datura. The flowers are like trumpets, and they can mute the worst aches and pains. He's made a tea for me with that a few times."

"I think I noticed that shrub growing close to the veranda when I was walking this morning." Perveen looked down the length of the table toward Rama, who was standing in the shadow of the doorway. "Was that datura?"

"Yes. But nobody should touch the plant who does not know." Rama's words came in a halting manner. "The seeds can kill."

"He is correct!" Vandana said, taking up a last forkful of potato curry. "But medicinal herbs are not the right thing to bring to a palace. Even if you brought good ones, they would suspect poison!"

"I don't think much of such plants as medicine." Dr. Andrews's face was disapproving. "Every plant grows differently. One cannot control for strength of dosage."

"We'll save Yazad's idea for someone else, then," Colin said. His plate was empty, and there was a gleam in his eye. "I've thought of something. I have an unopened crate of books that was delivered before the monsoon. I believe it includes several books for children. You can choose some to take to the prince and princess."

"What's your opinion, Vandana?" Perveen was feeling desperate to bring something.

Vandana tilted her head to one side as she considered the idea. "That would be entirely acceptable, if the books are brand-new and from overseas. And as for the maharanis, I'll be able to help you. I still have trunks from my last trip to Europe that are full of delightful trinkets."

"I couldn't take things from you." Perveen felt apprehensive, though she imagined whatever Vandana was offering would be just right.

"I wouldn't worry," Colin said, giving Vandana a warm smile. "Thank you, Vandana."

"Done!" Vandana clapped. "Come for breakfast, and I'll tell you more about the palace as well."

"What is your exact relationship to the palace?" Perveen asked. She didn't want to mention Vandana at the palace if she was a controversial person, and judging from her made-up face and hair, she was likely just that.

"She's a royal cousin," Yazad said, as if he couldn't tolerate being left out of the conversation. "She visited often in child-hood. But now my wife would sooner throw her jewels to our peacocks than go to that palace. I've told her to let bygones be bygones, but she wants nothing to do with them."

"Is it because your parents were upset about your not mar-rying the maharaja?" Perveen asked.

Vandana gazed at the candelabra on the table as if searching the flames for the answer. At last she spoke. "They were. But I prefer this life. Who would be daft enough to wish to become an Indian queen? When you enter Satapur Palace, you'll see what a closed life the late maharaja's mother and widow must endure. They live in that zenana from the day they enter as brides until they die. Yes, a maharani is given jewels—but what's the pleasure in wearing them if you're always home? Meanwhile, a maharaja can travel every-where he fancies."

"Some maharanis break purdah and travel," Perveen said. "Consider Suniti, the maharani of Cooch Behar. She became a social fixture in London. And isn't her daughter-in-law, Indira, a known party girl?"

"I've met the Cooch Behar women during my time in Europe." Vandana ran a hand through her glossy hair, which hardly moved. "That kind of free living only happens if the dowager maharani is not strong with the brides entering the household. This one is very powerful. She has kept the late maharaja's widow, Mirabai, in check."

Perveen was fascinated by the story. "Do you think that Maha-rani Mirabai wants to live in purdah?"

Vandana shrugged. "I never met her. But she's from the state of Bhor, and her parents allowed her more freedom. Apparently, she was given her first hunting rifle at age five and rode horses every day. She was not in purdah until she came to Satapur."

"You speak as if being maharani of Satapur is like imprisonment," Roderick said. "It's actually a dream for most women to have everyone at your beck and call."

"Sounds like a dream for you, my dear!" Vandana said, and everyone laughed.

Roderick flushed red.

"Purdah is not a privilege but a life of restriction," Vandana said in a sober tone. "The maharani has the responsibility to travel a few miles to worship at the family temple—but when she goes, her palanquin must be curtained. Nobody should see her face."

Colin leaned back in his chair and spoke quietly. "I understand that purdah is common for Mohammedans, but why would Hindus do such a thing?"

"We Hindus have deep-seated belief in the possibility of contamination by lower castes," Vandana said, turning to him with a more serious expression than before. "That's the reason untouchables aren't allowed in Hindu temples—and many Brahmins become angry if even the shadow of a lower-caste person crosses their path. The second reason is that if the public doesn't know the faces of the maharanis and princesses, they have a better chance of escaping harm if enemies ever enter the palace."

"Right now in Bombay, Gandhiji is speaking out in favor of untouchables," Perveen pointed out. "And we no longer have a society where one king would try to steal another's kingdom."

"Not kings—princes," Roderick cut in. "The rulers of Indian princely states are referred to as such because they are subject to George V, our own King and emperor."

Perveen was irritated by his fawning correction. But his presence reminded her of the rashness of invoking the name of Mohandas Gandhi in a government house. She needed to change the conversation right away. She turned to look at the physician, who appeared on the verge of nodding off. If only she could ask him some direct questions about the deaths of Prince Pratap Rao and his father. However, that was too confidential to discuss in front of others. She spoke in her most respectful voice. "Dr. Andrews, I'm interested to hear how you manage to practice medicine in princely India. Who pays you, and where is your surgery?"

Raising his head, Dr. Andrews said, "I'm employed by the Indian Medical Service and report to the Kolhapur Agency. I live and work in a small bungalow close to the village. Half the building's taken up by a waiting room, surgery, and ward for those needing overnight care. There are two nurses and some other assistants. Having served in India since 1885, I have sometimes worked with no aides, so I feel quite fortunate the maharaja added funds to my operation."

"Are your staff Indian?" Perveen was intrigued by the possibility there were some local jobs that were better than peasant labor.

"Yes—and they are always trying to suggest I use Rama's herbs instead of proper medicine." The doctor sighed. "We had an Irish nurse here for a while, but she couldn't stand the isolation."

"Yazad and I invited her to the estate—but she never came. I guess she thought too highly of herself to become friends with Indians." There was hurt in Vandana's voice.

"Could it have been that she was cowed by your social status?" Colin asked gently.

"Oh, was that her secret confession to you? You did like her, Colin!" Vandana said sharply.

Colin's face flushed. "I am not in that game, Vandana."

Perveen was surprised to feel the same brief flash of pique that she had experienced earlier while pondering whether other women traveled alone to the circuit house. If she hadn't known better, she would have thought her reaction was jealousy.

Dr. Andrews stood and pushed in his chair. "I'm not much for gossip. I'll take my leave because I must start early tomorrow."

Perveen was alarmed. If the doctor left now, she'd have no chance to ask about the deaths. She folded her napkin and rose. "May I stroll with you, Dr. Andrews? It's very dark."

"There is no need," the doctor said brusquely. "I will carry this lamp to the stable."

"Oh, that's a good idea! I'll walk alongside and bring the lamp back with me." Perveen was determined to get her conversation and followed the doctor out, ignoring the bemused expression on Vandana's face.

Perveen had thought it would be quiet outside, but there was a cacophony of sounds: chattering insects, and distant wailing—small cats, or great ones? The dog named Desi trotted close to Perveen as they proceeded down the moss-covered path.

"What's this nonsense?" Dr. Andrews sounded affronted. "Have you a worry about your health?"

Hastily, Perveen said, "Not at all. I only wish to know more about the autopsies you performed on the late maharaja and his older son."

"A most unusual request. Why is that?" His voice hardened.

Struggling not to sound defensive, she said, "I'm visiting the palace at the request of the Kolhapur Agency. I think the deaths of a ruler and his successor—less than a year apart—are unusual."

The doctor was a small man—maybe five feet six inches. But he managed to draw himself up and look down at her. "But that is confidential medical information."

His tone reminded her of a judge's reprimand.

"The government expects me to make a decision about the maharaja's education," she countered. "If there is a possibility someone murdered the older brother, it is an argument for having him go abroad."

"An animal killed Prince Pratap Rao, not a person. Didn't Colin tell you?"

"Yes, but what do you make of the fact that the maharaja and his son died just eleven months apart?" As if to punctuate her statement, Desi whined and looked up at the doctor.

"A coincidence, pure and simple." The doctor's voice was mild. "The maharaja Mahendra Rao was fatally infected after inspecting a village where cholera was just starting to take hold. Two servants tending him died of the same contagion. Other servants and family members fell ill but recovered after taking medicine."

Perveen smashed a mosquito that had settled on her arm. "A tragedy, indeed. And what more can you tell me about the death of Prince Jiva Rao's older brother? Mr. Sandringham was vague, and I saw few details in the papers he showed me."

The doctor pressed his lips together reprovingly. At last he said, "The prince was eaten by a tiger or leopard. Nothing a lady should hear about."

"If the prince was very badly mauled, how could you make an identification? Were you sure about it?" Perveen pressed.

"Who else would it have been? The young maharaja and his uncle, Prince Swaroop, both wore boots with the royal insignia. Those boots were still on the corpse. The clothing was mostly gone, but the remnants were that of the riding costume the boy had donned earlier in the day. I knew his size and skin coloring—I was his doctor."

Perveen stared into the darkness thinking that the doctor had a good point. "I understand. But what about the circumstances leading to this killing? How could the leopard drag a child away without anyone intervening and shooting the animal?"

"Because the maharaja liked to do exactly as he pleased. The men on the hunt told me the boy was anxious that his uncle, who is a skilled hunter, would get the killing shot instead of him. The maharaja had a tantrum and insisted on being the only one allowed to carry the gun. He'd had training, but how skilled can a thirteen-year-old be?" The doctor sighed, shifting the lantern he carried as if his right hand pained him. "The men around him knew they served at the boy's pleasure. So they walked alongside him without any guns, although more weapons were in the carrier bags on the horses."

"Let me take the lantern," Perveen said, reaching out for it, and he let her. "Leopards are shy creatures, aren't they? Why would they venture into a clearing?"

"I think the boy went ahead just a bit too far. The animal saw him and was emboldened."

"Who gave this report?" she asked, realizing the brass lantern's handle was quite warm.

"The same royal uncle I mentioned: Prince Swaroop, who searched for him in vain. I confirmed the story during a separate conversation with Mr. Basu, the tutor, and this fellow who serves as a kind of court jester."

The hot metal handle was becoming bothersome, but Perveen held fast, not wanting to distract the doctor. "How devastating for everyone to witness the boy being dragged off by the animal."

The doctor tilted his head, as if considering the question. "They didn't witness that. They realized the boy had gone ahead and then couldn't find him. The noblemen and grooms searched all night, with added reinforcements from the palace guard, and into the next day. The next morning, Prince Swaroop came across the child's remains. He was the one who brought the bad news back to the palace. I worry for Maharani Mirabai's health since the death."

"Oh dear." Perveen's anxiety was rising like the heat in the lamp handle. "If Maharani Mirabai has a health problem, that may also be government business. She is a ward of the court, due to her husband's passing."

"I have not seen her in two years, but from reports, she may· be suffering from melancholia."

"In what way?" Perveen was somewhat skeptical. Melancholia was used to explain everything from alcoholism to social withdrawal—especially when it came to women.

"In the years before her husband's death, she would travel to visit other royals in a purdah car. She appeared at state events—veiled, of course. That is no longer the case. She is said to be overly protective of Prince Jiva Rao and Princess Padmabai. She doesn't entertain visitors or even make prayers at the royal family's temple. Her relationship with her mother-in-law is reported to be unpleasant."

"Who is providing you all this information?" Perveen spoke quickly because the lamp handle was becoming unbearably hot, and she could hear that someone else had exited the bungalow and was walking across the veranda.

He coughed and said, "Owen McLaughlin, the last Satapur agent. He had strong relationships with a number of people at the palace, including the current prime minister, Prince Swaroop, whom he appointed."

Perveen had many other questions for the doctor but knew the time was limited. "Is there any modern medicine for melancholia? Perhaps I could bring it."

"If only that were the case!" he said. "There is no such medicine."

Perveen put the lamp down on the path, knowing he had no more need of her assistance. Her hand felt as if it was burned. "Maybe one day."

Looking from her to the lamp, the doctor shook his head. "You aren't used to the hardships of mofussil life. I worry that you won't be able to tolerate the trip." He paused. "You need a cloth soaked with cold water for your hand."

She felt mortified at both his words and the fact that she had forced herself to hold the lamp too long. "It's not a serious burn."

"You will also be burned if you ask too many questions. That's what I was told the last time I was with the royals." His voice was low and almost ominous.

Was he threatening her? "Lawyers must ask questions. That is why the Kolhapur Agency requested my help."

The doctor reached into his horse's saddlebag and withdrew from it a small, unlit lantern with a leather-wrapped handle.

Opening the lantern's front panel, he produced the candle from within and held its wick against that of the hot lantern sitting on the ground. Once it was lit, he muttered, "I strongly doubt you'll learn more from the Satapur palace than I did."

So he had probably asked questions after the death and been rebuffed. That was why he was on the defensive. Laying aside her growing skepticism, she said, "It was very kind of you to speak with me. Good night, Dr. Andrews."

"Good night, Miss Mistry." He mounted the horse with surprising ease and gestured for her to hand him his own lantern. "In any case, I wish you Godspeed."

8

BETWEEN THE LINES

After the doctor's departure, the night closed around her like a black silk hood. Her old fear of being trapped in a dark, small place arose within her, taking her breath away. She was imagining what it would have been like for Prince Pratap Rao to catch up with the leopard he'd planned to kill only to find himself the prey. Had the animal cradled him for a moment before sinking its teeth into him? She had heard the big cats did something like that to calm their quarry into submission.

The tapping of heels and Vandana's voice pulled Perveen away from the imagined horrors. "Perveen, call out if you're there!" From a distance, a bobbing light came toward her. "We were looking all over for you!"

"Present!" As she called out, she realized she sounded like a schoolchild.

"So the doctor's gone already?" Vandana said. Yazad was at her side, and Perveen saw that he held the same kind of metal lantern but in a gloved hand.

"Yes." She was glad they hadn't arrived in the middle of the tense conversation.

"Very good. Tomorrow morning is our breakfast. Come whenever you wish—just don't forget!"

"I will be there." Perveen resolved to organize her questions in advance. "It's so dark. Will you be able to ride home safely?"

"We know the way quite well, and the circuit house groom can walk in front with a lantern. Unless he's gone off with the doctor?"

"No. Dr. Andrews left alone."

Mohit, the young boy who'd helped her in the morning, stepped out of the shadows and spoke in polite Marathi. "Sahib and memsahib, shall I bring your horses?"

Perveen hadn't known anyone else was in the vicinity. She looked Mohit over, wondering how much he'd understood from her conversation with Dr. Andrews. Hopefully not enough to carry tales to the village.

"The question is if you can find your way back through the garden to the veranda," Yazad said to Perveen. "Now that we have found you, we must return you to Colin. He was eager for you not to miss pudding and to choose those children's books."

"I can see the veranda from here," she scoffed. She didn't like being babied. "And look. There's a light coming our way."

She was disappointed to see Roderick Ames rather than Colin in the glow of another approaching lantern.

"See you early tomorrow!" Yazad said.

"Good night." Perveen gave the lamp that had burned her hand to Mohit to put away.

"What were you talking to the doctor about?" Ames's voice was authoritarian, as if he had caught her breaking the rules.

Even though the stable boy might know the topic of her conversation with the doctor, she'd no intention of telling Ames. Walking briskly up the path to the veranda, she said, "I told the doctor good night, just as I did to the Mehtas. I suppose I shall say good night to you as well."

"Yes, you should go to bed," Roderick countered. "Tomorrow will be very tiring for you."

As she glowered at Roderick, Colin appeared on the veranda. "Good, you're back. Rama will take offense if you don't try the pudding. Roddy, how about you? Would you like another cup of coffee, or perhaps something stronger?"

"No. I'm heading off at six tomorrow." Roderick bowed slightly to the two of them and then headed along the veranda to a door that presumably led to his room. She noticed he had a cloth napkin between his hand and the lamp's handle. Everyone seemed to know how to handle the lamps except for her.

"Tea or coffee?" Colin asked as he ushered Perveen into the dining room. "Rama prepared both."

"Tea, please. And I'll try that caramel custard. It looks very creamy," Perveen said, settling down at the table. At her place alone, there was a small glass bowl containing a golden pudding.

Smiling at her, he said, "I hope you found the meeting with the doctor valuable."

She hadn't learned much except that the doctor had little confidence in her. "It was a good strategy for you to invite him and the Mehtas—although I was rather surprised that you shared my travel plans with everyone."

Colin raised his eyebrows. "Everyone knows that when the circuit house requests a palanquin, someone is going out on official business. I think it's better for people to know the correct information than for rumors to spread."

"I hope you're right." Through the window, Perveen saw a white flash: Desi loping across the lawn. "He's a lovely dog. I'm sorry that he's caged all day."

Colin looked taken aback. "Desi's on night shift, roaming the property and keeping us safe. He's a South Indian breed called a Rajapalayam; they are known as the king of dogs. He is very strong and energetic and is a born hunter. Without his cage—I prefer to call it a garden house—he wouldn't take time to sleep. It's set in the shade, it has water, and if he barks, Rama or I take him out." Clearing his throat, he said, "What do you think of the custard?"

"It's very good. The taste is a little different."

"Rama uses goat's milk, which is supposedly very good for the digestion. It's in our tea and coffee as well. I've become used to it and probably wouldn't like cow's milk anymore."

"We make do with what we can."

"That reminds me of the gifts for the royal children. I've been looking through them." He indicated a wooden crate that she had noticed earlier resting on a side table.

"Why do you have children's books?" she asked.

"I had the London office send me English books, and a Bombay bookseller provided a small load in Hindi and Marathi for possible use in a village school."

"But there is no school." She was glad for a moment to talk about what she'd seen in the village. "Why is that, when the last maharaja wanted one?"

"Prince Swaroop, the prime minister, hasn't moved forward with any plans, although the Agency would be willing to assist." Colin's voice was flat, and she sensed this was a matter he was displeased about.

"I see. And it's eight years till Maharaja Jiva Rao can begin to make decisions, isn't it?"

He nodded, looking somber. "I still wanted to have the books here. One never knows if a missionary might come through and see fit to start something. There's plenty of room here at the circuit house to have a schoolroom."

"But if the school were on these premises, you'd run into the problem of behaving as if the British are running Satapur." Perveen paused, because an idea was taking shape. "Do you think that if the maharaja went to this hypothetical school at the circuit house, it might be close enough to satisfy the dowager maharani, and English enough for his mother?"

His eyes widened. "I doubt the maharanis would accept the idea of the prince's mixing with peasants. As far as schools go in India, there are already a few colleges designed entirely for sons of the nobility."

Perveen was disappointed at his rejection of the idea, but she understood what he was saying. In Bombay, parents cared tremendously about sending their children to schools with the most affluent members of their own community. This was ultimately even more important than the religion of the school's teachers. "I'd like to know the names of those schools for royalty."

"They are mentioned by Mr. McLaughlin in letters in the file. Before you dig into the letters, can we look at the books together?"

Her pudding finished, Perveen joined Colin at the crate. He had pulled out a book with a turquoise cover and an intriguing gold design depicting an animal she couldn't identify. "*The Wind in the Willows*. I read hundreds of English books growing up, but I don't know this one."

"It's a story about animals. Before I came to India, my nephew always asked me to read it to him." Colin smiled wistfully. "I don't miss England much, but I miss him."

Paging through the book, she was careful not to let anything brush the sections of her fingers that had been scorched by the hot lantern. "It looks like a very whimsical novel set in a forest— that's perfect, isn't it? If there's enough time, I can translate some of the story into Marathi for Maharaja Jiva Rao, and his tutor can teach the rest during his English language lessons. Now we need a book for Princess Padmabai."

"I was working on that idea when you were outside," he said, picking up a small book with a colorful cover from a stack on the table. "What do you think of *The Story of Little Black Mingo*?"

Perveen turned the pages, and her misgivings grew. "I don't think this is the right choice."

He looked puzzled. "Why? I specifically ordered it because it's set in India."

Perveen pointed to the cover, which had a crude drawing of a barefoot brown peasant girl with a thatch of curls dressed in a fragment of a blouse and a ragged skirt. "Look at that figure on the cover—it's like a cartoon, the very opposite of the lovely animals in *The Wind in the Willows*. When the little princess realizes this is supposed to be an Indian child, she might feel embarrassed to know this is how outsiders see the country."

"I hadn't thought of that." Color stamped Colin's high

cheekbones. "As I mentioned, I'd heard of the book, but I hadn't ever seen it until now. I agree with what you're saying."

She had rejected his choice—and instead of objecting, he had agreed. This was most gratifying, and she wanted to reassure him that some of his books were good choices. Lifting up a book of rhymes written and illustrated by Kate Greenaway, Perveen said, "*Marigold Garden* might be a good choice. Every Indian child is familiar with marigolds, and the illustrations show girls wearing variations of traditional English dress. This is good preparation in case she's ever sent to school in England."

Colin took the book in his hands. As he paged through, he said, "There are no plans that I know about for the princess's education."

"Why not? In a few years, the maharani might wish for her daughter to be close to Jiva Rao. She could attend a nearby girls' school in England."

He seemed to stiffen. "Are you predisposed to both children being educated away from the palace?"

Perveen considered her words carefully. "Not at all. As you know, I haven't met the prince yet, so I have no idea yet what's right for him. But in my experiences visiting secluded women, it's seemed that home education has not served them as well as schools have. And the lack of socialization isn't beneficial for the development of a kind and cooperative personality."

"That sounds logical." Colin looked at her intently. "But promise me you won't go into the palace saying these things straightaway. I don't want you to be tossed out."

"I won't force my ideas on anyone." Perveen felt as defensive now as when the doctor had spoken to her. "Now that the books are sorted, I'll turn in for some rest. I only hope to wake up to some good news tomorrow about the palanquin."

"Very well!" Colin began piling the discarded books back into the crate. "When he went to the village to pick up things for dinner, Rama heard the men have returned with the repaired palanquin. They will be here for you tomorrow at ten o'clock."

She felt relief wash over her. "Thank you. And ten o'clock allows loads of time for my breakfast with Vandana!"

"One last thing. I've got something else for you to bring to the palace." He walked across the room and rummaged in a cupboard, then came back holding a tin instrument. He clicked something and a huge golden beam shot out.

She was surprised. "Is that a battery torch?"

"An Eveready from America," he said with pride. "Although I brought it from London. It's a companion to the lantern I use for walking at night. I thought you might like to have it."

Perveen was hesitant to take his prize possession. "I've heard about such torches but never had one. If the trek tomorrow will be during daylight, I don't know that I need it."

"It's for nighttime emergencies: perhaps you will find reason to find something in the dark. Let me show you the glove catch," Colin said, putting it in her hands. "If you hook the pin in the catch like this, the light will stay on."

His hands brushed hers as he showed her how to operate the battery torch. She felt every sense go on alert at his touch. She was so consternated that the flashlight slipped, and she barely caught it before it hit the floor.

"Sorry!" she said. "I'll be careful with it."

"Is your hand all right? It looks red."

"I touched something hot a little while ago. But it's fine."

"Sorry we don't have an icebox." He paused. "Don't keep the light on if you don't need it. There are three batteries inside, and they will expire within a few hours' use."

"I understand." She unhooked the catch so the light went out. That brief charge had not entirely faded from her hand, and she knew it had nothing to do with the burn.

She had given her hand to the railway conductor when she got out at Khandala the day before. She had put coins into the weathered hand of the candy seller in the Satapur village. Those were the kind of touches that many women wouldn't have engaged in, but they hadn't flustered her.

This was different. She'd experienced the same physical surge at Colin's touch as when she'd watched him stretch into a yoga exercise. It was a dangerous feeling.

9

A PRINCESS'S EYE

*P*erveen slept deeply, waking only once, when Desi went into a loud barking spasm. Was something happening outside? She felt too comfortable to worry much, and the soft sound of bare feet walking along the veranda reassured her. Rama must have gone out to look after things.

She didn't stir until the cock crowed. Five o'clock again. Marveling at his consistency, she draped a robe over her nightdress and padded barefoot into her adjacent bathroom to begin her toilette. She was surprised to find her bath was already half-filled with warm water.

"You're early!" she said as a slender boy stepped through the half-open bathroom door meant for servant use that opened to the garden.

"Sorry, memsahib." He put down the pail of hot water he was carrying and turned away from her. He must have felt chagrined about her state of dress, because he moved almost out of the door.

"Are you Hari?" she asked, realizing he must be Mohit's contemporary.

The boy nodded, still looking anxious.

"Don't worry, Hari. I'm delighted to take a bath early," she said with a yawn. "Did Rama tell you that I am leaving early today?"

"No. I didn't see him. Because the garden door was open, I thought it was all right to come."

"This door was open?" Perveen looked at the small door from the bathroom to the garden, which she was sure had been latched the night before. To think anyone could have come inside and gone through the bathroom into the place where she was sleeping! Perveen turned and walked back into the bedroom. Her trunk rested on the low wooden stand halfway across the room from her bed. She'd begun laying clothes inside it the night before. Alarmed, she approached it with a feeling of dread. The clothes seemed jumbled. She was almost certain that someone had dug their hands deep into the case. But maybe she was wrong. As she picked through the clothing and the folders of papers, it didn't seem as if anything was missing. The books for the children were there, and Colin's heavy torch. But then she realized what she didn't have.

The Kodak Brownie.

She scanned the whole room in case she'd made a mistake about where she'd left it. After all, she'd had a glass of wine. Her thinking could have been off.

Still—no camera.

"Bath is ready!" Hari called from the bathroom.

She thought of asking whether Hari had taken the camera, but she found the idea that he'd stolen it too unbelievable. Hari's face had shone with innocence and eagerness to please. Yes, a camera was probably worth more than he was paid in a year—but why would he or Mohit or Rama, for that matter, risk losing good jobs? Serving the circuit house was a long-term, secure future.

After Hari departed, she latched all the bathroom's doors. But she felt reluctant to undress and get into the water. She did so, feeling exposed, as if the thief were still there.

When had this happened? It could have been when she was in the garden with the doctor. That was easier to accept than the thought that an intruder had stepped into the room where she was sleeping. She'd been lying in bed in a locked room—he could have done anything. If her parents knew such a thing had happened, they would demand she return home immediately.

Now she remembered Desi's barking. Perhaps he'd been

warning of someone who'd stolen onto the property. A thief from the outside who would never be identified.

Perveen quickly pinned up her hair and draped herself in the same blue-and-gold sari she'd worn two nights before. Stepping out of her room, she scanned the veranda for Rama before remembering that he was probably leading Colin in exercises on the bluff. And then the worst thought came: What if the midnight intruder had been Colin or Roderick Ames? They were the only other people staying in the house. But what on earth could either man want in her luggage? She was supposed to be protected at the circuit house, but it was no safer than a cheap hotel.

As she walked along the trail toward the Mehta estate, she felt a knot of anger tightening within her. She couldn't limit her suspicions to only the men in the house. Vandana and Yazad could have an interest in the papers relating to the palace. And Dr. Andrews had warned her not to ask too many questions. Had he returned to investigate whether she had evidence of anything that could put him in a bad light?

Perveen guessed that she was arriving too early for breakfast with Vandana. Most upper-class Indians breakfasted around ten, and it was not yet seven. But she was desperate to get away from the circuit house and to speak to Vandana about her serious concerns.

The gate of Heaven's Rest was open. Either someone had gone out, or her arrival was anticipated. Perveen decided the latter because she didn't have to explain herself; the two durwans in pale blue uniforms waved her ahead on the long stone path leading up to the estate's front door. An Indian maidservant dressed in a French-style black gown and white lace apron showed her through a highly polished marble hallway out to a garden with a wide veranda. Vandana was lounging in a planter's chair, smoking a cigarette in the stylish black holder she'd used the night before. Although she wore a blush-colored peignoir and nightdress, her eyes were lined in black and her lips painted a deep pink. It was unsettling to see someone in nightclothes wearing full makeup.

"Welcome, my dear! So glad you were able to come." Vandana gave her a smile of welcome.

"I'm glad that I'm not too early for you." Perveen slipped into the empty chair next to hers.

Vandana patted Perveen's hand. "It is early, but I rose to say goodbye to my husband. And I know you were eager to get an early start as well."

Perveen surmised that a sweet matrimonial farewell was the reason her hostess had painted her face. "I found out the palanquin's been repaired—but I'm not in a rush. I shall depart the circuit house around ten."

Vandana inhaled from her cigarette holder and blew out a smoke ring. "From your expression, I see you're eager to travel. The prospect of a palace stay is enticing to most people."

"Of course." Perveen kept her voice casual, but she caught the patronizing tone of Vandana's comment. The Satapur lady was accustomed to such grandeur; Perveen, despite her degree and travels, was not part of that world. "Before we have breakfast, I've something to ask you."

Vandana nodded. "I am expecting many questions, and I will assist as best I can."

"Someone went into my room last night and removed my camera. Do you know anything about that?"

Vandana put her cigarette holder down quickly. "No. Why would I?"

An outright rebuttal should have been expected; but Perveen felt at a loss to answer the woman's counterattack. Awkwardly, she said, "I don't know. I just thought I'd ask everyone who was at dinner."

Vandana shifted in her chair, no longer looking comfortable. "You offered up that camera to Colin's cook last night. Perhaps it was just too intriguing for him!"

Perveen answered quickly. "I truly don't think Rama would steal."

Vandana picked up her cigarette, smoked, and then addressed her. "What does Colin think happened?"

"I haven't spoken to him yet."

"But you asked me." A tic at the edge of Vandana's left eye had started to quiver.

Perveen clearly understood that she'd offended Vandana. "I didn't mean to accuse you. But you were there last night. You might have seen someone coming from my room—"

"I did not. Did you come here for breakfast or an investigation?"

"I came because I like you. And I hope you'll tell me more about the palace." Perveen looked straight at her—and after a moment, the tension in Vandana's face eased.

"I like you, too. I do hope you find the camera before you leave for the palace." Her voice was soft.

"Yes. And I will return to the circuit house after the palace— so if it turns up, Colin will give it to me."

A bearer dressed in the same crisp blue cotton as the Heaven's Rest durwans stepped onto the veranda. In a low voice, he said, "Breakfast is ready, memsahib."

"We are having Yazad's favorite, kande pohe. It's a local specialty."

"It's very popular in Bombay." Perveen was relieved not to be presented with a fussy French dish. "I'm eager to try the Heaven's Rest version."

"Come!" Vandana said, leading the way, her silk gown elegantly trailing after her.

A table with a long white cloth was set up on the veranda on the other side of the house, which overlooked a tennis court. Perveen settled down to enjoy the food. The dish, a mixture of pounded rice, tiny chilies, bits of tomato, curry leaves, and spices, was delicious, especially with a fried egg served on the side, and a big saucer of the same purple berries that had been served at the circuit house but dusted all over with white sugar.

Just as she had the night before, Vandana put out her cigarette before eating. She encouraged Perveen to eat heartily. "You never know what the food situation will be. Maharanis often go on fast for religious reasons."

"I see. And because they are of a different class, they might want me to eat alone," Perveen thought aloud.

Vandana pressed her pink lips together. "They might. Tell Rama to pack plenty of water and the right kind of food for the trip. Rice and puris and certain vegetable preparations won't spoil."

"Where's Yazad-uncle?" Perveen asked.

Vandana's long-lashed eyes widened with excitement. "He wanted to look at a site with Roderick before he went to Lonavala. He has an idea about where to place a proper road."

So when Yazad had said "see you in the morning," he'd not been speaking to her, but to Roderick Ames. Now her curiosity was piqued. "Why would your husband wish to build a road?"

"We've seen how the land collapses during the rains. A real metaled road could allow us to get our crops out on carts—and also help with postal delivery and other needs." Vandana shrugged. "It would help us and others, too."

Perveen understood that the Mehtas must be far richer than she'd imagined. "Doesn't the royal family need to approve such a thing?"

"It's an improvement that could be shared by the whole community. I doubt they'd mind." She looked at Perveen. "You could put a whisper about it into the younger maharani's ear. I expect she's more accommodating than the old dowager."

Perveen realized all manner of intrigues were circling the palace without the maharanis' knowing. Awkwardly, she said, "I don't know that I can speak about that."

"Why not?"

"I have been sent to do one job. It's to understand the needs of Satapur's maharaja."

"His needs?" She raised a thinly plucked eyebrow. "That poor baby maharaja. It doesn't matter. Forget what I said."

From the stiffness in Vandana's tone, Perveen knew she'd taken offense. But after breakfast was finished, she led Perveen into a sitting room furnished with uncarved, curvilinear pieces that would only be fashionable in Europe. A stack of small fancy boxes decorated a shiny mahogany table. Immediately Perveen recognized the insignia of her favorite watchmaker on one. The others were velvet and leather boxes that she imagined held delightfully luxurious items.

"Yazad adores England and visits every few years. But he has a weakness for French accessories. If he hadn't come to Paris to buy his first Longines watch, we'd never have met."

"Were you at school there?"

Vandana hesitated a moment. "No."

"What then—family travels?"

"I don't tell many people, but I was working in Paris." After a pause, Vandana added almost slyly, "I danced."

"My goodness! How marvelous!" Perveen spoke effusively to cover her shock. She did not think upper-class women, let alone noblewomen, could dance. But Vandana's hair was short—clearly, she was a rebel. "Was it the ballet?"

"No. I did traditional Indian dances, performing with the Royal Hindustan Orchestra. We were quite successful, if I say so myself."

"How did you learn? Did your parents allow it?"

"No. I have good eyes, don't I?" She looked coyly through her lashes at Perveen. "Every palace has dancing girls who live in the zenana. Young girls play together, regardless of caste."

"And you must have talent!" Perveen added.

"A talent for physical movement—and opportunity," Vandana said smugly. "I was shopping for myself at Hermès twelve years ago when Yazad crossed my path. He recognized me from my theater performance the night before and rushed up to kiss my hand."

"What a fairy tale!" Perveen sighed, imagining it.

Vandana's big eyes flared. "It's true!"

"I believe you," Perveen assured her. "I just meant that it's such a romantic story. To meet another Indian so far away—to find true love—and, now, for you to be enjoying India together."

"It's not the dream I had when I was young—but it has turned out to be my karma," Vandana said. "Go on; choose something."

"I feel dreadful taking anything," Perveen said as Vandana began popping open various boxes. "I know you must have bought these things for yourself."

"Oh, these are not for me. I don't go to anyone's residence without a gift, except when I visit Colin, who cannot accept anything because he's in the ICS. Look at these—four cigarette cases from Cartier."

Perveen eyed a beautiful gold cigarette box inset with sapphires. "Do the maharanis smoke?"

"I've no idea about the younger maharani, but the dowager probably wouldn't let her." She picked up a slim rectangular orange box. Opening it, she said, "These are very fine riding gloves from Hermès. I've heard Mirabai is a passionate rider."

"What size are her hands, though? Do you know?"

Vandana knitted her brow, revealing lines that Perveen hadn't noticed before. "I hear she has a slender figure, and that usually means narrow fingers. Why don't you try them?"

Perveen could barely get the pale gray kidskin gloves halfway over her fingers. "They're quite narrow!"

"They will stretch," Vandana promised. "But also take a larger pair that fits you, just in case you're invited to go riding."

Perveen nodded because she knew the gloves she'd brought were crudely made in comparison. "Thank you very much. What about the dowager maharani?"

"As the elder lady, she must have a very special gift." A gleam came into her eye. "I've got an idea."

Vandana exited the sitting room and came back a few minutes later with a red box embossed with the name *Cartier*. She opened it to show a creamy moonstone pendant in a rose gold setting.

"My goodness—that is spectacular," Perveen said. "How can you give it up?"

"It means nothing to me," Vandana reassured her. "I bought it in Paris, but I'm sure the stone is from India. Moonstone is semiprecious, but this soft, milky shade makes it unique."

"Yes, it's very special." Perveen took a deep breath. "Somehow I must pay you for it. And the gloves." She hadn't the financial resources with her and disliked asking for anything extra from Colin.

Vandana lit a fresh cigarette for herself and smoked before answering. "Don't be silly. The government wouldn't approve such expenses."

"But this is too valuable to accept—"

Vandana held up a hand as if to stop further protests. "It's a tribute a royal would approve. Let's not speak of it again—this was paid for long ago and is the least of my concerns."

"I feel very awkward doing this," Perveen confessed. "This is so far from my everyday experience of how to conduct legal business."

"Take it," Vandana ordered. "All I ask is that in exchange you return to Satapur soon and stay with me for a few days. It gets very lonely here with no women around."

"I'd adore that," Perveen said with sincerity.

After twenty more minutes of pleasant conversation, Perveen left for the circuit house in a horse-drawn tonga commanded by Vandana's driver. With apologies, the driver stopped at the point where the wide path ended by the hill leading up to the circuit house. Perveen disembarked and walked the final ten minutes.

As she came close to the veranda, her attention was drawn to eight men sitting in the grass around a rough-looking bamboo contraption: two poles with a four-foot-square box fixed between them. One side of the woven box was partially open for air, but that purpose was defeated by grimy beige curtains. She had hoped for strapping men to hold the palanquin, but the carriers had very thin frames. Scars on their legs told the tale of how many hard miles they'd traveled.

Perveen made a calculation. She weighed at least nine stone—126 pounds. Her trunk was at least twenty more pounds. Although eight men were there, she'd been told that just four would carry the contraption and switch at intervals with the others. It would be hard, heavy work along the narrow paths and steep slopes of the mountain range.

After a whole day of wishing for it to arrive, she now found the palanquin was the last thing she wanted to ride in. But she could hardly voice a complaint.

10

THE WILDS OF SATAPUR

$\mathcal{P}$erveen had packed up and locked her trunk earlier in the morning, so it didn't take long to get herself and her belongings out to the veranda. Colin was there, dressed in his usual linen shirt, cotton trousers, and high boots. It was a practical uniform that made him look more like an explorer than a bureaucrat.

"The morning sun's done a bunk," he said, looking out toward the fog-draped hills. "I hope it reappears."

"It would be much better if it doesn't rain. I know the journey is at least three hours." She felt uneasy about the weather on top of all she'd experienced that morning. She wanted to tell him about the intrusion in her room but didn't know how to bring it up without sounding as if she was accusing the servants.

"Three hours in good weather. If it rains, they'll have to shift to a longer route, to avoid going through a waterfall." Colin gave her a sympathetic look. "Your expression is dubious. I hope it isn't Yazad's stories of bandit terrorists."

"No. It's just that those men who'll carry me look quite thin. I'm more worried that the weight of me and my luggage will do them in than anything else."

He laughed. "You weigh less than I. And I'm certain you'll return in a few days telling me about the splendid pictures you snapped in the forest."

Not without a camera.

"I'll miss you," Colin continued. "Not just when you're away at the palace—but after you leave me for Bombay."

Perveen absorbed the words, wondering if this warmth he felt for her had led him to snoop about in her trunk. Could he have taken the camera? It was a dreadful thought, but she needed to raise the issue. Carefully, she said, "I've enjoyed the food and atmosphere at the circuit house. However, I must mention something that's gone wrong."

"Of course. What is it?" He was no longer smiling.

"Between yesterday evening and five o'clock this morning, someone removed my camera from my trunk."

His eyebrows shot up. "Are you certain? Might you have left it somewhere?"

"I'm absolutely sure that I put it in my trunk."

With a serious expression, he said, "I will speak to Rama about this."

"Please don't accuse him," she said quickly. "It's so unlikely he took it."

Colin nodded in agreement. "I wasn't going to accuse him. He has been with me for over a year, and I trust him with my life. But he needs to know so he can make his own investigation."

Looking down the row of closed doors on the veranda, she spoke in a low voice. "Of course, Mr. Ames was here."

Colin frowned. "He's stayed here many times, and nothing's ever gone missing."

Perveen imagined that an engineer on a government salary could afford a camera. And the previous night, he'd made a comment about knowing how to take a picture. "I'd still like to speak with him before I go."

"That won't be possible. I heard him leaving his room before sunrise." At Perveen's startled expression, Colin added, "He said yesterday he would depart early. Taking advantage of morning temperatures is the usual pattern for official travel."

"He was doing something this morning with Yazad Mehta, I heard."

"What's that?" Colin's voice was surprisingly sharp.

Perveen didn't want to get in the middle of the talk about

building the road. "Something that took them away from Heaven's Rest. I'm not sure exactly."

"Ames didn't tell me that." He shook his head. "I only hope that he isn't doing a side project for Yazad Mehta. The hydroelectric dam is a government project. But one can't work privately for an Indian. That's a rule for all of us in the civil service."

Just as civil service officers couldn't take gifts. "How well do you know the Mehtas?"

"I've known them ever since I arrived here. Why do you ask?"

She blushed. She didn't want to share her suspicion that the Mehtas were counting on him to turn a blind eye to their development actions when she did not know all the facts. After she returned from the palace, she would try to learn from Vandana if her husband really hoped to go forward with the metaled road.

Colin's voice cut into her thoughts. "Perveen, we've got something else to talk about."

"We do?" She wondered if something she'd said had caused offense.

"I'll be in Bombay for two weeks in November." His eyes seemed to glow as he looked at her. "All of the area's political agents have been called in for a meeting with the governor's councillors."

"That may mean Sir David," she said. "I'll have to prepare you for him. He's got a misunderstanding of who you are."

"All right." Colin shifted his posture in the way she'd noticed before, as if he was looking for grounding. "My days are likely to be filled with official business, but I want to invite you to a lecture on India's man-made waterways at the Asiatic. As I said, I'm part of a club there called Thinkers for the Future. Would your family allow you to attend a Thinkers for the Future lecture with me?"

"I certainly am free to attend lectures," Perveen said after a beat. "But I don't know if it's a wise idea."

"Why not?" His eyes bored into hers.

Perveen struggled to figure out what to say. "Is this lecture invitation social?"

"Yes, it has nothing to do with the ICS or the Kolhapur Agency. It would be lovely to go together. I could call for you at your home."

She could predict her parents' reaction. Trying not to cringe, she said, "The social life in Bombay is less free than the one you lead here. I'll have to give my regrets."

He regarded her, his face coloring the way it had when she'd pointed out the problem with the unsavory children's book the previous evening. "So you're saying that we can be friendly here but not in Bombay? Even though you yourself socialize freely with Alice Hobson-Jones, an English councillor's daughter?"

Perveen looked straight at him. "A woman who hopes to maintain a respectable image within the legal community can't go around town with a bachelor of any nationality."

"Not even if his intentions are honorable?" Colin was scrutinizing her. "I said that I would call on your parents first."

Perveen felt panic rush up in a wave, threatening to take her breath away. "No. You mustn't."

"What is the main problem about me?" His voice was tight.

"I don't know what you're talking about."

"Is it that I'm a peg leg, or simply that I'm English?"

Perveen felt her heart break at the ugly words. "Neither! You're a very fit, bright, and ethical man!"

"If you think that, why wouldn't you give me the same chance at friendship that you would any other person?"

She had tried friendship with a highly attractive man once before—and it had failed on many levels. This was a lesson she could not afford to forget. Sadly, she said, "We live in a world with rules governing both our behaviors."

"For God's sake, this isn't Oxford. The chaperone laws are gone!"

But she made her own laws. She had wrapped herself in a code of behavior that surrounded her as securely as her sari. Grimly, she said, "I chaperone myself."

"Why?" he retorted. "If you trusted me enough to stay here, why can't you see me again? You know that I'm not married."

The way he was pushing made Perveen's irritation rise to the point where she could no longer mince words. "Bully for you. I'm not as fortunate."

"What?" His eyes widened as he absorbed the information. "Are you saying that you're married?"

She didn't want the ICS knowing, but she had to stop him. "Yes. It's confidential information for your ears only."

He faltered, leaning to the left as if he'd lost his balance. Righting himself, he asked, "Do you mean—you're actually Mrs. Mistry? Why didn't you say that?"

She shook her head. "My estranged husband has a different surname. I use my maiden name for professional work."

"What about your husband? Doesn't he mind you traveling about like this?" The questions came out rapid fire.

"That is not your business," Perveen said tightly. "In the time we've wasted arguing about spending time together, the sky has begun looking even darker. I'd best get on my way."

Colin looked at the sky and nodded. "I want you to travel safely."

She had to protect herself—not just her body, but also her heart. Slowly, she said, "When I return in a few days, I think it's better that I accept Vandana Mehta's offer to stay the night with her."

Colin's eyes narrowed. "Have you forgotten the report that you're due to give me? We've got business to do."

"That is the reason I came here!" Perveen felt like weeping. Everything had gone so terribly wrong. This was why women weren't supposed to travel without their husbands or fathers; whomever they met would regard them as available. All the old stories were proving true. "I never came looking for a friend or a beau. I will pay a call on you the next morning and present my report. Then I will go straight to Khandala Station."

He gave her a scornful look. "All right, then. I wouldn't want you to stay where you don't want to be."

Perveen thought of the space in the circuit house visitors' book where she was supposed to write comments. What could she say after all that had happened? She would not leave a lie saying that the experience had been pleasant. She'd leave the area by her name blank.

Rama carried her trunk to the palanquin, along with a tiffin box. His mouth was drawn downward, making his wizened face look even older. She wondered what he disapproved of—her swift rejection of Colin, or her decision to stay with the Mehtas?

Perveen took a rupee from her purse—standard behavior for a guest staying in another's residence. A bit of money was thanks for the extra work cooking and cleaning. But Rama put his hands behind his back.

She had offended him. Perveen put the coin back in her purse and turned to the waiting carriers. The ones at the front, who had seen the rupee she'd offered Rama, smiled broadly. She imagined the carriers were anticipating good tips. However, she planned to pay only at the end of a successful round-trip journey. This was the way her father had taught her was best.

Perveen climbed into the little box, which smelled of sweat and something organic she couldn't define. Was it rotting bamboo? A dead mouse? There was an array of slightly damp cushions and dark hairs on the thin mattress on the palanquin's floor.

She decided to lay out a shawl between herself and the surfaces and made sure the end of her sari covered the back of her head as she leaned back on the lumpy cushions. One of the bearers pulled the curtains shut, buttoning them down the center.

"No!" She put a hand on the curtains. "I'm not in purdah. I want to look out."

"But you could fall." Lakshman's expression was dubious.

She shifted her body so she was as close to the curtained opening as was possible in the hellish little box. "I will be very careful. If it gets too difficult, I will button up the curtains, though cotton cloth will hardly keep anyone from falling out."

"You must not touch it. You must call for us to stop."

Perveen grumbled her assent. Then Lakshman disappeared from view, and the men hoisted up the palanquin on their shoulders. It felt like there was unevenness between the front and back, with the front a bit lower than the back, so she had to hold the sides to keep from sliding into the wall. The angle was exacerbated by the fact that the beginning of the journey was downhill.

Perveen tried to ignore the uncomfortable rising and falling of the palanquin. Having parted the dirty curtains on the palanquin's left side, she had an approximate two-foot-square picture of the outside world. The growing mists were thick, allowing a view of only about twenty feet. All she could see were small, twisted ironwood trees that seemed to range on forever in the distance.

As the palanquin approached the village where she'd been the day before, people came out to stare at the palanquin. Feeling embarrassed to be the burden on the carriers' backs, Perveen shrank back from the opening and closed the curtains. Despite her declaration that she was not in purdah, she didn't like being gawked at.

Children's voices sang out, "Give, mother, give!" Their litany continued at the exact pace of the palanquin. They weren't going to leave. She felt heartless ignoring them, so she tossed out two paisa coins, which were swiftly caught. On a whim, she also threw out a pencil from the box she had holding half a dozen. The pencil could be used by a person working in a shop, or perhaps by someone trying to learn writing.

After the village, the journey continued through a green valley and then into a different kind of landscape. The trees became more varied; there were large peepuls, with heart-shaped leaves, and black plums. Despite the isolation, the jungle was noisy, filled with sounds from singing birds and clicking insects. Parrots screeched, and other unknown animals howled, making her skin prickle. She believed it was too early in the day for cats to be prowling. If a tiger sprang out of the trees, she wondered, would the men try to beat it off—or would they drop the palanquin and run? What would she do if she were carrying a palanquin with a stranger inside? Would she make an instant decision to protect that person with her own life, knowing both might die?

It was too frustrating a philosophical question to ponder. Maybe Colin's Thinkers group could take it on. Better to think about such things in libraries than in the jungle itself.

After about an hour's ride, she spied a small Hindu temple with a stone statue of a female, arms bent and fingers touching in a classic dancer's pose.

Abruptly, the men dropped the palanquin. She hadn't been prepared for how hard the landing would be and rubbed her bruised tailbone. Gingerly, Perveen crawled out of the window, inhaling the good smell of champa flowers. But she pulled back her hand quickly as she almost touched a gigantic brown spider. "My God!"

Lakshman picked up his lathi and struck the spider so hard the palanquin made a cracking sound. As he swept away the smashed legs and torso, she felt the shaking in her body slowly subside.

"Thank you." She was no longer sure she should climb out, but it had been an hour of claustrophobia and jouncing, and she knew she needed a stretch. So she took the hand Lakshman offered and clambered to her feet.

"There—see it? The altar for Goddess Aranyani. Will you make an offering?" Lakshman's voice was eager.

Perveen remembered what Vandana had recommended about leaving an offering. She suspected Lakshman had brought her here with the expectation she'd leave something of value that the team could later scoop up for their own benefit. She didn't like the idea of this; it interfered with her plan to tip them fair and square at the end of the journey.

She hesitated and then came up with an excuse not to give. "I'd better not do it. I'm not a Hindu."

"It is for safety. Religion does not matter!" His voice was urgent.

"To my priests, it would matter." Standing before him in the unfamiliar terrain, she felt tense. Would he see through her excuse?

He nodded and went to the men. They conferred for a while, shooting her disapproving looks, and then Lakshman walked off toward the statue. He put something inside a bowl set in front of Aranyani. Perveen guessed it was the money she'd paid him for assisting with her trip to the village the day before. He had given because he believed the protection of the goddess was essential. A feeling of guilt swept over her, and when he came back, she said, "I will give you and everyone else baksheesh at journey's end."

He shook his head as if her words were tiresome. "Memsahib, we will all eat now. Please take your tiffin near that kombadnakhi tree."

They'd been gone from the circuit house for only an hour, but she didn't think the men would be happy if she ordered them to keep going. They had put the palanquin down; they wanted to eat.

Picking up the brass meal container that Rama had given her, she surveyed the small tree, which had a mass of exposed roots that reminded her of claws. "What an interesting-looking tree."

"Kombadnakhi means 'the hen's tree.'" Lakshman spread out a light bamboo mat on the ground. "Sit here. There are many creatures about."

"Are there wild hens in these woods?" she asked as she opened the top section of the brass tiffin box to find two puris and two hard-boiled eggs.

"No, memsahib. The tree is named that because its roots are like hen's claws." Smiling slightly, he curled his fingers into claws. "When the roots are chopped, they are used to heal wounds. Also good against scorpion bite."

Was he trying to help, or just make her nervous? Probably both. Moving on from the boiled eggs to a serving of kitchuri, Perveen ate with her right hand because no fork had been provided. She listened to the birdcalls, trying to distinguish what was new to her, and what was familiar. A number of parakeets were flying about, cawing like her parrot, Lillian. She thought she heard the sound of koels and the faraway tapping of woodpeckers. A family of bonnet macaques scampered right up to her, stopping to regard her food with beady, avaricious eyes.

"I shall leave you something," she said, trying to make peace before they sprang onto the mat.

"They do not understand language," a bearer said, smirking as he passed her.

That was obvious, but she had hoped the tone of her voice would cause them to scramble off. It was an unpleasant feeling to have the monkeys circled around as if she were their prey. In the end, Lakshman shouted and waved a stick, and the monkeys loped off.

Perveen was embarrassed he'd rescued her. "How far to the palace?"

"A little more than two hours." Lakshman gestured with his hand. "I looked at those bushes. No snakes."

It took a moment for Perveen to understand his meaning. She hadn't used the outdoors as a privy since a childhood trip to the mountains. It was unsanitary and also embarrassing that the men would know what she was doing. But as she walked hesitantly to the designated area, she knew that Lakshmant must have guided hundreds of travelers to do the same thing.

When she returned, the carriers had surrounded the palanquin, the ones who'd guarded before now taking the poles. She sucked in her stomach to crawl through the narrow entrance into the palanquin box. Lakshman called out, and the box rose up sharply.

Thunder rumbled, and the sky became dark. It was just her luck to get caught in the last edge of the monsoon. Raindrops began pounding the palanquin roof, and she drew the curtains closed. The men moved more slowly through the forest now, being careful about what was underfoot. They kept singing, though. She could understand only a few words of their Marathi-based dialect, but she sensed the song was cheerful and meant to keep them feeling strong.

They continued for another hour, and toward the end, an argument broke out among some of the men about whether they should stop or keep moving. Lakshman was in favor of pressing on, but the men complained so angrily that she felt herself becoming nervous. And then, suddenly, the men stopped, and the palanquin dropped, unevenly, with a splintering sound.

The men clustered together, shouting and arguing. Unlike the previous time they'd stopped, Lakshman didn't come to the window to help her get out. Was it only because it was raining? With a sinking feeling, she listened to the rumble of his voice among the others'. After a long five minutes, she got out to see that the pole on the right side had cracked and was barely in one piece. The palanquin bearers were sopping wet, and the way rain was falling on her, she knew she would soon be just as bedraggled.

"Oh dear," she said in English. Some rough Parsi curses also came to mind, but the bearers wouldn't have understood those either. She wondered if the break had occurred when Lakshman had hit the spider on the palanquin with his lathi. Perhaps it was her fault for overreacting.

Lakshman's thin lips drew down in a grimace. "The new bamboo piece has failed. But no worry, madam. We can carry on holding it carefully."

She shook her head. "But it's bound to completely break since it's already started."

"We must go on. It is not safe to stay a long time in this part of the forest."

Perveen looked around the rain-drenched landscape. "Surely we can shelter somewhere and wait out the rain."

"No." His answer was sharp. "My brother saw remains of a monkey that looked like it was eaten by big cats. Tigers and leopards hunt at night. We should go on."

Brushing water out of her eyes, Perveen asked, "Would it be easier to carry the palanquin without my weight? I can walk, and perhaps someone can carry my trunk?"

"But your shoes."

She glanced down at her kidskin boots. "These are strong enough for walking and to guard against snakes."

He still looked wary. "It's not right for you to walk."

"We must go. I don't want to be eaten by a tiger any more than you do." Perveen tried to laugh, but it didn't sound convincing.

"Please let me talk to the others."

She could hear their voices, a rumble of disagreement and anxiety. She nodded, and he took leave.

"Four men will journey to the nearest place to get what's needed for repairing the palanquin," he said upon his return. "The others will carry your trunk to the palace. I will walk beside you."

"So we'll reach the palace in less than one hour's time, then?" she asked hopefully.

Lakshman shook his head. "No. That hour is running time. We cannot run if you are walking with us, and the weather is bad. It will take two hours or more. Depending on you."

All because she'd screamed at a spider. Feeling humble, she said, "I'll do my best."

A few minutes later, Perveen was trudging along, her shoulder feeling the weight of the legal satchel holding her most necessary papers and the gifts for the royal family. The heavy rain made her clothes and boots heavy, so as she walked, her back and hips ached. She recalled Colin's long stretches, and how his arm muscles had bulged when he'd done the yoga exercises. If only she had such strength and balance, walking on the wet, uneven terrain wouldn't be so difficult.

As she walked, keeping her eyes on the path ahead of her, she saw how many roots there were—how many holes and ridges and places to trip. So many depressions were filling up with water, it was hard to know how deep the water was until she stepped in. If she twisted her ankle, she'd become an impossible burden. The men who had jogged so surefootedly with the heavy palanquin weren't singing anymore; she imagined it was because their songs were fast-paced and she was forcing them to walk slowly. Or maybe they hated the rain, too.

She wondered if Colin had ever endured a failed palanquin ride. The ordeal of slogging through mud might be impossible with a wooden leg, but if he chose not to use it, his cane would also get stuck. Thinking of this made her step a little more quickly. Eventually, her journey would end.

The dark rain cloud was both in front of them and behind, and rain continued falling in tiny, cold knife pricks. She imagined it was probably raining at the circuit house, and that Colin was worrying about her.

When they came out of the trees, her boots were filled with mud. But the journey appeared to be almost done. Ahead lay what looked like a sentry's tower.

"We're almost there!" Perveen said, pointing to it.

"No," Lakshman said. "That's an old hunting tower."

"Should we wait there for the rain to stop?" she asked hopefully.

Lakshman wiped water from his face before answering. "The Satapur royal family used to hunt here because it is a good place for tigers and leopards. We are not so far from the palace. We should go on."

Lakshman wanted to protect them all from predators and naturally wished to finish the job. She tried to form a picture in her mind of a bright, comfortable palace filled with lights and warmth. She had everything to look forward to, if she could just keep her feet moving.

After some time, she saw, through a break in the trees, a faraway wall. The wall stretched on. It looked like a walled city, but she was afraid to hear it was another place they couldn't stay.

Lakshman smiled for the first time. "That is Satapur Palace! This the place where you wished to come."

She was too fatigued to answer, but his words made her legs move faster. As the fog cleared, she saw the wall was the facade of a giant gray stone palace punctuated with a series of towers topped by onion-shaped domes. The palace was so huge that it was surprising to see its massive arched entry protected by only two durwans. She guessed they were guards from their bloodred livery, although they were not standing at attention but squatting under the entry's filigreed brass roof to shelter from the rain.

It took fifteen minutes from first sight to reach the palace wall. With a wide smile, Perveen rushed the last hundred feet to get underneath the entryway roof. But she realized that her movement looked like an affront, because the durwans cried out and grabbed their bayonets.

"Do not worry, brothers! She has come to visit the maharanis," Lakshman said quickly. He had run up behind her.

"It cannot be." One of the guards spat sideways as he regarded their party. "Who are you?"

Perveen realized that she was too bedraggled to look like anyone's idea of a lady lawyer. And while she had not explicitly been summoned, she could reframe what the maharanis had asked of Colin. Firmly, she said, "Mr. Sandringham, the political agent, sent a letter about me. I am P. J. Mistry, Esquire. I came here at the maharanis' request for assistance."

At the last word, the men looked at each other. Then they

turned their backs to her and had a brief muttering. One of the men pushed open the door and went through it without a word.

"I think he is going to ask the maharanis if your story is true," Lakshman said to her. Perveen saw the worry on his face. After all, Colin had been turned away the last time he'd come. If Perveen was rejected, the hard journey would be for naught.

The guard came back with a dour expression. He beckoned to Lakshman and spoke to him in a quick, sharp manner. When Lakshman came over to her, his expression was grim. "They say no. The maharani received the letter, but she said not to admit you."

"Does she not realize I'm a woman?" Perveen was horrified.

"The guard says that she knows this now."

"Why is she refusing me, then?"

He kept his eyes low. "I don't wish to speak in disrespect."

"Speak! We have all traveled too far in terrible conditions to endure nonsense."

"The maharani looked out the window and told the guard you were too dirty to come inside." He gave her a look of anger, and in it, she sensed all the times that he was not allowed to set foot inside a building because he was poor and the wrong caste.

Perveen looked down and saw that the bottom half of her sari was brown from the spray of wet earth. The rest of the sari was plastered to her body, and rivulets of water ran down into her eyes. The fine clothes she'd packed into her case to wear at the palace would never be seen, just like the gifts she carried.

The gifts! There was a risk, if she handed them over, that they would disappear with the guards. But she didn't know what else to do. Perveen reached into her satchel and took out the two boxes wrapped in gold paper. "Bring these gifts to the maharanis and say they are from the lady who's come to help with the maharaja. Please tell them I'm only in this dreadful condition because the palanquin broke. I apologize that I had to get out of it and walk."

The guard nodded quickly. She guessed that he understood

what it was like to stand in the rain for hours. He went through the gate again, and she hoped for the best.

The rain poured down. The waiting seemed interminable. How many people were looking at the moonstone and the gloves? Perhaps the gifts were being laughed at as inferior; she would still be sent away to humiliate the Indian Civil Service.

But they needed her—didn't they understand? The letters from the maharanis had been filled with demands.

When the durwan returned, he no longer had the boxes. However, he was accompanied by a handsome, clean-shaven man in his early twenties wearing a red silk sherwani coat and coordinating tight-legged pajamas. Under the wide brim of his umbrella, the man had a thin, clever face that seemed oddly familiar.

The dashing man crooked a finger toward Perveen.

She hesitated. She knew she should not follow an unknown man's beckoning, but the circumstances were strange. Perveen moved forward, keeping her back straight, pretending she was striding down the halls of the High Court with her father.

She folded her hands in namaste, and the man reciprocated.

"Mistry-memsahib, I have arranged everything," he said in a warm voice that was the opposite of the guards'. "I have spoken to the maharani. She will allow you to come in."

11

ENTRÉE TO THE PALACE

"Are you the children's tutor?" Perveen asked in a haze of gratitude as she walked through the gate alongside the gentleman who'd allowed her in.

"Ha-ha!" Her rescuer gave her a look of delight. "Do I look eighty years old?"

Belatedly remembering what Colin had said about the tutor, she felt embarrassed. "Not at all, sir."

He broke into gales of laughter. At the end, gasping, he said, "I am just twenty-four. And it makes me laugh to hear you call me 'sir,' when I am the buffoon."

"Buffoon?" she repeated, not understanding.

Extending his long, gold-embroidered scarf to one side, he made a grandiloquent bow. "My name is Aditya. Everyone calls me Aditya-yerda, though, or Buffoon."

"Crazy Aditya?" she translated aloud. It seemed like an inappropriate title for such a sharp-looking young man.

"I don't take offense at Yerda," he answered with a wink. "Since turning fifteen, I have entertained the maharaja and his guests with jokes and stories. Come this way."

They were standing on a veranda facing a stone courtyard being pounded with rain. It seemed they were going to have to travel straight across. But out of the veranda's recesses, a bearer appeared with another large umbrella and began walking alongside Perveen.

Thus protected, she followed Aditya across onto another covered stone veranda, and then through a door into a dark, damp-smelling hallway. Tall doorways and ornate mosaics set into marble walls were the only things that felt palatial; without light and furniture, the hallway was depressing. She turned her attention back to the buffoon.

"I think you have a most unusual and historic profession!" Perveen said, thinking back to the deck of cards she'd scrutinized at the circuit house. Aditya's costume was more refined than the tight red harlequin suit shown on the joker card, but his position was similar to the one it depicted.

"These days there's very little to laugh about, but I am still here. It's because I'm the only one Rajmata trusts," he added with satirical gravity.

"Rajmata." She remembered Vandana speaking the same word. "Does that mean mother of the ruler?"

"Yes. But the lady we still call Rajmata is old—the dowager maharani. She did not like having her title changed. The younger one we call the choti-rani or rani-sahib."

"Thank you for explaining that to me." It was interesting that Mirabai was called the little queen even though her own son was the maharaja. Perveen imagined the whole palace was behaving with deference to her mother-in-law. Did the younger queen feel belittled by the title?

She also wondered who was in charge of the palace decorations. She'd anticipated this palace would be the grandest place she'd ever visited, but while the hallway had fine stone mosaics and elegant brass filigree work near the ceiling, there was little furniture: just a few heavy carved chairs and a locked cabinet. Looking up, she saw a row of grand Belgian crystal chandeliers, but none of them were lit.

"Rajmata wanted you to stay near her in the old palace, but Choti-Rani said you must stay in the new because it has electricity and piped water."

"So we are inside the original old palace?" She imagined the new one was better maintained.

"No, this is the new structure that was made for the late Maharaja Mahendra Rao's marriage to the choti-rani. We already passed through from the old palace."

She could imagine her sister-in-law's shock if she could see the condition of the palace. "And . . . I'm staying here?"

"Upstairs in the very best guest quarters. Right down this hallway, you will find a stairway."

Climbing the wide marble stairs, which were slippery with moisture, she hoped she would remember the way out.

"I said you must be very comfortable—or you would give the government a bad report about the palace." Aditya looked at her as if assessing what she would do.

"It is quite elegant here." She felt her breathing become labored as the dark rise of stairs stretched ahead. "When are lights used?"

"Electric light is only turned on after dark, for the rooms which are being used." He shrugged. "It was different in the late maharaja's time. But he knew how the crops were growing and how much revenue he would have."

"The maharanis aren't being told that?" Perveen stopped on the stairway landing to catch her breath.

"Choti-Rani has asked, but the palace minister doesn't have answers. So everyone worries." His glance seemed to show both frustration and contempt. "Please enjoy yourself here. In the new palace, there will be no birds flying through your room at night, and no snakes in the bath," he added with a cackle.

She looked behind her, belatedly remembering her luggage. "I have a trunk. The men who followed my guide took turns carrying it."

"Your bearers have given it to our staff." He had finished climbing the tall stairway without losing breath.

They faced a long hallway with tall, unscreened windows on one side with a view of the courtyard, and dozens of doors on the other. It reminded her of a hotel, except that each doorway was made of well-polished, patterned brass with multiple locks. The doors were exquisite, and Aditya explained that using brass rather than wood was both a show of wealth and protection against invaders.

She was eager to explore this new world, but the palanquin bearers were still on her mind. "Will my bearers be fed and sheltered?"

Aditya's eyebrows went up. "You are kind to think of them. Remarkable, even!"

"They did so much," she said, wondering whether he was being sarcastic. "Right now, I could still be in the jungle in a broken palanquin. Because of them, I made it."

"Do not worry!" He sounded bemused. "I will make sure they stay in the visiting servants' quarters until your departure. What is this about the palanquin breaking?"

She was too embarrassed to tell the story of her fright at the spider. "One of the carrying rails split. The rest of the team will come with it once it's repaired."

"The tiny bamboo bridge over the Satapur River has held the weight of many men," Aditya said with a chuckle. "Tell me, what kind of palanquin breaks under the weight of a lady?"

"I was told the palanquin broke for another reason two days before my ride," she said sharply, because she guessed he was commenting on her sturdy figure. "The carriers made a repair, but it didn't hold fast."

"I see. With luck, the clouds will clear tomorrow, and they will come." He smiled warmly at her. "Tell me any problems or questions you have. I will help."

"That is most kind." They had walked to the end of the long hallway and turned right to face another seemingly endless row of doors.

Perveen asked, "Where are we now?"

"We are still walking through the section for lady guests. In past times, during party seasons, hundreds of people would come. Ladies stayed here."

"Is it a zenana?"

"Of sorts. But I am in rooms with the maharanis without them minding." Aditya cast a sidelong glance at her. He had almond-shaped eyes that reminded her of Vandana's, although his had a golden-brown flecking that was different. "What have you come to ask them about?"

Perveen imagined that a court jester was most certainly a gossip, so she was careful with her answer. "The government asked me to listen to whatever the maharanis tell me. I was sent because they would not meet with Sandringham-sahib, the current political agent for the state."

"May your ears hear the truth!" he said as he stopped before a door with a lamp lit next to it. "And what happens when you leave?"

"I'll tell their tale to the government."

"So you are really a storyteller, just like me!" he said as he turned the doorknob. "Are you paid in rupees or jewels?"

"With a regular salary—" She broke off as she saw the room to which he'd brought her. The vast chamber was floored in black and cream marble tiles set in a diamond pattern, with scattered rugs made from the skins of tigers and leopards. Milky glass panels framed by gilded woodwork ornamented twenty-foot walls. The only addition to the spectacular walls was a large tinted photographic portrait of a serious-looking man with a broad mustache and a rakishly tilted pagri. The heavy ropes of pearls around the gentleman's neck, and the fact that the portrait was draped with a garland of jasmine, made it obvious that he was the late Maharaja Mahendra Rao.

"This room is lovely!" Perveen continued her inspection, knowing she would send letters to her family and Alice all about it. The guest room's furniture was ornately carved ebony. This included a wide four-poster bed dressed in silk quilts; a very tall, mirrored almirah; and a washstand that was carved with designs of snakes and flowers. She could hear the sound of water running like a waterfall in the distance and looked toward an arched doorway, where a young maid stood gaping at her.

"Your maid is called Chitra," Aditya said. "She is making a bath for you because Choti-Rani asked for you to bathe four times."

"Why four?"

He winked and said, "In the palace, it is not our right to ask such things."

She nodded. Aditya was candid and would probably be her closest ally during this visit. She felt almost regretful when the men arrived with her luggage and he took it upon himself to leave.

"Your bath is ready, memsahib," Chitra said in deferential Marathi. "I will unpack your clothing."

"Thank you. I do hope the clothes inside aren't wet." Perveen went to the trunk and opened it with the key she'd kept in her satchel. The tissue on top was damp, but everything underneath was dry.

"I shall iron everything for you!" Chitra said enthusiastically, as if the clothes had revealed the guest was not as vulgar as her appearance might indicate. "Memsahib, which sari will you select for the evening meal?"

"I've never eaten at a palace," she confessed. "How fancy will this dinner be?"

"Not very. The maharanis are widows, so their dress is quite simple. I think this will do." Chitra pointed at a blue silk sari with Chinese embroidery. It was a classic gara that had been part of Gulnaz's wedding trousseau, the very best sari Perveen had brought.

"Very well." Perveen swallowed, hoping there would not be any occasions more formal. "My friend said that in the old days, things were very gay here."

"Who is your friend who stayed here?" Chitra asked while beginning to unwind the sopping-wet sari Perveen was wearing.

Perveen realized she might be identifying herself with someone who had disrespected the late maharaja. But she could not retreat from what she'd said without being dishonest. Stepping out of her petticoat, she admitted, "Her name is Vandana. I think she's a distant relative to the royal family."

"Vandana is a common name. I don't know of her." Chitra's eyes shifted to Perveen's waist. "What is that wet string?"

Perveen realized that the maid had noticed the thin white cord she always wore wound three times around and knotted in front and back of her sheer undershirt. "It's called a kusti. In my religion, it is a kind of"—she struggled for the right word—"armor."

Chitra's eyebrows rose. "There are old suits of armor in our palace vault. But that cord does not look very strong."

"The kusti protects Parsis from going down the wrong path. It reminds me that no matter how difficult things are, I must speak the truth and do what is right." This was the core of Zoroastrianism. Many Zoroastrians said prayers three times a day while working the kusti through their hands. Perveen was not as observant as that but wearing a kusti had felt especially comforting on this journey. It provided guidance for an honest investigation and also linked her to her beloved family.

Chitra nodded. "Such protection is very good," she said, giving Perveen a hand as she stepped over the high edge of the long marble tub.

The water was scalding hot. She inched herself down into it, feeling a mixture of triumph and relief. Her journey had almost collapsed along with the palanquin—but she had pressed on and made it. She'd been turned away at the palace gate, yet she'd convinced her way inside. An old Parsi saying her late grandfather had often uttered came to mind: *The sword belongs to the one who uses it.* He had explained the proverb meant a man who behaves with force will prevail. During her hard day, she'd seen the advice also applied to a woman. And if she acted with resolve, she'd certainly solve the dispute about the maharaja's schooling.

Perveen picked up a facecloth and scrubbed herself. The water turned brown, and she was glad when Chitra's knock told her it was time to get out. She shivered in a towel, watching as the grimy water disappeared down the sparkling silver drain. Chitra scrubbed the tub to sparkling white and then refilled it. The process was tedious and took half an hour. Perveen got in again, and the second bath was lovely. When she climbed out, she had a strong desire to finish drying herself thoroughly and get into bed. But she couldn't; there were two more ablutions to go. She would continue bathing, because if she disobeyed the royal instructions, Chitra would probably report it.

As if sensing Perveen's reluctance to keep bathing, Chitra offered her a succession of beauty pastes to apply to her face and hair while waiting for her next bath. Turmeric paste went on first, followed by a thin mask of buttermilk. For her hair, it was a shampoo of amla followed by coconut oil.

The third tub of water was tepid, rather than hot; she guessed that the palace's stored hot water must have been running out. Her fourth bath was cold.

"Are you all right, memsahib?" Chitra inquired anxiously as Perveen jumped out of the tub moments after she'd rinsed off the final hair and skin treatments.

"Yes. Are there any more towels?"

This time, Chitra wrapped the largest, thickest towel Perveen had ever seen around her and began drying her. Perveen felt like a small child but was unable to stop the maid. Wrapping a second, slightly smaller towel around Perveen's head, Chitra instructed her to get in the bed, which turned out to be warmed at the head and foot by brass bed warmers. Moving the top one to the side, she saw that it was engraved with a ring of millet surrounding two tigers. She had seen this emblem on the top of the letter from the dowager maharani, Putlabai, but the letter from Mirabai had been on unmarked paper. She wondered if that was significant.

Perveen's worries were overtaken by a need to rest. Cocooned in cotton, she napped until Chitra arrived forty-five minutes before dinner to help with her dress and hair. The lady's maid had a device Perveen had never seen—a long brass clamp—that she pulled through Perveen's hair, so it came out in waves. Chitra arranged Perveen's long, wavy hair into a style that cascaded just past her shoulder blades. Alice would have snickered at such frippery, but Gulnaz would have sighed with admiration.

"This is very nice," Perveen said. "Usually I wear my hair pinned up."

Chitra gave a half smile. "In the old days, my maharani had many splendid hairstyles. Now she is a widow and very simple. I wish you to look special because tonight you will dine in the zenana. It is inside the old palace, the place where ladies lived for more than one hundred years."

Perveen was eager to meet everyone, but she could guess the two maharanis might not be candid if they were in the same room. "Will the maharani Mirabai and the children take their evening meal there?"

Carefully, Chitra moved the hot iron to a side table far across the room. When she returned, she answered Perveen's question. "I don't know if the choti-rani and the children will dine with you. But because you are a visitor, and the rajmata is the head of the palace family, you must pay respects to her first. Now, where is the jewelry you will wear?"

"I don't have much. A pearl necklace and earrings and bangles that match." Perveen had reasoned none of her jewelry could compare to a princess's, so she'd chosen to be simple.

Just as Chitra finished clasping a pearl choker around Perveen's neck, a knock sounded. Aditya, the buffoon, was waiting. He'd changed his costume to a dark green paisley kurta pajama. On his head, he wore a small orange pagri set at a rakish angle. A diamond the size of a grape glinted from the turban's edge. But the most dramatic ornament of all was alive: a small gray monkey dressed in a matching green jacket sat on his shoulder, peering at her.

"Who is this?" Perveen exclaimed in delight.

"He is called Bandar." Aditya chucked the monkey under the chin with his finger.

"Yes, I can see he's a monkey. A bonnet macaque." She tried not to sound impatient. "Does this bandar have a personal name?"

"It's Bandar," he repeated. "At this palace, we call things as they are."

Just as Aditya was called Yerda or Buffoon—rather than by his name. He played a role at the palace that couldn't be forgotten.

"Does your monkey do tricks?" she asked.

"Oh yes! You will have to see. But mainly he is my little friend."

As if to emphasize his master's words, Bandar nestled closely into Aditya's shoulder and peered at Perveen.

She smiled at the monkey and was heartened to see him smile back.

The walk from the new palace to the old meant crossing the same courtyard she'd hurried through before. The water had been ankle deep on her way in but had now run off into gutters, and the rain was lighter. Nevertheless, a bearer walked alongside her, shielding her with an umbrella. Another servant hurried alongside the buffoon but was unable to get an umbrella fully over the tall man's turban.

As they entered the old limestone palace, the buffoon flicked his wrist. The men nodded at him and walked away.

"How many servants are here? I fear I won't be able to keep them straight." The only one who'd spoken to her was Chitra.

"Rajmata has about twenty working in the old palace, which is more difficult to clean. Choti-Rani has fourteen in the modern palace. The children have two ayahs, a groom to help with riding, and their tutor. And outside guards . . ." He trailed off as he looked at her suspiciously. "What does it matter to you?"

"I noticed the palace seems very well cared for," she said

hastily, although it wasn't the whole truth. She had expected at least one hundred servants for a royal dwelling.

"And how do you know about the standards for palaces?" he asked with a chuckle.

"I don't know very much. I've only been to Kensington Palace. It's the smaller palace in London," she added, in case he didn't recognize the name. Perveen and some other students from women's colleges in Oxford and Cambridge had been invited to meet the Countess of Athlone, but the lady had only briefly greeted the cluster and continued on to more important business.

"I know George V." He wrinkled his large nose. "His beard is too thin!"

Perveen was startled. "You've met the King of England?"

"At the Delhi Durbar in 1911."

She'd seen a film of the royal durbar that had occurred a decade earlier. George V and Queen Mary had visited throughout India, and the climax had been a giant assembly of princes in Delhi. More than two hundred maharajas had attended.

"Our maharaja had a twelve-gun salute," he said with pride. "And afterward, we went hunting with His Majesty in Nepal. I was just a teenager, but the maharaja insisted that I come along."

"For your jokes?" Perveen asked.

He gave a wistful smile. "I was special to him."

Perveen heard love in Aditya's voice and decided not to ask him why the late maharaja had been considered important enough for the British to recognize him by firing off twelve blasts. From what she'd heard, smaller states typically received nine-gun salutes. If Satapur was so important to the British, why had they allowed contact to lapse as long as it had? She also saw another reason Mirabai might want to send her son to England. She probably hoped that experience would give him the kind of insider status that his father must have enjoyed.

"The zenana durbar hall," Aditya announced, gesturing at a wide arch leading into a gigantic, high-ceilinged room. Perveen stepped into it, her eyes drawn to the tall marble walls and columns inlaid with precious stones set in mosaic designs and illuminated by candles glowing in sconces. There was a long mahogany table with perhaps thirty chairs around it and five place settings at one end. Despite the room's grandeur, there was an unpleasant smell of dampness and decay that made her want to hold her nose.

"I'm too early." Perveen's watch read five minutes after eight o'clock: one and a half hours earlier than typical dinnertime in Bombay.

He dropped his voice. "Don't you see? Rajmata is already here."

12

A ROYAL FEAST

$\mathcal{P}$erveen followed his gaze and saw a tiny woman nestled into a mahogany chair far too tall for her. The maharani's chair had a cushioned back embroidered with the same crest she'd seen on the Satapur coat of arms: two tigers standing on their hind legs facing each other, while encircled by sheaves of millet grain. The emblem was several feet over the woman's gray head. Yet despite Maharani Putlabai's short stature, her face and body were very round, reminding Perveen of a laddu sweet.

"Come!" The elderly woman's voice was not at all sweet. "I have been here a long time. In the old days, people waited for the royal family. Today, the royal family must wait."

"I am very sorry, Rajmata!" Aditya's voice turned singsong. "The rain spirits held fast to our feet."

Perveen eyed the dowager maharani, who was dressed for mourning in a white raw silk sari. She knew from the documents she'd read at the circuit house that the dowager maharani was sixty, which meant she potentially had many more years of life. The dowager maharani had a single gold bangle on each wrist. They glowed in the light of a dozen candelabras spaced along the table.

The rajmata was looking closely at her. Perveen wasn't sure how grand her show of obeisance should be, but remembering the preparation for Kensington Palace, she bent her head and curtsied.

"Rajmata, my name is Perveen Mistry. I am a lawyer the government asked to respond to your letter of concern. Thank you very much for admitting me."

Maharani Putlabai continued to peer at her. "Are you a Muslim?"

Perveen sensed the apprehension in the queen's question. In the seventeenth and eighteenth centuries, Maratha warlords had fought long and hard against the Mughal invaders who'd taken most of the subcontinent. Could the dowager maharani, who had been born generations later, still harbor a grudge? Uneasily, Perveen said, "No, I am a Parsi. Because my family's ancient history is in Persia, my first name is also common for Muslim girls."

"A Parsi! That is why your sari is so gaudy. Sit down." The lady stretched her finger toward a chair to her right.

Gaudy! The colorful Shanghai-embroidered birds and vines on the lustrous sari were considered tasteful in Perveen's community. Nervously, she proceeded forward, almost tripping on her way to the oversized mahogany chair.

Aditya also took a chair along the opposite side of the table but several spaces away from the gold-edged Limoges china place settings. As he did, the monkey ran down his arm, stopping on the table to survey the scene.

Maharani Putlabai angrily clapped her hands at the monkey, and he leapt down to the floor. Perveen was glad the monkey was off the table, but she was surprised that the buffoon was allowed to sit with them. The court jester seemed to be more of a courtier than a servant.

"Our esteemed guest is a solicitor from Bombay," Aditya told the dowager maharani in an unctuous tone.

"And how does a solicitor from Bombay come to me with my moonstone pendant?"

Perveen looked more closely at the maharani and saw that she wore a thin gold chain ornamented with the moonstone pendant. Perveen had missed seeing it straightaway because the milky-colored jewel rested against the white silk of the maharani's sari.

"That suits you very well! I'm so glad you like it." She would give plentiful thanks to Vandana when they met again.

"How did you get my pendant?" the rajmata asked again, as if refusing to be deterred.

"It is from France," Perveen added. She hoped she wouldn't be forced to admit another person had purchased it and passed it on to her because she hadn't thought ahead about gifts.

"From France?" she said, raising eyebrows that were thick and surprisingly brown given her white hair. "My son always said it was the country he most wished to visit. But this is no French stone. It's my very own Indian moonstone, given by my favorite aunt as one of my wedding presents."

Perveen was confused. "Are you saying that you already have a moonstone like the one I gifted you with?"

"You are an idiot!" Straightening in her seat, the tiny lady glared at Perveen. "I know this is my pendant, the very one that's been lost for at least sixteen years. Indian gold is eighteen or twenty-two karat purity, and European is just fourteen. This is twenty-two karats and for that reason, it's clear this is an Indian pendant."

Perveen's thoughts were in a jumble, and she felt herself begin to sweat. Had Vandana recalled that the dowager had lost her beloved pendant? She might have thought a replacement would be welcome, but the old lady's aged brain was too confused. If only Vandana had told Perveen the history! The situation was awkward, because the maharani probably assumed Perveen had bought the pendant from a crook dealing in stolen goods. For a lawyer, this did not look good. And it was a huge distraction from the issue of the maharaja's education.

Taking a deep breath, Perveen acknowledged, "I don't know much about gems, but it might be a moonstone that came from India. And many Indian royals have their gems put into fancy settings at French jewelers."

"You are a gem of a lawyer to have brought this!" the buffoon cut in with exaggerated courtesy. "Now it is our responsibility to gift you."

"Don't speak for me!" thundered the dowager. "Why should I bestow gifts on a woman who lives in a thief's pocket?"

Perveen's face flushed. "I don't want anything. I cannot accept gifts as a government employee."

"Oh? That's not what the last political agent said!"

Perveen was confused for a moment before remembering Colin's predecessor. "Do you speak of Mr. McLaughlin?"

"Yes. He always chose a very fine gift from the palace treasury at each visit. He would have taken the maharaja's crown if he could."

"Oh." Perveen did not say it sounded like corruption, but she would take the matter up with Colin later. Were so many jewels given to the political agent perhaps the reason for the twelve-gun salute?

The dowager maharani rearranged the pendant above her sari so it was placed dead center. "Now tell me about how a woman gets to be a solicitor."

As she moved her thoughts away from the botched gift giving, Perveen's shoulders relaxed. There would be no surprises when she told her own story. "I studied law at the University of Oxford in England. I met the qualifications for becoming a solicitor, so I returned home and took up work in my father's practice."

"England." The dowager sounded pensive. "I don't believe its schools are any better than ours in India. What do you think?"

"I believe it depends on the institution," Perveen answered. "There are excellent ones in both countries, and for certain subjects, it is better to study here. Do you wish to discuss your sentiment about your grandson's education?"

A servant dressed all in white, holding a silver tureen, stepped into the room, but the old lady flicked a hand at him, and he hastily reversed. Turning her attention back to Perveen, she said, "It is not a matter of sentiment but truth. My grandson should not go far away when his dharma is to rule here."

Her words were true to the letter Perveen had seen. But she

needed more from the maharani than a polemic. "I read this opinion in your letter. Would you be kind enough to tell me about the intellectual requirements for a maharaja?"

The dowager maharani cocked her head to one side, as if considering the question. In a strong voice, she said, "Knowledge of crops and of counting, and the ability to write a good proclamation and to hold one's strength in public. The boy can learn all this from his tutor. Basu-sahib was excellent enough to teach my own husband and sons, so why not my grandson?"

Perhaps the maharani wasn't as confused in her mind as Perveen had believed when they were talking about the moonstone. "And how old is Mr. Basu?"

"Almost eighty years. He has a lifetime of wisdom."

This made her uneasy. Mr. Basu would probably be good on Indian history, including the Maratha Wars. But what about current thinking in science and the humanities? "He sounds very experienced. But how is he keeping up with modern knowledge that is expected for young men today?"

Maharani Putlabai looked sternly at her. "It is not only information that makes a good tutor. It is love of family. Do you know about the death of my son two years ago and my older grandson last year?"

"Yes. I was very sad to hear about the tragedies, Rajmata." Perveen felt she should say more but didn't know what wouldn't be twisted by the wily dowager. "May I know how long it has been since your own husband died?"

"Ten years," she said. "That is a portrait of him taken five years before he passed."

Perveen looked at the wall and saw a hand-tinted photograph in a heavily gilded frame. He was a white-haired gentleman with a curling mustache, a different maharaja from the one in the guest room portrait. At the maharaja's feet was a slain tiger. The so-called curse caused royal men to die early, but it appeared that this one had lived a long life.

Pointing a small, arthritis-gnarled finger at Perveen, the dowager maharani said, "Today, his two grandchildren are all Satapur has left. And they come to me every day looking for the love and companionship their mother denies them."

Perveen remained silent, not wishing to sound as if she was taking sides.

Even though Perveen hadn't contradicted her, Maharani Putlabai continued. "There was no need for you to come. Everything could have been settled if my letter had been read by that new gora in the circuit house."

"Mr. Colin Sandringham," Perveen said, disliking the maharani's use of the derogatory word for foreigner. "He read the letter after it was finally delivered, but he cannot respond without confirming everyone's feelings about the matter. As you know, without a ruling maharaja on the throne, this entire family are wards of the government. The Kolhapur Agency has requested I carry out this protection."

"So you, a lady, are appointed to protect us?" Maharani Putlabai sounded shocked.

Trying not to appear argumentative, Perveen told her, "They sent me because I am an Indian who speaks Marathi, because I have experience practicing law, and I will not violate your purdah custom. I will listen closely to you and to the choti-rani because we can sit at the same table."

The white-dressed servant had come back into the room. With head bowed, he whispered, "Rajmata, they are here."

"Very well." Maharani Putlabai nodded at him, then said to Perveen in a contemptuous tone, "Tomorrow you will meet Basu-sahib. Then you will understand the children are learning all that is necessary from him."

There was a sound of running feet, and Perveen's attention jerked toward the doorway. A little girl wearing a lacy pink frock raced straight into the room, clutching something tightly to her chest. A taller boy wearing a navy brocade coat embroidered in gold was in pursuit. He stopped short when the girl had reached the rajmata's outstretched arms.

"She took my binoculars!" the boy accused, his face contorted with irritation. "She'll smudge them up with her fat fingers."

"They're not his—they're ours. It's my turn."

"Children, they don't belong to either of you. They're mine." Maharani Putlabai held out the binoculars to the buffoon. "Put these away in my quarters."

The maharaja and his princess sister were beautiful, with golden-brown eyes; fair skin; dark, curly hair; and a manner as lively and mischievous as that of any children Perveen might see in Bombay. She was amused to learn the old queen cared so much for her binoculars. She was probably busy spying out from the line of tall arched windows of the old palace. No wonder the dowager didn't want to move to the new palace; it would deny her a front-row seat on the world.

"But I want them!" the boy whined.

Maharani Putlabai hesitated. In a softer tone, she said, "Wagh, it is dark now. Kindly wait to play with them until tomorrow morning."

Perveen's head swiveled between the grandmother and grandson. Even though she had addressed him with a nickname that meant "tiger," her verb tense had been formal. She was speaking to the child as her king.

Aditya rose to take the binoculars from the dowager, but from his quick steps and tossed head, he seemed annoyed to be sent off to put them away. However, Perveen was glad to have one less person in the room. An audience could influence Maharani Putlabai to hang a bit tougher in order to save face.

"Who's the lady?" Princess Padmabai looked shyly at Perveen.

"Yes—who?" Prince Jiva Rao echoed in a more imperious tone.

"The British sent her to us. You will call her Perveen-memsahib," the dowager said, standing up as if to assert her power over the boy. As she did so, Padmabai was bumped off her lap and giggled.

As the maharani reseated herself with the assistance of two bearers, she said dourly to the maharaja, "Perveen-memsahib wants to decide your education."

"Perveen-memsahib, are you our new teacher?" Prince Jiva Rao looked at Perveen suspiciously.

"No, don't worry about that. I actually am a lawyer—have you heard of this job?" When he shook his head, she said softly, "My job is to listen to everyone and help them find ways to agree. My full name is Perveen Mistry. If you like, you can call me Perveen-aunty—"

"They must call you memsahib," insisted the rajmata. "Because you are working for the British."

Was this a dig? Perveen imagined the royals weren't happy with the British because of having to tithe so much of their state's wealth. It was a shame she couldn't tell the rajmata her private feelings about British rule. Looking at Jiva Rao, Perveen said, "I am very new to palace life. Your Majesty, what would you like me to call you?"

Padmabai piped up. "Everyone calls him Wagh. When he was young, he cried as loud as a tiger!"

"And the tiger is part of our coat of arms. However, that is a nickname just for family. To say, 'Maharaja' is respectful," the dowager maharani told Perveen.

"Maharaja Jiva Rao?" Perveen asked, trying to find a way to connect with the boy.

"No! To say his name to his face is disrespectful! Simply say, 'Maharaja.' And for his sister, say, 'Rajkumari.'"

"Actually, Mr. Basu calls them Prince and Princess. That is another appropriate choice."

Perveen turned at the sound of a pleasant low voice speaking a mixture of Marathi and English. The tall woman walking toward the table in quick, athletic steps wore a lemon-yellow sari as demure as Maharani Putlabai's, but made of fashionable French chiffon, just like Vandana Mehta's. There the similarity between the women ended. Maharani Mirabai's skin was darker, and had a slightly weathered look that was unusual for an upper-class woman. The princess's large dark brown eyes were magnetic, but there were fine lines around them, just as there were lines on either side of her thin lips. She was not a classical beauty, but she was slim and looked strong, which surprised Perveen. She had imagined Mirabai would resemble the maharanis in miniature paintings, who spent their days lolling in bed or at tables laden with delicacies.

Perveen's attention was distracted by Mirabai's companion, a tall snow-white hound with a bright pink nose. The dog was a virtual copy of Desi, the guard dog at the circuit house. But unlike Desi, who was a fast-running outdoor dog and not particularly social, this one had a house pet's manners, walking confidently to Perveen and nosing around her.

Perveen put her hand out for the dog to sniff, and he wagged his tail as she scratched under his neck. His fur was silky soft and had a faint perfume. Was it sandalwood? Close up, she saw that his collar was studded with what looked like real rubies.

"Ganesan likes you!" Padmabai chirped. "See his tail going quick-quick!"

Most dogs approved of Perveen—even the skittish ones. She reasoned that animals could identify the humans who wished them well. Bowing her head to the junior maharani, she said, "I am Perveen Mistry, the lawyer who's come on behalf of the government. Thanks to both you and your mother-in-law for your welcome into the palace. I believe we will be able to resolve any conflicts if we work together."

Mirabai gave Perveen a nod and went to sit in the chair next to her daughter. Perveen noticed that Jiva Rao had bounced into the chair on Putlabai's left. The pecking order was clear. Even the dog knew his place. He lay down on the marble floor on the open side of Mirabai's chair.

A series of bearers entered, first carrying finger bowls. When Perveen's bowl was set before her, she dipped her fingers with pleasure in the warm water, which had a floating slice of lemon and a tiny rose in it. Elegant, indeed.

After the finger bowls were moved, the bearers returned carrying steaming plates. Perveen closed her eyes for a moment, savoring the rich smell of saffron and sweet onions that wafted in the air. She was so hungry. She wondered who would be served first: the maharaja or the dowager maharani. She was startled when one bearer placed a large steel thali plate on the mosaic marble floor, and each bearer holding a tureen squatted down to leave a small scoop on it. The dog began moaning, but Mirabai sternly told him to stay. At last, she gave him the command to eat, and he sprinted to the plate.

"Parsis say to always give the first bite of food to the dog!" Perveen was determined not to show that she was taken aback.

Maharani Mirabai's eyes widened. "You also fear poisoning?"

Perveen felt jolted. Was there a reason to fear poison in the palace? She'd thought such stories of treachery were only historical. Tongue-tied, she failed to come up with an answer.

"Your people also have enemies near them?" Mirabai persisted.

Perveen knew she'd better explain the custom. "Actually, we offer food to the dog first as a kindness toward animals. That is part of our religion."

"The poison worry is silly, just as the slobbering dog is," muttered the dowager maharani. "It used to be that dogs stayed outside. She took him in just after my son died."

"Ganesan looks like the South Indian breed called Rajapalayam," Perveen said, trying to distract the senior maharani from further disparagement of her daughter-in-law. "The Satapur agent keeps a dog that looks similar at the circuit house."

For the first time, Mirabai seemed to really look at Perveen. "It is correct that my dog is a Rajapalayam. He was gifted to us by the last agent at the circuit house after my husband's death."

This meant it was probable that Ganesan was related to Desi—very likely a brother or son.

"Ganesan means 'one who watches and keeps guard,'" said the maharani Mirabai.

"He is like an older brother!" Perveen said, then realized how thoughtless that was given Prince Pratap Rao's death.

Mirabai scowled, and the dowager maharani said, "As if a dog could take the place of a child!"

In the short time they'd been talking, Ganesan had quickly cleaned the thali of every scoop of food. He looked up as if asking for more.

Mirabai nodded at the bearer standing silently by the table's edge. "Go ahead." To Perveen, she said, "Normally, I wait a few more minutes—but the children and I will eat this food."

The bearers moved first to Mirabai and stood with the array of dishes, ready to serve. "Only rice, dal, and yogurt for him today," Mirabai instructed the bearer. "He is not well."

"Again? He needs meat for strength," the dowager objected, but Mirabai shook her head. Perveen noted that neither of the women took meat, and guessed it was because they were widows. Princess Padmabai was allowed everything. She chose lamb curry, potato curry, paneer kofta, saffron pilaf as well as plain rice, dal, cucumber raita, and stir-fried fenugreek leaves. Sweets were served at the same time, in little bowls; she took a rice pudding and gulab jamun balls.

Perveen ate all that was offered to her and used her right hand, following the lead of the dowager maharani, although silver was set around each place. The food was excellent, showing the signs of a careful cook who spiced things on the lighter side.

Mirabai ate in the British fashion, as did her son, who was using his fork and knife in a slapdash manner. Princess Padmabai used both methods interchangeably, spearing potato curry with the fork in her left hand and mixing rice and yogurt together with her right. Perhaps it was to appease both her mother and her grandmother, who ate elegantly, not a bit of food coming past her knuckles.

"What a delicious meal. It's hard to pick a favorite, but the lamb curry is especially tasty," Perveen said after she'd sampled all.

"Is that so?" the dowager shot back. "Do tell us, what is the Bombay standard?"

"There are many different cooking styles in Bombay," Perveen said, sensing that she was being told she hadn't the right to make pronouncements about the palace food. "My ancestors came from Persia hundreds of years ago, and some of the old recipes are still cooked. We eat rice with raisin and nuts, and we put sugar in our curries."

"The royal cuisine uses upward of forty or fifty spices per dish," boasted the dowager maharani.

"In rainy season, any food can become sickening," Mirabai said, looking at Perveen. "It's probably due to the rains that Wagh fell ill. That is why his diet is limited today."

"When was that?" Perveen asked, tearing off a bit of paratha.

"I was in bed all of last week," Jiva Rao said with a yawn that revealed half-eaten rice in his mouth. "It was so boring! And only soup to eat."

"Soup I made for you," Mirabai said, giving Perveen a significant look. "His stomach is still not ready for rich food."

"It was bad soup," the maharaja continued in his whining tone. "Then old Basu kept telling me to read, but I could hardly see the words. And my head hurt."

Perveen focused her attention on Maharani Mirabai, who was urging her daughter to finish her dal. "Was a doctor called to see the maharaja?" Perveen asked.

The younger queen shot a sideways look at the dowager. "It was not her wish."

Putlabai swirled yogurt and rice together as she spoke to Perveen, not looking up. "Dr. Andrews only comes too late. Calling for him is as good as wishing the person dead. My priest can take care of ailments."

"I hope to meet your priest," Perveen said evenly. It was appropriate for her report to include whether the prince had access to reliable medical care. Some Hindu priests were experts in Ayurvedic medicine, but others knew very little and as a result could do quite a bit of harm.

The dowager ate noisily and took a long drink of water. "It is a shame, but that cannot be. Our priest has gone on his village tour—he gives blessings to people at temples in small towns once the weather is good enough to travel."

"The citizens must be grateful for the special visitor." Perveen wondered if the dowager had sent the priest away in order to avoid his being interviewed by her. Turning to the prince, Perveen said, "Maharaja, are there any books you enjoy reading?"

"The *Mahābhārata*," Jiva Rao mumbled in a flat tone. Since he'd lost hold of the binoculars and been served the plain meal, he seemed less lively.

"And, of course, the history of every Maratha ruler—not just of our state, but of the dozens of others." The grandmother reached out and pinched the boy's cheek approvingly.

Watching the prince squirm, Perveen asked, "Do you study the *Mahābhārata* in Hindi or Marathi?"

"Sanskrit! The original language come down from Brahma," said the dowager maharani Putlabai sharply.

"There is very little English teaching," muttered Maharani Mirabai, as if this displeased her.

"Just because you came from Bhor, it doesn't mean you are better than us!" snapped her mother-in-law.

"I never said such a thing." There was a clattering sound as Mirabai's fork dropped to her plate. "We both know the maharaja wished to have his sons speak fluent English. Only then can they advocate with strength."

"But Basu teaches English very well!" The dowager maharani thumped a tiny fist on the table, making a fork rattle and the grandchildren snicker. "Are you saying that your late, esteemed husband didn't learn to properly speak?"

"I didn't say that." Mirabai spoke crisply. "He was the most intelligent man I ever knew. But he did not have the right accent for those English people. When he spoke, they would laugh behind their hands. He might have been able to get more if he'd sounded like this lawyer lady does."

How quickly a stiffly uncomfortable situation had turned into an all-out argument. Perveen realized both of them were looking at her, as if she should become a third warrior. She needed to defuse things. "Actually, I haven't spoken a word of English to anyone here. I did study at Oxford, but I have never tried to affect an accent. There are so many accents in England, anyway, that it is pointless to say one is best."

"That is not true in our case. There is only one accent for men in the ICS. That is the one my son needs to learn." Mirabai took up her fork again and began picking at her food.

"I speak English! The weather is raining." Princess Padmabai spoke English in a stilted but sweet voice. "When rain falls, I take umbrella. Who has taken umbrella from me? The dog has taken!"

Despite being the youngest, Padmabai already had the skills of a peacemaker—as well as the confidence to try out her English. Perveen felt a flash of admiration, which was just as quickly followed by regret. The rajkumari's destiny was to marry a man of royal blood.

Smiling at the girl, Perveen asked in English, "Why did you say that Ganesan has taken the umbrella?"

"Dogs can't hold umbrellas!" Jiva Rao shot back in Marathi. "He's just lying there."

"The dog puts umbrella in mouth and brings umbrella to the queen!" Padmabai said in English but using the officious tone of her grandmother. Then she picked up a kofta and threw it in her mouth.

"You have good aim and also good English, Rajkumari!" Perveen praised.

Princess Padmabai laughed, but Maharani Mirabai pursed her dry lips. "My son is also clever, but he needs the company of more boys to make him interested in learning. Too many women around weakens a man."

Perveen nodded. She didn't agree at all—but she understood that her praising the daughter before she'd said anything positive about the son had offended Mirabai. "Maharaja, may I ask what your favorite subject is?"

The boy pushed food around on his plate but did not answer.

"Do you like reading history, do you prefer calculating sums— or something else?" She remembered what Colin had said. "Aren't you good at drawing pictures?"

He paused, and when he spoke, his voice sounded more relaxed than Perveen had heard in the time they'd been together. "A maharaja has no time for drawing pictures. I like flying kites. Aditya-yerda brings them for me, and when the sun shines, I can run and get the colors so high above the wall walk. Up with the birds."

"Her question is not about playing!" said the dowager sharply. "It's about the important things Basu-sahib teaches you."

Jiva Rao grimaced and spoke in a sulky tone he'd used before. "I don't like Basu. He's too old and always coughing."

"He coughs so much and doesn't use his handkerchief!" chirped Padmabai. Then she proceeded to do a demonstration.

Her grandmother pointed a scolding finger at the child. "You are very lucky he can't hear your rudeness! And this meal is done."

At her words, the bearers, who'd been waiting along the walls, came forward to remove the plates. As they performed their duties, Perveen tried again to forge an alliance. Looking at both queens, she said, "If it's permitted, I'd like to give the children some small presents after dinner."

Padmabai bounced in her high-backed chair. "I knew she'd bring us something! Guests always do!"

"Did you bring me a kite?" Jiva Rao fixed an eager gaze on Perveen.

"No, sorry." Perveen suspected that Jiva Rao was going to be very disappointed to receive a book.

"She gave me back the Satapur moonstone." The dowager maharani caressed the pendant resting on her chest. "What did she give you?"

"She brought me gloves."

From the flat sound of Mirabai's voice, Perveen sensed the gift had been too little. Anxiously, she said, "I hope they fit you—"

"They're big in the fingers. As if someone already wore them." Mirabai looked warily at Perveen. "Are the children's gifts in the guest quarters?"

Perveen nodded, almost certain the young queen would find fault with the books she had chosen. But there was no way to change things now.

Mirabai sighed. "We shall go together—after the finger bowls come again. Princess Padmabai's hands are a mess."

13

A MIDNIGHT VISITOR

The wrapping paper Colin had offered for the children's presents had a gay Christmas design of green holly leaves and red berries. Perveen hoped the Satapur royal family would not be offended by the paper's connection to a Christian holiday, nor its age. When she was at the circuit house, Perveen had smoothed out the paper's creases—it had clearly been used before—and wrapped the books as best she could, tying official red government document tape to make bows. But she shouldn't have worried. The children took no notice of the paper and ripped it straight off to examine the books.

"My children are too excited. I'm sorry." From her position lying on a divan, Mirabai watched them toss the paper across the marble floor. Chitra rushed to pick up every piece.

"I don't mind," Perveen assured them. "Let them enjoy the surprise."

Jiva Rao quickly paged through *The Wind in the Willows.* When he looked up, his expression was mildly interested. "Why are these animals wearing clothes? And what are they?"

Padmabai, who had been looking over his shoulder, made her own assessment. "His animals wear boys' suits. It is very strange!"

"How amusing. Will you bring both books to me?" Mirabai asked.

Perveen followed them and stood over the small family group. She was glad that the dowager hadn't come—she would have soured the situation.

"You are getting a look at typical English dress for gentlemen,"

Perveen said. "I can read a bit of each book to both of you, if your mother thinks there is time."

"Why not?" Mirabai gave her a faint smile. "But their English is not strong."

"Then I will translate to Marathi." Perveen began reading, though a few of the words were untranslatable. In the corner, Chitra sat giggling behind the hand held over her mouth.

"Is this forest in England as big as ours in Satapur?" Jiva Rao interrupted midsentence.

"This forest in the book isn't real, so it's hard to say. However, the line of mountains that includes the Satapur jungle is many miles longer than even the island of England itself."

"That is true," Mirabai said, shifting on the divan so she could look directly at her son. "The Sahyadri mountain range—which is also called Western Ghats—starts all the way down south in Travancore and runs up through Gujarat. That is the place where Perveen-memsahib's people arrived many centuries ago."

"Have you studied geography and history?" Perveen said with interest.

"Oh yes. I had a proper education at a convent school, unlike my poor children."

The queen's lobbying for an overseas education was unsubtle. And it was understandable that a bright woman who retained so much of her education held a similar education as an important goal for her children. Perveen went back to reading aloud until she was interrupted by a knock at the door.

"Probably *her*, trying to send them to bed," muttered Mirabai.

Chitra gave the maharani an apologetic head bob before rushing to the door to answer.

But it was not the dowager maharani. Aditya the buffoon stepped into the room with Bandar on his shoulder. Seeing the assembled group, the monkey jumped to the ground and scampered up to them, settling in Padmabai's lap just inches from Perveen. Despite having been charmed by Hanuman's family and

Bandar on Aditya's shoulder, Perveen wished she could move a little farther away. She could not help feeling that one of the strange gargoyles carved into the stone exterior of the Bombay High Court building had come to life.

"And what are you people doing together?" asked Aditya, coming over to glance at the book. Perveen wondered if he was miffed not to have known the postdinner plan.

"Just reading," Perveen said with a smile as the monkey reached out and grabbed the book from her.

Aditya wrestled the book from his pet and rapped him on his head. "Silly Bandar! You cannot read."

"Bandar must be jealous we are looking at other animals!" said Padmabai with a giggle as the monkey climbed back on Aditya's shoulder. "Aditya, you should buy Bandar a flat driving cap like Toad wears."

"Do Satapur's animals—the ones outside the palace—also wear clothes?" Jiva Rao asked Aditya.

"The tiger is our royal animal. Perhaps in the forest, there is a family of royal tigers wearing our colors!" The buffoon drew back his lips over his teeth to imitate a snarling tiger, and the two children laughed.

Mirabai's face was unsmiling, and Perveen wondered if she was remembering how her eldest son had died. It probably was painful each time her second son was called by his nickname, too.

"Next time you ride through the forest, look for any animals wearing clothing," Jiva Rao commanded Aditya. "You can take Rajmata's binoculars."

"She won't give them up. She's too busy watching from the old palace for invaders." Aditya put imaginary binoculars to his eyes and drew his mouth down in a perfect imitation of the dowager's sour expression. Again, the children laughed, but Mirabai's frown deepened.

"She may also be looking for Swaroop-uncle! He always brings wonderful gifts!" Padmabai said, peeking anxiously at her mother. The princess moved close to her, and Mirabai responded with a gentle smile.

"You must see your uncle often," Perveen said. After all, he was the prime minister.

"Very often. He has no children, so he loves us very much." Jiva Rao's voice had a happy ring.

"One could call it love. I call it something else." Mirabai's tone was ominous.

What exactly did Mirabai think her brother-in-law's motivation was? Her cryptic comment, obviously meant for Perveen's ears, had left Jiva Rao and Padmabai both appearing downcast.

Perveen was glad when the buffoon spoke up. Brightly, he said, "Don't you think it is time to close the books? I came to take the maharaja and rajkumari to bed."

"You are not their ayah. It is not your duty," Mirabai responded, stroking Padmabai's hair. Perveen guessed the maharani had wanted the children to stay with her a bit longer.

"Rajmata told me." He ducked his head apologetically. "As you know, she will be watching from the gallery of the old palace to see if the light goes on in the nursery."

"Well then, it's better to go. You may read more with Perveen-memsahib tomorrow." Mirabai turned to Perveen. "And you shall see Mr. Basu teaching them his pitiful lessons."

"What time are their lessons?" Perveen asked, noting that Mirabai had chosen to be obedient to her mother-in-law's order regarding the children even though the lady wasn't there.

She shrugged. "They study sometime after breakfast."

"If it's not raining, I'll fly my kite instead. I will let you see it." Jiva Rao sounded magnanimous.

"I'd like that so much." Perveen smiled at him. She was getting an impression of the real boy who lay underneath the gold-embroidered royal costume. He liked animals and the outdoors; and he wasn't comfortable with all the restrictions and formalities his elders wanted him to observe.

"Come along, little ones. You may take your books to your room." Aditya bent to pick up the books from the ebony coffee table while Bandar kept a tight grasp on his shoulder. Perveen stared at the monkey's hands, realizing they looked very human. She had noticed this about monkeys before, but in this situation, the way the monkey's hands clung to his owner reminded her of a child with a parent.

The children rose reluctantly. Both hugged their mother and Chitra before going to the door.

"Might we trade books tonight?" Princess Padmabai asked Perveen. "Jiva Rao can read my book, and I'll look at *The Wind in the Willows*."

"No! What do I want with pictures of girls?" Jiva Rao scoffed.

"I shall take both books if you keep arguing," Mirabai warned. Although her words were strict, her gaze was affectionate.

As the children took their designated books from Aditya, Perveen spoke to Mirabai. "Will you stay five minutes? I'd like to speak with you alone."

"No." The maharani arose, ignoring Chitra's outstretched hand. "I am too tired, and tomorrow I rise very early."

From the maharani's wary expression, Perveen realized Mirabai might have taken offense at being asked to do something. Or perhaps it was melancholia that caused her to live in constant fear. "All right. Good night, then."

Mirabai took a last glance around Perveen's room. "I did not inspect this room before you arrived; it smells musty. You must open the doors to your balcony tonight to air it. When a room is closed up, it fills with mold. That is what happened to the old palace. It reeks of centuries of mold."

"Ah," Perveen said, remembering the smell that had hit her in the durbar hall. "The trouble is that it's raining at the moment—"

"The rain will stop. Then you will enjoy the fresh air."

Once she was in her nightgown and had had her hair braided for the night by Chitra, Perveen slipped out to stand on her room's sheltered balcony. The chatter of tree frogs and crickets and pounding rain filled her ears like London traffic. But unlike in London or Bombay, here the sky was very black; the only light was a low-down pinpoint in the distance. Perhaps it was a guard's lantern. This thought made her remember Lakshman and the other men who were sheltering in servants' quarters. They were likely to be fast asleep after their tiring journey with a palanquin on their shoulders. They would not be worrying about the dark mountains surrounding them, or anything else.

Perveen had not been afraid at Colin's bungalow, a small property in the heart of the forest—yet she'd not been safe, because someone had burglarized her room. Since that discovery, she had been on edge. Perhaps it was because of Mirabai's talk of poison and hints of an unscrupulous brother-in-law; or it was because Putlabai had been such an antagonist. In any event, Perveen was more alone than she had been in a very long time, even in the secure palace complex filled with servants and guards.

She wondered if the dowager maharani felt that way, too. She'd been a widow for ten years, and suddenly suffered the deaths of her son and eldest grandchild. Her loneliness, and fear of other losses, must have been overpowering.

Sadly, the dismissive manner in which the dowager treated her daughter-in-law and Perveen was common. Perveen knew the secret anger that came from being on the receiving end of an older woman's scorn. She would have to work hard not to react to Putlabai the way she had to Behnoush Sodawalla, her own faraway mother-in-law. A divorce from Cyrus would have meant a final departure from that woman and a tremendous psychic relief. But Perveen hadn't been able to attain a divorce under Parsi law, just a legal separation.

Perveen took a deep breath and reminded herself she was not living in the past. She would be more careful about her words, about looking out for poison, and about sticking to her assignment. She withdrew her notebook from her valise and began making notes of what the two maharanis had said during the dinner. She wanted to be very clear about what each lady wanted, even though it would be impossible to please both.

That task took about half an hour, and when she was finished, she did not feel ready for sleep. Spying an ornately carved mahogany bookcase across the room, she went to see what it held. The books were in a mix of English, Hindi, and Marathi literature and, curiously, some books on mathematics and geography. There was nothing about the state itself. Perveen chose a lavishly illustrated edition of the *Mahābhārata* and carried it to bed, where she read the Hindi text by candlelight until she was tired enough to snuff out the flame. Too many names of sages and princes filled her head; she wondered if that was the reason Prince Jiva Rao was bored. She closed her eyes, let the sound of insects fill her ears, and drifted off.

It was still black out when she awoke. The room was silent— almost silent. She heard a soft sound: moving fabric and very light breathing.

Someone had entered her room at the circuit house, and she'd not heard. But this time she wasn't missing it. But who had come? Should she give away that she was wakeful? That could force a confrontation. If she lay still, would they take what they wanted and then go?

Panic rising, she realized that this might just be wishful thinking. The person walking toward the bed with very soft steps could be an assassin sent to stop her from making the decision about Jiva Rao.

Fear swelled inside her, and she went immobile. She imagined Colin's horror when she never returned. But the thought of him made her recall a secret weapon. She reached beside her pillow for the battery torch.

"Who's there?" she shouted, sitting bolt upright and shining the light into the blackness.

"*Bhagwan ke liye!* For the sake of God, hush!" a woman's voice fiercely whispered back.

Pointing the yellow light in the direction of the voice, Perveen saw Mirabai. Her face was tense, but to Perveen's relief, she was not carrying a knife or gun.

"You told me to keep the balcony doors open so you could break in!" Perveen was angry with herself for being so naïve.

"It is not breaking in when it's my own home," Mirabai retorted. "And you said to me that you wished to talk. Put that light away from my eyes."

Perveen swung the light away and passed it over the room. She wanted to make sure Mirabai hadn't brought any companions. Perveen had been so frightened that her body was still tight and trembling.

Swiftly, Mirabai moved to the desk and lit the lamp's candle. Looking at Perveen, she said, "The electricity doesn't run late at night. We have a limited amount."

Perveen tried to gentle her voice, although she was still agitated about the intrusion. Mirabai was wearing salwar trousers under a very short sari—all in a soft beige silk shot through with gold thread. The fact that the maharani was wearing clothes that permitted her to climb like a man spoke of how daring this intrusion had been. "Why come at night rather than in the morning?"

Mirabai sat down in one of the velvet easy chairs. Instead of leaning back, she kept her back straight, as if formality was another form of defense. "Do you believe that I love my son?"

"Of course!" Perveen did not think the show of concern at the table had been false. But she needed to hear more from the maharani. Resolutely, she pulled back the mosquito netting around her bed. Swinging her feet down onto the soft fur of a rug, she stood and crossed the vast room to sit in the matching chair across from Mirabai. She saw Mirabai glancing at her plain white cotton nightgown. Perveen's sister-in-law had begged her to bring a fancier gown trimmed in lace, but Perveen had protested that there was no need to worry about contact with royalty during bedtime hours.

"I love my son," Mirabai repeated, and now Perveen was close enough to see that the lady's eyes were shining with unshed tears. "Sending Prince Jiva Rao to England will mean I will miss precious years with him. But I know it's the only way to keep him alive."

A shudder ran through Perveen. Since she had read Mirabai's letter to Colin, Perveen had wondered what the queen had meant about her son's physical safety. And the dowager was also concerned. This was something the maharanis agreed on, and possibly the way for Perveen to broker a resolution. Softly, she said, "Choti-Rani, you wrote to the Satapur agent about education. That was your main argument. Are you saying now that is not quite true?"

She looked steadily at Perveen with her luminous gaze. "I am also concerned about education. He's learning very little from Basu. But in the end, what matters is life. And I am afraid as I've never been before."

A chill ran through Perveen. Not wanting Mirabai to see her reaction, Perveen went to the almirah and found her silk wrapper. Tying it on, she returned to her chair. "What reason have you to fear for him?"

"His older brother's death wasn't an accident. It was intentional." She took a deep breath before continuing. "I believe someone wishes to exterminate my children. I don't know who, but I sense it. It is as real as the rain falling outside, as the air that I breathe."

To call for an investigation of the past, Perveen needed hard evidence. "Please tell me the reasons you believe Prince Pratap Rao's death was not natural."

"Just listen!" Mirabai's hands clenched the chair's armrests tightly. "The day that my eldest son was taken hunting, I was here at the palace with my other children. In the morning, we prayed together in the palace temple. First we prayed to Shiva, the destroyer of evil. He is our main deity. We have a side temple with a stone statue of Aranyani, who protects the forests. I always leave flowers and fruit for her, too. But this time, when I looked into the statue's face, I saw tears on her cheeks."

Perveen was careful not to let her facial expression change. Her initial reaction was skepticism, for anyone could accidentally drop water on a stone statue, or water could run from a leak in the ceiling. But what if the tears were real? Aranyani was a force Perveen did not know.

"I should have showed this wonder to the children. But they would have asked me what it meant. And I thought tears might mean something had happened in the forest." Looking down at her lap, she twisted the bangles on her left wrist. "Late that afternoon, I climbed the stairs up to the top of the palace. There is a parapet walk where one can see very far over the forest."

Perveen nodded, not wanting to interrupt.

"The hunting grounds are five miles from here. I didn't hear a shot, but I knew something must have happened, because I saw vultures circling in the sky."

"There are a lot of birds in this area."

"Vultures eat what has already been killed," she said. "I have seen it many times, because I hunted from my childhood up through the time my husband passed away. That particular afternoon, I thought the presence of vultures meant that the leopard or tiger had been killed by my son, and the skinned carcass had been left for the birds. It greatly relieved me, and I expected they would be home in a few hours."

"Who does the skinning?" Perveen asked, because the idea the maharani was presenting in calm language was upsetting to picture.

"Not my son," Mirabai said with a sympathetic look at her. "The grooms who went along are used to that. They take off the hide to be the trophy of the one who shoots it, to serve as a rug." She paused. "The rugs in this room were the work of my husband."

"I see." Perveen was not about to admit she felt sorry for the leopard and had avoided stepping on the rug. She knew that animal trophies were synonymous with royal life.

"But no leopard or tiger was ever killed; the men on the hunt all confirmed it." Mirabai's voice trembled as she continued the tale. "My brother-in-law said my son got lost in the woods that day and was killed during the night by a leopard or perhaps another animal. But as I'm telling you, I saw the vultures circle early that afternoon. Now I believe they had come for my son."

In her own religion, Zoroastrianism, vultures were an integral part of the death process. After funeral rites, bodies were carried to a tower so the birds could consume the flesh. It was simply a way for humans to give back to the world without contaminating the earth or water. But Perveen knew this was not a time to talk about her own people's appreciation of the great birds. She needed to untangle Mirabai's confusing theory without causing further emotional upset. "I understand what you are saying to me. But could an animal have killed the late maharaja and run away afterward? Then the vultures would have come."

"That could be, but I never saw his body." Mirabai unleashed her death grip on the chair to wrap her arms tightly around herself, as if for consolation. "My brother-in-law said it would be too upsetting for me to see. My mother-in-law and her lady-in-waiting washed his body without telling me. And then he was taken for the funeral."

"I can see why you have questions," Perveen said, nodding.

"I asked to have my son's clothing returned. I was told it was all gone. But animals don't eat cloth. There would have been scraps!"

"Do you think someone on the hunt shot your son?" Perveen asked.

"The doctor's report did not say he was shot. Prince Swaroop and Aditya both told me the doctor's report said he was not shot. But it could not be confirmed entirely, because the gun was not found."

This was interesting information. "Besides Prince Swaroop and Aditya the buffoon, who else was on the trip?"

"Three or four grooms. I don't know their names, but two were from our palace and two from Prince Swaroop's household."

"Did Prince Pratap Rao show any signs of being nervous before the leopard shoot?" Perveen wondered if the young maharaja might have sensed someone on the trip had bad intentions.

"Yes. Very nervous!" Mirabai's words came out in a rush. "He was crying, and when I asked why, he told me he thought that Prince Swaroop would bag all the animals, as had happened before. He wished so much to have his very own leopard rug. Many princes even younger than he was have killed leopards and tigers and have their skins as trophies in their nurseries."

This was not the kind of detail Perveen was after, but Mirabai's words gave credence to the doctor's account of the boy insisting on carrying the only gun. Perhaps he had dropped or left it somewhere in the forest because he found it too heavy to carry. The darker idea she didn't voice to Mirabai was that someone had cornered the boy, hit him with the gun, and then gotten rid of it.

The junior maharani leaned forward, looking intently at Perveen. "So my son was anxious—and I was hoping he'd have his chance. He was just like me—always carrying very strong feelings. I wish now I had said, 'You are too young to succeed. Stay home today and go hunting another time.' Then I might still have him!"

Perveen heard the raw grief in Mirabai's voice and felt a resurgence of her own sadness. She knew how it felt to wish one's actions had been different. "I am deeply sorry that you lost your oldest son. And I'm not sure we'll ever know the truth of what happened."

Looking grim, Mirabai shook her head. "He is gone, and nothing will bring him back. Now all I can do is protect Jiva Rao. I spoke of rainy season sickness to placate the rajmata, but I tell you, last week he was poisoned by someone in this palace.

He is only with us today because I recognized the signs and made him drink yogurt."

Perveen was sympathetic, but the number of Mirabai's murder theories made it hard to take her seriously. "Why do you think it was poison—not an upset stomach?"

Mirabai closed her eyes tightly for a moment. When she reopened them, she said, "The woods are full of many plants. And now that so few of us are living here, sometimes the food served in my own palace comes from the old palace, where *she* stays with her servants—the ones who've always hated me. He fell ill after taking lunch there with her, when I was away. I did not know he would eat there—and I had Ganesan with me. I like him to run alongside while I ride."

"So if Ganesan was with you, he was not able to taste the food!" Perveen's swift realization was followed by doubt about the maharani's choices. Surely she could have one dog to stay with her son, and another to protect her while she was riding. "Do you usually take Ganesan out during the children's meal-times?"

"Never. I did not expect to be out as long as I was. The rains came, and to avoid flooded places, I had to find another way back to the palace. I was stupid to ride when the sky was so dark." Her face clouded over.

Perveen could not believe the maharani's theory—not when the dowager was also worried for the same child's safety. "What reason would a grandmother possibly have to poison her grandson? She must love him very much."

"There are many different kinds of love. And the question is, whom does she love best?" Mirabai looked intently at Perveen. "My son is not the quiet, obedient child she would like him to be. And if he died, my brother-in-law could ascend to the gaddi. Prince Swaroop is the son she coddled over the years. He was always her favorite."

"I'm not sure the throne passes that way," Perveen said. "If a royal line is extinguished, I believe the Kolhapur Agency might become involved."

Mirabai's lips parted as if she needed to take in some air. "Are you certain? Which man has such a right? Is it the viceroy, or King George himself?"

Perveen didn't want to give a pronouncement that could be interpreted as her own decision. She parried. "I don't know. I think that discussion about succession is done with a great deal of consideration."

"You may be right." Mirabai sounded stoic. "After all, the British arrange royal marriages."

Perveen was startled. "Do you mean your own marriage wasn't arranged by your parents?"

"The Kolhapur Agency administrator wrote to the dowager's husband proposing me as the bride for the next maharaja of Satapur. It took a few years for everyone to agree—and of course, I never saw him before the wedding. I was sixteen. I had just finished tenth standard." She cast an eye at the mahogany bookcase across the room. "Those are my old schoolbooks."

Now the odd assortment made sense. "Why aren't they in your own rooms?"

"My mother-in-law didn't approve of them. She said there was no use for such books after I became a maharani. All I needed to know was the culture of the zenana." Giving Perveen a sly look, she added, "I do still get newspapers. They were delivered in my husband's day whenever the postal cart could get through, and I saw no reason to stop getting them."

"But this is princely India—not ruled by the British. Why would royal families let the British control their children's marriages?" As the question left Perveen's lips, she realized the dowager Putlabai's distaste for Mirabai might originate with the marital choice forced upon her son. Probably the dowager would have preferred one of the Satapur area's noble daughters.

"If royal states don't comply with these gentle suggestions, the amount of tribute we pay to the government might rise. Besides, I know why I was chosen. My father had never argued against the government, and he'd allowed me to go to the boarding school in Panchgani they suggested. Neither my mother nor I maintained purdah. At one time, I was considered a model for Indian womanhood." Her narrow lips twisted as she spoke the last words. "But now I sit alone in this palace, because the dowager says if I break purdah, the people will be unhappy."

Perveen's mind was working. Clearly the royal women did not observe purdah in the traditional sense within their own home; it was a matter of show to people in the state. Mirabai's inner rebellion made her think of Vandana, who also felt alone. Perhaps these two spirited women would find an easy kinship. Casually, Perveen said, "I met a charming woman who lives about twelve miles from here. She is named Vandana Mehta and has some past connection to this palace. I asked Chitra about her, but she didn't know her name. Do you know of her?"

Mirabai's brow furrowed, and she was silent for a moment. At last she said, "I do not know her, but I never visited this palace before I married. And Chitra probably doesn't know her because Vandana may not be her original name."

Perveen was intrigued. "Why do you think that?"

"Many of us Hindu women have our names changed by our husband's families. When I came here in 1905, I was no longer called by the name my parents gave me."

"And what was that name?"

"Keya." She spoke the name very softly. "In Sanskrit, it means 'monsoon flower.' I was born during a very hard monsoon. But tell me—you said the lady's married name is Mehta. Is she married to a Parsi businessman?"

"Yes! He is Mr. Yazad Mehta. I met them both at the circuit house." She wondered if being in business was a social disqualifier.

"I once heard the buffoon speak about that man." Mirabai put a hand over her brow, as if her head ached. "He wishes to make hydroelectric dams all through these hills."

"What do you think of that idea?" Perveen had noted the dramatic reaction.

"It would be sad to see nature ruined. If forests are cut down, the animals lose their homes. Aranyani would not like it."

Perveen was perplexed. "But don't you enjoy electricity and running water in this palace?"

Mirabai shifted in her chair, as if it had become slightly less comfortable. "We have our own electric plant within the compound that supplies the power. The rajmata said we must have a modern palace to make visitors comfortable, but there is no need for others to have such things. The villagers could not afford to pay for electric light—so why install it? I am sure that is what she would tell you."

Perveen knew the palatial luxuries of electric light and piped hot water should have made her feel more comfortable than she'd been at the circuit house, but they did not. She thought of the thin, desperate people in the village, the burned buildings that hadn't been restored. Mirabai was telling her in no uncertain terms that the state believed this was meant to be. She reminded herself reluctantly that this was not her affair; she had come solely to decide the maharaja's future.

Noticing that Mirabai looked as tense as when she'd arrived, Perveen tried to reassure her. "I am not involved in advocating for electricity. I will just discuss your concerns for the maharaja's education."

"You must tell the British to approve him for schooling in England. I don't care which school—just that he has eight years to grow strong in body and mind." Mirabai rose to her feet and shot a glance toward the closed door. Turning back to Perveen, she muttered, "If God wills it, she will die during that time. Her health is not good: she eats too many sweets. In eight years, my son will be eighteen. Jiva Rao can then take proper charge without being hampered."

"I see." Perveen knew from experience it was a mistake to count on people to behave the way one hoped. There was also a real chance that Mirabai could take on the same negative role in the household as the dowager had done.

"I shall go." Mirabai nodded at her and then crossed the room toward the balcony.

"Why not use the door?" Perveen suggested. "It's safer than climbing outside!"

"The guards in the hallway would see me," Mirabai said, reminding Perveen of the many unseen watchers. "By the way, my bedchamber is just below this room. In case you must see me."

Perveen knew there was no chance she'd climb the castle's exterior for a chat with the maharani. As Mirabai went to the railing, Perveen stood anxiously on the balcony and clicked on the bright torch to help the maharani see better.

"No!" Mirabai said under her breath. "That light can be seen by anyone below!"

The queen truly had no privacy. Hastily, Perveen shut off the battery torch. "God protect you."

Holding fast to the holes in the damp marble, Mirabai dangled her feet and moved her hands down the balcony wall. She tilted her face up one last time. She hissed, "Don't worry about me. Worry about my son!"

Mirabai vanished, and in the next moment, there was a soft thumping sound.

"Are you safe?" Perveen whispered over the balcony, praying for an answer back. The thump had made her own body feel as if it had fallen.

"Yes!" came a fierce whisper from below. "But never speak of this route to anyone, especially not the children. I don't want them trying it!"

14

THE MAHARAJA'S WORD

Perveen squinted at her Longines watch. Was it really just six o'clock?

No. The night before, she had forgotten to wind the watch. The room was bright with sunshine, and the grandfather clock near the doorway said nine-fifteen.

She'd awoken slowly, feeling exhausted from the previous day's hard journey and the broken sleep that had followed the maharani's midnight visit. Even though nobody had told her breakfast was at a certain time, Perveen had a dreadful feeling she'd missed it. She might also have missed a chance to see Mr. Basu teaching the children, which was exactly what she'd come to evaluate.

The curtains were open, and a wide ray of sun slanted across the bedroom floor. The large cream marble tiles were set in a pattern with small diamonds of black onyx. This floor was a modern one and very different from the smaller marble tiles and semi-precious stones inlaid into a complicated mosaic in the dowager maharani's grand dining room. Despite its darkness and the smell of mildew, the jewel-like setting of the old palace had appealed to Perveen's imagination; but that was because of her childhood illusions about the grandeur and power of India's royal families. Putlabai and Mirabai had both schooled her in the limitations for royal women in princely India when there was no adult maharaja to summon guests for parties, or to take the women out and about.

A rose-colored cup of lukewarm tea and three biscuits waited on the bedside table. The maid had drawn Perveen's bath, and it, too, was lukewarm. From the temperature, she guessed that Chitra had probably come with the water more than an hour before.

Perveen took a quick dip in the tub and dressed in a lime-colored sari embroidered with curling vines and blush-colored camellias, one of the most elegant Gulnaz had packed for her. It smelled damp, as if the rain had soaked through the suitcase during the long, wet journey. Today, though, the sun was shining, and even though she needed to go downstairs, she went to the balcony for a quick look.

The guest room balcony was on a corner, giving her a grand view of the north and east as she surveyed the landscape. Rolling green hills were like arms cradling the valley, but in the east, where the morning sun was shining, there was a small settlement of tiled-roof buildings. She wondered if this was a village that funneled its population to work in the palaces. Toward the north stood an impenetrable forest of green trees, large and small. That forest was probably where Prince Pratap Rao had been killed. The royal family's losses were as much a part of the land as the thousands of trees.

Perveen went to the desk and picked up her leather-bound folio holding her legal notebook and two well-sharpened pencils. She went through her room, closing the door behind her and wishing she had a key to lock it. In the hallway, sunlight streamed in through a row of tall, arched windows, making the marble floor shine. A thin man in his twenties dressed in a red palace uniform jacket worn over a lungi sat slumped with his back against the wall at the far end of the hall; he halfheartedly rose as she approached. She had thought her chamber was in an area just for women, but she must have misunderstood.

"Where is Chitra?" she asked, because it seemed very strange that the maid who'd been so attentive the night before had not lingered to help her.

"Rajmata called for her. Is something wrong?" His expression was wary.

So there weren't enough maids on duty to have one stationed near a guest. "I am quite all right. Where do the children have breakfast?"

"In the nursery. But they've already eaten."

She bit her lip, sorry to have missed them. "Are they at lessons?"

"Maybe." The guard looked uncertainly at her. "It changes every day."

"What about the maharanis?"

"Rajmata went for prayers at the temple and is just coming back to her zenana. Choti-Rani has gone riding."

She nodded, thinking to herself that Mirabai's definition of being a purdahnashin was different from the one she knew.

"Chitra told me you should go to the inner garden. She has arranged for you to have breakfast there."

"Which garden?" The palace had a maze of small green spaces in and around it.

"Once you reach downstairs, you will see a big arch. You will find the garden there."

Perveen thanked him and started on her way down the staircase. The pearl-embroidered slippers she'd borrowed from Gulnaz slipped on the polished marble, so she grabbed fast to the bannister. Her calves ached from the difficult slog through mud the day before, and a subtle pain girded the muscles in her back. She did not feel as strong as she needed to be.

She had to investigate a number of large arches before she found the right one that led to a dining room and adjacent garden. A bearer led her into a modern dining room with walls decorated with a line of large painted portraits of men with fancy jewel-studded pagris, all set at a forty-five-degree angle. Even if their coats hadn't been draped in diamond and pearl necklaces, she would have known they were the past three ruling maharajas from the confidence in their golden-brown eyes.

The furniture was ornate, curlicued Chinese mahogany, and a thicket of Belgian-glass chandeliers hung from the high ceiling. A long table was laden with many silver chafing dishes. The sight of the breakfast made just for her was overwhelming. She would hardly be able to put a dent in it.

On the far side of the dining room, a pair of tall arched doors opened to a charming geometric parterre garden. The rectangular sections were filled to bursting with red roses, orange marigolds, and white datura blooms. Peacocks strutted along the gravel paths that ran between the garden beds. A round pond was completely covered with lotuses. It made an exquisite, romantic scene.

"The rains may be hard, but they feed the flowers," Perveen said to the gardener she came upon, who was crouched under a rosebush.

Looking startled, he bowed his head.

Perveen continued to a round cast-iron table. The table was laid for one with silver and a porcelain plate, and there was a brass vase filled with white roses. She felt grateful someone had remembered her. The pretty setting for one looked more inviting than the dining room's mahogany table, which was long enough to seat forty people.

"Please be seated." A bearer dressed in fresh blue livery, with a pleasant round face, approached with a pot of tea on a silver tray. "Choti-Rani recommends that people eat outside when there is sun!"

Perveen imagined that the senior maharani would have disagreed with that idea because sun darkened the complexion. What did the lady think about having a daughter-in-law so brown from daily riding?

Perveen picked up the Limoges plate from the garden table and turned toward the dining room to go fill it at the buffet.

"No! I must serve you," he corrected her pleasantly. "What does memsahib wish to eat?"

Perveen awkwardly handed her plate to the bearer. Mirabai

was worried about poisoning. Perveen was unsure whether to take that seriously. She thought about asking for Ganesan, but she realized that the dog must have been accompanying his mistress on her ride. There was no other choice than to follow the bearer to the dining room, where he announced the dishes with pride. He pointed out vegetable cutlets cooked to golden perfection, a thick dal laden with sweet raisins, a rich curry of cauliflower and tomato, and pohe, the same beaten-rice dish Vandana had served. It must have been an area specialty. There were also puffy puris and crisp parathas, velvety scrambled eggs and plain hard-boiled ones, and a tall pitcher of fresh lime juice.

This was the kind of spread Perveen normally would have welcomed with gusto, and it was late enough in the morning that her stomach felt empty. But recalling Mirabai's warning, she reluctantly said, "Please give me two hard-boiled eggs and one puri."

"Only that?" The bearer looked affronted.

She felt pressured but was determined not to show it. "Oh! How about that banana? I'll peel it myself."

"You are choosing like the Englishman who used to come here," he said curtly.

"The last agent, Mr. McLaughlin?" The man had obviously been quite a presence here at the palace.

He nodded. "His stomach was sensitive, so he only ate English food. But you are Indian. You must eat the food. The cook made it knowing that you were a guest from far away. There is pohe here, a palace specialty, and a raisin dal, and a cauliflower curry—"

"I'll try the pohe," she said, not wanting to cause the cook undue offense.

The bearer smiled with satisfaction.

In the garden, with the plate set out and the tea beside her, Perveen began her meal. But after the bearer stepped inside, she quickly scooped the pohe under a tuberose bush. She felt too nervous about it.

As she peeled the banana, a monkey loped toward her. She tossed the peel to him, thinking he looked almost identical to Bandar, the pet monkey who rode on the buffoon's shoulder. Both creatures were gray with cream faces. She wondered how it was that one monkey was chosen as a dressed-up pet and the other lived as a scavenger. Was the pet monkey really more fortunate?

A shriek cut through the garden's stillness, distracting her. The noise sounded happy, and as high-pitched laughter followed, Perveen guessed that she was overhearing Padmabai playing somewhere higher up in the palace. Very likely she was with her brother.

Perveen glanced up the garden wall and caught sight of a flash of red streaking through the sky. It was a kite. The children must have been running along the roof of the new palace. In her mind, she saw them tumbling off, and the worry cut her appetite.

As the servant came out with more tea, Perveen pointed in the direction of the kite. "Are the prince and princess safe playing on the roof?"

He seemed bemused by the question. "Of course. They aren't alone."

How did a waiter working a dining room know what was going on above him? "If their mother is out riding and the dowager maharani is in her zenana, who is with them?"

"Probably their ayahs." He shrugged as if it didn't matter.

But she hadn't heard an adult voice, and that made her nervous. Pushing her half-empty plate aside, she stood. "Will you ask someone to take me to them?"

What she saw on the roof was alarming. Prince Jiva Rao was racing along a flat walkway that ran along the edge with the kite held high. Only a three-foot-high stone wall protected him from the open sky. Padmabai ran behind as fast as she could on her short legs.

"Please stop! Both of you!" Perveen called out as the bearer who had led her up the narrow, steep staircase to the roof made his exit.

Jiva Rao was startled and stopped short. Padmabai continued on her course and knocked into him. Perveen screamed as they fell down in a pile just inches from the low wall. Both children cried out in shock. As she ran to them, feeling mortified that her sudden command had caused an accident, she heard another voice.

"What nonsense to shout at them!" Aditya the buffoon snapped. "They were only playing!"

"This roof is a dangerous place to play kites. They are close to the edge. It was—" She heard herself sputtering, knowing it wasn't a good argument. She should not have yelled out and shocked the children.

"There's a little wall around the edge, and we always play here," Jiva Rao said, holding out his hands for Aditya to pull him up. Scowling at Perveen, the prince spat out, "You have no right to be here. I banish you!"

Perveen was shocked, but her temptation to tell off the child was swiftly replaced by her knowledge that doing so wouldn't be effective. "Maharaja, I'm sorry for startling you. I only came up for a chance to see you in more of your daily activities."

"The day's activity is what the esteemed maharaja wishes," the buffoon said, giving her a wink. The gesture told her that his annoyance at her arrival had worn off.

"Maharaja, do you always take lessons when you wish?"

Prince Jiva Rao pursed his lips as if he'd tasted something foul. "When it rains, I sometimes do the lessons."

"Look!" Padmabai was on her knees, holding on to the roof's edge and staring down. "Someone's coming. Another visitor, and not in a palanquin. A car!"

Perveen walked carefully over and looked down, trying to ignore the fear of falling that gripped her. A bright green car was moving along a very distant road. Why hadn't she seen this road when she had traveled the day before?

"It's Uncle!" Jiva Rao said with a look of joy. "That's his Mercedes Cardan."

"Yes," Aditya said, standing at the edge and squinting into the distance. "Our prince and princess have sharp eyes. Prince Swaroop and his entourage are coming."

Jiva Rao shoved the kite string into Aditya's hand. "Let's go."

"You see him—but he is not near. It will take twenty minutes or so for your uncle to reach the gate." Winding the kite string around his broad hand, the buffoon gave Perveen a mischievous glance. "I think he heard about the lovely lady lawyer and came to see!"

Perveen felt perturbed that this might be the case. "Who could have told him? Does the palace have a telephone?"

"No. Why do you ask? Are you already wanting to call the English?" He snickered lightly.

He had deflected her query into a joking accusation.

"Even if I wished to call the Satapur agent, he doesn't have a telephone!" Perveen snapped, just before realizing she was appearing too defensive. "I was only wondering how the prince learned I was here."

"We can only send messages by letter," the buffoon said.

"Or you ride a horse to bring people messages! You are always going here and there!" Padmabai looked cheekily at him, and after a moment he smiled.

Perveen guessed that after the popular uncle arrived, the royal children would be even less willing to study. "Since the prince will be arriving in a bit, will you please show me your lesson books? It would be nice to have that finished for the day, wouldn't it?"

Jiva Rao frowned, but Padmabai beamed. "Oh yes! They are in our desks. I'll show you mine."

Mr. Basu's classes were taught in a grand room on the first floor. With a glossy black-and-white marble tiled floor and fifteen-foot windows overlooking the garden, this was like no schoolroom Perveen had ever seen, although it had a blackboard and real teak school desks with chairs. A globe rested on a stand, and framed maps of India and the world hung on a wall decorated with ornate plaster moldings. But the most surprising element of the royal schoolroom was a framed picture of Mohandas Gandhi. The spiritual leader's kind eyes behind plain spectacles were a welcome sight to her, but seemed out of place given that Satapur was supposed to be in full support of British rule.

The children trooped in ahead of Perveen and began to giggle, first behind their hands and then more openly. Jiva Rao and Padmabai looked at Perveen's face for a reaction to the elderly gentleman sprawled out on a teak planter's chair, his legs on the long arms. Perveen smiled, too. She'd seen lawyers sleeping in the same posture inside the Ripon Club, but it was very incongruous here in the palace.

Jiva Rao's giggles turned to ribald laughter, a surprisingly powerful sound for a child to make. The sleeper gave a start and opened his eyes. He blinked a few times, and the lines running on either side of his mouth grew deeper as he came more fully awake and reached for his spectacles. "What's this about?" he said. "You are disturbing me."

Perveen spoke up because he hadn't seemed to note her presence. "Good morning, sir. Are you Mr. Basu?"

"Yes, yes!" he answered, and she saw his cloudy eyes finally focus on her. Sitting fully upright and adjusting the quilt on his lap, he said sternly to the children, "Who is this woman?"

"She's Perveen-memsahib," Padmabai said, dancing from one foot to the other. "She brought us books!"

"My name is Perveen Mistry." Perveen thought about adding "Esquire," so the tutor would understand she was a lawyer, but didn't want to seem pretentious. "The Kolhapur Agency sent me as its representative to visit the royal family."

"And for what reason are you visiting?" The tutor looked slightly dazed, as if he was still half asleep.

Perveen realized that her arrival might be a shock to a man in his seventies who was accustomed to an easy schedule. Gently, she said, "A decision must be made about the maharaja's future schooling. In order to do that wisely, I would be grateful for your insight."

"Are you a governess? I have no need of assistance." He pushed away the hand she offered as he slowly moved his legs off the chair.

Watching the man pause, trying to gather strength before standing, she could sense how flustered he was. "I am sorry for the confusion. I'm not going to work here. I am a lawyer who practices in Bombay. I'm helping the Satapur political agent make the decision about the maharaja's higher schooling. I only wish to chat with you and review the maharaja's academic work."

"Uncle is coming. Therefore, we will show her the lessons quickly and then go to him." Jiva Rao spoke as if he were already a ruling maharaja.

"May we read the books that Perveen-memsahib brought us?" Padmabai asked. On the way down from the roof, she had fetched both from the nursery. Now she thrust them at the tutor.

"Ah," he said. "*The Wind in the Willows* by Kenneth . . ." His voice faded off. "And *Marigold Gallery* by Kate Green. We must check with Rajmata to find out if these foreign books are allowed."

He was having trouble reading the titles and the authors' names, Perveen realized with shock. If the milky film she saw in his eyes was cataracts, this could be the reason.

"But Rajmata doesn't read English!" protested Jiva Rao.

"I know our mother doesn't mind," Padmabai said, grabbing back both books and holding fast to them. "Please, sir!"

Mr. Basu blinked again. "Very well," he said grumpily. "Why don't you look at those books while I show the lady your lesson books?"

"I don't like her seeing them. You must tell her I will not go away to school." The maharaja kicked sharply at the leg of Basu's chair.

Basu's shoulders jerked, and the boy laughed.

"Maharaja, why don't you want to try school?" Perveen had noted the childish behavior but was determined not to show a reaction.

He nodded. "I haven't been there before, and I won't ever go."

Perveen suddenly regretted asking for the maharaja's opinion. She'd created a situation where there would be a battle of wills. It would have been much easier to quietly observe and make the obvious conclusion herself.

As Mr. Basu led Perveen away from the children, his shoulders seemed to drop. Was this from relaxation or sadness? He showed her into a dark parlor that was crowded with damask-covered Victorian furniture.

"These are my private quarters. Everything was furnished for me by the late maharaja."

Hearing the pride in his voice, Perveen did not comment. She regarded a huge chandelier with so many large crystal teardrops hanging from it that it crossed the line from expensive to gaudy.

"Belgian glass!" he said, as if she would not have known.

"Magnificent," she said, thinking that chandelier and the gilt-framed portrait of King George and Queen Mary showed his clear comfort with European ways. Yet Mr. Basu had seemed to disapprove of Maharani Mirabai's past British teachers and didn't want the children reading foreign books without the dowager's permission. This was a strange contradiction—and Gandhiji's picture in the classroom added to the mystery.

Mr. Basu handed Perveen a pair of slim composition books. She watched him slowly seat himself in a Queen Anne chair. He gestured toward a velvet settee, and she settled herself there.

"Would you like tea?" he asked. "I can call for it."

Perveen shook her head, thinking that he seemed bent on drawing her attention away from the matter at hand. "No thank you. I don't want to take too much of your time. I only wish to get an idea of the maharaja's academic progress."

"You are holding the maharaja's work over the last year. I'm sure you will find it sufficient. It is the same course of study taken by his father and uncle."

"Just these two notebooks?" Perveen flipped through them, noticing many blank pages. "How often do you teach him?"

"When he wishes. It is an hour or so every several days. I am always waiting—as you saw—but he's not eager to come. The princess will do the work. She wants to learn to read, to do sums, and so on. She has the gift of her late father's intellect that would have been better given to her brother."

Perveen ignored the pang of sadness for the princess his dismissive comment had elicited and paged through the first composition book. Jiva Rao had completed mostly half-page statements that were much simpler than what she remembered doing at his age. The clearest things about them were the titles, no doubt copied from the blackboard. *What Is a Ruler's Duty? What Is the History of England?* Jiva Rao wrote in neat Marathi script, but his sentences were overly simple and showed a lack of thought.

"Do you lecture first and then ask him to write a summary?" she asked.

"Exactly." He looked pleased with himself.

"So—your teaching schedule is about an hour a day?"

"Oh no! I work very hard. I am on duty six hours a day for them, even if they do not come to me." He held his bony hands in front of him, raising a total of six fingers, and she suddenly could imagine how dully he taught mathematics. "The princess sometimes stays longer—she thinks numbers are a game, and she always wants to learn more. That is why she is unusually advanced. I am often telling her to go away and only return with her brother. He must not be overshadowed."

Padmabai might pull ahead and know more—even though she was three years younger. That would be unseemly. "What do the maharanis think about the progress of the children?"

"They know I am doing well." He leaned forward slowly, as if his back pained him. "I am carrying on tradition the way the rajmata wishes. The younger maharani may complain sometimes, but where is she? Always out riding or reading the newspaper."

In a neutral tone, Perveen said, "Choti-Rani mentioned to me she went to a convent school."

He nodded. "Yes, some girls' boarding school in Panchgani. She thinks boarding school with British teachers is the only way to get a prestigious education."

"It could be that she thinks that a school environment could improve Prince Jiva Rao's attitude toward learning." She studied the tutor, trying to think of a way to trigger reflection without making him feel insulted. "Were the late Maharaja Mahendra Rao and Prince Swaroop as challenging to educate as the maharaja?"

"Not at all—and that is because they always came to class on time. If they didn't come, their father would have punished them!" He lightly struck the armrest of the settee for emphasis and then winced. "He was a stern ruler. Satapur thrived in his day. No laziness among the fieldworkers or any royal children."

"Do you see any differences in temperament and abilities between that generation and this one?"

He gave her a knowing look. "With a pair of brothers, one is always a leader, and the second a follower. The late Maharaja Mahendra Rao was eldest and took to leading because he was the crown prince. Prince Swaroop knew he hadn't such responsibilities. He'd be granted a small palace in another district with surrounding lands that would provide some wealth, but never the power of his brother. That is why he was less studious, and to this day is easily led to selfish ways."

That was quite a bit of editorializing, but it lined up with what

Perveen had previously heard about Prince Swaroop. "Turning to more recent years, how was it to teach Jiva Rao and his older brother—when that brother was alive?"

"You speak of Prince Pratap Rao, who died a year ago." His voice dropped as if he was afraid of being overheard. "I must not speak ill of the dead, but the truth is that he did not like to work at his lessons. Prince Jiva Rao's manner was cooperative; he loved his brother and tried to bolster him in his studies."

Perveen didn't understand, because Jiva Rao had not presented himself as studious. "How does a little brother support an older one in his studies?"

He sighed, as if her questions were a cross to bear. "Imagine that I asked the two boys the question 'What is the name of the king who ruled Satapur from 1680 to 1720?' If Pratap Rao gave a mistaken answer, Jiva Rao would do so as well—even though he might know the right answer. He did not want to shame his brother."

Perveen thought it seemed less an instance of support than of fear of being resented by others for knowing more. She had felt the same at the Government Law School when she was a green eighteen-year-old, a lone female afraid of causing waves amongst the resentful male students. "What were the boys' ages at the time you noticed this behavior?"

"I cannot recall. It was always so." From his slumped position, the tutor gazed at her with his failing eyes.

Perveen wished to urge him to retire, but she imagined that Basu was afraid of life outside the palace. He had been there so long, it was almost as if he also were in purdah. Turning her attention back to the issue of the children, she said, "And now we see Princess Padmabai being eager to learn, and Prince Jiva Rao less so."

"It is not a matter of lack of brain!" Basu said, wagging a gnarled finger at her. "After the last maharaja died, Prince Jiva Rao gave up. He never tried to memorize the history of the maharajas anymore. He made no corrections on his work. It was as if he gathered up his brother's worst traits of laziness. Perhaps he believes stepping into a maharaja's slippers means taking on the flaws of his elders."

Mr. Basu's diagnosis had nothing to do with his own waning skills as a teacher. Perveen also wondered if Prince Jiva Rao had perhaps lost interest in academics due to grief over his brother's absence. He also might be lonely. She asked, "Who visits the palace?"

Wearily, he shook his head. "What concern is that to you? I thought this interview was about education."

"I'd like to know if the children have friends. A brother and sister growing up alone is a rather deprived situation."

With a snort, he said, "This is the first time anyone's described the Satapur palace as a place of deprivation! But they sometimes see their uncle."

"Yes, as we know he's arriving imminently. What could be the reason?"

"He bears the role of prime minister—but that is not anything that matters for you. You claim the British sent you to find out what I'm teaching the maharaja. It is nothing they would disapprove of. I did not put the portrait of that rebel in the room."

He was obviously referring to the picture of Gandhiji. "Who placed it there?"

He bent his head. "Choti-Rani. But you must not talk about it."

Perveen was feeling more respect for Maharani Mirabai by the minute. "I shall not be reporting about any of the palace decorations. I asked you about Prince Swaroop because I'm trying to understand whether the children have regular visits from anybody. Their welfare is important to the government."

"That's right," a cool voice said from the door. "You want us to raise a most obedient prince of George's empire."

15

A SUDDEN DEATH

*P*erveen turned in surprise to see a tall, dark man with a stiffly waxed mustache standing at the door. He looked a little older than thirty and was dressed in a dark purple silk sherwani coat over black trousers and slippers that were studded with what looked like rubies. He had a side-tilted turban set at the same rakish angle as in all the portraits in the family gallery. It was decorated with a lavish ruby brooch. She knew instantly that this debonair man must be Prince Swaroop.

Mr. Basu struggled to his feet. "Your Highness, may I present Miss Perveen Mistry? The Kolhapur Agency sent her."

"I'm very pleased to meet Your Highness," Perveen said, not sure whether to hold out her hand for him to shake. After all, he lived in a world where the women observed purdah. She brought the hand out slowly, and he stepped forward and pressed it to his lips, as a Frenchman would. Vandana might have approved—but Perveen recoiled. It had been a long time since any man had kissed her, and she did not enjoy having a stranger take such a liberty.

"Miss Mistry, I'm very relieved you arrived safely. Yesterday was dreadful weather for traveling." The prince's pronunciation had a shortened, imperious sound, similar to that of the dowager.

"You knew I was coming?" Perveen asked.

"Of course. My mother told me about the letter from the government. I am only surprised to see that you are not a male." He gave her a slightly mocking look. "Still, I am glad they sent you. Our family has received far too little attention from the authorities."

Did he not understand that Colin had been turned away? Perveen spoke in a neutral tone. "I understand your concern. The current political agent has tried to visit twice, but I believe his gender barred him."

"It was actually a different reason." He lowered his head and moved closer, as if he was about to share something confidential. "The new Satapur agent has a deformity that my mother believes would bring bad luck, if he were admitted. Purdah was a more palatable excuse."

"I've met him, and I assure you he has no deformity. He had a foot amputated," Perveen said, feeling her anger rise. "If anything, he behaved heroically, sacrificing his own safety for that of a child."

"What's gone is gone. You have met the challenge. In fact, my mother wishes to see more of you. She has asked for you to join us at lunch in the old palace at two o'clock." He beamed at her, as if this was delightful news.

Perveen doubted the elderly queen wanted to entertain her; more scolding was sure to come. "Thank you for telling me. That would be lovely."

"And how long are you staying?" He smiled again, and she had the dreadful thought that maybe he did want her on the premises. The kiss on the hand could have been a taste of overtures to come.

"Just until I've gathered all the information for my report." She paused, thinking about the chance she had to speak with the man who might become maharaja if his nephew died. Despite not wanting to encourage further intimacy with this casually mannered nobleman, she decided she had to interview him. "Have you children of your own?"

"No, I'm afraid my wife is cursed." He smiled tightly. "A prince may take a second wife, but McLaughlin-sahib made it clear to me that such an action would be undesirable."

Perveen couldn't tell him she disapproved his blaming his wife for infertility, but she could ask more about the Kolhapur Agency's puzzling directive. "Why would the British care about the doings of a nobleman who isn't in charge of a state?"

He frowned at her last words. "I am a prince—not a mere nobleman—and I wish they didn't care. In the end, they married me off to a beautiful woman who was barren, and they gave my brother someone who's ugly but still provided him two sons. He was the fortunate one."

"He may have had three children, but he's certainly unfortunate to have died." Perveen needed to change topic to avoid showing him how offended she was by his words. "Is there a marriage contract in place for Jiva Rao?"

"I've never heard of one. Have you?" Swaroop looked questioningly at Mr. Basu.

Prince Swaroop's arrival had brought so much energy that Perveen had almost forgotten there was a third person in the room. Now she turned to look at the elderly tutor, who was leaning on a cane and regarding his former student with a wary expression. "Nothing from the British yet. Your mother suggested a certain betrothal for him a few years ago, but the princess's parents did not want it for their daughter."

The prince scowled, as if his own honor had been attacked. "Which family thinks they are too good for my nephew?"

"She would not tell me. Most likely, the family did not wish to enter discussion because it is the British who must approve the choice. Isn't it so?" Basu turned to Perveen for agreement.

Perveen felt awkward, because she didn't know anything about the Kolhapur Agency's policies or attitudes toward royal marriage. "I have not heard about any matrimonial plans, but I can ask about it when I return to the circuit house."

"My brother was twenty-seven when he married, a father at twenty-nine, and thirty-three when our father passed into his next life." Swaroop's eyes narrowed. "To the British, this was perfect timing. I believe they called him 'a seasoned man.'"

"Yes, indeed." The tutor looked at his former student with approval. "A ruler who has a wife and sons is judged more stable than an unmarried boy."

Tilting his head down to Perveen, Prince Swaroop addressed her. "Surely you can tell us whether the British approve of my nephew ascending the gaddi at eighteen."

The interview she'd expected to lead was turning against her. But there was still great potential for added information from the bitter prince. Forcing a benign expression onto her face, she said, "In their eyes, I think education is the most important issue. But could we talk about the situation a little more? I should like to know your opinion."

His expression brightened. "Certainly. I will show you the palace gardens while we are having our talk."

"If you are finished with me, I shall return to the children's teaching." Mr. Basu sounded unwilling to go on the walk. Perhaps he sensed that the prince wanted to speak with her privately and give an unfavorable opinion of him. But then she remembered the agreement the maharaja had made with both of them to study only until the prince's arrival. If Perveen kept Jiva Rao waiting too long to see his uncle, he might be less agreeable with her for the rest of the visit.

"I believe the maharaja wants to see you very soon," Perveen said to Prince Swaroop. "Let's not take a very long route while we have our talk."

"You are good at telling people what to do," the prince said as the two of them walked out of the dark palace and into sunshine. "That is the way it is with Parsis. The women dominate the men."

Now she really wanted to explode—but then he could call her an emotional woman. So she gave him a hard look instead.

"I will show you this courtyard garden." He reached to put a hand on her elbow, and she moved it out of range. "There is a pond with many lotus types."

"Yes. I noticed it at breakfast." In the pond between the floating lotuses, two black swans made a lazy progression. She hadn't seen them earlier, and they struck her as slightly ominous. Two black swans, just like there were two widows in the palaces.

But the prince was looking past them. "Isn't the fountain fine? It's Italian. Two hundred years old and imported in pieces to be reassembled here. My father chose it as a gift for my brother when he was planning the new palace."

Perveen wanted to stop ambling and find a place to get down to business. She seated herself at the iron table where she had dined earlier, hoping he would take the chair across from her. He did.

"It's quite lovely here," she commented as she opened her notebook. "You must be glad that the position of prime minister frequently brings you to visit your childhood home."

"It is so different now. More than half the servants are gone— not because of lack of funds, but because of the widow's lack of interest."

Perveen caught his use of the term. Surely he wouldn't speak of his own mother that way; she was respectfully called Rajmata by everyone. "Do you mean your sister-in-law?"

He nodded. "She lives in a dreamworld always reading news-papers inside or riding horses outside. My mother was very different. She was a champion hostess; there were grand parties here, in the day."

"So your mother did not observe purdah in your childhood?"

Smiling, he shook his head. "The general public cannot look upon her, but she was friendly with both ladies and gentlemen who were related to us. For these big parties that brought in wealthy strangers, she would sit behind a carved sandalwood screen. She would make comments from behind it that everyone could hear."

"But today the purdah is more extreme, because they are widows?"

"As my mother says, it is the way it must be, yet"—he spread his arms wide, bidding her to look at the beautifully trimmed hedges and flower beds brimming with scarlet and pink—"what a waste not to share this with others."

Perveen knew that he meant other elite friends, not the people of Satapur. He was hinting that if he had control of the palace and could arrange for parties, he'd greatly enjoy himself. But that was a matter that could not be changed. She needed to return to the matter of Jiva Rao's education. Looking out at the pond, she said, "I've a question for you about the tutor. Mr. Basu told me he enjoyed teaching you and your brother very much, but he's having more trouble getting Prince Jiva Rao to keep up with his studies. I imagine that you remember what it was like to be his student. Do you think this trouble is due to the prince's personality or the teacher's style?"

He stroked his mustache as he pondered the question. Then he spoke in a measured tone. "That is an interesting question. Teachers will always be annoyed by a prince behaving like the boy he is, rather than a future ruler. The maharaja's antics remind me of my own," he said with a small smile. "Basu has sound knowledge, and I don't know if another teacher could do any better."

"Boarding school is a possibility. There are many teachers there."

"Ah yes. If he goes away to school, he won't be guarded the way that he is here. That could be dangerous." He paused, as if continuing to mull over the question. "Yet he would study under many teachers and make some friends who could prove helpful later in life. He could even find himself chums with some of your people."

"What do you mean by that?" Perveen felt her hackles go up.

"The Parsis are the wealthiest community in India."

She would not address that because the point was the maharaja's education. Striving for a mild tone, she said, "Boarding schools usually have students with various religions and even nationalities."

"But Parsis are the ones behind hydroelectric power, steel plants, and so on," he persisted. "I am in Bombay often—I meet them at the racetrack and hear stories."

She wanted to defend her community, to retort that Parsis were more than just hard-nosed business types, but she could not let herself get derailed. "It sounds as if you would like him to make connections that could lead to change for Satapur."

"It is embarrassing to be the only princely state in the western region without a full-service railway station. A railway track was laid during my father's reign, but when my brother ascended, he was too busy furnishing the new palace to provide the capital needed for trains to go on the tracks. Everything stopped."

"Since you arrived in that splendid car, surely there must be a road?"

"You saw my Mercedes Cardan." He gave a smile of pride. "Yes, there is a rough road that runs between our palaces and out to the hunting lodge and on to Poona. But there should be more roads in addition to a full railway."

"But you are prime minister. Have you considered moving forward?"

He shook his head. "Not without permission of the sleeping bear."

"I don't understand."

"The Satapur agent is in a deep sleep, not wanting to do anything substantial until the maharaja he guards comes of age. Then the agent will assure my nephew the government will build wonderful roads and dams and a railway as long as he pays more in taxes and crops. He will not know any better but to agree."

This was a different way of looking at Colin's relationship with the state. "You are not so fond of the British."

"Nor are they of us. To the English, we're a nursery of spoiled children." Prince Swaroop's words were delivered with a sad half smile. Perveen wondered how many times he'd felt belittled. She'd heard maharajas bought fleets of Mercedes and Rolls-Royces to prove they had more wealth than the British officers who controlled them.

She could bet that at an English school, some students would be rude to Maharaja Jiva Rao. But the prince would also develop friendships and social skills that would serve him well. And if the school was a good one, he'd receive a broad liberal education. In her case, it was after her studies in England that her dedication to the freedom movement had solidified.

Perveen could have shared this, but she doubted the prince wanted Indian independence, because it would surely end the princely states. Even though he resented the sleeping bear.

"I don't have access to the accounting books here, but it's possible that some of your family's assets could pay for improvements without taxes needing to be raised. Are there any unused palaces in the state?"

"Of course. And we have a house in London and several properties in Poona and Bombay. But to sell those would mean losing face."

He didn't want to give up these properties, and it made sense for such a big, expensive decision to wait for the future maharaja, the true ruler. Who knew what the situation would be in eight years' time? "May we talk more about the maharaja? Do you notice a difference in his mood and behavior since his brother's death?"

"Of course. It has saddened the whole family. That is to be expected."

He was regarding her as if she were slow, and that made her finally decide to confront him. "I hear that you were with the hunting party when Pratap Rao died."

"Yes, and I blame myself for the events." His voice was somber.

"In what way?" Perveen's pulse quickened. What was he about to confess?

"He insisted on carrying the hunting pistol and running ahead." Prince Swaroop's fingers moved restlessly on the edge of the table, as if he was uncomfortable going back to this memory. "The doctor's finding was that he fell down and was stunned—perhaps hitting his head on a nearby fallen tree. This was why he did not answer our calls. And his vulnerability led the depraved animals to find him."

She thought about what Mirabai had said about the suspicious nature of the death. Why wouldn't Prince Swaroop, who'd been on the scene, have the same misgivings?

Perhaps because he was the cause of the so-called accident.

Trying not to show her apprehension, Perveen asked, "And then—the next day—were you the one who found him?"

He looked searchingly at her. "Is your concern about a prince who's already died or one about to ascend the throne?" When she remained silent, he said, "Did you know that if the British believe there's corruption or disarray in a state without a ruling maharaja, they have the right to take it as a possession?"

He could have been going on the offensive because he feared she suspected him. But truly, there was no evidence. Perveen took a deep breath and spoke in a gentle tone. "I have not heard any such talk."

"Such land grabbing has happened many times on the subcontinent. It's how the British took half the land."

"You are correct about that point." Perveen could have talked about military force, and about pressure put on landowners to gift or sell the British property, but that would hardly do for someone hired by the British, even temporarily. She would stay professional. "I greatly appreciate your taking the time to talk to me. You have been so very helpful."

"You are brave to travel alone," he said patronizingly. "I wonder what a lady solicitor can do when she is alone in a princely state with none of her people to back her."

It sounded almost like a threat. As Perveen stared at him,

she wondered how she would get away if he wished her to be destroyed. One would think he'd fear British retaliation, but she could always fall ill, or have an accident. She swallowed, pushing down her fears. "As a representative of the imperial government, I feel as secure in protection as the viceroy himself. However, I'm not so sure of the maharaja's safety. I saw him running along the palace rooftop with the buffoon. Highly dangerous behavior!"

"But the roof is the best place for flying kites!" Prince Swaroop said with a mischievous smile.

Perveen understood why Jiva Rao liked his uncle. Smiling despite herself, she looked past the prince at two large-winged white birds swooping through the trees and landing on the court-yard grass. "Are those vultures?"

The prince stood and walked a few feet from the table to look at the birds, which were pecking at something. "Yes, the white vultures that are common to this area. But don't watch them. Their behavior is disgusting."

It was too late; she'd followed him closely enough to see the scavengers huddled near the tuberose bush where she'd thrown the pohe earlier in the morning. They pecked energetically at a gray monkey who lay on its back, its limbs stretched tautly as if paralyzed. Its dilated pupils stared blankly upward.

16

AN UGLY SIGHT

As Prince Swaroop shouted for a servant to come and clean things up, Perveen retreated to her chair. She was nauseated both by the sight of the carnage and the certainty that the food she had thrown under that very bush had caused the demise of the gray monkey she'd seen earlier playing happily in the garden.

Prince Swaroop came back to her with a hand over his mouth and nose. In a muffled voice, he said, "What a stink. The creature gave up all he'd eaten, along with his life."

"Do you mean that you saw vomit?" Perveen asked.

He nodded and sat down heavily, as if his body hurt.

She decided to trust his word, rather than go over to look. Now she thought about how the waiter had urged her to eat the palace specialty. She wanted to identify him. "Do you know everyone who works in the palace?"

"Of course. They were either here when I was growing up or are the children of such servants."

"A very round-faced young man waited on me this morning. I don't think I saw him waiting at the table last night."

The prince looked quizzically at her. "Were you eating in the new palace or the old yesterday?"

"The old palace." She felt herself sweating as she had a new thought: Was the urge to vomit due to horror at the monkey or an actual poison within her?

"The old palace waiters are different. There are different kitchens for the two palaces, so the food is delivered more quickly and to each maharani's taste."

Mirabai was the one who'd been worried about poison, and this poison had probably come from her kitchen.

In the next moment, the same round-faced man who'd served her in the morning emerged through the dining room doors into the garden. Head bowed, he addressed Prince Swaroop. "You were calling for someone?"

"There's a dead monkey here. You are not taking care of the grounds!" Prince Swaroop shook a finger at him in the same autocratic manner characteristic of his mother.

The bearer took a few steps toward the bush, looked at the monkey, and shuddered. Returning to Swaroop, the bearer said, "But I cannot touch that. It is the job for a sweeper."

Was that the real reason? Or did the bearer know there was some kind of poison spread about? He had been bossy toward her before, but now, with the prince present, he was entirely deferential.

"Get a sweeper, then!" The prince sounded exasperated. "Don't you see how sick this sight is making our guest?"

"One minute," Perveen said weakly through her nausea. "What is your name?"

"Lalit," the waiter answered, nervously shifting from one foot to the other.

There were many reasons the monkey could have died. If she falsely accused Lalit of poisoning the breakfast, he could lose his position. She needed to know more. Looking from the bearer to the prince, she said, "I must learn what made a vigorous animal die so quickly: whether it is from natural causes, illness, or something else. It is all part of my survey of the safety of the palace for the maharaja."

"Get a sweeper!" Swaroop directed Lalit. Then he waved his arms angrily at the vultures, so they hopped several feet away from the carcass. When the bearer was out of earshot, the prince turned his attention back to Perveen. In a churlish tone, he asked, "What is this all about? You had not spoken of investigating safety before—just education!"

The prince had not yet arrived at the palace when she'd break-fasted. He could not have placed poison into the food with his own two hands, but she didn't trust him. In a reasonable tone, she said, "The maharaja is an official ward of the government. Of course his safety is my concern. His mother told me yesterday that he fell quite ill from food served to him last week. And I know that monkey was in very good health an hour ago."

From a few feet away, one vulture watched them with blood-shot eyes. The vulture seemed eager for a chance to return to its meal. Perveen stared at the vulture, knowing there was no way to communicate that the meal it wanted so dearly might result in its sickness or even death.

"The strong prey on the weak. That's how it always happens," the prince said over her shoulder.

"Another possibility is a cowardly person has used poison to achieve his or her aim," Perveen answered tartly. The prince gave her a sharp look but didn't answer.

Two men dressed in shabby lungis appeared carrying a small broom and a bundle of newspaper. Prince Swaroop pointed toward the bushes, and the sweepers began their unpleasant task.

Perveen understood that with animals, power determined who ate dinner and who became the meal. But that was not how human societies were supposed to work. The Satapur royals didn't have the right to dispatch someone who threatened their autonomy. Not in the twentieth century. She decided to remind Prince Swaroop of this. "Your Highness, we are both supposed to be protectors. You were appointed prime minister to take care of people's well-being. I am a lawyer sworn to protect my clients."

"I am doing just that, but your theory of intentional poisoning is—hysterical!" He half-shouted the last word in English.

"I am not the one with a raised voice," Perveen said evenly.

He sucked in his breath, and when he spoke again, his voice was normally pitched, but cold. "This is too hard a job for the Kolhapur Agency to have given a lady. I'll call for tea now, and then you can be released. Don't worry—I can arrange for the royal palanquin to take you, since you have none."

"No thank you! There is no problem whatsoever with my continuing this job." She wanted nothing he had offered her. And how could she abandon the maharaja? If someone wanted her dead, it probably meant he was at risk. She needed to stay long enough to deliver the school recommendation and convince the maharanis something was afoot within the palace.

Prince Swaroop shook his head, as if at a petulant child. "If I cannot convince you the monkey's death was an act of nature, there is no point in talking to you about anything."

Perveen got to her feet. The anger she felt toward the prince had made the nausea subside. As she looked toward the palace, she felt relieved to see Aditya standing inside the doorway.

"Good morning! I see you have met the children's uncle. What do you call him in the English storybooks—Prince Charming?" Aditya laughed merrily, clearly having no idea how charged their discussion had been.

"Escort memsahib to her room," Prince Swaroop ordered. "She's feeling poorly after having seen the ugliness the men are cleaning up over there."

"What happened?" Aditya regarded the sweepers bent over by the bushes.

"A vulture was eating a dead monkey." The prince scowled, bringing the ends of his stiff mustache downward. "It is a natural occurrence in the forest but not inside a palace—so our guest wants an investigation."

Aditya's friendly expression froze. In a faltering voice, he asked, "A monkey died?"

Perveen realized what he was afraid of. "He was not dressed in clothing. Don't worry."

"Let me see!" Aditya hurried to the bushes and pushed aside the servant who was shifting the animal's corpse into a newspaper bundle. Then he came to an abrupt halt. "Aiyo! It's my Bandar!"

"It can't be," Perveen said, feeling her head spin. *Please let it not be true.* The death of a pet was entirely different from that of a wild monkey.

Prince Swaroop came to stand over the grieving buffoon, who was kneeling by the corpse. "You are mistaken, Aditya. He is an ordinary gray bonnet monkey, not yours."

"No, it is he!" Aditya's retort was anguished. "I know the white mark between his eyes as well as the birthmarks on my own body. He is mine."

"Your pet, Bandar, wears a coat. This one is clearly an untamed monkey!" Prince Swaroop argued. Even though she disliked him, Perveen longed for him to be right. If only Bandar would pop out of hiding; then the buffoon's tears would stop.

"This morning, before I could dress him, he ran from me. He was angry I took a biscuit away from him." Aditya burst into wrenching sobs. "Why did he have to die? He's only three. Bonnet monkeys live more than thirty years."

She could have elaborated on her suspicion about the poisoned breakfast dish. But that would mean she'd have to admit throwing pohe in the bush and being the agent of Bandar's death. Aditya had seemed to be the most natural and friendly person within the palace, but if he learned her actions had led to his pet's death, he would never forgive her. She already could not forgive herself. Perveen had missed her pet parrot, Lillian, many times since she'd been away. And she took comfort that large parrots like Lillian lived more than fifty years; Perveen was counting on having a long-term friend.

As guilt washed over her, she saw Swaroop looking at her with concern. Wordlessly, she shook her head. If she declared to Aditya she thought there had been poison, it would add to Swaroop's impression of her hysteria.

"What happened to him?" Aditya wailed. "How could this be?"

"He was dead before we came outside, so we do not know exactly. I suspect the monkey fell sick and the vulture took advantage." Swaroop kept his gaze averted from Perveen.

Aditya's eyes hardened. "Where did the bird go?"

"Over there." Swaroop pointed to the corner where the vultures waited.

Angrily, the buffoon rushed toward the large birds, pulling from the folds of his clothing a short, sharp dagger. Sensing danger, the vultures all rose, screaming out warnings, and flew off.

Perveen's heart pounded as Aditya shouted a stream of profanity at the birds. When they were out of sight, he turned to address the tiny cluster of bearers waiting with terrified expressions in a corner of the garden. In a low, ragged voice, he said, "Bring a fine cloth so I can wrap Bandar. Then I'll take him to the temple for a proper ceremony."

The buffoon loved Bandar enough to seek religious cremation by a priest? She had not known Hindus would do such a thing. But then again, there was a monkey god, Hanuman. Perhaps Bandar could be buried at a Hanuman temple.

Swaroop's voice was warm in her ear. "He's very upset. Let us leave him here. I shall escort you to your room."

"That is not necessary." Feeling sick, she turned to walk back into the palace. But despite her declining his offer, Swaroop strode beside her down the gleaming marble floors of the new palace.

"This way," he corrected her when she paused. She followed, because the many turns and great rooms opening up along the halls had confused her. Her upset about the monkey had distracted her from her memory of the route.

As they continued toward the wide staircase she had walked down earlier in the day, she asked, "When Choti-Rani returns from riding, will you please ask if she could come to see me?"

He gave her a tight smile. "Remember, she keeps purdah. I cannot go to her."

She had no idea if the laissez-faire purdah customs practiced by the maharanis really excluded brothers-in-law. But Mirabai might insist on keeping purdah from Swaroop because she disliked him. Whatever the reason, the prince's comment reminded her that the maharanis were cut off from society in general. As she and Swaroop started to ascend the stairs, she asked, "Does she have any voice to the outside world?"

"Oh, she lets her feelings be known. Mr. Basu is supposed to write letters for her, but she wrote her own letter to the government. Your presence is the response."

"Your own mother also wrote. If the two didn't have opposing ideas, I would not have been called." Perveen had climbed about twenty steps, and there were two more flights ahead. Looking sideways at the prince, she added, "I heard from Mr. Sandringham that he receives letters from a palace officer. Do you know whether the choti-rani speaks with him?"

"She does every day. Didn't he tell you?"

Perveen was perplexed. "I haven't met anyone with that title."

"The children's tutor, Basu, also serves as palace officer. He has worked inside the palace for over forty years. He knows what to tell the servants and how to settle disputes among the constituents."

Perveen felt breathless, both from the climb and from the news that such responsibility was in the hands of the fatigued old man. "Has Mr. Basu been teaching and managing palace affairs all that time?"

"Only since the former palace officer, Jaqinder Dhillon, decided he'd like to work for me."

"Why did Mr. Dhillon leave his important post for your place?" Perveen noted that his expression had seemed to become less confident.

"Why should I tell you any of my business?" he fired back. "You were saying your concern is about my nephew's safety."

Having a trusted palace official gone would have destabilized the situation there. And it had obviously slowed down the administration of the state. But should she throw fire on fire? No, it would not bring about anything helpful.

They had come to the guest wing, and she saw the door to her room was open. She didn't want him to follow her in. Trying to sound reasonable, she said, "We don't know what does or does not matter until we have all the facts."

"From the health of monkeys to the names of the lowliest servants!" He shook his head and looked down with a most patronizing smile. "You ask about the most unusual things. What an investigation this will be."

Not responding to the insult, Perveen stood with her back toward the open door, both blocking entry to the prince and signifying the end of their walk. "Thank you and goodbye."

Prince Swaroop gave her a surprised look, as if nobody had ever told him that he was dismissed. But he whirled around on his heels and strode away, his slippers pounding the floor in a way that made her insides jump.

Chitra was standing at the open almirah when Perveen entered. The maid turned around and looked calmly at Perveen. "You are back for a rest, memsahib?"

When she had arrived at the palace filthy and wet, Perveen had appreciated Chitra's kindness; but now she worried about what the maid had been up to. "What are you doing with my things?"

"I was only putting in the clothing that the dhobi finished ironing. Your clothes from yesterday."

As Chitra held out the freshly laundered white lace blouse that had been a sodden mess the day before, Perveen relaxed slightly. "The laundry was done quickly—yet it was still raining when I went to sleep last night."

"Yes, but we have a warm room where clothes hang to dry." Sounding proud, she added, "The dhobi's iron is burning hot!"

Perveen went to the almirah to look at the perfect rectangle of unwrinkled silk. She had been worried that Gulnaz's sari was ruined, but it was more lustrous and smooth than when her sister-in-law had given it to her.

Chitra spoke quickly, as if she feared Perveen was angry. "Your blouse and underthings and nightclothes from last night have also been washed. Would you like me to send off the gara sari? It is not at all soiled, but I could have it lightly pressed."

Perveen could hardly think of clothes at that moment. Tightly, she said, "No, too much washing and the color fades. Tell the dhobi that this laundry service for my clothes worn in the rain was appreciated. I'll give you some baksheesh to give to him."

Smoothing the top of the folded gara sari with her hand, Chitra offered a small smile. "Memsahib, I have good news for you. Some men have arrived with your palanquin."

Perveen closed her eyes, making a silent prayer of thanks. She was not one for regular formal prayers, but at the moment, the arrival of the necessary transport seemed providential. "That is wonderful to hear. But is the palanquin mended?"

Chitra nodded. "They have left it near the gatehouse. The men will wait as long as needed, and then they will take you home."

Perveen pictured the long rainy night in the forest they must have endured. "The poor fellows must be starved. And so tired!"

The servant looked at her curiously, and Perveen recalled Aditya's surprised comment about her concerns. Probably it was rare for someone to comment on servants' hardships. "They were tired, yes, and they have already been given food to eat."

Perveen suddenly was panicked. "From which kitchen?"

Looking puzzled, Chitra said, "We servants have our own kitchen. It is a hut near the old palace. We are a different caste from the royalty. Actually, we are many different castes. But we must take different food and use different plates."

"Are leftovers given from either of the main kitchens?"

"Never. That food is too fine for us. It is taken to the temple near the palace for devotees." Chitra gently closed the door to the almirah and locked it. Then she put the key in Perveen's hands. The gesture seemed to be one of reassurance, and that gave Perveen the encouragement she needed to press on.

As Perveen took the key with a nod, she said, "I have another question. I know the maharaja had a stomach illness last week.

Today, I saw him running very close to the edge of the palace's roof. Has he had any accidents or other illnesses?"

Chitra ran her tongue over her lips as if they'd suddenly gone dry. "I don't know."

"You see him every day, don't you? What do you recall?"

"Children fall down. They get sick. I cannot keep track of it." She hung her head. "I'm sorry."

"Never mind." Perveen could not decide if Chitra was stalling her or speaking honestly. She would not force her view on the girl, who clearly had been trained to please.

Looking shyly at Perveen, Chitra said, "Memsahib, the bearers are asking how long you will stay here."

This was a tricky question to answer. Perveen wanted the men to be prepared to go quickly, but she didn't want to miss out on learning a little bit more about whether poisoning might have occurred. "If they are feeling well, I'd like to leave sometime this afternoon."

Chitra's face was anxious. "So soon?"

It surprised her that Chitra seemed to wish she'd stay longer. "I've finished my observations of the maharaja, but I need to have a conversation with the maharanis."

The lines around Chitra's mouth relaxed. "I am glad. Rajmata has asked you to join her at two o'clock. After that, there will be a special meal because of Prince Swaroop's visit! You will taste the finest mutton curry and masala fish from our river. These are his favorite dishes."

Now Perveen understood Chitra's desire for her to stay—it was so the royals wouldn't be angry with her. Yet the lunch presented too great a danger. "I will gladly visit the rajmata at two, but I must regret missing the lunch in order to reach the circuit house before dark."

"Yes, memsahib."

"Chitra, you are an expert lady's maid. How long have you served at the palace?"

"All my life! My mother is also a princess maid, because she waits on the rajmata. The women in our family line are born for this work."

Perveen noted the pride with which Chitra had spoken the title "princess maid." "Is your father in service to male royalty?"

"He is a bearer at the royal hunting lodge. We don't see him very often." Her voice was low and held a hint of sadness.

"That is a shame you can't see him. How long has your mother been working in the palace?" Perveen asked.

"She began doing small jobs for other princesses who aren't here anymore when she was six. When one of those princesses left, she was given the position of service to the rajmata."

Perveen realized the princess who left might have been Vandana. In any case, Chitra's mother was a longtime observer. Perveen would have liked to speak with her—but if the mother's loyalty to the rajmata was strong, it was unlikely such talk would be confidential.

Chitra was looking at Perveen as if expecting more questions. Perveen ventured, "So Basu-sahib was here as a tutor to three generations. "

Chitra started to polish the brass base of the oil lamp on the table. "Yes. Rajmata likes him very much."

Watching her, Perveen said, "I heard that Basu-sahib also has the position of palace officer because the man who had that role—Jaqinder Dhillon?—left to work for Prince Swaroop."

"Yes. Sardarji ran away." There was contempt in Chitra's voice.

"Ran away?" Perveen mirrored the maid's emotion. "Why?"

Chitra rubbed at the lamp with vigor. Without looking up, she said, "I'm sure Prince Swaroop invited Sardar Dhillon to go to his place. Prince Swaroop always favored the palace officer. He gave him much baksheesh whenever he visited."

"So maybe he thought he'd earn more money there?" That was quite a normal reason for a person to change jobs.

Chitra shrugged. "I think he wished to leave. This place suffers from a curse. Our maharaja had lost his life to cholera, and a year later his son was killed during the hunting. This palace became a very sad place."

"Would you go away, if you were given a chance?"

Chitra's eyes widened. "Are you saying you would take me to Bombay?"

Perveen realized she sounded like she wished to poach the maid from the palace. "No. My words were clumsy. I was just wondering if you've thought of going elsewhere, either to work or to get married."

Chitra stopped polishing altogether. She gave Perveen a look that was almost angry. "Outside of this palace, there are a thousand girls who dream of taking my place—and perhaps one hundred of them have some blood connection that could allow it. But if I leave the palace, what becomes of me? My father has no money for a dowry. I would be nothing."

Maybe she had wanted to go to Bombay. Perveen felt heavy with regret for Chitra and all the longtime servants at the palace. She told Chitra she wished to rest but to return shortly before her meeting with the dowager.

The maid insisted on drawing closed all the long silk draperies—a formidable task since the room had sixteen windows. Once alone, Perveen opened the curtains closest to the desk and sat down with the legal notebook she'd been carrying all morning.

Slowly, she turned the ruled pages. The observations she'd noted the previous evening were penciled in a careless manner. She'd been weary, and it had been tricky to work by candlelight. Today she'd taken her notes in the presence of the children and Mr. Basu and Prince Swaroop. These were easy to read. The trouble was what importance to assign the opinions of the people to whom she'd spoken, because while some of their points seemed valid, others were very questionable.

She needed to write with the goal of bringing the women to

agreement. But how could she do that when their minds were as separated as the two palaces? Also, she would have to face them without showing her suspicion that one of them might have tried for her poisoning.

Her favorite Parker pen was set up in its holder on the desk's blotter, and nearby rested a small folio with palace stationery bearing the Satapur coat of arms. Soberly, she dated a piece of the stationery and wrote two paragraphs. The first was her recommendation regarding the maharaja's education and her rationale for that recommendation. She signed the statement and copied it on a second piece of paper in Marathi. Then she wrote a third statement in English, with some added paragraphs about what had happened after breakfast, and the fears about Pratap Rao's death that Mirabai had privately expressed. This letter would be for Colin's eyes only.

Each letter went into an envelope. There was a small container of stamps, all featuring the likeness of Maharaja Mahendra Rao. Wondering when stamps would be reissued featuring the new maharaja, she pasted one on the envelope addressed to Colin Sandringham.

A knock on the door startled her. She called out, "Who is there?"

"It is Chitra again! Sorry to disturb your rest, but the time is ten minutes before two."

Perveen opened the door and thanked the maid for the notice.

Bustling in, Chitra looked at the bed, which showed no signs of untucked covers. "You did not rest."

"I remembered some writing that I had to do."

Chitra eyed the envelopes Perveen was holding and the Parker pen in its holder "I wish I could write. Then I could send a letter to my father at the lodge. The postmen drive everywhere bringing letters when the weather is good."

"I also wish you could do that. Will you please close the door?"

As Chitra did so, Perveen sat down on one of the lounge chairs where she'd been with Mirabai the night before.

"You're not in trouble," Perveen reassured her when Chitra returned to stand before her with a bowed head. "I only want to ask you about some palace history."

Chitra mumbled, "Even if I could read, I would not be allowed to touch the history books in Basu-sahib's rooms."

"Earlier, you mentioned a curse. I would like to know more about it."

"Yes." Chitra looked anxiously toward the closed door to the hall. "But it is a long story, and your presence is requested by the rajmata in just a few minutes."

Perveen looked at her watch. "This won't take long, and I need assistance with my hair since I didn't have your help earlier this morning. Not long curls like yesterday—just a simple topknot."

Chitra's face colored. "I am sorry I wasn't here this morning. I will do my best."

Perveen settled herself at the ebony dressing table fitted out with a mirror that stretched six feet upward.

"I might make some mistakes in the story. I know what my mother has told me." Chitra began to pull out the pins from Perveen's hair. "It all began with the late maharaja."

"Maharaja Mahendra Rao?" Perveen asked.

In the mirror, she saw Chitra shake her head. "No. It was during the time of his father, Maharaja Mohan Rao, who was married to the rajmata. In the old days, life here between family and servants was more free."

Perveen thought Chitra's word choice was odd. "How was it free?"

"There was more enjoyment." The maid picked up Perveen's silver-handled travel hairbrush and began brushing out her hair. "Mother says there were more than two hundred servants; we were a town within the palace! Three buffoons made jokes, and there were twenty musicians and dancers. The rajmata and her husband arranged many parties, and nobles came to visit."

"It sounds very exciting," Perveen commented. This was the palace Gulnaz had expected for Perveen.

"Yes. But the trouble was that one of those palace dancers fell in love with the late Maharaja Mahendra Rao when he was a young man—before he became a ruler."

Perveen felt her pulse race. Yazad had hinted that Vandana was supposed to marry Maharaja Mahendra Rao. "What was this dancer's name?"

"My mother says not to speak her name because it brings bad luck." She brushed Perveen's hair more slowly. "The maharaja was just at the age of getting married. So it was wrong for him to be attached to the dancer. Especially wrong for her to be carrying his child."

"But maharajas often have courtesans, and sometimes extra wives."

"Such behavior looks bad to the family of a bride, if a maharaja is not yet married. And this dancer was not a young girl. She had done this kind of thing before with maharajas and other guests. She wanted to trap him."

Perveen considered things. Could the dancer be Vandana? If so, she was far from the noblewoman Yazad believed her to be.

"My mother said that the late maharaja also loved this dancer. But she could not stay in the palace. There was risk to the line of succession because he did not have a proper wife and heir yet."

"Mirabai was chosen for him by the Agency," Perveen remembered aloud.

"Yes, yes." Chitra nodded. "And his parents knew that they must not complicate that match."

"So—how is a curse involved?" Perveen's thoughts returned to what Roderick had said about the maharajas dying too young.

"The dancer was in the palace one day smiling and busy. But then she was gone."

"Does your mother think the dancer was killed?"

"Maybe. Why would she willingly leave, when she loved the

maharaja?" After a pause, Chitra added, "Haunting and curses come when there's an unjust death."

If the dancer had died, Perveen's burgeoning theory about Vandana was useless. "Did anyone see the woman being harmed or hear stories about that?"

Chitra put down the hairbrush and looked into the mirror, her eyes serious. "I cannot give facts, because from what I've heard, the dancer was not human. She is a spirit, the daughter of the mountain goddess, Aranyani. The dancer had power to place nazar on the palace's maharajas."

"Nazar" was an Arabic-origin word, but Perveen wanted to know Chitra's interpretation. "Do you mean the evil eye?"

Chitra took Perveen's hair in her hands. "Yes. Your people know about it?"

Perveen nodded. She did not want to get into the fact that she didn't believe in it, because she didn't want to stop the story. "Please tell me more about the goddess."

"Aranyani is a powerful protector of animals. People say she can also touch the sun, so the crops grow well after the rains." Chitra's voice was as strong as her hands twisting Perveen's hair. "When Goddess Aranyani is happy, the maharaja can give the British their nuts and grains and still have enough left for the villagers."

"All right, then." Perveen tried to pull the story together in her own mind. "The dancer disappeared, maybe going home to her mother, the goddess Aranyani?"

Chitra paused to gather up an errant strand of Perveen's hair. "My mother says that Aranyani wouldn't take her daughter back, nor could she return to the palace. Therefore, the daughter haunts the forest around it. She can follow the royals to the edge of the forest, where she told a leopard to kill Prince Pratap Rao. And before that time, she was responsible for killing his father, who had not fought for her to stay."

As Perveen's topknot grew larger, so did her questions. But she had to be careful not to sound disbelieving. "I was told the maharaja Mahendra Rao died from an illness he caught in a village."

In the mirror, Chitra's face was serious. "Cholera is a sickness carried in water. And these goddesses have power over water."

"Do you think that Prince Jiva Rao's life could be saved if he leaves this area for a little bit?"

Chitra shook her head. "Not if his fate is written."

Perveen had written the legal opinion on Jiva Rao's educational plan. Since that matter was finished, she could not help being curious about the dancer—whether she was a young Vandana, and, if not, what the wealthy woman's exact connection was with the royal family. She would privately ask Vandana a few more questions before returning to the circuit house.

A knock at the door made Perveen jump.

"Oh! It must be Aditya-yerda," Chitra said. "He told me he will come to bring you to Rajmata for the meeting."

"Just a minute!" Perveen called out. Then she picked up one of the three envelopes. Should she give it to Aditya or Chitra to post for her? She wanted the letter to be sent without being read first. She wasn't sure of Aditya's reading ability, but Chitra was illiterate, which would ensure more privacy. "Chitra, I have a special request."

"Yes?" The girl's eyes were on the envelope.

"The next time the postman comes, give him this letter. It is most important."

She nodded. "I will do that."

"Please do it quietly, without telling anyone. I don't want any delay." She reached into the cloth purse she wore on a ribbon under her clothes and gave the girl two annas. "I am thankful to you for the good care during this stay."

A letter in the post was her secret insurance policy for informing Colin about what she thought should be done about the maharaja.

In case she didn't make it back.

17

AUDIENCE WITH TWO QUEENS

"Will you go in?" Aditya asked.

The two of them were standing just outside the zenana durbar hall.

"Certainly," Perveen said, but she heard the waver in her voice. Right then, she imagined the maharanis felt expectant. They would be tense, but not angry. That could easily change.

Softly, he said, "I was afraid when I came here at age eleven. But there were so many servants to comfort me and teach me what I needed. They told me, 'Act as if you belong, and you will belong.'"

"That is good advice!" Perveen gave the buffoon a slight wave as she stepped inside. He stayed outside the room, as if he knew that for this event, such was his place.

The durbar hall was as dim by day as it had been the previous evening when Perveen had stepped nervously inside for dinner. The grand room's long windows were covered by geometric-patterned marble jalis that let in just enough light to reveal that the long dining table had been moved to one side of the room. The dowager maharani was seated at the room's center on an ornate gilded ebony throne, with Mirabai ten feet off to the side, half-hidden behind a column. Perveen craned her neck to see that the junior maharani was rigidly perched on an ordinary upholstered chair, although a relaxed Ganesan sprawled on a small rug at her side. The room was vast, and Perveen could imagine that assemblies there could hold more than one hundred.

Near the entrance to the room, four women sat cross-legged

on large floor cushions. They wore jewel-toned silk saris with
wide borders shot through with gold. They could not be servants;
perhaps they were ladies-in-waiting to the rajmata. The rajmata
hadn't invited them to dinner the previous evening, but it was
very likely that they were there now because they were meant to
serve as witnesses.

The big white dog raised his head and looked appraisingly at
Perveen as she approached. She felt a similarly powerful gaze on
her back from the ladies-in-waiting as she stepped forward to
address the queens. Perhaps they were scrutinizing the foreign
manner in which she'd draped her sari.

Remembering how awkward it had felt to curtsy the day
before, Perveen resolved to do better. When she was about fifteen
feet from the rajmata, Perveen stopped and rested her briefcase
on the floor. She folded her hands together and placed them at
her chest and then raised them to her forehead, in a respectful
namaste.

Mirabai was looking affectionately at Ganesan, but the dowager maharani watched Perveen, all the while holding a golden
scepter studded with rubies and moonstones in a death grip.

Perveen wondered if she should have bowed her head. She did
so, realizing that her feelings of awe at being before royalty had
changed to something else: pity. She now saw the royal women
as the survivors in a very wealthy, lonely family. They were a
mother-in-law and a daughter-in-law locked into an unhappy
union they hadn't chosen, and the only way the rajmata could
affirm power over the choti-rani was through the manipulation
of Prince Jiva Rao.

"What is that you have carried in?" the dowager maharani
Putlabai asked curtly.

"My legal briefcase. I brought it in case I need to refer to
information within." The truth was, she hadn't felt safe coming
without it. She didn't want the briefcase to be an obstacle to her
departure if she had to leave hurriedly.

"A case made from what?" the dowager responded.

Perveen glanced at Mirabai, silently asking for guidance, and saw an expression of dread. Then Perveen understood. She should not have carried anything made from the hide of the animal sacred to Hindus. Only the buffoon had seen the leather briefcase when she entered, and he had let her pass. In a quiet voice, she admitted, "It is bridle leather from England."

"In our state, the only leather allowed is that from water buffalo or goats."

"Sorry, I did not think. Inside there is a paper I want to give you—"As she fumbled with the latch, all the papers fell to the mosaic floor. The ladies behind her giggled as she scooped up the papers, separating out the one she intended to read.

After the case was closed again, the dowager said, "Someone must take that foul thing out."

Behind Perveen, the women began arguing—nobody wanted to take it. Perveen's anxiety surged as she thought about the many confidential government papers inside. If only she had left the case in her room and just carried the recommendation in an envelope. But it was too late for regrets.

Aditya eventually stepped through the door. After conferring with the ladies-in-waiting, he carried out the briefcase. Perveen thought of how she was going to have to confess to Colin she'd put the government's documents at risk. But how much English could the buffoon read—and would he look through her things in public?

"Now we can begin." The maharani pointed a long finger toward the women waiting behind Perveen. "Bring her cushion!"

A lady rose to her feet and came forward carrying a flat cushion covered in blue velvet, gold braid around its edge. She laid it near the room's center, facing the throne, heightening the sense that Perveen's position was that of a supplicant.

"That is too far away." The dowager maharani frowned at the lady. "Let her come close enough for my tired eyes to see."

"Thank you," Perveen said as the girl placed the pillow just five feet before Putlabai. Despite Putlabai's complaint, her eyes had been strong enough to focus on Perveen's leather briefcase. The lady's eyes were sharp as an owl's—very different from those of Mr. Basu.

Perveen remembered how easily Colin had sat cross-legged on the ground during his yoga practice. This was the dowager's position, but Perveen hadn't the same flexibility, so she settled on the cushion with her knees together and her feet tucked under one hip.

She turned her attention from Maharani Putlabai to Mirabai. Why was the younger queen on a chair and not a cushion? Perhaps it was a statement of her middling position—that she was not high enough for the zenana throne, but she was respected enough not to be somewhat elevated.

The dowager went into a coughing spasm. Perveen wondered about her health, but she stayed quiet.

"I called you here to tell me what you think about our family." The dowager's voice was scratchy and hard to understand. "But I wonder how much you could learn. I hear you took ill at the sight of a dead animal and had to rest."

Perveen imagined the buffoon was likely still near the doorway, hearing his pet referred to in such a cold way. She took care with her words. "Yes, it was a shock to me. What sadness for Aditya to lose his dear little friend."

"He wishes to perform rites for the creature tonight. Since you are emotional, you may attend the ceremony."

Perveen had no intention of being around through the evening, but she'd share that information later. "Is a religious cremation customary for animals?"

Caressing the jeweled scepter, the dowager shook her head. "It is not. However, that monkey was like a younger brother to Buffoon. Two playful little fools!"

Mirabai spoke up from behind the column. "I cannot bear to

think of Ganesan dying, but he risks his life every day. He should have the same honor when his life ends."

"You took the dog with you this morning on your ride!" Putlabai chided. "You are always taking him. Do you not care about the protection of your son?"

"While our lawyer guest is here, he's fine." Mirabai stretched down an arm to stroke her dog's white head.

Perveen's heart sank. Did Mirabai want her to stay? She decided she'd better make her intentions clear. "Rajmata and Choti-Rani, I've prepared my recommendation. It is here in my hands."

"At last. You have been wasting our time. Speak!" the dowager commanded.

Remembering how she'd planned to compliment both of them, Perveen ran her tongue over lips that had gone dry. She wasn't in the right frame of mind for it. "Rajmata, I would like to first compliment you on the care you've taken with both your grandchildren. Your knowledge of the proper traditions for monarchs has been passed to them. I have seen how Princess Padmabai loves books, and your grandson knows so much about Satapur's history."

"Yes, it's true." The dowager maharani shifted on her throne, looking more at ease.

Perveen's gaze turned toward Mirabai. "And I understand that as the mother of the future ruler, you have allowed him to enjoy being a boy. Flying kites and enjoying animal life are natural at his age. And your hope for expanding his circle of friends is sound."

Mirabai nodded very slightly, but she did not smile. She must have understood the decision wouldn't be straightforward. Ganesan seemed to have picked up her mood and uttered a low growl at Perveen as she held up the paper.

"I have written my recommendation in both Marathi and English to serve as a permanent record for you to keep in the palace." Perveen bent her head to read the words she had written in very formal language less than an hour before. "The document reads as follows: 'I, Perveen Mistry, a partner at Mistry

Law, Bombay, working on behalf of the Kolhapur Agency, gratefully accepted access to the Satapur palace from October tenth to eleventh, 1921. During this time, I sought interviews with many residents of the palace, including Maharani Putlabai, Maharani Mirabai, and the maharaja's tutor, Mr. Arvind Basu. His Highness Prince Swaroop is not a household resident, but, as uncle to the prince and as prime minister, had an opinion.'"

"My brother-in-law's opinion has no bearing on this! He would only take her side," sputtered Mirabai.

Perveen raised her voice and continued reading. "'Most important, I spoke with and observed the maharaja Jiva Rao. I found him to be a healthy, intelligent young man of ten years. He excels in verbal communication and confidently asserts his will.'"

This was a delicate way to get around the fact that he did not have polite social manners. Perveen continued, "'The maharaja knows Marathi history well and has a special interest in animals and the outside world. However, he is unwilling to participate in a daily lesson plan, and his tutor has given up on pressing for such a study schedule including more than very basic subjects. To fulfill the maharaja's potential, I recommend that his education expand to include modern biology and science, mathematics, writing, and literature. If he achieves fluency in English, that will put him in the top tier of Indian rulers.'"

"What are you saying about changing his lesson plan?" the dowager maharani interrupted, sounding irritated.

"Just give her a minute!" Mirabai snapped.

Putlabai's sharp eyes narrowed as she turned to look toward her daughter-in-law. "You! Disrespectful!"

Perveen was stunned when Putlabai took the jeweled scepter and threw it with a shaky arm toward the column. The heavy scepter landed with a crash inches from Mirabai. The younger maharani screamed in shock, and Ganesan sprang from his place and rushed the short distance to stand in front of the dowager. He bared his teeth and growled.

Now the dowager screamed and put her hands over her face. Her fleshy arms shook.

"You deserve it!" Mirabai muttered. "Ganesan knows your true nature. You throw this symbol of our land and family like it's a stick that means nothing. It means everything—and so does my son."

Ganesan was continuing to menace the dowager, barking and showing his teeth. The ladies seated on the cushions shrieked, and one small woman ran forward, gasping and half-crying as she retrieved the scepter from the floor. Several moonstones had fallen off and remained on the mosaic tiles.

"Please call him off!" Perveen begged Mirabai. The rapprochement Perveen had hoped to bring about had gone terribly awry.

Mirabai gave Perveen a resentful look, then clucked her tongue. "Ganesan. Stand down!"

As quickly as he'd taken off, the dog trotted back to her. Perveen was impressed; he appeared to be a very well-trained guard dog with the ability to scare off attackers. The lady-in-waiting returned the damaged scepter to the rajmata, who clutched it and looked venomously at Mirabai. It was as if she were a small child who had forgotten she'd started the fight.

"Good, Ganesan!" Mirabai said, smiling as she patted his back.

Perveen calmed herself, and then continued. "'An excellent education for the maharaja can be obtained at a number of fine schools throughout the world. However, it is too late in the academic year for the maharaja to be granted a place at a suitable school in Britain. The best possibility is for him to enroll at one of India's many fine boarding schools. By studying inside India, he will gain a richer knowledge of biology and history that is specifically useful to governing—'"

"Studying in India!" Mirabai cried out in English. "How could you go against me? Over my dead body will I allow it."

"What is she telling you? What secrets are you keeping?" the dowager complained in Marathi. A wailing came up from the ladies-in-waiting. Perveen couldn't guess which maharani's side they favored, but she understood that nobody liked her recommendation.

Striving to ignore these outbursts, Perveen soldiered on. "'If he lives at boarding school, the maharaja will become acquainted with other nobles and young men destined for important roles in Indian politics and business. He will have true friends he can turn to when he is making decisions about moving Satapur forward. He shall also benefit from schooling side by side with some British students and having British teachers. He will learn the English language to the point of fluency.'"

"His English is the first point, not something that should be mentioned at the end." Mirabai's voice shook with emotion. "How can he study here and speak like an Englishman? And you went abroad for your education. Why do you recommend him staying in India?"

The dowager maharani cut into the conversation. "India is best, but he should not study away from home. Basu teaches him everything that is necessary."

"I noted in my report that Basu-sahib can't make the maharaja sit down and study," Perveen said, afraid the conversation was going to be an endless circle of the queens' restated desires. "And Basu-sahib doesn't really have time for tutoring when he's also performing the duties of a palace officer."

The dowager muttered, "Perhaps a new teacher could be brought—"

"No!" Mirabai protested. "She said he needs to meet others who will become his friends and assist his interests later on."

At least Mirabai approved of some part of Perveen's plan.

"What good is that if he leaves Satapur and dies? You saw what happened to your beloved husband and your older son when they left these walls," Maharani Putlabai said darkly.

"We can pray for the maharaja's safety, but we can never know what might happen. He could die within these walls, too." Perveen paused, because she was going to ask for something that wasn't in the original Agency plan. But she was the guardian; she had to do it. "Because of this, I would respectfully like to ask permission to take him with me to the circuit house until the school admission is arranged."

Mirabai exhaled. "I want him to travel away from here properly. Not with you in a dirty palanquin. He must go in a royal procession. Otherwise the people will be worried."

"What are you saying? I tell you, he is safe here!" thundered the rajmata. "You have no reason to steal him."

Perveen needed to speak the truth if the rajmata was to understand. Taking a deep breath, she said, "There may have been poison in a dish prepared expressly for me this morning. I did not eat it, but I believe that Bandar could have gotten into it. And that is why he is gone."

Putlabai glared at her. "If you believe this, why didn't you tell my son? His Highness only said you were weak and worried."

There was a murmur and rustling in the back; the noblewomen were discussing this. Perveen felt anxious, knowing that the buffoon was outside the door. Would he guess that she'd allowed Bandar to eat the food?

"Who do you think poisoned your food?" Mirabai demanded.

Perveen spoke evenly. "We cannot know for certain whether it was tampered with. But I suspect such an act might have been undertaken by a person who didn't want me to write the educational recommendation."

The maharani looked intently at her, and when she spoke, her voice was soft. "So someone wished to kill you. Yes, it sounds like a matter of poison."

Perveen did not feel reassured by the choti-rani's sympathy. She might be trying to manipulate the situation, to steer Perveen toward declaring her mother-in-law the culprit.

Trying not to look distrusting, Perveen pulled up the sides of her mouth into a half smile. "Now, I have listened to both of Your Highnesses. I understand from you that my recommendation is not what either of you had envisioned; however, I hope that you take some time to reconsider it. An important aspect of this plan is that the maharaja can grow up with continued love and guidance from both of you and return home on holidays. And there are good boarding schools with British faculty in Panchgani, which is relatively close. Have you heard of St. Peter's School?"

"But the only English who go to boarding schools in India are the children of shopkeepers and missionaries," Mirabai hissed. "He is not part of that class."

Perveen had been starting to build a respect for the younger maharani, but she had no patience for Mirabai's prejudice. "The British have built several small boarding schools expressly for Indian princes, but they have not been well regarded. I believe that if the school we choose has the right kind of environment, the prince will feel comfortable. And having boys around him on playing fields and in classes will make him more excited to study."

"Your plan pleases nobody." The dowager maharani shifted in her seat and began coughing again.

"You speak of asking many people—but why didn't you ask my son?" Mirabai demanded.

"Yes. He will surely wish to stay!" Putlabai snapped.

"We did speak together. He told me he doesn't want to go away," Perveen said. "But he has not been anywhere except his uncle's home, and that was years ago. I have confidence he will be very excited by the company and activities at a well-run school inside India."

"If he comes back for holidays here, he could die. Either along the way or inside these palace walls." Mirabai looked imploringly at her. "Please send him to England."

Perveen felt a heaviness in her heart as she realized that not a single person in the palace would be supportive of her recommendation. "I am so sorry. I have been ordered to make the decision that I believe is best for the prince's emotional and mental well-being. And the first school he attends is just the start of his formal education. He might go to England later."

"Never!" thundered Maharani Putlabai.

Perveen had one last card in her deck. "Please think about this for a few days. If you still disagree, you can write to the Kolhapur Agency. A legal hearing will occur where you can plead your case."

"Plead?" the dowager maharani repeated incredulously. "Did you forget to whom you're speaking? A queen does not plead for anything."

"'Plead' is not a term of disrespect, but a legal term. It means to argue for yourself. Often, people who do so employ a lawyer."

"And I don't suppose you can recommend one?" Mirabai huffed.

"You can ask Mr. Basu or Prince Swaroop for advice. It would be a conflict of interest for me to give you a name. But I must inform you that I am the only lady lawyer working within a thousand miles. It will have to be a man."

Mirabai put her hands to her head as if it hurt. "You know that we don't speak to men except for a few who work in this household or are our relatives. You were sent here to help us because you were female, and you did not!"

Perveen's heart was pounding hard as she realized she'd have to refuse them in a world where nobody ever did. "It pains me that I could not find a solution that pleased both of you. But my task is to consider the prince's need to grow into a wise and compassionate young man."

"Give me the papers you read from," Mirabai commanded. "Both of them, English and Marathi."

Perveen went forward and handed them to her. Ganesan raised his long nose to sniff at the papers, as if he found them suspicious.

"It is all lies!" Putlabai said, looking at her daughter-in-law, who was intently reading.

Mirabai raised her head and regarded the rajmata. Perveen remembered an expression she'd read in a cheap English novel. *If looks could kill.* That was the manner in which the younger queen was regarding her elder.

Perveen tried to still her inner discord without success. Shakily, she said, "I understand your feelings and will tell the government it may expect a rebuttal from you in writing."

"Enough of this useless chatter! I let you in because I trusted you," said Putlabai. "You disgust me with your behavior. Go!"

Perveen felt chastised, but she knew things would have been much worse if the dowager had denied her exit. It felt unsettling to be leaving Prince Jiva Rao behind. She'd proven a very poor guardian, indeed.

As she walked out, she heard a whimpering sound. It was the dog, Ganesan.

Was he upset with her, too?

18

WESTWARD HO!

The circuit house lay to the west, which made Perveen's departure a race against the sunset. Would the men walk fast enough to reach the destination before they were trapped in darkness? She remembered how many unexpected bluffs there had been along the route, and she prayed the palanquin would not break again. Its failure on two previous trips was not a good omen.

Before she'd climbed into the litter, she'd said her goodbyes to Aditya, who had handed her back the briefcase Maharani Putlabai had ordered him to take out of the zenana. Looking sadly at Perveen, he'd said, "Thank you for caring about Bandar. And it's too bad they did not listen to your ideas."

Perveen was grateful for his kindness. She told him, "Perhaps time will allow them to think more."

The buffoon's shoulders had sagged, and his face had looked ravaged. He'd appeared entirely different from the sly, joking man of the previous day. In a low voice, he'd said, "I heard you say you think Bandar was poisoned."

"It is a possibility. I've no idea who the poisoner could be," she'd hastily added, remembering the knife he carried. She did not want him trying to administer justice.

"Go soon, before the maharanis tell the guards not to allow it," he had said in a low voice.

So she'd gone straight out—without looking for the children to say goodbye and pushing down her feelings of unease.

It had been a relief that her luggage was already loaded

inside the palanquin. But before she climbed inside, she'd asked Lakshman to show her the repairs. Both carrying poles had been changed to heavy pieces of blackwood.

"It's heavier than bamboo, so it shall not break. But it takes more effort to carry." His mouth had pulled down in a weary frown.

Those words seemed to hint at trouble. "I do hope you had enough rest," Perveen said.

"We who walked with you were taken care of these last days. But the men who came this morning had little rest and meager food."

Chitra had said the food had been from a kitchen just for servants. "What kind of food did they receive?"

"Some rotis and dal. Then someone else brought pohe—"

"No!" she cried aloud. Realizing there were palace guards nearby, she blushed.

"I told them not to eat it. It was not freshly made, and I wished the men not to fall ill before walking again."

Thank God. All she could do was smile at him, grateful for his shrewd thinking. But why someone would poison these men— who were no risk to anyone—was beyond her.

Except for the fact that if they fell ill, she would not make it back to the circuit house.

She climbed into the litter and pulled the curtains closed so she would not be seen by the dowager, who was surely at the window with binoculars. In her mind, Perveen apologized to Mirabai. And then, without realizing she was doing it, she reached inside the waist of her sari and found her kusti. Perveen moved her fingers along the sacred cord and began a private prayer for both the prince and princess.

The men lowered the palanquin just a half hour into the journey. She could hear them grumbling, and she felt a rush of irritation. Weren't they concerned about the timeliness of the journey the way she was? Or had they lowered the palanquin because it was close to breaking again?

Lakshman came around to the window to speak to her. "The men are too hungry. They must eat."

Hungry men would not be strong, and she herself felt famished. "I understand. Where's the nearest village?"

"No village," he said, his hands moving to fix the pleats in his lungi. "But just ahead is the old hunting lodge. It is where the royals used to hunt, before the tragedies. That is where we got the wood to fix the palanquin. The people did this work and must be paid."

So this was the real reason for the stop. But it raised another question in Perveen's mind. "Why didn't we pass this hunting lodge when we traveled to the palace?"

"We came near it. Remember, you noticed the hunting tower. The way toward it often floods." He made a diagonal gesture with his hands, indicating a slope. "That is why we go on the longer path to avoid it during rainy season."

"Very well." An idea was forming in her mind. "I don't mind stopping there."

The men shifted their duties, the ones who'd been carrying her giving their spots to the ones who'd flanked the palanquin. It seemed the palanquin was moving faster after the decision to go for food.

Thirty minutes later, they had arrived. The hunting lodge was an extraordinary place, a timbered building that reminded her of some grand homes she'd seen in the English countryside, yet with Indian detailing: arched windows and a heavy brass door. The stucco was peeling and showing signs of disrepair, and the grounds had been planted with vegetables that she guessed fed the lodge's staff, now that royalty no longer came to hunt. As the palanquin approached, a half-dozen children dressed in a strange assortment of rags and aged palace uniforms ran out of the lodge, followed more slowly by a few men.

The palanquin was set down more gently than in the past, and Perveen emerged, wrapping her cashmere shawl over her shoulders before taking the brass cup of chai offered to her. The tea was hot but not sweet enough. She almost asked for sugar but then realized they probably had none. This place was far from any village, and if these people lived at an abandoned lodge, there was no employer who could make it possible for them to buy such a luxury.

A sturdy man in rough peasant clothing was making millet rotis—millet, the grain that comprised part of the emblem of the royal household. She drank her tea and took the roti that was given to her first, a mark of respect. The bearers were served next and ate hungrily.

After finishing her roti, she inquired about paying for the palanquin's repair. An old man wearing a faded blue palace uniform quoted a price of six annas—much less than she'd expected.

"Blackwood is a very fine wood," Perveen said after giving him the coins. "If you have a grove of such trees, you could sell the lumber to carpenters."

"Blackwood doesn't grow here," the elderly man said, peering at her through eyes watery with cataracts. "It came from a broken carriage that was left behind a year ago."

"May I come inside the lodge?" Perveen asked.

The group of men frowned and began muttering to Lakshman. He stepped forward and spoke in a low voice. "Baburam says no. It is their own place now, not for looking."

"I won't report about what they've done with furniture and all that. It isn't my concern. I just want to see where Pratap Rao was brought—after the tragedy." She looked entreatingly at the aged Baburam, who hesitated and then nodded.

All the windows were open to fresh air, but their ornate iron grates were dappled with a mixture of spiderwebs, dust, and dead-insect debris. Long gray cobwebs hung from large old chandeliers and the tops of the ornate moldings running along the ceiling.

Except for a long mahogany table, most of the lodge's furniture was gone. The stucco walls had empty, pale spaces where pictures had been removed. However, a tall portrait of a previous viceroy of India, Lord Chemsford, remained. A black line zigzagged over his long nose and down to the bottom of the portrait.

Was this a sign of wear or a subtle piece of political commentary?

Perveen turned from the dour English portrait to Baburam. Quietly, she asked, "Were you present the day of that hunting trip when the prince was killed?"

Baburam nodded. "I have been here for fifty-two years. I was there then, as I am now. Keeping things safe."

Perveen reached into the purse she kept tied around her waist, just below her sari's pallu. She pulled out two annas and put them in his palm. "There must have been a lot of rushing around the night before with the search party. Do you recall that?"

Taking the coins and putting them in a pouch at his waist, he nodded. "We all searched. Prince Swaroop called for us to go out carrying torches. But we didn't find him that night. It was the next day."

"Who found him?"

"The prince. He carried the boy in with his own arms. He was weeping as if his son had died."

"And what else happened?"

"He told the engineer to ride off to fetch the foreign doctor. As if the foreign doctor could bring life to him!" He shook his head.

"The engineer?" Perveen repeated his words, feeling a shock course through her. "What was his name?"

"He did not say. He was a dark Anglo-Indian."

Perveen mulled over the fact that Roderick Ames was friendly with the Satapur royals and had never said a word about it at the circuit house dinner. Or maybe the situation was different; he could have been riding by and volunteered to help.

"Had you seen this engineer before with Prince Swaroop?"
Baburam shook his head.

"Who else was on the hunt?" Perveen asked.

"Prince Swaroop led it; also the buffoon was there, and six grooms and four beaters."

"Beaters?" Perveen repeated the unfamiliar word he had said in English.

"These men chase the wild animals out of hiding."

Perveen felt sorry for the animals, but she needed to keep her focus on the people. It sounded as if there had been many men who might have had a chance to kill the prince—and also to find him. "Why would Prince Swaroop ask the engineer to fetch the doctor?"

"I was not there, so I cannot say. But a British doctor is always required to declare cause of death for a maharaja," Baburam told her. "He did not come until the next day, delaying the religious rites for the prince. And that brought misfortune. It is why the family still grieves."

Dr. Andrews might have been involved in a surgery or treating patients and been unable to leave immediately. But this delay was probably a chief reason both maharanis disliked him. She suspected that the physician had warned her not to ask questions because he didn't want her to get an alternate view of his performance. What might he have missed? "I would be grateful to see the room where the maharaja was placed."

Baburam's expression became wary. "I should not."

That reaction made her all the more certain she needed to see it. She took a deep breath, and felt the kusti tight around her waist, reminding her of her duties. "Please. I need to know more about the prince's death. It's all for the sake of the family line."

"The maharaja was laid down in the old nursery room," Baburam muttered. "I do not wish anyone to see it, because it is not clean."

In her opinion, the whole lodge was not very clean. But he

probably meant something different. "Are you telling me the room has been left in the same condition as at the time of his death?"

He gave a small nod. "I have not gone in there. But nobody would touch his things. Bad luck."

An untouched room could tell her many things. "You do not have to go inside with me. I will take the risk upon myself."

Baburam closed his eyes, as if in prayer. When he opened them, his voice was barely a whisper. "May your god protect you."

The hunting lodge's upper floor was dominated by a long, wide corridor. Its wall was hung with animal skins and heads that made her turn away. So much for Aranyani's protective powers. Perveen asked Baburam if there was a zenana wing, and he shook his head.

"Not many women have come here," he said. "The choti-rani was the only one."

As she continued exploring the lodge, she decided the structure reminded her of a lodge she'd once visited during a house party with Alice in Cotswolds and she guessed that Maharaja Mohan Rao had been inspired to create a setting that would impress British visitors. Many of the doors were half open and revealed furniture draped in dusty, mildewed coverings. There was evidence of animal nests here and there and also of human habitation—not on the beds, but on mats on the floor. This was a sign the servants who'd stayed were observing propriety.

At the end of the hall was a door that was shorter than the others.

"The nursery you wished to see," Baburam said in a low voice.

Inside, there were two canopied beds and a cradle. Only one bed had linens; on it was a small pile of decaying textiles.

Perveen moved slowly toward the bed. "All these things are still here? Why?"

The bearer said, "The old clothes were defiled and would bring bad luck. There was no reason to take them. His body was taken to the palace for the rajmata to bathe."

"Not his mother, though," Perveen said, remembering Mirabai's sorrow.

"No. Prince Swaroop said she was too upset after the death of her honorable late husband the maharaja. She could not see the body." Baburam looked past her, his face very grave, as if he was remembering the hard day. "After his body was cleaned and dressed in new clothing, the rites were performed on the lake, and he went to his next life."

Perveen put out a hand to lift up one of the pieces of cloth, hoping this would not violate any rules. It was a pillowcase that still had a black hair clinging to its underside. The prince's hair. Feeling the eyes of the men on her, she folded the cloth and put it aside.

Next she lifted up a small pair of cotton drawers, mostly decayed, as well as a cotton vest. Cotton jodhpurs torn into long strips covered in a mix of dirt and smudges of blood. The sight of the browned bloodstains made her heart beat faster. A small green velvet pagri decorated with sapphires was intact—as if it had fallen from his head.

Perveen was impressed that as poor as the men staying in the lodge seemed to be, they had not sold the pagri. Her next thought was about what wasn't there.

"Where is the jacket or shirt the prince was wearing?"

He shook his head. "There was no jacket."

Another thought came to her. If a leopard had eaten the prince, wouldn't all the clothes in front of her be heavily stained in blood? She saw a few rusty smudges, but the chief damage to the jodhpurs, aside from the large tears, was small, sharp, incisive marks—almost as if a stiletto blade had sliced into the cloth.

Maybe the marks did not have a human origin. She recalled Mirabai's comment about seeing vultures in the sky the day before the prince's body was discovered. Were these punctures vulture pecks? If so, it meant that the prince was probably dead but not mauled when the birds came to him. He could not have been killed by a leopard, as Dr. Andrews had posited.

And why was the jacket gone?

Perhaps because an unmarked jacket would have given away the truth that there had not been a leopard or tiger attack.

"Please," she said, knowing she was likely going to be refused, "I need to take these clothes with me."

"But they are not yours," Baburam said. "And it is bad luck."

"The government must see them," she said. When he didn't respond, she said, "You have a picture downstairs of a very powerful Englishman."

He looked at her warily but did not answer.

"I don't wish the new viceroy, Lord Reading, to ever come here," she said emphatically. "I hope that my bringing these clothes out to his officers will keep them from coming here to look for them. I hope that it will keep all of you safe."

Baburam's look of resistance faded. He did not protest as she took off her fine shawl to carefully wrap around the garments.

By the time they set off again, the sun had dropped to less than half the height it had been. Lakshman was visibly annoyed by her detour upstairs with Baburam. It had taken about twenty minutes. They had at least an hour and a half's journey left and perhaps an hour of light.

"Do your best," Perveen said. She knew there were lamps on the front of the palanquin that could be lit. She hoped they would be enough to safely illuminate the path and drive off animals of prey. She kept the palanquin curtains open to be of assistance in looking for animal movements in the distance. But as she looked for glowing eyes in the darkness, she thought about the danger of people. Vandana and Yazad, who felt they were rich and entitled enough to act outside of societal boundaries. Roderick Ames, who seethed at being shut out of both Indian and British society. Prince Swaroop, who could not rule Satapur because of being born second. Even Aditya, who had produced a knife in a sudden moment of rage, seemed capable of being a danger.

The memory of the defaced portrait of the old viceroy also hung in her consciousness, just as it had hung on the wall inside the lodge. She wished she'd asked Baburam if he knew who'd marked it so boldly. She could only guess it had been a nobleman, because who else would take such liberties?

Darkness had begun to fall by the time they'd reached the village where Lakshman had brought her a couple days earlier. Small cooking fires outside the huts glowed like beacons, showing the way. As they proceeded from the hamlet into the forest, the light disappeared. She saw the outline of the wooden sign that she knew marked the proper path toward the circuit house. That landmark should have reassured her that the journey would come to a safe close, but it also reminded her of the awkwardness ahead. She had pledged to Colin that she wouldn't overnight at the circuit house. Now she understood that her fierce reaction was because she'd been afraid of herself. She'd longed for something both emotional and physical, as real as the curve of his strong back when he'd exercised, as real as the sweat shining on the skin of the men who carried her. She knew if she kept on seeing him, she would continue feeling like that—and it wasn't right.

She poked her head out of the palanquin and called to Lakshman, "Pleas' stop when you get to the Mehtas' bungalow."

He turned to look at her without slowing his rapid pace. "You told me to take you back to the circuit house."

This was true. "After you've dropped me at the Mehtas', you can go to Mr. Sandringham and say I'll come tomorrow."

He didn't answer, and she wondered what would happen. The palanquin bearers had kept moving steadily throughout the exchange. But when they'd drawn alongside the gate of the Mehta bungalow, Lakshman called out for the palanquin to be lowered.

Glad that he'd accommodated her request, Perveen climbed out. A series of aches from two days of riding in a palanquin and a postal cart before that had settled into her back, hips, and neck, making her feel very old. Gingerly, she approached the Mehtas' guards. Trying to sound pleasant, she said, "I was here just two days ago, and I've come to call on the burra memsahib."

"Name?" The older guard, a tall fellow with a bristling mustache, spoke crisply.

"Perveen Mistry, Esquire."

"They cannot see you," he answered firmly, and the second guard nodded in agreement.

"Why?" she challenged.

"The burra sahib has been gone for business since yesterday. And the burra memsahib is not feeling well."

Perveen could not tell from the guard's tight expression whether he was merely putting her off. "That is worrying. When did she fall ill?"

"For some time."

A day earlier, Vandana had been the picture of health. Skeptically, Perveen asked, "May I see her to ask if she'd like the doctor to be called?"

"She wishes no visitors."

Was the senior guard telling the truth about this? Very likely he was saying whatever Vandana had told him to say, and Perveen couldn't force her way in. Looking intently into both of the guards' faces, she said, "You must call Dr. Andrews. Please let memsahib know that I am worried about her. I'll be at the circuit house and will return if someone sends word that she'd like my company or to see the doctor."

As the palanquin continued on toward the circuit house, the sky turned from dark blue to a deep purple and finally to black. She raised her voice so Lakshman could hear her. "Why not light the lamps?"

Lakshman jogged back to answer her. "Too much oil for too short a distance." Then he gave a sharp cry. "Aiyo! Stop!"

The palanquin jerked to a halt, and from the tongue-lashing he gave the carriers, Perveen realized they had come very close to the edge of a bluff. Yet he wouldn't put on the lamps! All she could do was pray as the palanquin moved on more slowly. All around, the sounds of animals and insects had grown to an orchestra. She thought this was too close to civilization for leopards and tigers, but there were plenty of unseen snakes.

Fifteen minutes more of slow, tense travel elapsed before the palanquin arrived on the outskirts of the circuit house grounds. No more unseen cliffs to worry about—just a steep upward climb. She had done this before, and she knew there would be lit lamps marking the gate.

"Set it down. I'll do the rest on foot." Perveen disembarked and walked, easily at first and then with more difficulty. Her heart was thumping from the exertion and the excitement of finishing the journey. Perveen shifted her briefcase from her right hand to the left as she passed through the unlocked gates of the circuit house. Instantly, barking arose, and Desi ran toward her.

"Desi!" she cooed, knowing he couldn't see her and counting on his recognition of her voice. She put out her hand, hoping also that he'd remember her smell. He did. Desi's warm, wet tongue greeted her, and his wagging tail slapped against her sari. Perveen laughed and said, "Show me the rest of the way, will you?"

Hurricane lamps on the veranda illuminated Colin nestled into a planter's chair wearing a white linen shirt and an Indian lungi of patterned blue-and-green cotton. As Perveen and Desi came into the light, Colin arose, taking hold of a cane. Instead of coming toward them, he went swiftly along the veranda and in through one of the doors. Perveen saw a gap where his prosthetic leg usually was. Probably he was departing because he believed his natural state couldn't be exposed.

On the other hand, he might have hurried inside because someone was there he needed to warn.

Perveen's mind flitted to Vandana. What if she wasn't in her sickbed at home, but had gone to Colin because her husband was away? It could be that the Satapur agent was involved in whatever scurrilous proceedings she had in relation to the palace. They also might be having an affair.

Perveen's face was warm. Why should it matter to her if the Englishman was involved with a charming older woman who lived nearby? Perveen could have mistaken his personal interest in her, which meant everything going forward would be fine.

"Will you ask sahib to come speak to us?" Lakshman's voice was slightly labored from the uphill walk. He and the palanquin bearers had arrived just behind her.

"Of course." She'd almost forgotten about them. "You all must be paid tonight."

Perveen had stepped onto the veranda when Colin reemerged from his room. He was wearing linen trousers and both of the sturdy boots she remembered from before. His expression was guarded. "Good evening," he said.

"Sorry. I've come back without warning." She felt stupid as soon as the words were out of her mouth. Obviously she had returned.

"Weren't you going to stay with the Mehtas?" he asked pointedly.

"Yes. I stopped there and learned from the guard that Yazad is away and Vandana isn't feeling well. She's sick in bed," she added, watching him for a reaction.

In the lamplight, his green eyes seemed to grow larger. "Was it very disappointing not to be able to stay there?"

Perveen glanced at Lakshman, who appeared to be listening closely. This was not a conversation she wanted repeated all over the village. "Of course not. I am prepared to let bygones be bygones. But first, the bearers must be paid."

"I'll do it," he said, reaching into the pocket of his trousers and pulling out some coins.

"What will you pay them?" Perveen didn't think it looked like enough.

"The standard rate. Two days' work is one rupee each and two rupees to Lakshman."

The men had worked above and beyond the call of duty to ensure her safety. In a low voice, she said, "Considering all that happened, I think they deserve more."

Colin pressed his lips together. "Unfortunately, I can't pay them more. The Agency says that if one group of palanquin bearers is paid more than another, it causes discord."

"Well then, you give the rupee to each of them. I'll use my own per diem fund for their baksheesh. When I make the expense account, I will explain all that they did to get me to the palace and back."

"So you were admitted?" His eyebrows rose.

"Yes, of course I was." Perveen turned away from him to dispense coins from the cloth purse. The tired men beamed as she put an extra rupee in each palm. In Marathi, she told them, "You solved problems nobody expected. You endured very bad weather conditions. And you moved fast, yet with care. From my heart, I thank you."

Lakshman and his crew left for the village, singing as they carried the now-empty palanquin away.

"They're very pleased," Colin said, gazing after them. "Now, if you aren't too fatigued, I'd like to make an apology."

"About their payment? There's no need—"

"Not that." Clearing his throat, he went on. "I'm sorry for how I behaved earlier. I thought about it, and I understand the position you're in."

She was flooded with relief. They would be able to work together; and she needed him badly, because of the danger to the royal children. "Thank you very much for that. There's so much we need to discuss, but my boots . . ." She trailed off, letting him take in the spectacle of her stained and dirty footwear.

He squinted at them and shook his head. "It looks like they're ruined. Can you just take them off?"

She felt awkward. "As long as it isn't violating circuit house propriety."

"Of course not!"

She bent to unlace the boots, realizing that her resistance to going barefoot was probably due to a desire not to be exposed. All Colin had seen of her until then had been her face and hands. She wanted to keep things proper, but it felt very good to have her damp, cramped toes uncurl and touch the veranda's clean tiles.

"Is anybody else staying at the circuit house at the moment?" she asked, hoping that nobody else would see her in such a casual state.

"How odd that you should ask." Colin grinned, clearly at ease with her again. "Roderick Ames came through at lunchtime."

Her worries about Roderick Ames were coming to a head. "Why was that?"

"Just said he was on his way back to Poona. While we were eating, I asked him if he knew anything about your missing camera."

"What was his reaction?" Perveen asked as Rama came out carrying a tray with water glasses and a small pitcher. His appearance with much-needed refreshment diverted her temporarily. She smiled at the silver-haired man and folded her hands in a namaste greeting.

Colin settled down in his chair again and motioned for Perveen to sit as well. "He said of course he would never pinch anyone's property, and he left without even finishing."

Rama placed the glasses on the table and asked, "Are you looking for Miss Mistry's camera?"

"Yes," Perveen said. "Do you know where it is?"

Rama lifted another item she hadn't noticed because it was

behind the silver water pitcher. As he handed Perveen her Brownie camera, he said, "This was set on the rock wall close to the place in the part of the veranda where you made your photographs. I just saw it at sunset today when I was setting out the lamps."

Yet he had waited to bring it until she was there—and conversation had turned to Roderick Ames.

"May I see it?" Colin looked at Perveen, who nodded and watched him take it into his hands. "I had not realized until just now this is the cardboard model. If the camera had been there since our gathering, it would have been ruined by the rains. But it is completely dry—so it must have been returned."

"That's right," Perveen said, her suspicions of Ames solidifying. "I was wondering something. Why do you have a friendship with Roderick?"

Colin's brow creased. "I would say that we are friendly to each other, but not close. Why is that a concern?"

"He's not terribly—pleasant," she said, struggling to find the words to express what she'd thought of his presence during the evening of the party.

"Very few social graces," Colin said with a small smile. "But I see virtually nobody except Rama over the long rainy season. If any visitor comes, I try to find some commonality, because it's such a relief to have someone to speak with."

"If you will please excuse me," Rama broke in gently, "I will go to make your tea."

"Thank you very much," Colin said.

After Rama had gone, Perveen said, "I wonder if the film is still inside."

Colin turned the camera over and paused. "A good question. The trouble is that if one opens the compartment to check, the film roll will be ruined."

Perveen weighed the value of the film's images of animals and Colin's friends against the chance to know what Roderick might have done. Shrugging, she said, "I can always take more pictures of monkeys. It doesn't matter; let me open it myself."

She took the camera from Colin, and as she'd expected, the film was gone.

"Why did you know the film would be missing?" Colin looked at her with something close to awe.

"Perhaps because Mr. Ames didn't want his image saved for posterity," Perveen said.

"He's just an ordinary civil service engineer." Colin kept his eyes on her, and when she didn't answer, he said, "You seem to know something about him that I don't."

"I heard from one of the old servants at the hunting lodge that Mr. Ames was on the scene when Prince Pratap Rao died. Quite a coincidence."

"He's never spoken about it to me. Are you sure the servant was correct?"

"He described an Anglo-Indian engineer, and what motive would this man have to lie about it?" Perveen looked around, feeling ill at ease. "Who else is staying at the circuit house today?"

"Except for Rama here, we are absolutely alone."

"I just wanted to be sure our conversation is confidential."

"Of course it is. And now let's not worry about Roderick Ames anymore. I want to hear what happened to you from the moment you boarded the palanquin."

"That's a good place to start." Perveen spoke about the palanquin's breakdown, watching his face grow long, then relax as she described how she'd made it to the palace on foot with Lakshman and four of the bearers. She had just been speaking about how the moonstone pendant had gained her admission to the palace when Rama returned. He set down a pot of fragrant tea and a plate of small green packages. Guessing they were rice pancakes wrapped in banana leaves, she gave a sigh of pleasure. "Panki! I thought this was only a Gujarati dish."

"Gujarat is not so far. Recipes travel through the mountains like the birds," Rama said with an elegant movement of his hand. "I will prepare a full dinner after this. What kind of chicken tonight?"

"I don't care what you cook. I could eat a dozen of these!" she declared, piling three panki onto her plate. She had been so busy at the lodge she'd eaten only one millet roti and was famished.

Rama beamed. "I shall steam more panki for both of you."

After Rama left, Colin looked at her with concern. "Weren't you fed well at the palace?"

She was so glad to be back she could chuckle about it. "Things started out well enough. But very quickly, it became my aim to avoid eating. Let me tell you!"

She told him about everything: from the atmosphere inside the palace to the business of the tutor also serving as the palace officer, from Mirabai's fears and the possible poisoning attempt to her own growing suspicions that Pratap Rao hadn't died from the exact cause the doctor had reported. The last part, she knew, was the most serious. It raised concerns both about the doctor's performance and about the possibility of murder.

But Colin didn't immediately address that. Looking sober, he said, "I feel bad for having sent you into such danger—and also feel quite lucky you were clever enough to survive and return to me. But I'm a bit worried about you taking the clothing from the hunting lodge. I've been told never to take things from palaces, and I imagine that restriction holds for other royal property."

"Owen McLaughlin took plenty from the palace," Perveen shot back. "And the government must see the clothing. It's prima facie evidence there never was an animal attack."

She went to her room, where Rama had brought the valise. Unlocking it, she took out the shawl-wrapped bundle of royal clothing she had placed inside it. Out on the veranda, next to the hurricane lamp's light, the holes in the clothing and the smudges of blood showed clearly.

"These holes in the jodhpurs look like pecking made by birds,"

Perveen said, pointing to the damaged fabric. "My guess is that local vultures came upon the prince's body—just as vultures fed on the dead monkey at the palace. The scant blood makes it seem that he was already deceased when the scavengers arrived."

Colin winced. "It is gruesome to think about. But I still don't understand the whole picture you are presenting."

Perveen took a long sip of tea before answering. Its heat warmed her, gave her the strength she needed. "Mirabai spotted vultures on the afternoon he went hunting, so he might have died close to that time. And if his killer had been an animal of prey, there would have been much more blood. Therefore, I suspect the agent of Prince Pratap Rao's death was human. The maharaja's body was burnt in religious rites the day Dr. Andrews confirmed his cause of death as an animal mauling. Thus we have no evidence other than the lack of more severe damage to the clothing."

Colin's cup rattled as he put it down on his saucer quickly. "That's quite an accusation."

"I agree, but I can't see another explanation. One thing that troubles me is we don't have the jacket. Sometimes what's not there is as important as what is there. And I think we can agree that a leopard would not eat the material of the jacket, nor could it undress the prince and move the jacket elsewhere." She paused, aware of Colin's intense concentration on her words. "Only a man could do that."

"Or woman!" Colin interjected.

Perveen thought about the theory of a woman killer. The most obvious possibility was Mirabai, who freely rode in areas outside the palace. And she was supposed to have suffered melancholia, although Dr. Andrews admitted he had not diagnosed this himself. Perveen reflected on the conversations they'd had together and did not think there was a strong chance of her being mentally ill or having the mindset to murder her child. Shaking her head, she said, "It could be, but is unlikely, given the number of men on the hunt who had ready access to the prince. In any case, I would like to speak to Dr. Andrews first thing tomorrow about whether he ever saw Prince Pratap Rao's jacket."

Colin exhaled slowly. "I will keep the late prince's clothing in a locked safe until we know what to do with it. So the new question is, who on the hunt could have murdered Prince Jiva Rao?"

"And where is this safe?" Perveen was hesitant to give up something so precious.

He answered without hesitation. "It's built into the wall behind the portrait of the Poona Agency administrator."

Feeling more relaxed, Perveen settled back in her planter's chair. It felt so good to be away from the palace and able to speak frankly. "The servant at the hunting lodge said that in addition to Prince Swaroop and the engineer, he saw a number of beaters and Aditya, who is the court buffoon. He's one of the few men the maharanis will socialize with."

"If it's true that Roderick was on the hunt, perhaps Roderick Ames took the camera because he didn't want the image of him with you and me to be seen by those people."

Perveen raised her eyebrows. "That certainly is a fanciful theory. It would require him assuming that I would have time during my royal visit to have the film developed."

"In civil service school, junior officers were told that many palaces have their own photographers and darkrooms. It's for reasons of privacy regarding royal images. Therefore, it's conceivable you would have snapped more photographs at the palace and someone would have offered to develop your film."

"That's an interesting idea, but Prince Swaroop must know he's in the civil service." Perveen thought some more. "Prince Swaroop arrived quite unexpectedly at the Satapur palace. Perhaps he learned about me because Roderick Ames stopped at his palace to warn him."

"Because the two were in league when it came to Prince Pratap Rao's death?" Colin shook his head. "I don't want to believe it."

Was he stalling on every possibility she provided because he had something to hide? "That is one theory. What I was thinking during the palanquin ride was a bit different."

"It's best to consider everything."

She remained silent. The other idea she'd had could hardly be shared with Colin. If he went to his superiors with it, her job would be finished.

"What is it?" Colin persisted.

Perveen sighed. What he did with the information was out of her control.

"Prince Swaroop told me that the British government reserves the right to take over princely states and add them to the empire. Do you confirm this?"

A guarded look came over his face. "Yes. It has happened in the past. But I've not heard talk about that regarding Satapur."

This didn't surprise her. "You live remotely and have been hands-off. I don't know if that was the case with Mr. Owen McLaughlin, who once held the position of the Satapur agent."

"So you are saying there might be a long-range scheme of the government to disable the ruling family and grab Satapur for the empire?" Colin said slowly. "And they placed me—an inexperienced officer who doesn't travel far and wide—in this position so I would not know to ask questions."

Perveen bowed her head. "It could be. But I doubt anyone in the Agency would act without orders from higher up. A portrait of the viceroy hangs in the lodge, and his face has been disfigured with black paint. I first assumed one of the servants did it. Now I realize it could have been Prince Swaroop, out of anger at this perceived situation."

Colin looked past her into the dark garden. "Either Swaroop or Mirabai could have defaced the portrait in rage, believing that the government killed Prince Pratap Rao. But if the prince's death is a government conspiracy, that seems to rule out the likelihood there's any poisoning going on in the palace. What do you say about that?"

"I don't know. It's just the same about Roderick Ames. I really don't know if he's involved, but I am concerned." Perveen let out a long sigh. "I don't know if I should have delved into so much about the past. The fact is, we are both responsible for Prince Jiva Rao's safety."

Colin's fingers drummed the planter's chair's long armrest. "If you are wondering about the likelihood of food tampering versus poor food hygiene, Vandana might have some ideas."

"I tried to visit with her on the way here, but she was unavailable. The guards said she was ill, though I don't know if it's true. I hope Dr. Andrews will check on her."

"Don't worry! Whatever Vandana has can't be too serious."

She felt annoyed by his certainty. "Why not?"

"This morning, I saw Vandana riding past the point where I do my yoga exercises."

Perveen remembered what the doctor had said about cholera in the village. "I hope she didn't go where people are ill. How long does it take for cholera symptoms to show?"

"She has no interest in the village—don't worry about that. I imagine she was taking a trail ride past the village to go into the woods. She's told me before that she likes to visit the Aranyani shrine."

Aranyani, once again. During dinner, Vandana had spoken of her belief in leaving offerings for Aranyani. Perhaps she had gone to bring money for someone. But these were ungrounded suppositions.

"We shall both call on her tomorrow." Colin held up the pot of tea, and she offered her cup for him to refill it.

"Back to the matter of Prince Jiva Rao's education," she said. "Because the maharanis disagreed with my recommendation, they may ask for a court hearing. Women in purdah are entitled to send representatives; perhaps one could be Mr. Basu, but I think he would serve as the dowager maharani's mouthpiece."

"Who would speak for Mirabai?" Colin leaned back in his chair, studying her. "Some other palace insider?"

"Prince Swaroop doesn't agree with her position." Perveen paused, thinking some more. "I mentioned Aditya, the court buffoon who seems to be almost like a family member—but he is not esteemed enough to speak in a courtroom representing a royal."

"I suppose we should not be tying ourselves in knots trying to help them after they rejected your decision. Which sounded like a logical one." Colin sipped his tea. "I wish I'd also had the chance to meet Prince Jiva Rao. He comes into maturity in just eight years! I think if we do well by him, he'll do the same for his state."

He had said "we." Did that mean he would continue calling for her to visit Satapur? Or was he thinking she was going to help the maharaja settle into his school?

Before she could ask about those things, Rama had quietly reappeared. "The boy has filled the tub in memsahib's bathroom. Perhaps a bath before dinner?"

Perveen thanked him. It was a good moment for an interruption; she needed some time to think over the difficult ideas she and Colin had discussed and also to soak her aching bones.

"Could dinner be ready in the next hour or so?" Colin inquired.

"Yes, but I must go to the village. We need some special vegetables and nuts for the dish that I have in mind." Rama looked at Perveen with a faint smile. "A welcome-back dish."

As Rama headed off with the money Colin gave him, Perveen departed to her guest quarters. She took a quick bath, willing herself not to think any longer about her dark theories. She had reached safety; she would rest, and then the next thing to do would become clear.

Perveen dried herself off and tied a fresh kusti around her waist. She had just finished draping herself in a gold-and-green sari when there was a tapping at the door.

"What is it?" she asked, bringing the sari's pallu over the front of her body to form the graceful swag that was essential to Parsi womanhood.

"The plans are off. We've got unexpected visitors." Colin's voice was a whisper.

A man did not whisper in his own home; something had to be wrong.

She opened the door to face him. "Who are they?"

Colin did not answer but pushed his way into the room, bumping a bookcase with his cane in his haste to enter. He muttered, "Prince Swaroop and several men from the palace."

"But—" She broke off, trying to think. Her growing theory about government interference was being challenged. She recalled what Baburam, the old man at the lodge, had said about bad luck. "The prince must have found out I took the late maharaja's clothing."

Colin's words came rapid fire. "I don't think they know about that. At least, they didn't say. Prince Swaroop says he and his men were trying to catch your palanquin procession. He was upset they couldn't find you."

Perveen shuddered as she realized that Prince Swaroop might have caught her en route if the group hadn't made the unexpected detour to the lodge. What would have happened then? "Did he give any reason for pursuing me?"

Colin leaned on his cane as if he needed its support. "He said the maharaja is missing."

At the words, Perveen felt a ringing in her ears. It couldn't be. "Are you sure you understood them? What exactly do they mean by 'missing'?"

He shook his head. "Prince Swaroop spoke English to make sure I understood. They think you've kidnapped him!"

19

THE INNOCENT ON TRIAL

*P*erveen had no response to give Colin. Of course, he knew she was innocent. But her head was filled with something Mirabai had said about her coming to the palace: *While our lawyer guest is here, he's fine.* Perveen had not taken that to heart, and the worst had occurred.

She slid her bare feet into a pair of clean sandals and went out. Thirty feet away, in the central section of the veranda, she saw three hulking men in hunter-green uniforms decorated in heavy gold braid. Green was not the color of the Satapur palace; it must have been connected to the prince's own staff. Her eyes swept over what the men had with them: swords, bayonets, long rifles. If they really believed she had Prince Jiva Rao, would they use force to try to get her to reveal his hiding place?

"Prince Swaroop is in the drawing room," Colin said from behind her. "I told him that nobody else was in the palanquin when it was unloaded. But he insisted on speaking with you."

"That's understandable." She thought about her conversation with the prince. He had never agreed or disagreed about his nephew being in danger at the palace. In fact, he had spoken about the risk of him living unprotected at boarding school. And now the maharaja was gone; blaming things on her was a way of keeping himself in the right.

Her legs felt heavy as she went into the drawing room. Prince Swaroop was sitting rigidly on the best piece of furniture in the room: a velvet settee with a rosewood back that stretched up to a ridiculous height. A second man was seated on a shorter side

chair. He was a Sikh wearing a stout, well-wrapped turban decorated with a sapphire pin. She noted there was no refreshment
on the tables in front of the visitors—a hospitality error. If Rama
weren't away in the village, the prince and his companion would
have been served.

Looking up at her, Swaroop said, "You will bring the maharaja."

"I wish I could help, but he is not here." She was upset to hear
her voice crack, which surely made her sound guilty. "And may
I please become acquainted with the gentleman you've brought
with you?"

"It's Dhillon, my prime minister." He arose from his seat and
walked toward her with quick, angry steps. "Where did you put
him, then? I heard you made a stop."

Backing off so they weren't as close, she thought about his
words. Maybe they had gone to the lodge already. The other
alternative was that he had spies throughout the area. "We made
two stops," she said, refusing to allow him the chance to correct
her on something later. "The first was for food and drink at the
old hunting lodge, and the second was at Yazad Mehta's estate
nearby."

Swaroop's eyes flickered from her to Colin. "I know Mehta.
Why would you see him?"

"I'm friends with his wife. You may know her from your childhood at the palace—"

He interrupted her. "It is because you knew such an estate is a
clever place to hide the maharaja."

"Miss Mistry would not do such a thing," Colin interjected.
He was standing at her side, and she was aware that while he was
much thinner than Prince Swaroop, he was an inch taller. His
presence had a comforting strength.

Perveen endeavored to sound logical. "If you go to the estate
and speak to the Mehtas' guards, they can tell you whether there
was a boy with me."

"You call him a boy? He is the maharaja!" Swaroop stepped toward the two of them in an unveiled menacing fashion. "We already stopped at the estate and spoke to the durwans. They reported that you got out of the palanquin to speak to them, and that they did not come near the palanquin to look inside. How could they know whether or not you had my nephew? They said you seemed most eager to get inside the estate, even though they told you the lady of the house was indisposed."

Reacting to the prince's aggressive movement, Colin stepped between the two of them. Firmly, he said, "Your Highness, please don't doubt Miss Mistry. She has worked very hard for the welfare of the maharaja."

Perveen felt sick, realizing how her assertive behavior could be twisted to look suspicious. "The carriers, who are ordinary village men you could speak with as well, unloaded me and my luggage here. They took away a palanquin that was so light that they were singing. Mr. Sandringham here was the witness."

"Yes, it is true. Your Highness, please walk through the circuit house and look," Colin said placatingly. "Once your mind is at ease that he's not here, we must put our heads together on how to best search for the maharaja. I am just as worried as you are."

"For the worst reason. To you he is the future puppet. You'll send him to that pathetic boarding school for royal boys where he'll be taught obedience to the British." Prince Swaroop looked around the parlor as if Jiva Rao might be trussed up beneath the sofa. Curtly, he asked, "Where are your servants?"

Colin looked uncomprehendingly at him. "My bearer, Rama, is my chief employee. He's gone to the village on some errands. Two village boys also work here. I'm not sure where Hari and Mohit are at the moment."

"Gone to the village!" Swaroop seized on Colin's revelation. "Is that where you're hiding him, among the peasants?"

"As we've explained, the maharaja did not travel here with me. Let's be logical." Perveen paused to swallow and put her thoughts together before continuing. "How could he leave the palace grounds without the guards seeing him? I know from past experience that a child in a large home has many places to play, fall asleep, or maybe get locked into—accidentally or not."

Mr. Dhillon spoke in a cool, modulated voice. "Miss Mistry, are you saying you believe he's safely in the palace?"

She looked at him, aware that he'd misunderstood, but grateful that he wasn't as inflamed as the prince he served. "I would not say that he's safe. Maharani Mirabai was certain someone was trying to kill Jiva Rao. If he can't be found here or at the palace, it's certainly possible that something worse than kidnapping has taken place."

Mr. Dhillon said nothing, but closed his eyes, and Perveen wondered if he was thinking that if he'd stayed at the main palace, Jiva Rao would not be in this predicament.

Prince Swaroop looked down for a long moment, and when he returned his gaze to her, she saw the bluster was gone. Was it because he knew he himself was in danger of being accused of kidnapping? Gruffly, he said, "I accept your invitation to look over the place."

"I'm most relieved. Go anywhere you wish!" Colin said.

After the prince and the sardarji had arisen and departed the drawing room, Perveen asked Colin, "Can you please tell me what the Agency has said about the next person in line to the throne?"

Colin nodded, as if he understood her suspicion. "There is no document with that information outlined. Prince Swaroop surely could petition for the right to reign, if Prince Jiva Rao is found dead. But it would most likely be rejected, because the laws of succession do not allow one to look backward a generation to appoint the uncle of a rightful heir. There was a direct line already established from fathers to sons: Mohan Rao, Mahendra Rao, Pratap Rao, and now Jiva Rao, in his brother's stead."

"What happens if Jiva Rao isn't found?"

"It's most likely that a regent would be appointed until the government chose a new maharaja. That is exactly what happened in Baroda. Most likely they'd choose a malleable and good-looking young man of royal caste."

Perveen reminded herself that there was still a chance Prince Swaroop held out hope of getting to rule. There were so many rumors about how the British oversaw states that it was entirely possible. In any case, she was sure that Swaroop feared society's judgment, because for a Satapur prince to vanish while he was paying a social call—twice—seemed more than coincidence. She considered all the drama and indignation that Prince Swaroop had shown them, and also the fact that, based on when he'd arrived, he must have ridden from the palace at nighttime—a hazardous situation. It all seemed to show a desperate concern for his nephew. But was it real—and when had he left the palace? She asked Colin, "Could it be possible to reach here safely riding most of the way in the dark from the Satapur palace?"

"I don't know. Are you thinking he set off earlier than you did?"

Perveen nodded. "He already told us he traveled via the forest path that I took to the palace. It could be that he went that way much earlier because he had something in mind. Perhaps he meant to apprehend me when I was defenseless."

"Dear God." Colin looked at her, his face more serious than she'd ever seen. "It would be crucial for Swaroop to appear deeply concerned if the surviving heir to Satapur has vanished. Especially since Prince Pratap Rao died when they were together on a hunt."

Perveen belatedly realized it had been too trusting to allow Swaroop to tour the circuit house unescorted. The prince, Dhillon, and the guards all had the power to plant evidence that could make it seem Perveen was the guilty party, with Colin as her accessory. Prince Pratap Rao's garments had been secured within the circuit house safe, but if they found them, what trouble could ensue? Perveen said, "I agree with you about his possible motivation, and I dislike the idea of them roaming everywhere without a witness. I'll follow them. But I need an excuse for it."

"You can open doors they cannot." Colin crossed the drawing room to a handsome campaign desk. From the middle drawer, he brought forward a ring of house keys. "All the unused bedrooms are kept locked, so they will need you to help with access. I'd go myself, but you move faster."

It was the second time he'd referred to his disability with her. But there seemed to be no griping about it this time; it was just a statement of fact.

Over the next half hour, Prince Swaroop searched the house. The prince demanded every almirah be unlocked, and Perveen complied. Following closely without comment was Prince Swaroop's minister, Mr. Dhillon. If only she could get him alone for an interview. She imagined he knew the truth. Was his loyalty truly to Prince Swaroop rather than Satapur?

After the house was finished, the royal party descended on the outbuildings on the property. As the prince strode by Desi, whom Colin was holding on a leash, the tall dog strained at the leash and growled. It was as if he recognized the maharaja's uncle for the dangerous force he was.

Keeping an eye on the men as they entered the stables, Perveen walked over to Colin. She had been ruminating over what they could do, and it was time to tell him what she'd concluded. Quietly, she said, "I must return to the palace. Somebody there may have noticed something that could explain what happened."

Colin pressed his lips together. "That's too dangerous. Our first duty is to inform the government and get direction from them."

She was not surprised by his reaction—but she was unwilling to concede. "I disagree with that plan. Kolhapur is quite far, and what could a cluster of British gentlemen do to find Prince Jiva Rao?"

"I'm looking for help closer by. The officers in Poona could offer us arms after they have received clearance from higher up."

"What do you mean, arms?" Perveen couldn't believe he was talking about starting a war.

"Military involvement is allowed in defense of the royal family. A military search of the palace is safer than you going alone."

"But where is the military stationed?" She felt more impatient than ever. "It could take days."

"There's a cantonment in Satapur very close to the palace. But official orders must be given before the soldiers can help."

"Ah. Even though Prince Swaroop is prime minister, he must wait for British orders?"

Colin kept hold of Desi's leash as the dog strained in the direction of the gates. "I'm afraid so. I propose that tomorrow morning we go to Khandala and then take the train to Poona. There's no time for sending them a letter. If I present the situation to the chief councillor by tomorrow afternoon, word could be sent to the cantonment by telegraph." He paused. "It would be best if I could get Prince Swaroop to come with me to give his side of things. But they'll certainly need to hear what you've told me."

"I'll write a memorandum about all that happened at the palace. But I won't join your trip tomorrow."

"And why is that?" Colin asked tightly.

"The administrators in Poona will only pay attention to you and Prince Swaroop. In their eyes, I'm just a woman." Perveen decided to push on. "Here is how I can be more useful. I could return to the palace in the hopes of locating evidence and also getting testimony from witnesses who would be too frightened of soldiers."

Colin shook his head. "It's too dangerous."

"You and your bosses didn't think that two days ago," Perveen retorted.

"Someone's coming," Colin said, looking toward the gates. Desi was focused on that direction, but his tail was wagging.

Perveen was not surprised to see Rama coming through. He put his heavy bags down on the grass. Stretching his arms, he said, "I see new horses at the stable. Are some people staying with us?"

"Yes. Prince Swaroop of Satapur, his prime minister, and three guards. It's an unexpected visit."

Rama's forehead creased with worry, but he nodded. "How many rooms should be prepared?"

"We don't yet know if Prince Swaroop will stay overnight," Perveen said, though she realized as she said it that, with the sky dark, there could be no other option for the royal party. The thought of sleeping under the same roof as Swaroop was disturbing.

"Look—they're coming back over to us," Colin said in a low voice.

Prince Swaroop and his followers were emerging from the stable. Now Swaroop stood before Perveen and Colin. In a more muted voice than he'd used before, Swaroop said, "As you can see, I didn't find him."

Perveen wanted to say, *I told you so!* but she was wise enough to remain silent. And she was grateful that they hadn't found Prince Pratap Rao's garments.

"You have our word, as the maharaja's guardians, that we are as anxious to find him as you are." Colin thumped his cane on the ground, as if for emphasis. "I propose we expand the search through the jungle and possibly inside the palace."

"We have already looked there," Swaroop said dismissively. "And tonight, palace guards and villagers are going with torches through the jungle."

Just as they had when the first prince disappeared.

"We could ask for the assistance of the military. What do you think about that?" Colin spoke in a way that made it seem as if the decision were up to the prince.

Swaroop frowned. "But that must be ordered by the British."

"Yes, that is true," Colin answered firmly. "If you come with me to Poona tomorrow, you can tell them what's happened, and I will confirm the details. But first, you must stay the night. There is no possibility of traveling in the dark."

The prince's face grew longer. Perveen imagined that he wanted to say no—but he could not get on his way given the lateness of the hour. He had to lie in bed with the British, at least for one night.

"My cook can prepare chicken in one of ten ways," Colin began in a cheerful tone. "Let me tell you . . ."

The long teak table was set for four, and Perveen set out white paper place cards that Colin produced from a desk drawer. It was clear using such cards was an unusual occurrence for him, and Perveen was better versed on the correct rules for seating than he was. He'd worried about whether the prince should get the head of the table due to his rank, but she had reminded him that according to the circuit house's copy of *Debrett's Peerage*, the honored guest, royal or not, was seated at the host's right. The card for Jaqinder Dhillon was placed on the opposing side, and Perveen put the card for herself at the table's foot.

In the hour before dinner was ready, Perveen watched Rama hurrying, making mistakes with serving, and she could only imagine how disconcerted the last-minute visitors had made him. Four boys from the village arrived to aid in preparing guest rooms and baths, and the three guards who'd traveled with the prince were shown to their quarters in one of the garden huts.

Perveen had asked Rama what he would prepare.

"I have plenty of rice and dal and greens. But a chicken that is just big enough for two cannot stretch to feed four as a roast. I'll make vindaloo."

"A good idea." Perveen had felt anxious, as if this were her own house that was lacking.

Once all were at the table, Colin opened up a bottle of claret. It was finished among the three men in ten minutes, so he asked Rama to bring another one. Prince Swaroop drank readily, and she felt nervous watching Colin pouring him more. She feared that Swaroop could turn angry and undisciplined, and if Colin kept pace with him, he'd be unguarded in what he said. Yet the prince was significantly amiable, and even joked that Perveen had run from the palace because she didn't want to eat with him but now had to dine with him after all.

This made Perveen, who had not taken a drop of wine, quite nervous. She was the only female dining with males, more vulnerable than in her father's worst nightmares. Trying to seem blasé, she said, "The lady I mentioned earlier, Vandana Mehta, is less than a mile away. It's a shame she's not available tonight to join us."

"And which number cousin is that? I have sixteen first cousins and scores more second and third," the prince said casually. "My mother is the only one who can keep track. She refers to them as 'your ninth cousin-sister' and so on."

"I don't mind us not having other guests tonight," Colin said, pouring more wine for the prince. "It would be uncomfortable making small talk when we know the maharaja is very likely away from home, either by himself or with someone who has a malevolent purpose."

He was right. Perveen felt like a dolt for getting carried along with Swaroop's chatter. After Colin's comment, the prince's face had darkened. Perhaps he'd realized he appeared not to be grieving enough.

Perveen considered what could make good table conversation at such a difficult time. "Your Highness!" she said, smiling pleasantly at Prince Swaroop. "Are your men carrying maps of the area that we could study in order to plan tomorrow's search?"

"We have no need of maps. I know every hill in Satapur. In fact, my knowledge of my land is what made it possible to get from the palace to this place so quickly," he said, spearing a piece of chicken. "Knowing the land, I drove back to my palace, and there I gathered my men, and we took our fastest horses. I haven't been here since I was twelve years old, and Mr. McLaughlin was sitting at the head of the table. He treated his royal visitors well. There were thirty servants in attendance including a French chef. We had a mutton roast and a cream cake, and he gave me my first champagne."

He was indeed disassociated from his nephew's disappearance. She was becoming fast convinced that the two princes disappearing while their uncle was around was not coincidental. But she did have someone else to ask about. "What do you think of the ICS engineer, Mr. Roderick Ames?"

"Who?" He swirled the wine in his glass, not looking at her.

"Oh, I had heard you asked him to fetch the doctor after Prince Pratap Rao was found."

The prince was in the midst of drinking and suddenly choked. His minister jumped up, took the glass away, and thumped him on the back.

"Are you all right, Your Highness?" Dhillon's voice was easy, as if he had seen this happen before. But Perveen sensed her words had caused the shock.

"Yes," he said sourly. "Now I remember. There was an Anglo-Indian ICS officer who saw us in the forest."

"What happened exactly?" Perveen asked, switching to Marathi. Colin's eyes flickered away, and she realized he was going to pretend he didn't understand a word.

The prince shrugged. "He was there, and I asked him to get the doctor. He knows where his home is. So he handed back his gun and went."

Perveen mulled over his words. They seemed to hint that the gun belonged to the royal party, rather than being an ordinary military-issue pistol.

"He said he was on the hunt with you." This wasn't true at all, but she suspected he'd agree with her.

Prince Swaroop shrugged. "Yes. He was interested in royal life."

"And how did he get close to you?" Perveen saw Colin digging into his food, and wondered if he had understood what the prince had just revealed.

"He set up an electric house for me. My palace may be smaller than the main one, but there are more lights there, throughout." He gave a small, smug smile.

Playing on this, Perveen put an admiring warmth into her voice. "As you can see here, not even this Englishman has electricity! What does one pay for setting up an electric house?"

"A few thousand. He certainly does not complain because he gets privileges like hunting trips. Although that was the very worst trip to go on." His eyes became damp, as if he was about to cry. High emotion was the impact of too much alcohol on some.

"Yes, yes," Perveen agreed. "But tell me—if he was doing work for you, and you had him on the hunt, why didn't you recognize his name straight out?"

"I don't like to see Indian faces with English names. I call him something else."

"And what's that?"

"Kuta."

It was a Marathi word that meant dog and showed her the depth of Prince Swaroop's rudeness. But it didn't rule out the chance that Roderick Ames had been the one who had killed Prince Pratap Rao—perhaps in exchange for a very large payment from Swaroop.

"Enough talk of the past!" Prince Swaroop said in English. He lifted his empty glass and looked around for someone to fill it. "We will search for Maharaja Jiva Rao. And this time, we must find him before it's too late."

As Colin hesitated, Perveen sensed his reluctance to allow the prince to become utterly inebriated. But in that pause, Rama came forward, picked up the bottle, and poured into the prince's glass until the bottle was empty. She shot a glance at Rama and saw sweat beading his brow. He probably had served the prince because he was nervous what would happen if the royal became angry.

"The search," Colin began. "Satapur is thirty-one miles at its widest point and forty-five miles running north to south. We have an official map of it, although the landscape might be different from what's on the map."

Perveen was distressed by the idea that the map was wrong. "Why is that?"

"During monsoon, waterfalls spring up. For example, when I first came here, there was a stone path from the village to the Aranyani temple in the forest. But after a few months of rain, every stone has been swept away. Today, trees have fallen where the path once was, and a ravine has been created that cannot be crossed."

The prince looked bemused. "You have seen this temple?"

"Yes." Colin shifted in his chair. "I've explored much of the state carrying the existing maps. When I find changes, I mark them. From that I can create new maps—unofficial ones."

"So the Kolhapur Agency gave a mapmaker this agent position?" The prince sounded amused.

Two red spots appeared at Colin's high cheekbones. "I was an ICS collector before this. Maps are my personal interest."

Perveen was going to suggest he bring out these maps for the prince to see, when she was distracted by a riot of barking.

"Someone has come." The prince attempted to stand but swayed so much that the Sardarji hurried around the table to hold him steady.

Colin looked unflustered. "It is likely one of the neighbors! Rama will go to check on things."

Rama had already put down his tray of puris and gone through the door.

Perveen felt nervous. "Will Desi bite someone he doesn't know?"

"Not likely," Colin said soothingly. "He listens to Rama's commands."

"Why is it that you have no durwan to guard the circuit house?" the prince asked disbelievingly. "There were guards in Mr. McLaughlin's days."

"Desi is all we need. To look at him, you'd think he is the fiercest dog in the world—so any wrongdoer would certainly run."

"There's a dog at the Satapur palace just like him. My man will go with your bearer and call my guards!" Swaroop said, and Dhillon hastened out. She waited, feeling tense, until she heard comfortable male conversation outside.

Two minutes later Rama and Dhillon returned with a tall man dressed in a blue sherwani coat and matching trousers, with the sideways-slanting Satapur Palace pagri on his head. For a moment, Perveen was confused, but then she recognized Aditya.

"Your Grace." He put his hands together in a gesture of respect to the prince.

"You must be from the palace. I am Colin Sandringham, the agent of Satapur." Colin rose to offer a slight bow.

Prince Swaroop waved a dismissive hand. "Don't bother with that! He is only the court buffoon."

Perveen gave Swaroop a scathing look and got up herself to greet the buffoon. As she neared him, she smelled a mixture of smoke and sweat. Trying not to wrinkle her nose, she said, "Please come in, Aditya, and sit down. Is there some news?"

"Yes. Take a chair—we will bring you food and drink," Colin said, because Aditya was still standing uncertainly in his spot.

But he remained standing. Edging away from Perveen, he said in stilted English, "I know you took him. But is he still alive?"

This was such a change from the way Aditya had spoken before—it was as if an old friend had been replaced by an unpleasant double. Earnestly, she said, "I did not take him. The honorable Prince Swaroop can tell you himself Maharaja is not here."

"It is true," Prince Swaroop said, following the declaration with a burp.

"He is not here because she's had him killed. Why else would he vanish after her visit?" Aditya demanded.

The buffoon had spoken a bit of English to Perveen before, but she realized now that he was fluent. Perhaps the hunting trip with King George had taught him quite a lot—or he'd been sitting in on the children's lessons with Mr. Basu.

Colin put down his knife and fork. "I see how much you care for him. But Miss Mistry has absolutely no reason to harm the maharaja. She's been employed by the Agency to keep him safe."

Aditya acted as if Colin hadn't spoken and looked pleadingly toward the prince. "Your Grace does not know how upset the rajmata is. A third death could kill her."

"How is the choti-rani?" Perveen asked.

"Who knows? She has gone riding. Her answer for everything." His voice was contemptuous.

Colin looked at Perveen with alarm. "It's nighttime. She cannot be riding in the dark—"

"Who knows if she returned?" Aditya said. "I came looking for Maharaja, not her."

Perveen noted the dullness in the buffoon's voice, and the haunted look in his eyes. She asked, "Before leaving, were you able to have the funeral service for Bandar?"

His eyes shone with moistness. "Yes. I performed the rites and sent him down the river. In his next life, he will be a great man."

"You are speaking of an animal's good fortune at a time like this?" Swaroop scoffed.

Quickly, the buffoon bowed his head. "Please forgive me."

"Is there anyone at the palace who might have taken the maharaja out?" Colin asked.

"We are all like a family; we love each other," Aditya answered after a pause. "And the dowager maharani asked the durwans if any visitors came to the palace. They said nobody came to the palace except for her and the bearers of the palanquin."

"Servants and ladies-in-waiting can leave the palace, can't they?" Perveen asked, thinking the enemy was most likely from within.

"After Maharaja Mahendra Rao's death, many servants were let go. The maharanis wished for fewer, deeply trusted people to serve." Aditya's words showed how highly he thought of himself, and how he wished for everyone to recognize his status.

Yet he had misunderstood her question. It was likely because he was weary from having traveled so far and in darkness. How had he made it? Perveen reprised the invitation Colin had made earlier. "If you'd like, Rama will set an extra plate for your meal."

Aditya nodded gratefully, but as he moved toward the table, the prince spoke in a snappish tone.

"No. He eats with the other servants."

Perveen's shoulders flinched. The maharanis both treated Aditya almost in the same manner they would a courtier, so she had expected Prince Swaroop would do the same. And Aditya's stony expression told her that he didn't appreciate being dismissed so rudely.

"Rama, bring this man's meal to the tea table on the veranda." Colin spoke quietly, and Perveen sensed he was trying to make up for the lapse of protocol without offending either side. "There is a washroom two doors to the left, just along the way."

The buffoon stalked out of the parlor.

Rama edged closer to Colin and murmured, "But there is no more food in the kitchen! Everything is on this table."

Colin's eyes darted to the scant food left on silver trays and bowls. "If everyone here has had enough, I'll have Rama prepare a plate."

Prince Swaroop pulled a chicken bone from his mouth and said, "This circuit house has gone to the dogs."

Rama went into the kitchen and came back with the kind of metal plate used to give food to beggars or workmen. She supposed he was using it because he understood the caste restrictions Prince Swaroop was pointing to. Not looking at the courtier or Prince Swaroop, Rama spooned leftover rice and vegetables onto it. There was no vindaloo left.

"So we are fed the same as servants!" Jaqinder Dhillon said in low Marathi to the prince.

"Sorry, but we were not expecting royal visitors," Colin shot back in the same tongue.

Watching Rama walk out with the half-filled plate, Prince Swaroop drained his glass. "Is there more? Or are the bottles as empty as the kitchen cupboard?"

Colin tilted the claret bottle. "It's empty. Tomorrow, breakfast will be at eight because we must set out for the train station by nine."

Perveen kept her eyes on the half-open door to the veranda. She didn't want to agree with any part of Colin's plan, but she wanted the prince and his men to follow along. Aditya, too.

She knew that with the men gone to Poona, she'd have a better chance at reaching the palace and finding out what she needed to know.

20

DIVERGING JOURNEYS

At sunrise the next morning, Perveen lit the candle at her bedside. After splashing water on her face, she dressed in the split skirt, blouse, and jacket she'd packed in Bombay. She filled a small bag with essentials: a flask of water, her notebook and pen, and the battery torch. Holding her boots in one hand and the pack in the other, she tiptoed quietly to the veranda. She did not want to make noise and wake anyone.

But someone was already waiting.

"Good morning," Colin said from the planter's chair that was his favorite. She noticed he was fully dressed in trousers, a white linen shirt, and boots.

"Good morning. No yoga today?" She had been counting on his being absent.

"No time for it. But look over there."

Although a mist was heavy, she saw movement in the jacaranda tree and recognized the monkey group. Hanuman dropped down to the grass, followed by four monkeys of similar sizes.

Despite her desire to get underway, Perveen couldn't help smiling. "His family travels together."

"Yes. They've always got company, and they can protect each other. We humans could learn from them." He sighed, then turned back to appraise her riding costume. "So what is this about?"

Perveen was mindful of the long line of guest rooms adjacent to the veranda. Tilting her head toward them, she murmured, "I'll talk to you in the garden."

Colin followed her over to the jacaranda tree, where there was an iron bench overlooking the hills. She seated herself on the bench and began working on putting on her boots. She'd noted that Colin wasn't using his cane. She wondered if he was feeling better than the day before or if he was trying to present an impression of strength for Prince Swaroop.

Looking at her lacing up the boots, he said, "Your dress makes me think you aren't planning on visiting the administration in Poona."

Perveen would not let him talk her out of her plan. "Yes, I have different intentions. I would like it very much if you'd meet me at the palace later on with whatever search party you can muster. I'll make sure that you are allowed in."

Colin had not seated himself. He kicked at a white stone that lay between them. Keeping his eyes on the stone, he asked, "The prince doesn't know where you're headed, does he?"

His question exasperated her. "Of course not. I don't trust him as far as you kicked that stone. Though I believe what he said about paying Roderick Ames to do a private job for him—did you understand that?"

"Mostly," Colin said. "And it's a conundrum for me. It is against ICS policy for us to take money from outside employers."

"You said that earlier. I have reason to believe that Roderick might also have explored working for Yazad Mehta. They went somewhere together the morning after we all had dinner."

Colin shook his head. "And if I say something about that relationship—I'll lose my friendship with Yazad."

"It's a hard position to be in."

"Yes. I would rather focus on another problem. What will I say to Prince Swaroop about your absence this morning?"

Perveen bent to pick up the stone, which had landed a few inches from her feet. It felt smooth and cool in her hand. It seemed arbitrary whether a stone was considered precious or not. It was the same with people.

"What you tell him is up to you. I don't think he'll miss my company at all. If you tell him where I've gone, though, he might chase after me instead of going to Poona with you."

Colin looked over his shoulder toward the circuit house, as if to check that no one had come out. "I could say you left word you were not in the mood to go to Poona. But I'm afraid it could be difficult for you to rouse Lakshman to get the men to carry the palanquin so early in the day."

"Lakshman and the bearers are too exhausted," Perveen agreed. "I was not planning on asking for their help. I rather hoped to borrow a horse from your stable."

Colin's eyes widened. "How will you recognize the way to the palace when you were inside a curtained palanquin the whole time? And horseback riding is difficult in certain parts of the forest."

Perveen would not address her own private fears. Instead, she said, "I kept the curtains open for most of my journeys. I saw quite a few landmarks. Also, there's a path worn through the jungle. The journey is quite simple to manage, as long as it's not dark."

A bright green parakeet swooped down from a tree, startling them both. Colin almost lost his balance.

"Do sit down," Perveen urged him, and he did, keeping a judicious foot of space between them on the bench.

"When you left two days ago, I was anxious that you wouldn't be allowed in. But now—my anxiety's different." Colin let out a gusty breath before continuing. "I'm quite worried about your safety. If you're killed at the palace, or on the way to it, what will I say to your husband? That I just sent you off completely alone?"

"Oh, shut up! He's not even in the picture frame!" The impolite words burst from Perveen before she could stop them.

But Colin seemed more perplexed than offended. "What does that mean?"

She hadn't meant to divulge anything, but she didn't want him using her husband as a tool against her. In a tight voice, she said, "That man is as good as dead to me. He's not part of my life. If I were killed, it would actually be to his advantage."

Colin leaned back as if to better evaluate her. "Are you saying that you live apart?"

"Oh yes." Perveen tried to sound nonchalant. "He's more than a thousand miles away. And I wish it were farther."

"You are divorced?"

Perveen was annoyed by his calm-sounding question. "No. I cannot divorce Cyrus, because the abuse he gave me was not severe enough. A Parsi woman can only get a divorce if the damage is quite severe—loss of an eye, or a limb."

Colin's face had paled at her words. She wondered if her speaking of a lost limb had made him think of his own loss. When he spoke, his voice was shaky. "But you live in British India and are a subject, just like me. Divorce is not impossible. Surely this could be brought to the court. What about adultery?"

"There is an adultery provision for divorce among Parsis; however the accused spouse must commit adultery with a person who is not a prostitute. And I don't have that evidence."

"I can't believe marriage is so restrictive for such a progressive religion," he said, frowning.

"The British approved the standing laws made by Parsi males," she pointed out. "Your government also upholds unfair family laws in other Indian religious communities: rules that keep daughters from inheriting as much as sons, widows from owning property, and men and women from leaving unhappy marriages."

Colin shook his head. "I didn't know about any of this. I feel like a fool."

She longed to put out a hand to touch his; it was clear he was shocked. But that would be improper. Softly, she said, "I'm trusting you with this information about me. The Agency might not have hired me if they knew of my tarnished past."

"They will not hear anything from me. I shall keep that confidential information close." He touched the front of his shirt, just over his chest. "And please know that I think you are a very brave woman to have found a way to leave. Thank God for that."

She felt her cheeks warming. "Can we please end this overly personal talk? I was on my way to the stable. If you are willing to lend me a horse."

"As much as I worry about you, I will not try to restrain you. Too many have already done that." Colin pushed himself up to standing again. "I need to make sure you get away before Prince Swaroop awakens."

Perveen could not begin to express how grateful she felt for his confidence. So she merely said, "I look forward to seeing you when you arrive at the palace."

Colin tilted his face to the sky. "The fog is lifting from the hills. I hope the weather stays fine for both of our journeys."

Perveen set off a half hour later with a shawl wrapped around her shoulders to protect her from the cool morning air. Her essential supplies were loaded into a saddlebag, including a small tiffin box with breakfast food that Rama had quickly prepared. Mohit was sleeping in the stable. Once roused, he helped Perveen mount the same horse, Rani, who'd carried her three days before. As she trotted downhill, it seemed that the small spotted mare finally understood what her nudges meant. She hoped Rani would be responsive and surefooted along the steep and wet sections she remembered from the palanquin ride.

As the path wound along the wall that bordered Heaven's Rest, the Mehta estate, Perveen saw the same guards who had been on duty the day before. As she came level with them, she pulled back on the reins to halt Rani. "How is the burra-memsahib?"

The senior guard glanced sideways as if he was nervous about something. "She is not well. The doctor has come."

Through the open gate, Perveen saw the same dark horse that

the doctor had ridden away from the circuit house. The saddle-bags were marked with a red cross, a detail she hadn't noticed earlier.

"We cannot admit anyone until he has determined it is safe," the younger guard piped up.

Suddenly, Perveen remembered what the doctor had said about two children getting cholera. How could it have spread here, to this walled estate? "Does she have cholera?"

"He has not said yet!" The older guard gave the young one a reproving frown. "But she has been very sick. When the sahib returns, he may not be able to come inside either."

Perveen was flooded with pity for Vandana. No matter how deceptive the woman might have been, she did not deserve this kind of suffering. And Perveen knew she could not go in to see Vandana; the risk of carrying germs to the royal family was too high.

"I will pray for her recovery at Aranyani's shrine's," Perveen said. Even though she was not a Hindu, making a quick Zoro-astrian prayer there would be a comfort, when she felt worries coming from every direction. "Will you tell her maid to tell this to memsahib?"

"That is her chief deity," the older guard said, and gave her a slight nod. Perveen said goodbye to them, now understanding that the tension she'd seen in their faces was not because they disliked her. They were frightened for their employer, and they probably realized that their own welfare was also at risk.

Perveen nudged Rani with her heel, encouraging the horse onward. Fog was sweeping in, and this seemed ominous. She did not know what she was heading into. She had no idea if Prince Jiva Rao was still alive, nor could she know that Colin's trip to Poona would go well and result in military support for the search.

Riding through the village, she saw many more villagers were out than the previous morning she'd been there. Perveen steered her horse carefully, keeping her head down and concentrating on the route. She hoped that the eccentric costume might keep them from recognizing her, but judging by the scrutiny, she doubted it.

As she continued on into the outer edge of the forest, where the trees were thinner and more flowers grew than deeper in the woods, she thought more about Vandana. If Dr. Andrews couldn't help her, it would be a tragic homecoming for her husband. Perveen wondered if Yazad knew anything about the moonstone pendant Vandana had manipulated Perveen into bringing to the rajmata. Perhaps he had been the one pushing the idea that it should go to the palace. But why? She needed to concentrate on catching the turn for the temple. She was also keeping watch for any signs of human movement—although she hardly expected that Jiva Rao could have traveled this far by himself.

Perveen rode on until she saw the crumbled pillars set a few hundred feet before the old temple. Gently, she guided Rani to walk onward. As they entered the temple grounds, Perveen saw that the brass bowl where Lakshman had left money before was brimming with wild orchids. Here, in the midst of the forest, Aranyani was being worshipped.

She coaxed Rani over to where a large dead tree lay fallen on its side. It was the right height to use as a step-down platform. She stepped off safely and brought Rani to the small stream near where the palanquin bearers had taken lunch.

"Don't leave me," she said, patting the horse on her flank before turning toward the shrine she had refused to approach before. It was a large cylindrical gray rock with an alcove carved into it. Inside there was a roughly carved black stone figure. From the breasts jutting forward, she knew it was an image of a woman, but there were none of the elaborate hairstyles or other artistic flourishes that were present in most religious statuary.

The cawing of a bird brought Perveen away from her wonder at the old statue and back to the present moment. Perveen wandered into a different part of the temple garden in order to face the hills. She felt for the kusti inside the waist of her skirt and began to move her hands along it, whispering her prayer. She prayed that Mirabai had found her son. As she prayed, she felt as if she was harnessing the energy of the thousands of animals and insects around her. She was not a believer in Aranyani, but if the goddess wanted to help her, she would accept it.

She had just finished when she heard a crunching sound on the ground. It was not a human footstep; it sounded like a larger animal.

Her stomach lurched as she turned slowly, fearing the worst.

But it was a man coming toward her on a horse. She stayed stock-still, because she knew she couldn't possibly get to Rani fast enough to get away. She could only hope it wasn't one of the two men she feared most: Roderick Ames and Prince Swaroop.

As the figure drew nearer, she saw he was small and humbly dressed. He had a shock of silver hair. Blinking, she called out, "Rama-ji, is that you?"

"Yes. Sandringham-sahib sent me after you. He did not want you to become lost."

Perveen smiled, thinking Colin had found a way to reassure himself of her safety. But Rama was not a palanquin bearer; how would he know the way any better than she did? When she broached the subject, he smiled.

"Along the route to the palace, there are different pieces of land. In one section, I know I will find a thicket of brahmi plants. In another, ashwagandha. I know these places."

"That is fortunate for me." Perveen was sincerely glad to have him accompanying her.

"I will bring my horse to the stream for a drink of water. And then I will make my prayers for the safety of the maharaja," Rama said, walking his horse to the stream. "It will not be long."

After Rama had walked to the temple, Perveen returned to the stream, where both horses had their heads bowed over the clear water. They drank on and on, even though it was not hot. It seemed as if the animals understood there was a complicated journey ahead.

Without argument, Perveen let Rama lead the way. Rani seemed happy to follow the slowly moving horse in front of her. After an hour and a half of slow, careful riding, the palace's high gray towers appeared in the distance. As they drew closer, Perveen sensed a difference. It wasn't until she was going up the stone path to the palace that she saw there were no durwans guarding the main entrance.

Rama, who had been riding just a few feet ahead of her, stopped. He held his horse's reins so she could draw alongside.

He looked at her and shook his head. "No guards. That is not good."

"There were guards there at the time I left. They might be away now because they are looking for the maharaja."

Perveen took a long drink of water from the flask and, from the saddlebag, took out her notebook and pen. These she tucked into the deep pocket of the split skirt, which was turning out to be a more useful garment than she'd ever expected.

Two peasant children emerged from the shadows of the wall. Each of them held a knife. Alongside them was the tall white dog, Ganesan. He growled at Rama, but when Perveen called out to him, he recognized her, barking happily and wagging his tail.

"So you are the guards today!" Perveen said in a friendly manner to the children, gesturing for the younger one to come closer and hold Rani's reins. He did so, and she managed to slide off. Ganesan half-jumped on her, and she petted him, cooing all the while.

"Where are the durwans?" Rama said to the children, speaking in the local dialect.

"The prince is gone. A fancy Parsi lady took him!" the younger boy said.

As Rama looked at her, Perveen took a deep breath. She realized that because of the strange riding clothes, she hadn't been identified. "I am the Parsi lady, but I never took the maharaja. I've come here to tell the maharanis that I don't have him. I will do my best to find him."

"Only family members are allowed inside." The older boy's voice wavered. "And this is not the ladies' gate. That is on the other side."

Perveen was surprised. She hadn't been told about a ladies' gate to enter the palace structure before. Could that gate have been the way the prince was taken from the palace?

"Can you kindly show us the way to the ladies' gate?" Perveen was using formal language that was not typical when speaking with poor children or servants. It was a gamble, and the younger child snickered, but she could see the older one felt pleased to be treated with respect.

"Your grandfather cannot go inside the zenana," the younger child said, looking at Rama.

"I would not disrespect the palace. But I shall walk alongside her to this gate," Rama said. His insistence on staying near reminded her that despite the fact that children were guarding the outside of the palace, she had no idea who might be waiting inside.

A few minutes later, they were standing outside another gate, but it was a curious one, about four feet tall.

"Is this gate meant for children?" Perveen asked.

"No. It is for the maharanis' protection," said the older child guard. "People must bend to go inside. The servant standing inside can see who is coming."

"If not a lady, cut off the head!" said the younger child with a giggle.

With a grinding sound, the bar over the small door slid up. The comment the child had made about cutting off the head didn't seem funny to Perveen. The fact that the door was being raised meant somebody was there on the other side, waiting.

Yes, she was a woman—but that hadn't stopped her from being targeted for poisoning. Was this archaic doorway part of another attempt to end her life? She glanced at the older boy, who was fiddling with the edge of his lungi and looking nervous. She could urge him to step through the gate ahead of her, but he would likely refuse for fear of getting in trouble.

She looked at Ganesan, who had not left her side since she'd arrived. He stood by her with a slowly waving tail. She put a hand on his smooth, warm fur and was glad to have a strong friend.

"Go ahead," she said, pushing on his hindquarters as he headed through the gate. He was deft and could avoid any knife. On the other side, she heard a woman's soft laughter; and in the next instant, she took a deep breath, bent herself in half, and crept through.

"Are you safe?" Rama called after her in English.

Perveen found herself in a vestibule that she remembered from her first night. The square room was largely unfurnished but had a lavish mosaic tile floor. Sitting on cushions was the same cluster of ladies-in-waiting she had seen in the durbar hall, as well as serving maids crouched off to the side. Keeping her eyes on them, she answered, "I am quite fine. There are a few gentle-women and some maids, but nobody else."

"The men are all away looking for the maharaja!" The speaker with a high-pitched, emphatic voice was the same petite, fair woman who had assisted the previous day when Maharani Put-labai had thrown her scepter.

Perveen raised her hands in a gesture of emptiness. "I did not take him. The reason I'm here is to help find him. May I know your name?"

"I am Archana. I am the rajmata's lady-in-waiting." From her tone, it was clear she saw herself as the zenana's executive officer.

"And how is the rajmata?"

Archana looked grave. "She has taken to her bed. We all fear for her health."

Although Archana's allegiance was supposed to be the rajmata, Perveen imagined Archana knew everything going on with both maharanis. That was the nature of zenana life. "Is the maharani Mirabai back in the palace?"

"Not back yet."

Perveen's concern was rising. If Aditya's account was accurate, this meant the junior maharani had been missing for more than twelve hours. "It is strange to me that she went out without taking Ganesan along."

Archana paused as if to ponder this. "It could be she knew the journey would be too long for him?"

Perveen was not satisfied. "Are the men who are seeking the maharaja searching for her, too?"

Archana regarded her with a patronizing smile. "Everyone wants to know where she is. But the men cannot approach her, because they don't want to break purdah."

Perveen mulled this over. "It would also be difficult for them to recognize her if they've never seen her."

"She dresses in her special suit when she rides. She would appear like a man to outsiders—but we would know her."

"A man's riding habit?"

"No, it is the livery of a palace messenger." Archana dropped her voice as if she thought this shameful. "She had the suit specially made for her. She does not think the rajmata knows about it."

Although, Perveen thought, Archana surely had told her.

"Memsahib, I am sorry to interrupt. Where shall I wait for you?" It was Rama, speaking from the outside.

"The front of the old palace, please." He would be able to speak to Colin and the others when they arrived, whether it was later in the day or the next morning. She also knew that if Rama needed to enter the palace, that would be the only gate where he'd be allowed in.

21
WHAT THE PRINCESS SAW

*P*erveen had spoken confidently to Rama, but inside, she still felt doubts. She hoped Archana and the other palace women truly believed she was innocent of kidnapping. And now the issue of a vanished maharani seemed as pressing as that of Prince Jiva Rao's disappearance.

"Will you come with me, memsahib? The dog cannot come along. Rajmata does not like him." Swiftly, Archana was moving toward an archway opening into the zenana's long hallway. Perveen wondered if she would be led to an interview with the rajmata, or something entirely worse.

"Wait. I must speak to her first."

Perveen wheeled about, startled because she hadn't seen Mr. Basu in the zenana. There was a long shadow behind the cream marble jali wall, though. "Is that you, Basu-sahib?"

"Yes," he answered in his wavering voice. "Please come through the door so that I can address you."

Perveen looked about in confusion. "I don't see a door." .

"Here." Archana unlocked a door crafted of the same marble fretwork as the rest of the jali wall. There was no knob, and the whole door had been fitted in so ingeniously, with the pattern matching the wall, that it was close to invisible.

Archana stayed behind in the zenana and closed the door as Perveen stepped through. Mr. Basu was standing in the darkened main hall. His head and shoulders were bowed, as if he was in mourning. Perveen wondered if he knew something that nobody else did.

"I never thought you would come back." His voice was heavy. "But it is good. If you are here, it must mean you did not take him."

His statement revived her hopeful feeling "You are correct. I am worried for the maharaja. Will you tell me exactly where people have searched?"

His narrow shoulders rose up and then dropped, making him look helpless. "Where haven't we looked? Through the palace, through the gardens."

"Is there a map of the old and new palace rooms? He could be hiding."

"I don't need a map," he said, the impatience in his tone reminding her of Prince Swaroop. "There are hundreds of rooms. The guards have searched them all. Now they are spread out through the forest."

How strange that she hadn't seen any while traveling with Rama. "How trustworthy are these guards? Do you know each and every one?"

"I do. They would have no reason to hurt their future monarch."

She moved closer to him and lowered her voice. "Would you say the guards in the old palace are more loyal to the dowager and the ones in the new palace to Maharani Mirabai?"

"It should not be that way, because it is one family." Sighing, he added, "I think this business of running after children is too much for my heart."

Noticing the sweat on his brow, Perveen said, "I pray your health will be fine. Take all the rest you need—I am here to manage the search. Your word as palace officer to give me authority will be helpful."

He passed a hand over his eyes and said, "Yes, you must look everywhere. If the maharaja is found, I will ask the maharanis if they will allow my retirement. An old teacher like me should not be living longer than his princes."

Perveen sensed he was hiding tears and felt a rush of sympathy. Pulling a fresh handkerchief from her pocket, she put it into his hand. "It must feel very sad to lose your maharajas. A different kind of sadness than what most feel."

The teacher pressed the cotton cloth to his eyes. "Yes. All the dreams I had for them to take their place in history are gone. And the shame is that with the maharaja Jiva Rao, I had not taught him enough. If he dies, he goes into his next life knowing too little."

"We should not expect the worst," Perveen said softly. "By the way, I have an assistant from the circuit house waiting for me by the front entrance."

Mr. Basu took the handkerchief away from his eyes and blinked. "An Englishman?"

"No. Rama-ji is an Ayurvedic doctor," she said, because identifying him as a cook or yogi would probably not get him through the gate. "He knows the landscape very well because he gathers herbs. If Rama-ji wishes to come inside to speak with me, will you please allow him to?"

"I will tell the staff," Mr. Basu said with a decisive nod. "Then I will wait downstairs in my study, if you need something more."

"I would like to see the rajkumari," Perveen said. "Will you please bring me to her?"

"Eh? Why her?" He sounded irritated.

"Princess Padmabai is missing both her mother and brother. The confusion must be so much for her. She may be very sad and frightened." Perveen was surprised she had to spell it out for him.

"That is not true. We hear that she has been playing all day," said Archana casually from the other side of the jali.

Perveen felt she was being blocked. "I would appreciate it if someone would bring me to her—"

Archana's voice answered her in the same maddening tone. "It is not possible. Nobody is willing to take you."

It was a struggle not to let her anger show. "You just heard that

Basu-sahib gave me clearance to search the palace. Because the princess no longer has a living father, I am her legal guardian. I am most concerned."

Archana's voice was cool. "I believe you. But nobody wishes to accompany you. They say you have put nazar on everyone."

Perveen was horrified. "I have no such powers. I am just an ordinary woman."

There was a long silence and then finally a soft voice. "I will take her."

There was a great murmuring among the ladies-in-waiting on the other side of the golden screen. Then the unseen Archana spoke again. "She is allowed."

The golden door within the wall swung open, and a middle-aged maid dressed in a modest blue-and-white sari stepped through. Perveen smiled at her encouragingly. "What is your name?"

Pressing her hands together in a namaste, the maid murmured, "Swagata. Everything bad that could happen to my family has already occurred. It does not matter if I sacrifice."

As they set off, leaving the old palace's halls and heading toward the courtyard, Perveen tried to reassure the maid, who had kept her head down and walked stiffly. "Swagata-bai, I will not cause you suffering. I only wish to be led to the princess."

"I will do that. But do not give me any money or papers."

Perveen walked along, thinking about what the maid had said. "Does this have to do with Chitra?"

Swagata looked sideways at her. "Yes. She is my daughter. Because of what you gave her, she was put in the palace jail."

Perveen felt jolted. "Where is this jail?"

"Underneath the old palace." Swagata's mouth twisted with worry. "It is wet and cold, and there are rats."

"And criminals?" Perveen could not hide her alarm.

"Nobody else is staying there now. But in the old days, the maharajas put thieves there. It has a very bad atmosphere."

Perveen felt dreadful about the request she'd made to post the letter—especially since she had made it safely to the circuit house before the letter had arrived. "I am so very sorry. I can't imagine who accused your daughter of doing something wrong."

"Someone was in the hallway outside your room. There are guards everywhere," Swagata said in a heavy voice. "It is only because they are hunting for the maharaja that they are not in every corner of every hall, listening."

Looking past the palace's columns into shadowy darkness, Perveen did believe they were necessarily alone. What she said aloud could be repeated. "What happened to Chitra was unjust. I will speak to Rajmata about it."

"After you see the princess?" Swagata's eyes were keen.

"Yes. Right after that."

On the new palace's first floor, the nursery door was open. Padmabai sat in the middle of a pink-and-green Agra carpet, bent over a large, fancy English doll. As she approached, Perveen saw that the child had a small pair of silver nail-scissors in her hand, and she had cut off half the doll's black curls.

Padmabai looked up when her ayah, a thin elderly lady, yelped at the sight of Perveen. Then the ayah spoke rapidly to Swagata in the same regional dialect that Perveen had heard among the palanquin bearers. Swagata translated for Perveen. "She was fearful at the sight of you. I explained that you did not take the maharaja. That you came back to help."

"I must ask Princess Padmabai some questions," Perveen said in Marathi to Swagata. The senior maid relayed this to the ayah, who settled down on the floor, keeping a suspicious gaze on Perveen. Perveen felt uncomfortable having the women there, because she knew they understood Marathi. "It would be very kind if you waited just outside the room. I'll call out for your help if the princess doesn't understand something."

Judging from both maids' expressions, Perveen gathered they

were reluctant to leave the remaining royal child alone with someone believed to have the evil eye. However, they couldn't blatantly disrespect a high-ranking visitor like Perveen.

Perveen closed the heavy door behind her and approached Princess Padmabai. Settling down on the carpet next to her, Perveen asked, "What is your doll doing?"

With a serious expression, Padmabai answered, "She is preparing. Her hair must be cut, and she will wear a white sari."

The young child might have remembered what her mother or grandmother had done after Prince Pratap Rao's death. So Padmabai had assumed the worst about Prince Jiva Rao. "I understand. Please tell me about what you did with your brother yesterday."

Pausing with the scissors, Padmabai gave her an annoyed look. "Everyone asked me that already!"

Perveen recalled that she was supposed to speak to any royal family member with respect. How could she do that and still elicit information? "You know that I wasn't there with them. Please tell me."

Padmabai began snipping again. "We played on the roof with the kite. Then Uncle came, and you went with him to talk. Then Aditya was crying because his monkey died. I cried, too. How could he die? It's not fair. And then my brother was crying."

"About the monkey?"

The girl looked at her but didn't answer.

She tried again. "What was the maharaja crying about?"

Padmabai shook her head vehemently. "I should not tell you."

Not wanting to frighten the child, Perveen chose her words carefully. "Princess Padmabai, I think your brother might be lost. It's very frightening for him. I must find him."

"Oh no! He is not frightened. He is going to a good place."

Perveen had a sudden awful thought of the jail that Swagata had mentioned. What if he knew about it and had gone there— and perhaps been trapped somehow? "Is it inside the palace?"

When the princess didn't answer, Perveen pressed on. "Please tell me the truth. You are such a smart girl that you must know the truth."

"I am not a girl!" Padmabai retorted. "I am a princess."

Perveen tried another approach. "Princess Padmabai, you play in many places—and the old palace and new one together have hundreds of rooms and even places underground. Could he be hiding in one of them?"

She shook her head.

"How do you know?"

"I watched from the roof when he ran away."

Perveen tried to hide her excitement because she didn't want Padmabai to realize she'd given up a major clue. "Your eyes are sharp, even when you don't have binoculars. How did he leave the palace when it is guarded?"

"He went through the little zenana door when all the ladies were taking their tea."

"That was clever of him. Where is he running?"

Padmabai remained silent.

"Why won't you say?"

"He told me not to tell anyone."

She changed tactics. "Why did he leave?" When Padmabai shook her head again, Perveen said, "It's important you tell me all that he said. I want you to be able to see your brother again."

Padmabai shook her head, this time so vigorously that her short braids flew out. "But you will take him away from our home to a school."

Perveen felt sick. Either the boy had listened outside the zenana durbar hall, or someone had told him about her conversation with the maharanis. "I won't make him go anywhere he doesn't want to be. I can promise you that. Do you believe me?"

Padmabai gave her a long look, and then finally nodded.

"Where was he going?"

"Uncle's palace."

As she'd expected, Swaroop was involved. "Did your uncle tell him to go there?"

"No. I told you, he went walking on his own."

She recalled the Mercedes Cardan that Prince Swaroop had arrived in. He could easily have picked the boy up en route, driven him the rest of the way to his palace, and left him confined there before racing off with a party on horseback to the circuit house. In this scenario, Swaroop could blame the boy's disappearance on Perveen.

"We know the way." Padmabai put down her doll and used her hands to point. "We can see the top of the palace from where we play kites."

The issue now was to understand the direction he'd headed. "I see you pointing, but I don't understand. Let's go up to the roof."

Both maids insisted on following when Perveen came out of the room and told them, "We're going up to the roof to look around. Can you please bring me Rajmata's binoculars?"

"But I have them," Padmabai said, pointing to a wicker toy box.

Up on the roof, a warm breeze caught at Perveen's hair. She followed Padmabai to the western side of the palace. The child pointed, and Perveen saw, after what looked like a few miles of trees, something brown poking up through them.

Perveen took hold of the binoculars and, after focusing, realized Padmabai had pointed to a chimney. The residence was closer than Perveen had thought. "Did your uncle ever tell you or your brother you could go to visit him there?"

"Of course he did. But our mother doesn't want us to," Perveen said in a sweet lilt.

Mirabai probably feared for their safety—and she herself could not go with them, as a woman in purdah. Gazing at the distant chimney, Perveen was struck by another thought. Looking at Swagata, she said, "When Prince Swaroop arrived yesterday, I saw him come from the other side."

"Yes! His palace is on the east," Swagata said, turning to point to the other side of the roof.

But Padmabai was standing on the western side of the roof, which overlooked the hilly forest that stood between the palace and the circuit house. Perveen put her hand on Padmabai's small shoulder. "Are you very sure he was on this side of the palace? The road is not there."

"I watched him leave through the garden going that way. Uncle's palace is there." Her voice was insistent.

Looking down at Padmabai, Perveen asked, "Do you remember the times you went to Uncle's palace before?"

"Yes," chirped the princess. "It's splendid like Toad Hall!"

Perveen smiled at the reference to *The Wind in the Willows*. "Toad Hall has a fireplace. Does your uncle's palace have one also?"

Padmabai looked at her blankly. "What is a fireplace?"

"It is a place inside the main house for burning wood for warmth in wintertime."

Padmabai's voice came more slowly. "I am not sure."

"The hunting lodge has a fireplace," Perveen said. "I saw it when I visited there yesterday. I think the lodge is the building with the bit of chimney poking up through the trees.

"The question is whether the maharaja could reach the lodge. It's about an hour's palanquin ride from here," Perveen mused aloud. Because the maharaja was a child, it would take him longer than an hour. There was an uneven, rough earthen path to follow. There were forks along the path, but it was conceivable the maharaja would have found the hunting lodge.

Perveen looked at the sky. It wasn't yet noon, and the earlier clouds had given way to clear sunshine. There was time and good weather for her to safely get to the lodge. But before that, she would have to tell the dowager maharani what she'd learned.

22

A POISONOUS WOMAN

The maids surrounded Princess Padmabai as she went down the narrow stair that led from the roof to the palace's third floor. Then the ayah took her back to the nursery while Swagata led Perveen down to the ground floor and then into the old palace.

As the two of them walked, Perveen said, "You are the rajmata's princess maid. You know her mood very well."

Swagata's lips were set in a hard line. "Yes."

Perveen guessed that whatever loyalty the maid might have felt toward the old maharani was overshadowed by the maid's resentment at how the dowager had jailed her daughter. "I will speak to Rajmata about Chitra, but I am trying to understand what her mood has been like since Jiva Rao's disappearance. Is she very angry? Is she sad?"

"She has not said very much. She asked for the servants to find clean formal clothing for everyone. That must be why the little princess was preparing her doll for mourning."

"Both of their lives have been marked by so much death," Perveen said. What she couldn't express yet was the question in her mind: Was the dowager maharani preparing merely because she was fatalistic, or because she knew something?

They went through the gold door again into the zenana. After passing the durbar hall, Swagata showed her to a steep stairway patterned with inset stone designs of lotus flowers and vines.

Gesturing to it, she told Perveen, "The dowager's room is up this way."

"She can walk up such steep steps?" Perveen had only seen the elderly woman sitting down.

"No. She is carried," said Archana, who looked down at them from the floor above.

"By women?" Perveen asked.

"Oh yes!" Archana delivered an overly sweet smile. "We would do anything for her."

Perveen thought about what Archana might be capable of as she followed the lady-in-waiting to the rajmata's chambers. Following in their wake was a phalanx of more gentlewomen, whispering among themselves, and Swagata, who kept several paces behind, as if mindful of her lowly status, yet determined to guard Perveen. The rajmata's bedroom was round, revealing that it had been carved out of one of the castle's towers. But it did not have the bird's-eye view that Perveen had expected. Instead, its small windows were shielded by jali screens that threw dappled light across the floor and bed. The royal bed was a simple charpoy made of ropes and canvas, although the covers were lush silk embroidered in gold. The rajmata lay on her back with her head and shoulders propped up on a bolster. Her eyes were closed, but when Perveen spoke to her, they fluttered open.

"Namaste, Rajmata." Perveen folded her hands together in the gesture of respect. "I came to help find the maharaja."

Swagata had taken a spot crouching by the room's door. Her eyes were fixed on the rajmata, as if she was afraid what might happen next.

A gnarled finger emerged from under the silk and pointed toward Perveen. "How can you find him when my men could not?"

"Because I've learned something from the princess that could help us know where to look," Perveen said.

"Impossible!" the queen shot back. "The princess already

was questioned. She did not see anyone take the prince, but it probably happened when she was playing with her dolls."

Perveen was not encountering the quiet, mournful rajmata whom Swagata had described. The queen must have distrusted Perveen so much that her behavior shifted in her presence. And she didn't trust the rajmata either.

"The good news is the maharaja might not have been kidnapped," she said, settling down on a velvet stool near the bed so the dowager could see her. As Perveen looked at Putlabai, she waited for the wrinkled-walnut expression on the lady's face to relax. It did not.

Maharani Putlabai heard Perveen's account of what she'd learned without interruption. At the end, the maharani reached out a frail hand toward her bedside. Swagata placed the cup of tea that was waiting there against the queen's lips. After she drank, she spoke. "There are two dozen men searching already. If the princess is speaking the truth, why haven't they found him?"

"It could be that he hid from them—or that he's reached the lodge, or that he's been helped by someone to reach your son's palace. Actually, it is possible that Prince Swaroop is involved in this disappearance." Perveen paused, letting the words sink in. "Just as he was involved when Prince Pratap Rao was lost."

"My son was innocent then and is innocent now. He would never tell the maharaja to make such a journey on foot." The rajmata shifted in her bed, and Perveen saw that although the woman wore a silk nightdress, the moonstone pendant was shining at the base of her throat.

Perveen decided that the least she could do was ask some more questions. Discreetly opening the notebook she'd carried in, she began writing. "When exactly did Prince Swaroop leave this palace?"

The dowager glanced at the notebook. "Yes, write what I say, because it is the truth. Sometime midafternoon. It was after the letter was read."

"The letter?" Perveen repeated, not understanding.

"My son brought me a terrible letter Chitra was sending out of the palace. It was to the English telling them that this palace is run by criminals."

She felt herself flush hot with embarrassment. "I wrote the letter, and it certainly did not say that. I included the information that I already expressed to you on the maharaja's education. I also mentioned the possible poisoning I described to you and other concerns Maharani Mirabai shared with me. Chitra should not have been jailed for agreeing to post this letter."

As Perveen was talking, Swagata had come forward from her crouch against the wall and prostrated herself on the floor. Not looking up, she murmured, "Please, Rajmata. Kindly let my innocent girl go back to her work."

"Do not tell me what to do!" the dowager shot back.

Disheartened by the reaction, Perveen turned to look over the assemblage of ladies-in-waiting and maids. The maids all had their faces toward the floor, as if they shared Swagata's pain, but a couple of the ladies-in-waiting had hands over their mouths, as if hiding laughter. Trying to sound neutral, Perveen addressed the noblewomen. "Here's a question for you. Who traveled here with Prince Swaroop, when he came in his car?"

"We are always staying in the zenana. How can we know?" Archana asked with a shrug of her narrow shoulders.

Perveen pointed to the jali windows. "The jali screens allow intelligent women to see and hear every visitor."

Beaming slightly, a chubby maid spoke up. "I have good ears and eyes! Aditya told us that he brought three guards."

"Did they leave by car?"

"Yes, they were going back to his palace on the good road. He wished to gather weaponry and horses from there for trekking through the woods."

The search would have been immediate if the men had used

horses and whatever weapons they wanted from this palace. Why had Prince Swaroop insisted on going to his own palace first?

Perhaps he had found the maharaja along the way and put him somewhere for safekeeping—or killed him. Perveen considered the idea and dismissed it. With three witnesses, it would have been a great risk for the prince to pull off any malign action.

But Roderick Ames had been in the hills over the past two days, so he was suspect. "Have you ever heard of an electrical engineer called Roderick Ames?"

The young maid shook her head. "No. Is he an Englishman?"

"He's actually an Anglo-Indian. And he was on the hunt where the last maharaja was killed." She looked toward the ladies-in-waiting. "Perhaps someone saw this man through the jali screen."

"I have heard the name. He is the man who went to fetch the doctor after the hunt," Archana said. "Remember, Rajmata?"

"The doctor who did nothing." The dowager coughed, a racking, dry sound. Perveen saw that the normally pale lady's face was quite flushed.

"It must have been a very painful time." Perveen remembered how Mirabai had been shut out of washing the prince's corpse, but Maharani Putlabai had not. "On my way to the circuit house, I stopped at the lodge. The servants have preserved the late maharaja's clothing, but there is no jacket. I wonder if you saw his jacket when he was brought back here to be bathed?"

Maharani Putlabai stared at Perveen for a long moment. "No, it was not there. He was carried inside by Prince Swaroop, and he'd already wrapped him in a silk sheet. After we bathed him, he was dressed in a new suit that I'd planned to give him for the next Diwali. The collar had rubies. I took the stones from my own collection, so he could always have a part of me with him when he wore it."

Perveen had not expected the dowager to be so forthcoming.

She stayed silent as the dowager continued, her voice gaining strength.

"The new suit was a little large for him yet—but there was no time for tailoring. It was time for the rites." The dowager pressed the moonstone at her neck, as if for comfort. "We traveled to the palace temple that evening, all of us except Mirabai, who was too weak to manage. I told Jiva Rao to light the funeral pyre, and he cried that he would not do it."

"Why?" Perveen asked softly.

She gazed past Perveen, as if seeing the tragic scene again. "He did not understand the custom. He feared that his brother would wake up and cry out from pain." Putlabai fiddled restlessly with the pendant. "I never thought I'd see my own son die. And after that, a grandson. I cannot bear to see Jiva Rao's corpse. I'd rather die myself."

"Rajmata, please don't speak like that. There's a very good chance we will find him!"

The maharani shook her head, and there was a sad half smile on her face. "If he is lost, the way to find him is to send the buffoon. He regularly travels carrying messages for me."

Perveen was heartened to know the dowager believed her words, but it was surprising that the maharani didn't know Aditya's whereabouts. "But the buffoon is not here. I thought you sent him to the circuit house, because he arrived there last night."

"Do not tell me I've done things I have not done!" The dowager struggled up to her elbows to better glare at Perveen. "Prince Swaroop promised he would find you—why should Aditya also go? This is a bad time for him to be away. The guards are gone. We have only children outside with knives that could be taken from their hands."

Of all the people she'd met at the circuit house, Aditya seemed closest to the children. So it didn't surprise her that he had gone looking for the maharaja, even without the queen's permission. "Aditya-yerda was at the circuit house yesterday evening, a few hours after Prince Swaroop arrived. Prince Swaroop thoroughly searched the property to verify that the maharaja was not there. Today the prince is traveling with the Satapur agent, Mr. Colin Sandringham, to Poona. They will ask for the military to join the search. That is how seriously he feels about the disappearance."

"But why Poona? We have a fine cantonment here. In the old days, they only served at the maharaja's pleasure." The dowager's voice was sour.

"Yes, those are exactly the men whom we want to join the search," Perveen reassured her. "The government must send orders for their deployment. Mr. Sandringham thinks Prince Swaroop can personally make the best case for it."

The dowager fondled the moonstone at her throat, which like her face was reddened. "My son is a good leader. If he had been in charge, none of these deaths would have happened."

Perveen decided to hide her disagreement on Swaroop's skills. "I hear that the maharani Mirabai is also out searching. That was very brave of her to go, but I am quite worried. She has been gone so long and not returned."

"The fool disobeyed me when she left. She broke purdah!" The dowager's voice was a snarl.

"Doesn't that always happen when she rides—breaking purdah, I mean?"

"She believes it is not breaking purdah if she is not recognized. I've been told she dresses as a man when she rides. She wears a royal uniform. But surely people know." She muttered, "To think I got rid of one bad woman only to get another."

There was an uncomfortable rustling in the back of the maharani's room, and Perveen wondered what her words had meant. *One bad woman only to get another.* Was she referring to the dancer?

"It has been hard for you." Leaving her notebook on the

stool, Perveen rose from and approached the queen's bedside. "What was her name?"

As the dowager stared at Perveen, the queen's face twitched. "Devani."

Perveen felt a surge of adrenaline because she knew that if she was careful, she could draw out the truth from the old woman. But she could not appear too aggressive. "A Hindu name. What is the meaning?"

"Devani means 'goddess,'" the dowager said. "But she was a demon. With evil eyes. I see her in you also!"

It was all coming together in Perveen's mind. Vandana meant "worship." Yazad's name, in the ancient language of Avestan, meant "divine angel." And they lived at Heaven's Rest.

"People told me not to talk about it, but you should know. Her evil eyes were always on my jewels."

"I brought back your moonstone pendant," Perveen said, trying to reassure her. "I am not a demon."

"Although it is not expensive, I always treasure the moonstone because it calms the emotions. For a young woman, the moonstone is said to be especially beneficial; that must be why she seized it. And her evil eyes trapped two of our family's men! How many more would she take?" The dowager shifted against the forest of pillows behind her. "I did it to save them. She is no more."

The words were cryptic. Had she ordered a murder? Perveen needed to know more but not put the dowager on guard. "Who took Devani away from the palace?"

"Palanquin bearers. Not in the palanquin with the royal crest—an ordinary one taken from the village. Isn't that what happened?" The queen peered into the back of the room. Perveen shifted her gaze to the group, which was nodding and murmuring assent. But Archana's mouth was grim, and her face seemed unhappily frozen. What did she know?

"Archana, pour me some more tea," the dowager

commanded, and Archana swiftly went forward to do as she was told. After the dowager had her fill, she coughed heartily. "Devani was a threat to all of us: my husband, my sons, and thus Satapur. She should not have come back."

Perveen could not tell whether the queen already knew the dancer was living in luxury just two hours' riding distance away. Because Prince Swaroop had spoken about Yazad Mehta, it was possible. "If I am guessing right about the lady, she did not seem vengeful. She was most insistent that I bring the moonstone back to you, although she did not tell me the history behind it. I truly believed she'd bought it in Paris."

"Devani is alive?" The dowager's voice came out in a croak. "You are telling me you saw her? What about her son?"

Perveen felt jolted. She realized that if Chitra's story about a dancer who was pregnant was true, there could be a child. And if that child was male, he could arguably have a claim on the throne. But this was all supposition. "I'm not sure if she's alive. I would like to investigate further. That can be done after we have found the maharaja."

The dowager squinted at her, as if she was searching for something. "Your speaking of this lady's survival can only be another sign of your nazar."

Perveen moved closer to the dowager's bedside, so Putlabai could get a better look at her face. "I came only to help your grandson and to try to help all of you find some peace and happiness."

Grimacing, Maharani Putlabai turned her face away from Perveen. "I am so very tired. My heart hurts. I want you to leave my room."

"Yes, you have done enough. Go!" Archana said, including Perveen in her gaze as she pointed to the door.

"You also, Archana. You have served me well. But I command you and all the other ladies to let me rest alone."

As she shuffled out with the others, Perveen took a last

glance at the reclined dowager. It was unsatisfactory having to leave this way without having secured Chitra's release from the palace jail, as well as with the half-drawn picture Perveen was getting of Vandana.

Outside the maharani's room, the ladies-in-waiting began dispersing, their voices raised as they talked about what was for dinner and which maids would arrange their hair. Perveen asked Swagata, "How long does she usually sleep?"

"Very short times. We could wait here in case she wakes," Swagata said.

"I will wait then, too." Archana glared sternly, as if she suspected they might go back inside the room.

Perveen was annoyed. She'd wished to ask Swagata some questions about Devani but felt censored by Archana's presence. In any case, she knew she should not be tarrying. The best course was to get back on her horse with Rama at her side and make straight for the lodge. Yet if she wasn't here when Colin arrived, he would be worried.

Perveen opened the notebook she had brought from her room. Leaning against a marble column, she turned to a fresh page without existing notes and dated it.

"What are you writing, another private letter?" Archana asked sarcastically.

Perveen looked coolly at Archana. "No, this is a document of record. I will keep it myself."

Archana shook her head and went back to stand close to the dowager maharani's doorway. Perveen decided to ignore her, because she had much to write. First, the information Padmabai had given her about Jiva Rao's intention to reach his uncle's palace and, second, the dowager's revelation that she had tried to kill a servant whom she believed was pregnant with a half-royal child. She would not mention her own thoughts about Vandana because nothing had been verified. Nor did Perveen have any hard evidence yet of whether Pratap Rao's death was foul play.

Perveen was still writing when Swagata tapped her on the shoulder. The senior maid's face was twisted with worry. "Archana thinks she heard the queen retching. She has gone in the room."

Perveen looked toward the open bedchamber door down the hall, and in the next instant, there was an anguished scream.

"Oh, my queen! Oh, my queen! What has happened!" Archana wailed from within the room.

All along the hallway, the closed doors to the rooms where the ladies-in-waiting had repaired for their relaxation creaked open. A sea of women flooded into the dowager maharani's chamber.

Perveen and Swagata pushed their way in along with the others. The dowager maharani was lying on her side in the bed, a pool of vomit in front of her. The dowager maharani's face, which had been flushed before, was now very red.

"Rajmata, Rajmata!" said Archana helplessly. Looking at Perveen, she said, "Rajmata has fallen very ill!"

All around her, the ladies-in-waiting rushed forward again to look closely at the maharani. Swagata's voice rose clearly above the worried chatter. "It could be poison. Choti-Rani always said there was a poisoner in the palace!"

Perveen's panic was now rampant. "Someone must fetch a doctor!"

"Our priest is the only one who gives medicine. But he is away at one of the villages!" Archana's pallid face had gone even whiter.

"Memsahib, weren't you saying there was someone who came with you?" Swagata asked.

Perveen had almost forgotten about Rama. She felt a wave of relief. "Yes! Can someone run for him?"

The assorted women looked at one another, but nobody moved.

"Do you not want help because you want her dead?" Perveen exploded in frustration.

Archana spoke stiffly. "This is a zenana. A woman's world. It is difficult to bring a man inside without the maharani's permission even for such matters. Our priest is known to us. Your man is not."

"But he is a Brahmin who knows Ayurvedic treatment. Come with me, Swagata!" Perveen ordered, and with the maid behind her, she hurried down the steep staircase, almost twisting her ankle as she went around a landing. She slowed slightly, not wanting to become a casualty. Then it was through the gold jali door and through a bewildering succession of long halls. As she hurried along, she wondered if the maharani had naturally fallen ill, or if it could be something else.

Perveen was sweating and breathless when she made it to the front gate. At first she didn't see Rama anywhere. Then she saw the horses' tails gently waving, and realized he was standing between them, stroking both.

"Rama, I need you!" she called.

He emerged from between the horses with a questioning look on his face.

"The dowager maharani has fallen ill. I need you to treat her."

His brow creased with concern. "What kind of illness? I may have something with me, or I could ask for something to be gathered."

"I don't know. It was very sudden. She sent everyone out of the room because she said she felt tired. Then she vomited and became pale. She is not responding to voices or touch, but she has a weak pulse." To illustrate, Perveen touched the inside of her own wrist, which was pulsing rapidly.

Reaching into the saddlebag on the horse he'd ridden and taking out two bottles, Rama said, "I have an ointment that can sometimes help people regain their wakefulness. The only other remedies that I carry while traveling are for snake, animal, and insect bites."

Perveen nodded. "I understand. Come quickly!"

He shook his head, looking down at his dusty sandals. "How can I? I am not clean enough to enter the room of a queen."

"Do not worry about your dress and shoes. You must come!" Tears of frustration came to her eyes. She could not force him to go against custom; she could only speak from her heart. "You saved Colin's life. You have a gift from God—he would want you to serve him and save the maharani!"

Rama undid the first few hooks of his rough cotton coat, exposing the sacred thread he wore across his skin from shoulder to waist. The palace attendants would understand that this humble-looking man was of the priestly caste. He spoke, and his voice held its usual calm strength. "First, I must thoroughly wash."

The maids showed him a washroom in the old palace, while Perveen waited impatiently outside. Looking uncertain, he disappeared through the door decorated in gold leaf designs. Perveen realized he had likely never been in such a splendid place and felt embarrassed by it.

At last he emerged, his skin damp with water and shining clean. He had cleaned the dust from his clothes, and his feet were clean and bare. As they hurried to the dowager's chamber, Perveen related a quick description of the dowager's collapse. "I hope that what I told her wasn't too upsetting. But she was also drinking tea when I was in the room, and she vomited. There could have been something—"

"I will look at her, and then we will speak again."

As they entered the upper zenana hallway, Perveen saw that Princess Padmabai was standing uncertainly by herself outside her grandmother's room. Seeing Perveen, she ran up and cried out, "What is wrong? Is Rajmata ill? None of the ladies will permit me inside!"

"We are not sure what's wrong. Rajkumari, kindly wait a little longer," Perveen implored her.

"I am princess. You must do as I say and let me in!" She stamped her foot just as her brother would have.

Rama bowed deeply and brought his steepled hands to his forehead. Softly, he said, "Because you are the rajkumari, you are the best one to say prayers for the rajmata. Do you know her favorite deity?"

"Shiva, the destroyer," she answered promptly. "I know many prayers for Shiva-ji that Rajmata taught me. She let me make prayer and give prasad at the shrine in her parlor."

Perveen was grateful for Rama's lead. "Please say your prayers for her at the parlor shrine. And we will come to pray with you very shortly."

Once the girl had stepped into the parlor, Perveen hurried into the bedroom, where the maharani was lying, surrounded by the same murmuring ladies.

"She no longer breathes!" Archana wailed when the two of them entered.

"Let him see what he can do," Perveen said, ushering Rama in before he could be refused.

Bowing his head, Rama put his hands together in namaste and proceeded toward the maharani on his damp feet. At the bedside, he first prostrated himself and touched the queen's feet. Such formality seemed irrelevant at a time like this, but Perveen imagined it reassured the servants and ladies-in-waiting.

It had been at least twenty minutes since she'd run from the room, and the queen did not look any better. Perveen no longer saw the rapid rise and fall of the maharani's broad chest. She watched Rama take hold of the queen's wrist, feeling for a pulse. His deeply lined face did not betray any emotion, and he didn't answer any of the shouted questions about the queen's welfare that came from the women.

Rama pulled the silk sheet over the maharani's chest and placed his hand over it as if feeling for a heartbeat. Looking at Perveen, he shook his head.

As his fingers went to the queen's temples, Perveen tried to calm herself. She remembered how he had used local plants to keep Colin alive. Surely he could use the same magic now.

Looking up at her, he said, "We are too late. She has left this world."

Perveen bowed her head. She had thought the rajmata was bullheaded and ruthless, and most likely a murderer. The queen's death was shocking. But Perveen did not feel true grief, because she had never seen a moment of kindness from the dowager to anyone around her. But she felt a deep sadness for the woman to have been so desperately unhappy. Perveen looked around the room of women, who were wailing and tearing at their hair and saris. They probably were feeling many emotions but had defaulted to an overdramatic reaction. Nobody wanted to appear disloyal.

Perveen took a sideways look at Rama, wondering if he'd purposely taken time with his ablutions to cause a delay. If Rama had been unable to save the maharani's life, his method of treatment could be blamed, leading to some kind of punishment, or at the very least social ostracization.

No, she told herself. Rama was a brave, exemplary man. Such connivance was not in his character.

Rama touched the queen's temples again and looked into her ears and nose. He drew out an arm from underneath the sheet, and as he did so, there was a soft sound of something falling. He reached down and picked up a small gold snuffbox ornamented with a milky moonstone.

"What is this?" he asked Swagata, who was standing closest to him.

Swagata wiped tears from her eyes. "It looks like her husband's snuffbox. He always used it. I did not know she had kept it."

Perveen watched as Rama placed the small container on the bedside table, thinking of Vandana's cigarette case. Vandana hadn't thought the dowager maharani smoked; but here she was using snuff.

Very gently, he opened it, exposing its interior, which held traces of a grayish-brown powder.

"Some hours earlier today, she asked to be alone to drink her cup of tea," Archana said in a whisper.

"Where is the dowager maharani's teacup, please?" Rama asked.

"Here." Swagata pointed to the cup on the bedside table. Rama stared into the depths of the teacup, as if it held answers waiting to be heard. Then he picked up the dowager maharani's right hand. On the thumb and two other fingertips were gray-brown smudges.

"Look," he said softly. "The same powder is on her fingers. From the color of her skin and the inside of her nose—and what you say about the heart beating too fast—it most likely is datura poisoning. But it does not lead to death in minutes. She could have started it earlier and then added more recently."

"The tea was fine. Others drank it with her." A lady-in-waiting came forward holding two cups; her hands were shaking so much the cups rattled in their saucers.

Perveen was full of questions but did not want to come off like she was the enemy. "It could be that she only added the datura to her own tea. Does anyone remember seeing the snuffbox with her before?"

The group responded to her question with silence, but Perveen noted some of the women were looking downward as if afraid of being identified. At last Archana said, "Yesterday, before her morning prayers, she asked to go into a storeroom where she keeps some valuables. I brought her there."

"What did she take?" Perveen asked.

Archana closed her eyes, as if trying to go back to the moment. "A number of things. Some jewelry, some boxes. I carried everything out at her direction."

"To this room?" Perveen was imagining the journey.

"Of course." The lady-in-waiting gave Perveen an irritated look.

All of this action had taken place before Perveen had awoken to the special breakfast prepared for her. She asked, "What happened next?"

"We went to the palace temple to pray."

"Straight there?" Perveen asked.

As if suddenly remembering, Archana said, "She asked to stop in the kitchen first. That was unusual, because we do not eat before praying, but she said she had a gift for the cook. She told me to go somewhere while she spoke with him."

Perveen felt a ringing in her ears and put her hand on the wall to steady herself. Here was the proof to go with what the dowager had hinted at: she herself was the one who'd put poison in the breakfast food. She'd very likely kept the container with her and wound up taking the poison herself. The question was whether she had killed herself from despair over Jiva Rao's disappearance, or for some other reason.

"Are you feeling sickly?" Swagata asked, looking anxiously at Perveen. "Did you touch that powder?"

"No," she said quickly. "But for reasons of safety and evidence for the police, the maharani's teacup and the snuffbox must be secured until the doctor arrives. Where can this be kept?"

"Basu-sahib has a safe," said Archana.

Perveen had almost forgotten about the palace officer. He needed to know that the dowager maharani had been the palace's poisoner so that he would not have any servants arrested.

Perveen opened the door and nearly knocked over Princess Padmabai.

"Is Rajmata still sick?" The princess's eyes were large in her small face.

"That was good of you to pray. I know how hard you tried. Your grandmother—" Perveen hesitated, not wanting to shock the child. "She became sick very suddenly. Rama tried to treat her, but she had already passed."

"Passed?" the little girl repeated, looking with confusion from Perveen to Rama. "Passed what?"

"She has passed from this world," Perveen said gently. "She has died."

"Like Bandar!" Padmabai broke out into sobs. "It is not fair. Everyone is leaving me."

Perveen could not stop the child from rushing into the dowager's bedchamber. Padmabai wailed and tugged at her grandmother, looking for a reaction. The maids rushed toward her, but Perveen held up a cautionary hand. She didn't want Padmabai to be denied her last sight of her grandmother. Although the grandmother had been cross while Perveen had seen her, it was clear that the princess had loved her.

Padmabai put her head against her grandmother's pale cheek. Then she stepped back and looked at Perveen. Softly, the princess said, "In her next life, she will be a butterfly. She will be red and white, my favorite colors. And she will always flutter near me in the garden."

"Yes." Perveen was touched by the child's words. Hinduism gave everyone a second chance, a way to regain life, but in another form. And a butterfly was a good metaphor for the dowager, who had once loved parties, but never wanted to stray far from her property. "What a nice thing for her to become."

"Aai told me that Pratap Rao is the wind that roars at night. It means he is telling us he's all right. And what about Wagh?" Her voice trembled as she spoke her brother's nickname, the one only palace family members could speak. "Will he ever come back, or am I all alone?"

"You will not be left alone. We cannot guess what God's will is, but we will do our best to find both of them." As Perveen finished speaking, she saw Rama give her a nod of approval. She felt bolstered knowing he was with her.

"Yes, both of them." Padmabai wiped tears from her eyes. "I want Aai. Where is she?"

The princess had been using the ordinary Marathi word for "mother." This touched Perveen's heart. She put aside decorum and held out her hand to Padmabai. "Let's look for her. I will take you on my horse, just like in a story."

After a moment, Padmabai took Perveen's hand. Looking up at Perveen, the princess said, "And when Aai and Wagh see us, they will be proud."

23

AT THE LODGE

erveen requested that Mr. Basu, Archana, and Swagata accompany her and Padmabai to the main gate. She wanted to make certain nobody would think she was taking the princess against her will. Also, Padmabai would see there were people who cared to wave back at her. What Perveen didn't share was the small possibility Padmabai might not return to the palace, if Mirabai was declared dead. Then Perveen and Colin would become the princess's guardians.

Perveen knew this was because of legal precedent. Cornelia Sorabji, India's first woman lawyer, had been guardian to a small number of orphaned princes and princesses. But although Perveen had developed affection for the little princess, the prospect of becoming a formal guardian was daunting. She took a deep breath and reminded herself not to let worries carry her away. Soon she'd be back in Bombay with a stack of boring contracts on her desk and her father nattering on in her ear.

Perveen concentrated on the present as the group walked together through the old palace, crossing the courtyard and halls that had finally become a little more recognizable to her. They passed through the gatehouse, where the horses had been watered and were ready to leave.

"Here is a document to give to Colin Sandringham when he arrives," Perveen said, presenting the pages of writing she had torn out of her notebook and placed in a palace stationery envelope. "It explains the two areas where the prince might be:

the forest toward the lodge and the vicinity of Prince Swaroop's palace."

"Very well," Mr. Basu said, turning over the envelope in his hands.

"Also, as palace minister, do you have the authority to release Chitra from the palace jail? The princess and I wish to see her before we leave."

"Yes, I do have the right. Archana will kindly bring her." The tutor turned to Archana, who looked defiant for a moment and then shrugged, turning around to proceed slowly through the gate into the old palace.

Watching her leave, Mr. Basu said, "She was the dowager's best friend. She is the one who will miss her the most."

Perveen thought about the way Archana had called out when the maharani had fallen ill, yet been so strangely resistant to medical help. "Archana may have known all her secrets, but in the end, I'm not sure she wished for the dowager's survival."

"With duty comes fear," Mr. Basu said, rubbing his damaged eyes. "I felt it myself teaching the children."

"Three generations of children. You saw it all," she said sympathetically.

"Yes."

"I have not asked you about someone in the palace who may have been a special friend to Maharaja Mahendra Rao."

"Which friend?" he asked absently.

Perveen resolved to be careful not to give away anything about her theory that the dancer was still alive. "A dancer named Devani. The dowager had her removed from the palace."

He raised a cautionary finger. "She went away and returned."

"What do you mean?" Perveen was perplexed.

"During the reign of Maharaja Mohan Rao, Devani went away for a regular holiday to her home village. But she did not come back after the month leave she'd been granted. We believed she had quit the palace. She was quite young—only fourteen or so—and was easily the best dancer in the group. Maharaja Mohan Rao sent a messenger to find her, and she was convinced to come back."

Perveen looked at Swagata. "I'm confused. The dowager told me she was sent off for good!"

"She was gone during that time and came back just as Basu-sahib said," Swagata interjected. "Then before Maharaja Mahendra Rao married, she was gone again and did not return."

"Yes," Mr. Basu said. "In 1905. She was a threat to his engagement."

This was just as Perveen had heard from Chitra. She would have asked another question, but Padmabai had wandered toward the horses. With Ganesan tagging behind her.

"Be careful you don't get too close!" Perveen shouted, because she feared that Padmabai might get kicked.

"Rama-ji is watching the horses for me," Padmabai called back. "But there are only two. Which horse is mine?"

Perveen went over to join her. "You and I will share riding the little spotted horse. Her name is Rani."

"Oh! She is a queen?"

"Only the best for you, Rajkumari!" Perveen said with a smile.

"My mother wants me to learn to ride," Padmabai said, looking up trustingly at Perveen. "But Rajmata said I should not. I could fall off and break bones."

"I will carry you on my horse. I won't let you fall," Perveen promised, hoping this would prove true.

Just then Chitra came running after them, sandals slapping against the hard stones. Swagata held out her arms. Her daughter ran straight into them.

The reunion was beautiful. As Perveen watched the two, she made a silent prayer that Padmabai would experience the same.

"Thank you," Chitra said, stepping away from her mother to prostrate herself before Perveen. "Rajmata and the prince said I had to be locked up because I was an enemy to Satapur!"

"You were very brave, Chitra. Please get up!" Perveen felt embarrassed to be treated like a ruler.

As she bounded up to her feet, Chitra said, "Is it true that Rajmata has passed away?"

"Yes. I saw it. It looks like it was suicide—a sin," Swagata added heavily.

Perveen had expected to see shock, but Chitra's face broke into a smile.

"Don't look like that!" Swagata chided her daughter. "What do you think happens to us when there are no queens to serve? We could be sent into the fields like peasants."

"Oh no. The choti-rani is now becoming rajmata!" Chitra's eyes glowed. "Because she is my mistress, I will become the head princess maid!"

"Do not forget I am your mother!" Swagata said, frowning at her.

"We have no time for arguments." Perveen didn't like seeing how baldly power was used by servants as well as royals. Turning to the palace minister, she said, "Basu-sahib, I would be grateful if you could organize what needs to be done for Rajmata's memorial service."

"I will do as I can, but it is a state event. And nothing can happen without Prince Swaroop. The son performs the rites for a mother." Mr. Basu's voice sounded confident, as if he was back in comfortable social terrain.

Rama led Rani toward a marble mounting block, and Perveen used it to step up and seat herself on Rani. Chitra lifted the princess to sit in the front section of the saddle. Perveen took her own cashmere shawl to securely tie the little girl against her body. "I know you must take Padmabai, but Ganesan won't leave. What shall we do?" Chitra looked anxiously at Perveen.

The tall white dog paced around the horse, looking up at Padmabai and barking.

"I hope he doesn't bite the horse's legs!" Perveen worried aloud.

"He won't hurt the horse. He wants to go along," Swagata said, putting a hand on her daughter's shoulder as if the boastful words of a few minutes earlier had been forgiven.

Perveen knew she should be feeling easier in her mind. Putlabai was no longer able to exert her poisonous will. Her son Swaroop was a repugnant man, but there was no indication he'd kidnapped Jiva Rao. Her mind should not dwell on morbid thoughts but focus instead on the most efficient way to locate Prince Jiva Rao. Taking the reins in hand, she asked the palace assemblage, "But is Ganesan strong enough to follow us for miles?"

"More than that! He used to hunt with the group," said Mr. Basu, who had slowly made his way toward her.

So there was no reason not to take the dog. Perveen looked down from her high perch to address Chitra. "Please get a rope to tie to his collar. Padmabai can hold on to it, and he will feel like he's with her—and not chasing us."

Chitra gave swift instructions to the children who had been guarding the palace, and the youngest one hurried off for a rope.

"Ganesan is coming?" Padmabai's voice had a happy lilt.

Perveen was glad for the opportunity to reassure the girl. "Of course. Did you know that at the circuit house, Ganesan has a brother dog?"

"A brother dog," she repeated, sounding impressed. "Older or younger?"

"You will have to decide about that. He is just as big, but not quite as clean. I daresay they would be happy to see each other again." Her comment was strategic. After the lodge, Perveen intended to bring Padmabai to the circuit house for safety.

"I would like to see the brother dog!" Padmabai's feet drummed against Rani, and Perveen had to hastily pull back the reins to keep the horse from moving. The boy reappeared with a rope, and Rama helped construct a leash tied to Ganesan's jeweled collar.

"Even if the princess drops the leash, he will follow," Chitra said. Looking soberly at Perveen, she added, "I am praying to Shiva-ji and Aranyani both that you find the young maharaja and my dear maharani. She is finally free to rule the zenana."

Perveen knew Chitra was talking about Mirabai leading the women, but Perveen could imagine that Mirabai might refuse to live that way anymore, since there was no longer a mother-in-law to obey. And there was something else. Women had taken charge of kingdoms and princely states before. Could Mirabai serve as regent? This prospect was something for the Agency to consider.

Rama swiftly mounted his horse and gestured to Perveen. "Let's travel before the sun is gone."

"We will see you again," Perveen said emphatically to Chitra. "I will send a letter straight to the palace in case there is a delay bringing home the children."

"Rama-ji, tell me, how far?" Padmabai called out to Rama shortly after they had left the palace.

"Half an hour more," he said. "Not long."

Padmabai bounced against Perveen. "But it's boring."

"You are seeing the world! How can that be boring?" Perveen could not keep the tension out of her voice. Padmabai seemed to have forgotten the seriousness of their quest. There was no telling whether Jiva Rao or Mirabai were at the lodge. If Mirabai was in a depressed state when she found Jiva Rao, she might have taken him on her horse, just as Perveen was carrying Padmabai. And because the maharani had disagreed with Perveen's idea to keep the prince in India, Mirabai might have decided not to return.

Or maybe, if Mirabai couldn't find Jiva Rao, she would end her own life. Swagata had said suicide was a sin, but the outlawed custom of sati—a widow's suicide following a husband's death—still occurred on occasion in rural areas. It was not outrageous to think a melancholic woman might want to die after the deaths of her husband and both sons in just a two-year period. That was far too much grief for anyone.

"Where is the lodge?" Padmabai complained as she fidgeted with Ganesan's leash.

"Just ahead," Perveen said, fibbing. "Be careful with the dog's leash. Don't drop it!"

"I must get off. The horse is too much up and down," the princess whined.

Perveen wanted to divert her. "Look at that banyan tree. Let's count banyans on the way to the lodge."

But these attempts to settle Padmabai weren't effective. Perveen made a frustrated face at Rama as the little girl kept complaining.

"Do not worry," he said, moving his horse along at a steady pace. "The lodge is near, and once she eats, she will be calm."

Perveen doubted how calm the child could be after having seen her dead grandmother. "The people at the lodge are very kind. They'll be very excited to meet Princess Padmabai."

"No!" Rama corrected her. "They will fear looking at a princess would show disrespect."

"Even so young?" Perveen was dismayed.

"Yes. We must shield her."

Perveen agreed to follow Rama's advice and dismount from the horses close to a stream that was just out of sight of the lodge. While Perveen let the horses drink their fill, Rama went ahead to the lodge to ask about the maharaja, promising Padmabai he would bring her something to eat. Perveen watched the princess dart around, looking at every dragonfly, beetle, and bird with interest. "Will Water Rat come with his boat?" Padmabai asked.

"I don't think so. He's in England!"

"That's a shame. Where can I make susu?"

Perveen had not planned a strategy for royal toileting needs.

Apologetically, she said, "There is no special room here like you have at the palace."

Padmabai hopped from one foot to the other. "Isn't there a thunderbox like Rajmata's?"

"We will go behind the tree. It's all right; nobody will see."

"Ganesan can come. He doesn't mind."

Perveen made sure the horses were tied fast before taking Padmabai.

"Where's Rama? He said he was bringing me something," Padmabai demanded after they'd returned.

Perveen checked her wristwatch. "It has only been ten minutes. He must be waiting for the food to be made. They make very tasty rotis here."

"I'm hungry!" Padmabai stamped her foot, and Ganesan gave a low growl.

But twenty-five minutes later, Rama had not returned. Perveen tried to imagine various scenarios. Perhaps he had fallen into an important conversation about the maharaja. She longed to walk closer to the lodge to look for Jiva Rao, but she was reluctant to bring the princess because of what Rama had said about people's expectations of purdah.

Sitting on the grass, Perveen stared at Rani. The horse looked back blankly as if to say she didn't know what was keeping Rama either. Rani shifted her feet, and the cashmere shawl lying on the saddle moved, too. With new eyes, Perveen looked at the garment. She could drape it over the princess. That would provide enough privacy—but would the child be frightened?

Perveen sprang up and took the shawl from the saddle. Chuckling, she tossed the red cloth over the girl. "Look at you now!"

"Aankh micholi!" cried out Padmabai.

The princess thought Perveen wanted to play blindman's buff.

"We don't have enough people," Perveen said. "This is a different game. Just follow me quietly. I'll take Ganesan with us."

Walking along the path to the lodge, Perveen nodded to a few peasants standing around. She tried to act as if it were entirely natural to be slowly leading a draped child with one hand, and a leashed dog with the other.

"We are looking for our traveling guide," Perveen said to the grizzled man from whom she'd bought millet rotis. There was a circle of dough cooking on his round griddle.

"Who is that?" he asked, flipping the bread. "A young bride?"

The shawl's red color must have confused him. "No. A child I need to keep safe."

He shook his head. "Who is this? You must tell me."

Swiftly, she realized that the draped princess could be mistaken for the missing maharaja. "No, no. It is not the maharaja."

"It's me!" Padmabai's voice came out cheerily.

In a low voice, Perveen said, "It is the princess, and I have covered her for the sake of privacy."

At that declaration, Padmabai pulled off the shawl and looked around smiling. "I smell such nice roti!"

The man groaned and clapped his hands over his eyes. "I saw nothing!"

"Will you please wear the shawl over your head again? It is not that you are bad—but the people here believe that they are being rude if they look at you," Perveen admonished Padmabai.

"You don't wear a shawl, so I won't," Padmabai declared.

Perveen would have liked to talk with her sometime about how women's rights differed according to rank and religion and family preferences, but this was not the place. Ignoring the princess, Perveen addressed the roti maker, who was edging away. "Bhaiya, please wait. I must find our guide. Didn't he come to you asking for food?"

The man stopped but did not turn around. "I saw that man, but the prince came out to speak with him."

"What prince?" She felt hope rising at the thought of the maharaja.

"Prince Swaroop. And he's in an angry mood."

"Where are they now?" Perveen wondered whether the prince had refused to go to Poona with Colin because he had suspected she was up to trouble. She scanned the area and didn't see evidence of a horse.

"They went off." He pointed vaguely toward the woods behind the lodge.

Perveen felt uneasy. Why would Rama abandon them? It could only be due to the prince's order.

As if sensing her unease, Ganesan began whimpering.

"Poor Ganesan," Padmabai said, peering down at him. "He is also hungry!"

The rotis man bowed his head. "What I make is poor quality. I cannot make food fine enough for a princess."

"Your rotis are very good, and she must eat." Perveen would have said more but saw that Padmabai had let the leash for Ganesan slip out of her hand. The dog was trotting away from them toward the woods.

"Ganesan! Come back!" Padmabai screeched, but the dog paid her no mind. His casual trot broke into a run.

"He may have smelled an animal," Perveen said. Seeing the fear in Padmabai's eyes, she added, "He'll come back soon!"

"What if it's a leopard or tiger? He could be eaten!"

Desperate to sound reassuring, Perveen said, "It won't happen."

"But my other brother was eaten up!"

Perveen opened her mouth to comfort Padmabai, but the girl had already started chasing the dog.

"Come back for your roti," Perveen shouted, but she knew it was in vain.

Padmabai, who had lost so much, was determined to keep her dog.

Perveen smelled smoke from the flatbread now burning on the griddle. The man had abandoned his cooking and had run toward the lodge. *Good. Let him get the others to help.*

She picked up the edge of her skirt and began chasing after Padmabai.

Padmabai was still in sight, and it wasn't too hard to catch up with someone with such short legs. However, the princess wouldn't stop and turn back. She was insistent on following the palace dog, who was now moving at a trot just fast enough that his rope stayed out of reach. Perveen grew even more frustrated as she followed Padmabai off the path and into uncut forest. Rama wouldn't know where they were, and they were hardly on track to find the maharaja, as she had planned.

Padmabai was moving steadily but, in an instant, tumbled and fell. This pause gave Perveen time to sprint a few yards and catch up with her. Perveen picked her up and saw a small, dirty gash on the child's leg.

"I'm bleeding!" Padmabai whimpered.

"It's all right," Perveen said. "We can clean that up. Really, we should go back."

"No!" the princess said, wiping tears from her eyes with dirty fists. "We must get Ganesan."

"You have such a lovely voice. Just call him," Perveen beseeched.

"He only obeys Aai and Aditya." The child scrambled up to her feet. "Hurry, hurry!"

This far from the path, everything looked the same—ironwood trees with their twisty, sinister limbs and ground covered by tangles of vines and fallen boughs.

One couldn't see snakes and other dangers when traveling off the path. Perveen wanted to tell this to Padmabai, but what was the point? The child was insistent on saving her dog from presumed danger. All in all, she was considerably more courageous than Perveen had assumed.

Perveen was so upset she forgot the rules. "Padmabai, you must—"

"No!" The little girl ran forward with a surge of speed that was surprising. Ganesan had paused, allowing his mistress to catch up and take hold of his leash. Then he resumed his trot, pulling her forward.

Perveen's breath became labored as she chased the dog and princess, who were gaining considerable distance. Perveen would have been able to catch the princess at her previous speed, but the sturdy dog was pulling the girl faster than Perveen would have expected. Adding to the trouble was the darkness of the forest. Through the dappled black-and-green shade, she worked hard to focus on the moving splotch of white that was Padmabai's fancy lace-trimmed dress.

When the girl suddenly veered off to the right, Perveen raced on as quickly as she could, but as she made the turn into the green, she could no longer see the princess. Just ahead was a small, oddly shaped building. It was a short tower with a barred window on the ground level. On the roof, there was a built-in bench.

Was this the hunting tower that she had glimpsed when traveling to the palace a couple of days earlier? She approached the tower, hoping that Padmabai had become curious and gone inside. A tower would contain her; and it was a relief to slow down. Perveen was entirely unfit for running.

Her ears perked at the sound of three sharp barks. Not barks of defense—the sound of happy greeting, she thought as she picked up the pace of her steps.

Perveen looked through an arched opening about five feet high. There was a room with a ladderlike stair at its center. She understood this was for hunters to climb in order to reach the rooftop for shooting.

She had to bow her head to get through the short doorway, bringing back the slight anxiety she'd had a few hours earlier when she'd entered the zenana. But nobody was waiting for her with a knife. As she entered the cramped space, she saw Ganesan standing on his hind legs with his front paws on someone small.

"He's so dirty. Make him get down!"

The imperious voice was unmistakable.

"Maharaja, I have been looking all over for you! Ganesan, stand down!" she called out in the way Mirabai had done. The dog obediently dropped back to all fours. Prince Jiva Rao's fine coat and trousers were covered in dirt, and his curly hair stood on end. As he saw her, his face fell.

"Don't take me!" he shouted.

"I won't take you anywhere you don't want to go." Perveen felt herself on the verge of tears. "I'm so sorry about your worries. And so glad Ganesan led me to you."

"I found him!" Padmabai said. She had crowded herself behind her brother and was petting the dog.

"And what about your mother?" Perveen asked hopefully. "Maharaja, is she also here?"

Before he could answer, a sharp whistle startled her. Ganesan's ears perked, and he whirled about. An Indian dressed in riding clothes with a holstered pistol at the waist had stooped to enter the hunting tower. Perveen put her hands together in a respectful namaste, and then her words of greeting died.

This was not Maharani Mirabai, or Roderick Ames. The person who'd come into the tower was about the same size as Prince Swaroop and had the same hooked nose and dark curls. But he was not the children's uncle.

He was the buffoon.

24

A FIERY FATE

No wonder Ganesan had happily run to be petted. But Perveen felt unsettled by the altered appearance of Aditya. Seeing him in this context, she recognized how similar his frame and coloring were to Swaroop's. Aditya also shared Jiva Rao's striking golden-brown eyes. How had she missed these resemblances all those times he'd spoken to her at the palace? It could only be that she'd allowed hierarchy to obstruct what was obvious.

Aditya smiled at her, but his expression was not friendly. "Why did you come to this place? You were supposed to go to Poona."

"Is that what they told you?" Perveen said instead of directly answering. She had seen the pistol in his holster and didn't want him to seize control of the situation.

Jiva Rao looked anxiously at him. "Aditya-yerda, don't let her take me away!"

"Don't worry," Aditya said. "She won't take you or your sister. You will stay with me forever."

Perveen didn't like Aditya's sharp insistence. Firmly, she said, "Children, my job is to keep you safe and bring you home. Aditya, we have much to talk about, but we must reunite the children with their mother."

"Did you know Aai went away?" Padmabai said to Jiva Rao. "And Rajmata has died."

Jiva Rao ceased all movement. "What?"

"It is very sad that your grandmother has passed," Perveen said, seeing the prince's stunned reaction. "We will look for your mother, just as we have searched for you—"

"You did nothing to find him," Aditya said coldly. "I caught him a few hours ago."

Perveen took note of the aggressive verb Aditya had used. Jiva Rao's eyes were slightly moist, and she couldn't know if this was because of the bad news about his family, or because of Aditya's strange behavior. If the buffoon had found the prince hours ago, why hadn't he told the servants at the lodge?

The dog barked, and the buffoon gave him a sharp rap on the muzzle. That act made it clear that Aditya had seized control of their only possible ally. Perveen did not know what attack commands Mirabai had taught the dog; even if she could guess them correctly, why would the dog listen to her?

Perveen scanned the tower for evidence of what the buffoon and prince might have been doing before her arrival. The round room was small and had very little in it: several unlit lanterns, a water jar, two camp chairs with canvas seats embroidered with the Satapur coat of arms, and a carved wooden chest. A brazier holding half-burned wood sat in the tower's center. Perveen could imagine the scene at a hunt—a prince and his aide could wait here, drinking tea until a great cat came pacing around outside, which could be glimpsed from the window. Then the prince would climb the central stair to the tower's top and get his shot.

In the darkness, something bright on top of the chest caught her eye. It was a golden box with a sparkling line of diamonds and a purple floral design. She had seen it before—had it been at the palace? Perhaps the buffoon had stolen it.

It was almost the same shape as the dowager's snuffbox. Edging closer to get a better look, she realized that it looked more like a cigarette box. And then she remembered Vandana displaying that very box at the circuit house and showing off all the extra cigarette boxes she'd bought at Cartier on the table in her home.

Perveen had smelled the faint odor of smoke when Aditya arrived at the circuit house.

The question was not whether he'd met with Vandana, but the purpose of the meeting.

"What are you looking at?" Aditya asked sharply.

"Nothing! This place is small, but it looks comfortable." She did not want him understanding that the cigarette case had shaken her. What she needed was to get the children to walk out of the tower with her. Only after they were away from Aditya could she put together the pieces of the puzzle.

"Who told you about this tower?" Aditya demanded.

"The palanquin bearers pointed it out to me," she said. "But it's a bit tight for all four of us. Let me take the children out— they need something to eat."

He moved more solidly in front of the doorway. Folding his hands across his chest, he said, "No."

"Why are you talking so meanly?" Padmabai gave him a petulant look.

"My princess, what would you like me to say?" The buffoon had a strange glint in his eyes as he looked at the princess. Perveen felt the hairs on her arms standing up.

Jiva Rao had settled against the tower wall, pulling his arms around his legs. He had made himself into a ball. Perveen wondered what had transpired between Aditya and the maharaja before she'd arrived. As if sensing the prince's distress, Ganesan trotted over and lay at the boy's side, but Jiva Rao kept his arms locked around himself.

"Aditya-yerda, stop being angry," Padmabai said, still behaving as if she hadn't sensed the quiet, coiled danger that Perveen and Jiva Rao both seemed to recognize. Climbing into one of the camp chairs, she demanded, "Tell me a story while I wait for my tea."

Aditya looked at her with an expression that seemed to hold years of irritation. Then he gave a cynical eye roll to Perveen. "Why shouldn't they hear a story? My own story is much better than your *Wind in the Willows*. Maharaja, will you kindly take the chair near your sister?"

Despite the courteous invitation, Perveen had a dreadful feeling that he was about to put Padmabai and Jiva Rao through something awful. His life story would probably be full of hardship and harsh opinions of the royal family. As Jiva Rao uncurled himself and dropped into the camp chair near Padmabai, Perveen asked, "What about the *Panchantantra*? Or Jataka tales?"

"No, no, no! Perveen-memsahib, you can read books," Padmabai explained in a grown-up voice. "Buffoon's job is to tell us stories that are not in books."

Aditya spread his arms gracefully and made a slight bow. "As you wish, my dear princess."

Perveen stood rigidly, watching the courtly behavior with a growing sense of dread.

"Two autumns ago, after the rains had stopped and the roads became hard enough for the postal cart to travel, the postmen brought a letter for me," Aditya began. "I could read my name on the envelope, but not much more."

"Because you haven't learned to read yet!" Padmabai said, grinning.

Perveen flinched, worried that Aditya would react badly to Padmabai's condescending words. But he winked at the child and answered her in the same falsely pleasant tone. "That is because I am not rich like you. And I was called to work at the palace when I was nine."

The buffoon was twenty-four years old, which put his year of birth around 1897. The maharaja Mahendra Rao was born in 1878, so he could have been the royal father who had passed on golden-brown eyes to Aditya. But the dowager's husband, Maharaja Mohan Rao, was firmly in middle age when Aditya was born. And hadn't Mr. Basu said that the dancer had disappeared for some months while she was a young teenager? Perveen was willing to bet the time span the dancer was missing lay between 1896 and 1897.

Aditya's voice interrupted Perveen's frantic calculations. "Now, please guess. Who had sent me a letter when everyone knows I cannot read?"

"Someone who doesn't know you!" Padmabai guessed. "How did you learn what it said?"

"Oh, I asked Pratik to read it to me. The letter said that if I came to the racetrack in Poona on a certain date, someone would meet me with a special gift."

"What did you do?" Padmabai drummed her feet impatiently on the earthen floor.

"Traveling to the racetrack was easy enough for me to arrange because, as you know, I am given free reign to travel and bring back gossip for Rajmata." He gave Perveen a knowing look, and she forced a smile. She could not let him see her fear.

"What was the gift?" Jiva Rao asked, his expression wary.

"A beautiful lady handed me a packet of rupees. I asked who she was, and why she was doing this. She confessed she was my mother! What a surprise that was for me. As everyone knows, I was raised by a buffoon family in a village. She asked them to bring me up while she was working."

Padmabai beamed. "Where did the beautiful mother work? Was she a beautiful lawyer like Perveen-memsahib?"

Perveen liked that Padmabai assumed there was a world of women lawyers, but she thought it was silly for Padmabai to call her beautiful. She certainly did not feel that way, with her face and hands smudged with dirt, and with bits of leaves and sticks crumbled into her riding skirt.

"This was her job." He rolled his arms, miming an Indian classical dancer. "For a while she had danced in the very palace you know so well, for all the maharajas who came to visit. But then—instead of fetching me out of the village, as would have been kind—she went to France and Switzerland. When my mother called me to the racetrack, she did so to beg my pardon and to say she always thought of me. And that if things had gone right, I would have been a maharaja."

"She was a dancer, and you became a maharaja." Not under-standing the significance of his words, Padmabai clapped. "It's a good story. But too short."

Perveen saw Jiva Rao's eyes flicker toward the doorway. She waited to catch his eye and gave him a slight nod of encourage-ment. She would throw herself in the buffoon's path if needed. But as Jiva Rao slowly began rising from the chair, the buffoon looked at him sharply. "Sit down. Your story is not finished."

"Yes, he is going to tell us about his royal place!" Padmabai trilled.

Sitting uncomfortably on the edge of his chair, Prince Jiva Rao looked contemptuously at his sister. "You fool, can't you see he's not talking about a different place? He wants to rule Satapur instead of me."

"You are more intelligent than people say!" The buffoon's voice was rich with sarcasm.

Perveen felt sweat beading on her temples. She had wanted to avoid a confrontation.

Padmabai shook her head so her braids trembled. "But Wagh is our maharaja."

"He would be—unless he has an accident." The buffoon paused, his eyes sweeping over Jiva Rao, whose jaw was set in an angry line, and Padmabai, whose face showed only confusion.

"My dear children, have you forgotten your dead older brother?"

"Let's not speak of him!" Perveen implored as Padmabai's eyes clouded over.

"It happened near here," Aditya said with an odd smile, and Perveen felt a chill run through her. It was wrong to smile when talking of another's death. "I searched harder than anyone else for Prince Pratap Rao. I made this whistle." He paused to bring his fingers to his lips and sent out a high-pitched sound that made Ganesan jump up and go to him. "The prince came to me. What a story he told!"

"He told you a story?" Jiva Rao asked, as if he couldn't stop himself.

"He said that he'd chased a small tiger, but its mother had come and bared her teeth at him before she led the baby away."

"He was very brave!" Padmabai said.

"No—he was afraid," Aditya said, patting Ganesan's back. "So frightened he dropped his pistol."

"Our older brother dropped a pistol? It cannot be. He was very strong," Jiva Rao said.

"It is a pretend story—don't worry!" Perveen said. But now she wondered if the weapon at Aditya's waist was that very hunting pistol. It was a howdah, which had thick barrels and was designed for personal defense against predatory animals.

The buffoon studied her for a moment and then gave a wide smile. "Believe what you choose."

"I want to know more stories about our brave brother. Nobody speaks of him. They want to forget." Padmabai's honest words made Perveen feel faint. She had a sense that the buffoon wanted to tell every detail of Pratap's death—or make it sound even worse than it was. The goal was to hurt the children in a way that couldn't be undone.

The buffoon gave her a contemptuous glance and then, for Padmabai, made an exaggerated display of shivering. "Look how cold Perveen-memsahib is! Shall we drink tea?"

Padmabai clapped. "Yes! Nobody has given me food, and I'm so hungry! Tea and rotis!"

"The roti man is nearby. He can make them for the children. They can go out together to request them," Perveen said quickly. If the royal children said they wanted something, he'd have to concur. She also wondered whether Rama might be nearby and could somehow intervene.

"Roti later. First we must take tea." Something about Aditya's insistence sparked a warning in Perveen's heart. The dowager had been the only poisoner at the palace—hadn't she? But she could not walk. She needed someone to provide her with the poison, and it could have been the buffoon.

Aditya took a box of matches from next to Vandana's cigarette box and struck a match against the half-burned branches in the brazier at the room's center. The flame took, and a small fire started. He poured water from an urn into a kettle and hung it on the half circle of metal set over the fire. As he went about the ritual, Perveen thought of quickly grabbing Padmabai and making a run for the door—but then she'd have to leave Jiva Rao, and because of his status, he was the most vulnerable of all of them.

Padmabai bounced in the camp chair. "Aditya-yerda, tell us more of the story. You said that our brother saw a tiger and dropped his pistol."

"Yes. He was most worried about where he had left the gun. I said it would be too dangerous to go back to look for it. He was frightened Prince Swaroop would be angry because it belonged to him. So do you know what I did?" The buffoon opened his arms so wide they spanned half the tower's width. "I said, 'Come here. Cry in my arms, and I will make it better.'"

"You always do that with him," Padmabai said, smiling at Prince Jiva Rao, who was looking as if he'd seen a ghost.

Perveen had an awful feeling about what might come next. She shook her head at Aditya. "Let's not talk of a real beloved person who is gone. It hurts them."

The buffoon scowled at her. "And I have not been hurt, a thousand times?" Turning back to Padmabai and Jiva Rao, Aditya raised his hands and began to mime for them. "I held my hand like a cup behind his head. That made it easy to push his head down into the earth. I held him there for many minutes, until he stopped moving."

"Stop it!" Perveen cried out in vain. This was far too cruel to the children. What would he pantomime next—the prince struggling for his life?

Jiva Rao would not see it, because he had buried his face in his own hands.

But Padmabai was still oblivious. In a curious voice, she asked, "Did you put his head there to see Mole?"

Aditya had confessed a murder, and while Padmabai was still puzzling it out, Jiva Rao's shoulders were shaking with sobs.

Perveen imagined that Jiva Rao understood that the reason the buffoon was being forthcoming was to bring terror right before the prince's own death. Yet she could not succumb to this feeling. She remembered the time her father had asked her to run the interviewing of a client he was fairly certain had committed first-degree murder. He had counseled her to sound relaxed and unafraid. But how could she derail this man?

He was a performer. And what came at a performance's end?

Perveen put one hand against the other and began clapping. "We must all clap for Buffoon and cheer him, too. What a story!"

Padmabai began slapping her hands together, but not Jiva Rao. He buried his face deeper into his hands, and Perveen had the dreadful thought that he probably believed she delighted in his brother's death.

Aditya gave her a condescending smile. "It will not work. Nobody can hear the sounds of two people clapping so far from the lodge."

What did she have left? The element of surprise. "Did I tell you I spoke with your mother?"

He looked startled for a moment and then shook his head. "You are not from this area. You can't know her."

"I certainly do know Vandana Mehta. We had a long conversation that I already put on record."

"She didn't tell me about you. But it doesn't matter."

"Actually, she matters quite a bit. She is well respected in government circles."

"But she is most likely dead by now. Datura takes less than twelve hours."

He was talking about the poison that the dowager had taken. So he must have procured it for her and kept some for his own use. She reminded herself that Dr. Andrews had made it to Heaven's Rest. Vandana might survive.

Trying not to show her agitation, Perveen asked, "Why would you do such a thing to your mother?"

"She always wanted to give me money and fine things from Europe. I had only one request—we had talked about it since before the last rainy season. Still, she would not change her mind."

"What was your request?"

"A simple thing. I only needed my mother to come forward and write a letter saying who my father was. She has important British friends who would believe her." Shaking his head, he said, "She was foolish, saying that she would rather stay with her husband than join me when I became ruler."

"Your mother left you before—and this was another abandonment," Perveen said, imagining his rage.

"My mother leaves. But she always comes back," Padmabai said, as if trying to cheer him up.

Perveen took a deep breath. "I know you have been very badly hurt. But that does not mean it is necessary to hurt others. That cannot ever bring happiness."

Aditya threw his hands in the air as if her talk was inconsequential. "And do you think I was happy before? When you saw me smiling and bowing, you thought I was enjoying life?"

"The rajmata created the situation that made your mother give you up," Perveen said steadily. "Now she is dead. Please let me walk out of this tower with the children. They have done nothing to you."

"Impossible!" His hand went to his weapon. "If the stupid boy sniveling in that chair lives, I will lose my claim to the throne."

Perveen shook her head. Aditya's desire was so off course it could never be granted—not even if every member of the royal family, Swaroop included, died. If she told him this, would it scuttle his manic plan? Swallowing hard, she began. "As a lawyer, I feel it is my duty to give you the correct advice."

His expression shifted, became more interested. "Yes, yes. I will need lawyers to help me."

Hoping he wouldn't explode, she said, "The trouble is, the claim you wish to make would very likely be rejected."

"Of course it won't!" He advanced toward her, speaking urgently. "I look very much like my father and my brothers. My mother is gone, but I will find others who can verify the truth about my mother and the maharaja."

"And which maharaja was your father?" Perveen kept her tone businesslike.

He paused, then said the name with reverence. "Maharaja Mohan Rao."

"So you are a half brother to Prince Swaroop."

"His *older* brother," he corrected with a raised eyebrow. "Once that information is widely known, everyone in Satapur will want me to rule."

"But my brother is maharaja!" Padmabai bleated. Jiva Rao's face was set in a despondent mask. He'd been taught enough about the history of the brutal Maratha wars to understand what Aditya had in mind for him.

Perveen had to change the conversation. "There is a bar to the plan you have in mind. The trouble is that the succession for the Satapur throne does not pass *between* the sons of Maharaja Mohan Rao. It passes through the descendants of the succeeding ruler, the late Maharaja Mahendra Rao."

Frustration tightened Aditya's jaw. "That's not correct! In our palace, succession passed between brothers just recently. British approved!"

"The reason that occurred was because Prince Pratap Rao had no offspring." Perveen continued to speak carefully and slowly, lest she confuse him. "The British and royals set up strict laws about the path of succession." Remembering what Colin had said about the maharaja of Baroda, she added, "They could even appoint an ordinary boy of royal caste from the area. But it would be important that both his parents were of royal caste."

Aditya's expression froze. After a moment, he said, "You are lying."

"I am not lying. The reason your mother wouldn't help you was because she knows this." Trying to calm him, she continued, "Your mother loves you and wants to help you—but she knows that such a plan would not ever be legally accepted."

His expression had re-animated into threatening. "You shall suggest to the Britishers that I be named the ruler."

Perveen shook her head. "I would not suggest someone who didn't let these children go free. A maharaja loves the people of his state. He doesn't kill."

It had been a risk to refuse him outright, but if he was going to take his anger out on her, it might allow for the children's escape. She watched his face sag with the comprehension that his ambition had been hopeless. And then he forced a smile.

"You have taught me something I didn't know, Perveen-memsahib. It is too much to think about. Let us have a cup of tea together."

"I will take one," Perveen said, thinking that maybe in the ritual of serving tea, she could stage an upset.

"I don't want any," Jiva Rao said, his voice shaky.

"Yes! I want a big cup!" Padmabai declared.

"This isn't your home. I'm not sure if the water is clean enough for royalty. Let me taste it to see," Perveen offered. She did not trust Aditya giving the children anything.

Padmabai stuck out her lower lip at Perveen. "But you promised we would stop at this place to have tea and eat!"

Aditya beckoned to Padmabai. "Listen. Do you hear the kettle singing? Princess, kindly take the kettle off its hook."

"What?" Padmabai asked in surprise.

"Yes. You are big enough to do it," said the buffoon encouragingly.

"No, you mustn't!" Perveen said, trying to step out to grab Padmabai and finding that the dog was blocking her. As Padmabai hurried toward the fire, Perveen called out, "Don't touch it. You'll be burnt!"

The buffoon laughed, and Perveen realized what he'd done: set up a situation where she would try to forbid the princess to do something, which would make Padmabai want to do it all the more.

Aditya stepped into Perveen's path, preventing her from reaching the princess as her small hand darted out over the fire and closed on the kettle's iron handle. Shocked by the heat, she screamed, and the kettle swayed on its hook. She lost her balance and pitched so she landed on the edge of the brazier ring.

Crying out, Perveen lunged forward, but Aditya grabbed her shoulders. "Stop! She will be taken by the fire, just like her brother will be." At Padmabai's scream, Ganesan had begun barking. Aditya kicked at him, and the dog shied away.

Perveen felt Aditya's hands gripping her shoulders, and although she flailed her arms, she could not break the hold.

"Help us!" she screamed, but she knew that Ganesan's barking masked her voice.

"Stop it!" Aditya sounded furious as he yanked one arm up behind her. From her shifted position, she saw that Jiva Rao was gone. Although the pain in her shoulder was excruciating, she twisted and squirmed as violently as she could to keep Aditya diverted. She made a silent prayer that the prince would not run into the forest but to the lodge, and that he would ask the men there for help.

Aditya was holding her by both of her wrists. Slowly, he began pushing her toward the fire beside which a weeping Padmabai lay on the ground, cradling her burned hand, with the dog hovering over her. The child was in so much pain she paid no heed to the scattered embers that were burning very close to the skirt of her lacy white dress.

Aditya whispered in Perveen's ear, "All you need to do is kick those bits of fire toward her. It would be an accident. You could not help yourself."

"No! I am here to protect them. I would never—"

"This is your last chance. You can be my partner. Make a fine document like you did for the queens. Change the dates. You can prove that I am the best choice to rule."

Perveen began to shake. She should agree with him, appease him, try to calm him down—she knew she should—but she felt frozen. The space was too small for her, and the fear too large. He would get the document from her, and after that, he would kill them all. So she said nothing.

"Say goodbye to them," Aditya said.

Between her breaths she called out, "Go, Padmabai! Go, Jiva Rao!"

She had forgotten their titles.

With a roar of rage, Aditya pushed her straight into the fire.

Perveen was enveloped in intense heat and the choking smell of the smoke. As she struggled to pull away, she saw flames were burning one side and one sleeve of her riding jacket. She did not yet feel the pain of burning but knew it would come.

Jiva Rao was pulling Padmabai toward the tower's door. Perveen quickly pushed against Aditya and raised her voice into a scream. It was not hard to sound frightened, and if the buffoon was focused on her destruction, he might not apprehend the royal children.

As she struggled against his superior strength, a thought flashed through her head. *This is what being the guardian means.* She had not expected to die for the Satapur children, but that was her fate.

Perveen screamed again, and she heard a commotion from somewhere behind her. Ganesan was barking very close by. With horror, she watched his head lower over her forearm and his teeth clamp on to it.

But the pain of a bite did not come. Instead, her arm was almost wrenched from the socket as Ganesan jerked her away from the fire. She rolled from one side to the other, desperate to put out the flames on her clothing. She realized Aditya was no longer holding her. As her gaze shifted, she saw legs in tweed jodhpurs disappearing up the tower stairs.

Why was Aditya going to the tower's roof rather than running out the door?

Because it was a hunting tower with excellent views.

Perveen stumbled to her feet and fell forward against the stairs. The first step was hard, because her arms felt so weak, and her balance was gone. But the second step came, and then a third.

Perveen was only three feet up when she felt strong hands on her arms. A fresh surge of panic went through her. In the fire and fear, she must have gotten everything wrong in thinking that the buffoon was up the tower.

"Perveen! Stop!"

Colin's voice jolted her.

"Perveen!"

She fell back against him, but the sudden movement pushed both of them off-balance, and they collapsed in a heap on the tower's earthen floor.

"Sorry," Colin said as he edged out from underneath her. She looked at him, feeling overjoyed at her rescue yet embarrassed to have come so physically close to him. All the things she had felt at the circuit house were still there.

She had to stop hyperventilating to speak to him. It was a struggle. "Am I on fire?"

"Not anymore. Good God, who did this?" Colin said, looking at the burnt sleeve and the panicked dog circling around her.

"Aditya—the man who arrived yesterday evening. Have you seen the children? Did they get away?"

"They are just outside this building being consoled by Prince Swaroop. Both are fine."

The three people Aditya most wanted to harm. Perveen whispered, "But Aditya's up on the roof! He can shoot them."

Colin looked up the ladderlike stair to the point where it ended in a square space open to the sky. "What are you trying to tell me?"

"This is a hunting tower," she whispered again. "And he's up there with a gun."

As abruptly as he'd come to her aid, Colin left her. He scrambled up and pushed his way through the doorway with more speed than she'd ever seen from him. Perveen could not move as fast; she bit back her pain as she used every aching muscle to drag herself out of the tower. She was stumbling many yards behind Colin, but she could clearly see the royal family in a clearing. Both children were hanging on to Prince Swaroop; Jiva Rao had his face buried in the prince's jacket sleeve. The young maharaja must have been crying. The three were so consumed by their reunion that they had no eyes for the man standing on top of the tower with a pistol in his hand.

Perveen's gaze swung from Aditya to Colin. He was ten feet ahead of her, walking slowly toward them. She knew from the fact that he was in boots that he was wearing his wooden leg. Did Aditya see him?

Her question was answered in the next moment.

"First one to move is the first dead." Aditya's voice rang out from the top of the tower.

Prince Swaroop raised his head from the children to look up toward Aditya standing at the tower's top. There was no sign of recognition in the prince's face, perhaps because Aditya's clothes were different from usual. Sternly, Swaroop called out, "Who are you?"

"You think I am nothing!" Aditya said. "But I am an older brother to you. You should respect me."

Prince Swaroop did not react to the words immediately. Squinting, he asked, "Is that—Aditya-yerda? In my riding costume?"

"I took it from your luggage at the circuit house yesterday evening! Everything that is yours should be mine." Aditya pointed the pistol at the two princes.

"Don't be silly. You don't even know how to shoot a howdah pistol. You are not of the warrior class," Swaroop said contemptuously.

Perveen winced, knowing how sensitive Aditya was to issues of status. Swaroop was teasing a scorpion without realizing how fatal the sting could be.

"You tell me this—the royal who only knows how to waste money and how to drink? You should drink to this!" Aditya cocked the pistol.

Perveen saw a small, lithe figure sprint across the grass. It was Rama, headed toward the royal family. Was his plan to shield them? She felt her heart break with the shattering sound of gunfire.

Perveen instinctively hit the grass, covering her head. When she realized she was safe, she unwound and looked toward the royal family. The children clung to Swaroop, and Rama had gone to the side of Colin, who had fallen in the grass.

Colin had once again sacrificed himself, she realized with dread as Padmabai screamed.

"Get down! Get down!" Swaroop was shouting. She felt hopeless and immobile. How many bullets were loaded in the pistol—could he finish them all off?

But when she glanced fearfully behind her to identify where Aditya was aiming next, she didn't see him. Perhaps he had fallen down on the roof, because she could see nothing more than his left hand clinging to the low wall surrounding the tower's roof. Had he collapsed after firing the first shot, or even shot himself?

"How . . ." she whispered to herself, but did not finish the question.

Stepping out of the brush was a short, slender woman wearing the blue costume of a palace messenger. She was holding a long hunting rifle. Her black hair was wild and unkempt, but the angular, nut-brown face was unmistakably that of Maharani Mirabai. And for the first time since Perveen had met her, she was smiling.

Swaroop's eyes widened, and Perveen understood he was confused by his sister-in-law's appearance. However, Padmabai and Jiva Rao whooped with delight.

"Mother, you got him!" Jiva Rao called.

"Three cheers for you!" Padmabai said, and then burst out crying.

It was a belated reaction, Perveen realized. All of Padmabai's cheerful banter had masked how frightened she'd been.

The maharani nodded at the stunned group of people regarding her. Then she calmly laid the gun on the forest floor and went forward with arms outstretched to her children.

25

A ROOM WITH A VIEW

"Perveen—you are the absolute end! How could you fall into a fire and barely singe a hair but manage to ruin my favorite sari with a turmeric stain? It will not come out, I am certain," Gulnaz teased.

"I shall make it up to you. The British are paying me well." Perveen smiled at Gulnaz, whose words belied her generosity. Perveen's sister-in-law had been with her at the Poona Hotel for the last three days. Because of her physical complications, she had decided it was better to spend the extra days in Poona to attend meetings with various administrators than to travel back and forth.

Perveen had been treated for just two days at Sassoon Hospital. Dr. Andrews had suggested she recuperate in the hotel, which was much more restful. She had a small first-degree burn, but her shoulder was sprained from being dragged from the fire by Ganesan. Her parents had come to see her and urge her return to Bombay, but she had refused. She wanted the fate of the Satapur royals settled before she left.

And the work wasn't so hard. At the moment she was ensconced in a comfortable velvet chaise with her notebook on her lap, working on a new recommendation. Gulnaz shook her head. "I keep thinking about that fire. So terrible. I can't believe you don't remember any pain."

"It was incredibly brief. My shoulder pains me when I lift my arm, but it should get better. I really shouldn't have to stay around here for the next two doctor's appointments. My government work will be finished before then."

"But I'm here, too, and you keep me from being out of sorts. I'm not used to town life," said a deep English voice from the door.

Perveen looked past Gulnaz to see Colin standing in the open doorway. Feeling her cheeks warm, Perveen said, "Oh, hello."

"You are here from the hospital or from the Agency?" Gulnaz looked him over with a disapproving air.

"I am neither of those. I'm Colin Sandringham, political agent at the circuit house." He walked toward her with his slight limp.

"Mr. Colin Sandringham is the one who recognized the circuit house horses tied up near the lodge. He stopped to investigate and found a dangerous situation underway."

Gulnaz looked sympathetically at him. "Mr. Sandringham, those travels must have been hard. Did you break your foot?"

As Colin's skin flushed, Perveen quickly returned to introductions. "Mr. Sandringham, may I introduce my sister-in-law, Mrs. Gulnaz Rustom Mistry?"

Colin had reached Gulnaz and put out his hand. "It's just an old injury; hardly bothers me at all. Mrs. Mistry, it means all the world to Perveen that you're keeping her company here rather than heading back to Bombay with the rest of them."

"I have been a hospital volunteer," Gulnaz said proudly. "That is why I thought of the crutches. Never mind. I'm grateful that you rescued Perveen without thinking of yourself."

"It seems the one who bore the most injury was the little princess," said Colin, taking the chair across from Perveen. "Her hands were scorched and there is bandaging that must be changed. I hear she screams to the high heavens, but if the care is continued, she will gain full function and have just a few scars."

"I'm glad to hear the prognosis is good." Perveen looked at Colin, who had surely come to talk about more than Princess Padmabai. "Gulnaz dear, I have some things to discuss with Mr. Sandringham that are confidential government business. Could we have some time?"

Gulnaz bit her lip. "I promised Mamma I would be with you to help—"

"I do need your help with communication," Perveen said. "Would you be kind enough to go up to the third floor and ask the maharani if she can join us for dinner this evening?"

Gulnaz looked skeptical. "Do you think the rajmata would accept hotel room service?"

That was what Mirabai was called, now that the dowager was gone; but it still made Perveen think of the old lady. Shaking herself, she said, "What is a palace but constant room service?"

"Here's something you could take with you." Colin held out a small package wrapped in brown paper. "These are a few more books for the children. I was going to present them myself, but they would prefer a lady visitor, I'm sure."

"Yes, I would be happy to bring them on your behalf," Gulnaz said. Perveen knew her sister-in-law was enjoying the chance to get to know the royal mother and children, who had taken the entire third floor of the hotel. Yet it was clear she was uncomfortable leaving Perveen alone in the room with Colin. Gulnaz disappeared with a crackle of starched silk, leaving the door wide open to the hall.

Colin sat down in a cane chair near the chaise longue. "You have a very protective sister-in-law. Is she older than you?"

"Yes. She was one class ahead at school." Perveen gave him a halfhearted grin. "She sorely wanted me to take on this job because she thought being in a palace would civilize me a little bit. But now she's the one who's spending more time with Maharani Mirabai than me."

"I wish you didn't have to do so much when you're recovering from your burn and sprain," Colin said, looking at the papers.

"Just small problems. They haven't stopped me from editing Vandana's testimony."

While Perveen was in bed at Sassoon Hospital, Vandana Mehta had sent flowers and a card offering her best wishes. And when Perveen was checking into the hotel, Vandana had also arrived. Very quickly, the ordinary hotel room booked for her by the government became a deluxe suite with a view of the Poona racetrack. "You must see interesting things while you are resting," Vandana had advised her.

Upstairs, with the doors closed, Vandana had gotten to the point. Looking seriously at Perveen, she had said, "You must think the worst of me. But the truth is, I was very ill. Aditya poisoned me because I wouldn't go along with his wishes that I tell everyone he was the maharaja's heir."

"Did you drink tea?" Perveen had asked.

She shook her head. "No. We both smoked cigarettes. I think he put something on the edge of my cigarette. It was inside the holder, so I couldn't see it."

"Were you feeling ill when you left the tower?"

"I was, and if my horse didn't know the way home so well, I would not have made it home. And then, thank goodness, you told my durwan to fetch Dr. Andrews. He had no idea what the poison was, but if he hadn't given me charcoal, I would have perished."

"I think they hesitated because they didn't want to hear the bad news that you had cholera." Perveen had reached out her hands to her. "I'm so glad you survived—and that you had nothing to do with Aditya's scheming. Although I do wish you had told me more about the situation before I'd gone to the palace."

"But I was just getting to know you." Vandana looked soberly at her. "I didn't know if I could trust you. My mother was a dancer, and my father a minor lord who has never acknowledged his connection to her or me. His legitimate daughter is Archana, a lady-in-waiting in the Satapur palace."

"I've met Archana. She is not very pleasant." Perveen thought about how a nobleman could go to a palace party, select a dancer for private entertainment, and enjoy himself without any thought of raising his offspring. And perhaps Archana's coldness to Perveen had been because the lady-in-waiting had felt her investigation was threatening the palace hierarchy. Still, a question remained in her mind about the moonstone. "Did you really steal the moonstone, as Maharani Putlabai claimed?"

Vandana took a deep breath. "I removed it from the rajmata's bathroom in the zenana when I was told I had to leave."

"What happened with the maharaja Mohan Rao?"

She looked down, an expression of pain coming across her face. "I was just fourteen. I did not try for it—he went after me, and even my mother said I must submit to him. They said it was an honor to be chosen. I was frightened because I knew I could not possibly refuse."

Perveen nodded. She understood how powerless a young female would have been against the wishes of all the adults around her.

"I fell pregnant, and my mother made up a story about my needing to tend to my grandmother, who was retired in our ancestral village. She feared for my safety because Putlabai would not want her husband knowing about the baby. In the village, I gave birth to the most beautiful little boy, with eyes the color of all the Satapur maharajas'." She looked past Perveen and out the window at the Poona racetrack. "The family that took him to raise were court-buffoon caste. They had not had their own son and were eager for one to continue the family tradition. They even kept the name I gave him, Aditya. I named him Lord of the Sun, because I wanted him to have something he could feel proud about, even if he would grow up to be an idiot or clown."

"How was it that you returned to the palace?"

"To my surprise, the maharaja missed me and sent a messenger looking. There was very little food and few comforts in the village, and everyone pushed me to return." Looking sadly at Perveen, she added, "Putlabai hated me, and I had to always watch food for poison, so I became very thin. My poor health was probably the reason I did not fall pregnant again! And I was aging. He tired of my body by the time I was seventeen. And inside my heart, I was always yearning for Aditya to grow old enough to come to apprentice as a buffoon at the palace."

"So you did not want to leave the palace in 1905," Perveen guessed.

"Yes, that is so. As I grew older, I concentrated deeply on dance and became the leader of the group. And there were so many interesting visitors from other countries coming to the palace. I learned to say a few things in English to them and even a few words of French and German. And then the maharaja's son fell for me. He had seen me dancing since he was a small child, and he had his heart fixed on me. I was lonely, and I must admit, it gave me pleasure to frustrate his mother just a little bit. He gifted me with jewels, saris, and other luxuries. I understood what it would be like to be married to a wealthy man who loved me."

"Was there a pregnancy?"

She nodded. "After three months, you could see the change in my shape, and gossip spread. I heard his parents wanted me banished. The day I was being thrown out, I ran through the zenana packing up all my dancing clothes and jewelry, which I thought I could sell later. I also took the moonstone necklace the maharani had accidentally left in the bathroom. I thought I could sell it to help with my survival."

Perveen was startled. "Was the plan for you to live in a new place? Maharani Putlabai thought you were killed."

"Yes, that was her plan. But one of the palanquin bearers who carried me off was crying. He told me they were supposed to drop the palanquin in the river." Vandana stared out the window again. "I gave each of them a piece of jewelry in exchange for my survival. I believed my relatives in the village a few miles away would hide me—and I'd get to see my son. But the people there were too afraid to let me stay with them, and the buffoon family wouldn't let me through the door." She shook her head. "I heard

Aditya laughing and playing inside their courtyard, but I could not see him."

"That must have been so painful. And you were pregnant and alone. An impossible situation!" Perveen said.

"I thought of ending my life—but I realized that was exactly what the maharani and her husband would want. So I decided that my revenge would be survival." Straightening in her chair, she smiled at Perveen. "In the next village, I found a midwife who fed me the proper herb. A day later I was no longer pregnant." She gave Perveen a long look, which told her of years of unspoken sorrow. "Then I was free. I went to Poona. Because I spoke some English, I was hired as an ayah for a British family. I worked three years for them, and when they were returning to England, they brought me along. But on the ship, I met some interesting people, three Indian musicians traveling to become part of a very popular troupe playing in Europe."

"The Royal Hindustan Orchestra!" said Perveen, remembering.

Vandana nodded, and an expression of pride came into her eyes. "They were intrigued to learn that I had once been a court dancer and challenged me to show them a dance. One evening, after the family I worked for was in bed, they set up their instruments and played on the deck. I had danced just five minutes when they implored me to join them. They assured me I'd earn more as a dancer in Paris than as a nanny in London. I got off the boat with the orchestra men in Calais. And then I reinvented myself as Madame Vandana of Royal Hindustan."

"It must have felt like a reincarnation," Perveen mused. "Yet you came back to Satapur."

"Being married to Yazad has been wonderful. We enjoy our lives so much!" Vandana said, her eyes playing across the prominent band of diamonds on her left finger. "After I'd heard the maharaja Mahendra Rao had died, I suggested to Yazad we buy a property in Satapur. To him it was practical, because he has interests in developing hydroelectric power in the area."

"But what was the reason for you?"

"I still often dreamed of my lost baby. I wanted to see him, to tell him I was sorry for leaving, to explain the circumstances." Grimacing, she added, "I did not know that jealousy would overwhelm him and he would regard the royal children as his nephews and niece rather than his superiors."

"Aditya received different messages about belonging to the family," Perveen reflected. "He became very close to the rajmata. She let him socialize in her private rooms and he played for hours with the children." Perveen paused. "Did the rajmata suspect Aditya was your son?"

"He said the rajmata never indicated this—but he came to believe that Maharaja Mohan Rao did know. Why else would he bring him to the Delhi Durbar? It was very special treatment." Shaking her head, she said, "After he lost his father, he could only hate the other sons—and grandsons. I didn't know until recently what he'd done to Prince Pratap Rao. I was horrified and frightened. I told him he should never do such a thing again."

Perveen believed her.

The fact that Vandana had given a prompt and candid account and had fallen ill from poisoning by her son made it clear that she was also a victim of Aditya's machinations. Nevertheless, Vandana had asked Perveen to record a statement of what had transpired with Aditya, painful as it was. The testimony would be kept private but could be used if Vandana was ever accused of wrongdoing. However, Perveen had been frank with her about the necessity of Colin's knowing more of her story, and she reluctantly agreed before departing for Heaven's Rest.

It was three days after the conversation with Vandana. Perveen decided that now—with Gulnaz gone and Colin sprawled comfortably in the chair across from her—was the time to address the matter. She got up, closed the door that Gulnaz had left open, and returned.

Colin raised his eyebrows. "Your sister-in-law won't like that."

"I was not exaggerating when I said we had a confidential matter to discuss."

"As do I," he said. "But fire away."

"We have not spoken alone since the shooting at the hunting tower. You saw with your own eyes that Aditya attempted an assassination."

Colin nodded. "And that the maharaja's mother saved the day."

"What are you hearing from the Agency about digging deeper?" Perveen was worried questions would arise about Aditya's motivation to kill the maharaja.

"It looks fairly cut-and-dried. Prince Swaroop was interviewed by several different administrators who see him as the most important eyewitness. The only question is whether Aditya had an accomplice. There was a fancy cigarette box found in the tower."

This was what Perveen had feared might be noticed. "It belongs to Vandana Mehta."

"What?" His eyebrows rose.

"Vandana reported to me that Aditya attempted to drag her into helping him make a claim to the throne because of her ties to the British. Obviously, she refused. For that, he poisoned her cigarette."

"Datura poisoning," Colin said, nodding. "I still don't understand why she consorted with such a knave while being married to my friend."

"I'm married. I'm consorting with you."

His face pinkened.

"Sorry, Colin, I could not resist." Perveen was glad she'd disarmed him. She did not want to divulge Vandana's blood relationship to Aditya unless it was absolutely necessary. "I think

Vandana missed the palace community. Sometimes one takes up with someone without understanding their character until it's too late. That was my own situation when I became suddenly engaged to a man no one in my family knew."

Colin gave her a long look, as if he had many more questions but had decided to hold back.

Both of them were holding back.

"Will the maharaja have to testify?" If this happened, the story about Aditya having royal blood might surface, and that could bring about the question of his mother's identity. If Colin learned it was Vandana, he might feel duty bound to tell Yazad, and such information could destroy a happy marriage.

"I am the children's guardian," Colin said. "I don't think it is in their interest to face long conversations with Englishmen. Do you?"

Perveen initially bristled at his statement about being the children's guardian; but it was true. He was the Satapur agent, and she had been brought in temporarily to surmount the barrier of purdah. And now—hearing what he was doing to shield the children and Vandana—she felt relieved. "That makes sense. If he wants to talk about things, he can speak to his mother."

"Now, that's the topic I wished to discuss with you."

He handed a copy of the *Times of India* to her. "There's been some coverage of what's being called 'the mysterious affair in Satapur.' It involves the death of a dowager, the kidnapping of a maharaja, and so on. In this newspaper, Maharani Mirabai is being lauded as a heroine."

Perveen glanced quickly at the sensational headline and then dug into the article. The report detailed a kidnapping of the young maharaja by a corrupt servant. The act of Maharani Mirabai to save her son's life was being cited as a model example of the strength of Indian women. This gave her an uncomfortable thought. "Does all this attention to Maharani Mirabai bother Prince Swaroop?"

"I'm not sure. Yesterday, he asked to be removed from his position as Satapur's prime minister. He went straight back to his flat in Bombay without waiting for an answer."

"Mirabai said he was quite overcome with grief when he performed the last rites for his mother," Perveen said. "He may need some time to gather his thoughts about all that has happened. But it will be a shame if he stays too long in Bombay. The children really do care for him."

"It could be that Prince Swaroop feels ashamed he wasn't the one who fired the shot that killed the villain."

"That's true. The article hardly mentions him and greatly praises the maharani." Perveen read the glowing praise of the queen's training with firearms during her childhood in Bhor that had led to years of hunting with her husband. She looked up to grin at Colin. "Apparently she bagged hundreds of birds, but she refused to kill leopards and tigers due to her affection for them. What this story doesn't mention is how she found her way to her children."

"I had an interview with her," Colin said. "She caught sight of you riding with her daughter. She followed you, taking a path through the woods, to make sure the princess was safe. She always carried a rifle when riding by herself. She did not understand what was happening in the tower until it was too late. She believed that if she stormed in, he would act quickly against the children. She had listened to you trying to talk him out of killing the children and concluded there was no more use for words. Therefore she bided her time until he came to the top of the tower and she had a clear shot."

So the maharani had patience. Wondering if Colin had the same reaction, she asked, "What do you think of the maharani's character?"

He thought for a minute before answering. "I'm sure she's more forthcoming with you, but I do like her. She's intelligent. She showed restraint in the situation when her children and you were in danger. She also had a great understanding of the challenges of the state and had some suggestions to make regarding the appointment of a new prime minister. All this was done in a very soft, pleasant manner."

A manner that would please the British—let them think she would be a compliant ruler. This was a good position to be in for a woman who wanted progress. Smiling, Perveen said, "You are making me think of a proposed change in Satapur's governance. The Agency has quite wide authority in that matter, doesn't it?"

"That's what I hear." His brows drew together. "But who is proposing the change?"

"You might be," she said with a smile. "One of the rights of the British government is to select a ruler for the state if no heir is fit for duty."

He nodded, looking warily at her.

"I think everyone would agree that it makes sense that the maharani be appointed the governing regent for Satapur until the maharaja ascends to the gaddi. If she likes, he could be educated at college before becoming ruler. She thinks her son deserves time to mature like her husband had. And look how popular she is with the country! This situation allows everyone to win."

Colin was quiet for a long moment. "I like the idea very much, but she's a woman nobody knows because she was in various states of purdah during her life as a maharani. Therefore, the Agency might argue back to us that the local population would be angry about a woman regent."

Perveen understood he was predicting what might happen in a private conversation he'd have with his superiors, so she offered an obvious rebuttal he could use. "Purdah was always a custom observed in deference to her late mother-in-law's wishes—not her husband's. The maharani's recent activities, such as riding through the forest to save her son and shooting dead a murderer, have proven her strength. People are praising her throughout India, and I imagine this story will play well in Britain, too!"

"I agree about the current perception of Maharani Mirabai." His voice was cautious. "But what about the supposed mental weakness that Dr. Andrews spoke of?"

"I never saw any weakness. I saw reasonable suspicion that her son's life was in danger—and now that the perpetrator is dead, she is not speaking of those matters anymore. She is quite ready to return to the palace after making an official statement of her desire for her son's education in a proper school."

"Still wishing for England?" Colin asked. "I guess there's nobody stopping her now."

"As I told you before, she rejected my suggestion of St. Peter's School in Panchgani. But since being here in Poona, she's heard good things about the Sardars' School in Gwalior, established twenty-four years ago by its maharaja. She hears a good class of Indians are studying there, and she will give it a chance."

"Let me think about it." Colin looked past her and out the window at the bustling street and, beyond that, the tall green hills. At last he said, "It's not unprecedented to have a woman rule a kingdom or state in India. Consider the Rani of Jhansi and, more recently, the Begum of Bhopal."

"That's right. And all of us, Indians and British, were under Empress Victoria's thumb when she reigned, and there could be another British woman monarch in the future." She hoped it might be a woman who'd support the idea of India's freedom.

He was silent a moment. "I'll introduce the concept of the maharani's taking over as a regent. Of course, I would need to remain at the circuit house as the political agent connected to Satapur."

"Certainly. You have a good working relationship with her now; and it will only strengthen," Perveen said.

"Life and death matters build relationships, I hope," Colin said, smiling at her. "In any case, when I speak to my director, I want you to be there with me. You will be better at arguing all the advantages. After all, you are the lawyer."

26

RIDING HOME TO RULE

*M*irabai, the maharani of Satapur, had no more patience for palanquins.

If her late father-in-law had been forced to build a railway for the sake of moving agricultural produce, why shouldn't the same track carry people? And it would start that very day with a new train painted in the colors of the crown—red and gold—bringing her home to Satapur. Roderick Ames, an engineer introduced by her brother-in-law, knew the railway people in Kharagpur who had managed everything.

The coronation was two weeks from Sunday. That word—"coronation"—made her smile. She had thought about it twice before—first for Pratap Rao, and then for Jiva Rao. Jiva Rao had lived, and although he would not take power for years, the formal coronation would reassure Satapur's population that the future would be good.

She had the first gift she had prayed for: her son saved.

The second heavenly gift was the removal of the twin poisons from the palace, the dowager maharani and Aditya.

But this third gift—to become the one to take charge in Satapur?

That she had not expected.

Perveen Mistry had spent many afternoons talking with her, first explaining the decision of the Kolhapur Agency in her favor and then going into the various roles of a regent.

But the Satapur train was her own grand idea. With regular trains, newspapers could come to Satapur every day. Just as people could leave to find work in the city, and businessmen could come in and start to build the schools and shops her husband had always spoken of. But she would take the train's maiden voyage home to Satapur.

While she waited on the platform, she sat on a fine cane chair with Chitra standing nearby, shielding her from the sun with a parasol. The parasol was a nod to propriety, because she had not wanted to wait indoors.

On the other side of the track, she saw a small crowd waiting to board the train to Bombay. A number of the people, especially the English, were gawking at her. At first she felt uncomfortable, remembering all that had been said to her about keeping pure through purdah. But then she thought about how they liked to see their own royalty so much. So she gave a small wave.

The applause and cheering told her the people did know who she was—and that they knew the Kolhapur Agency had decided to appoint her as regent. Two days ago, she'd seen Jiva Rao happily settled in Gwalior, and Padmabai was going to attend the same girls' school she had loved so much. It would be better for both of her children to have the attention of good teachers and friends their age. That was how she'd felt when her husband was alive, and it was now even more true, because she'd have scant time for anything other than governing. But she would not compromise on her morning horse rides; those would continue as a necessity. Riding had pulled her from depression before, and she knew that surveying her state on horseback would settle her before the difficult decisions of each day.

Across the platforms, a familiar figure with a specially draped sari caught her eye. Mirabai raised her lorgnette and saw it was indeed Perveen, who was reaching into her briefcase for something or other. The woman was entirely too consumed with papers, Mirabai thought with affection. Then a new figure swam into her gaze—a tall foreigner with a slight limp.

Mirabai recognized him as Colin Sandringham, the

Englishman who was the political agent for Satapur. He had met with her several times, and after they had both overcome the awkwardness, she had wound up talking with him for two hours about the things that she wished for Satapur. Some of these ideas would be shared with the Kolhapur Agency. But not all. It was better that way, he'd said.

Now she looked at Perveen, who was putting a paper in Colin's hand, which he examined and tucked into his jacket's breast pocket. Mirabai could tell from the way that Colin's face was turned toward Perveen that he was talking about something quite serious. Perveen listened but had her body half-turned away, as if she didn't want to hear.

What were they talking about? Surely nothing to do with the Satapur crown. That was all settled.

And then Mirabai understood. They were having trouble saying goodbye to each other. He was English, she was Indian, and of course they could not be together; but in some way, they had bridged that impassable river.

"Your Highness, the train is due in five minutes," said Archana. "Whom do you wish to ride with you in your car?"

"Swagata and Chitra," Mirabai said, enjoying the shock that creased the noblewoman's smooth brow. But why shouldn't she spend the ride ensconced with the two women she trusted most at the palace? They were going to help her plan a large party, just like in the old days. It would be as good as a coronation.

The Bombay Mail arrived with a large clatter and blocked her view of Perveen. The train stood for five minutes. As it pulled away, she saw that Colin Sandringham was still on the platform. His eyes followed the train until it was completely out of view.

But all was not lost, Mirabai thought with a smile.

Colin Sandringham was duty-bound to attend her party.

And she would add one more name—Perveen Mistry, Esquire—to the invitation list.

GLOSSARY

Aai: mother

Amla: berry with ayurvedic properties

Avestan: the language of Zoroastrian scripture

Ayah: child's nanny or maidservant to a woman

Ayurveda: systems of plant- and animal-based medical treatment and disease prevention

Bandar: monkey

Beater: someone who drives animals from hiding for a hunter

Brahmin: the highest caste in Hinduism, that of priests and their families

Datura: genus of nine species of poisonous, night-blooming plants in *solanaceae* family

Dharma: behavior and conduct for the right way of living

Dravidian: relating to a family of languages spoken in southern India and Sri Lanka, or the peoples who speak them

Durbar: gathering of nobles within a royal palace

Durwan: guard

Gaddi: throne

Gandhiji: respectful term for Mohandes Gandhi

Gara: heavily embroidered silk-satin sari; the embroidery is usually done in China or Gujarat, and these saris are historically favored by Parsi women

Jali: decorative wall meant to provide privacy and limited observation, usually in zenanas

Kande Pohe: popular breakfast dish in Western India featuring beaten rice, onion, and spices

Karma: the result of one's behaviors

Kolhapur Agency: British colonial government's grouping of 25 princely and feudal states in Western India that later became known as the Deccan States Agency

Kumar: prince

Kusti: Zoroastrian's sacred cord that is worn wrapped around waist

Kurta pajama: man's clothing of tunic top and coordinating drawstring-waist trousers

Laddu: round chickpea-flour sweet

Lathi: stick used for fighting

Lungi: male garment; a rectangular cloth worn around the lower torso

Mahābhārata: epic story of the Bhārata dynasty to be read after the Rāmāyana

Maharaja: ruler of a Hindu state or kingdom

Maharani: mother or wife or daughter of a ruler

Maratha Empire: Western India's warrior clans who defeated the Mughal rulers and dominated much of the Indian subcontinent from 1674 to 1818

Marathi: language spoken by Maratha people

Memsahib: polite address form for a woman of upper class, mostly for Europeans, but also for wealthy Indians

Mitha paan: sweet and sharp-tasting betel leaf delicacy

Mofussil: rural area

Monsoon: rainy season lasting several months

Pagri: turban

Parsi: Indian-born follower of the Zoroastrian faith

Poona: important town in British India

Puja: worship celebration

Purdah: a style of living in some orthodox and Muslim and Hindu homes where the women and children stay in a separate section. Women in purdah can visit with other females but they do not show their faces to men outside the family

Rajkumari, Kumari: princess

Rajmata: mother of the ruler

Rāmāyana: ancient epic poem that tells the story of Prince Rama, his wife Sita, and the demon king Ravana

Choti-Rani: a maharani married to a maharaja who lives in a household where there is already a rajmata

Roti: whole-wheat bread cooked on a griddle; its plural is rotis

Sahyadri Mountains: ecologically diverse mountain range running parallel along Western India from Gujarat down to the southern tip of India; the British called it the Western Ghats

Sardarji: respectful term for a Sikh gentleman

Satapur: fictional princely state within the Kolhapur Agency

Sherwani: fancy long coat with a banded collar worn by men

Susu: urination

Wagh: another name for "tiger"

Yerda: idiot or fool

Zenana: section of a home designated for women only

ACKNOWLEDGMENTS

The Satapur Moonstone is set in a fictitious state within the actual Kolhapur Agency, an administrative group run by British India that oversaw the life of royals in many small princely states in Western India. Although Satapur is a pretend place, my aim was to present a realistic portrayal of royal life in pre-independence India. This would be an impossible task were it not for the assistance of scholars, friends, colleagues, and family in the United States and India.

Firstly, I want to thank Amrita Gandhi of New Delhi; Madhu Kumari Rathore, and her daughter and granddaughter, Suneeta and Shalini Rana, of Falls Church, Virginia; and Nigel Sequeira of Baltimore, Maryland, for sharing knowledge and their connections with some of India's royal families. I continue to appreciate the insights of legal historian Mitra Sharafi; Jehangir Patel, editor of *Parsiana*; Perzen Patel of bawibride.com; and Farida Guzdar, a Parsi friend nearby.

Kudos to my trustworthy driver, Namdev Shinde, who safely transported me via car and horse to Matheran, Lonavala, and Khandala in the Sahyadri Mountains. I also appreciate Manjiri Prabhu for introducing me to her beautiful and culturally rich hometown, Pune, and connecting me with India's writing community.

Vicky Bijur, my longtime agent, has my eternal gratitude for encouraging me to write the Perveen Mistry series and bringing it to its main home at Soho Press and overseas to India, Italy, Finland, Korea and perhaps even more. Anyone who has worked with

Juliet Grames knows that having her as an editor is like having an inspired and protective angel by your side. I am indebted to Juliet, Bronwen Hruska, Paul Oliver, Monica White, Rudy Martinez, Rachel Kowal, and the rest of the gang at Soho Press, as well as the committed, energetic Penguin Random House team who convinced booksellers to take a chance on Perveen.

I am thankful for Ambar Saihil Chatterjee, my editor and dear friend at Penguin Random House India, as well as his colleagues in publicity, Varun Tanwar and Smit Zhaveri.

Every Perveen Mistry book starts with historical research, and I was fascinated by several memoirs from bygone days: Cornelia Sorabji's *India Recalled; The Hill of Devi* by E. M. Forster; and *The Autobiography of an Indian Princess* by Sunity Devee, Maharani of Cooch Behar. I learned about the management of India's kingdoms by the Indian Civil Service in *Princely India and the British: Political Development and the Operation of Empire* by Caroline Keen. A fascinating look at the personal histories of several pioneering princesses can be found in *Maharanis* by Lucy Moore. *The Raj on the Move: Story of the Dak Bungalow,* by Rajika Bhandari, helped me imagine the circuit house down to the ten versions of chicken. I continue benefiting from the kind assistance of David Faust, librarian for South Asia and Middle East Studies at the University of Minnesota.

As always, my family in India and the United States have helped me make a road map of how and where to search in India for the missing pieces in my stories. From the bottom of my heart, I thank the Banerjees, Parekhs, and Parikhs for the contributions you have made to my writing over the last decades. There are many of you—and you know who you are! Last but not least, to my nuclear family, Tony, Pia, and Neel, I love you all so much and am grateful to you for pulling together and walking the dogs while I'm on the mean streets of Bombay with Perveen.

I welcome conversations with readers about India. Send me a message by visiting http://sujatamassey.com or by sharing your thoughts in the public comments on my Sujata Massey Author Facebook page. To find out when I am running special promotions or touring in your area, sign up for my occasional letter delivered straight to your inbox at http: sujatamassey.com/newsletter.